CAUGHT BETWEEN LIFE . . . AND DEATH

Shivering, Ben clung to the life jackets, floating in the pitch-darkness. He didn't know what had happened, but guessed that the terrorists had returned. He told himself that they hadn't discovered him and blocked his exit from the water tank permanently: they'd have pulled up the life jackets . . . wouldn't they?

When the sound of gunfire and stomping feet came through the top of the tank, he had to fight down the panicky urge to climb up and batter his way out through whatever was covering the access hole. He hugged the life jackets, eyes closed, gritting his teeth, until the feeling passed.

Breathe, Gannon.

Just keep quiet and breathe.

CRASH DIVE

John McKinna

AN ONYX BOOK

ONYX
Published by New American Library, a division of
Penguin Putnam Inc., 375 Hudson Street,
New York, New York 10014, U.S.A.
Penguin Books Ltd, 27 Wrights Lane,
London W8 5TZ, England
Penguin Books Australia Ltd, Ringwood,
Victoria, Australia
Penguin Books Canada Ltd, 10 Alcorn Avenue,
Toronto, Ontario, Canada M4V 3B2
Penguin Books (N.Z.) Ltd, 182–190 Wairau Road,
Auckland 10, New Zealand

Penguin Books Ltd, Registered Offices:
Harmondsworth, Middlesex, England

First published by Onyx, an imprint of New American Library,
a division of Penguin Putnam Inc.

First Printing, June 1999
10 9 8 7 6 5 4 3 2 1

Dedicated to the commercial divers of the Gulf oilfields. This books is for you, guys.

And especially for Teresa, my wife.

ACKNOWLEDGMENTS

Thanks to my parents, for keeping the house full of books.

My agent, Jimmy Vines, for his integrity, support, and enthusiasm.

My editor, Joe Pittman, for his skill and encouragement.

PROLOGUE

The warm Lebanese wind carried the scent of burning cedarwood to the guard's nostrils. He shifted the hefty Chinese-made AK-47, adjusting the strap to relieve his cramped shoulder, and strolled slowly to the open archway in the wall surrounding the house. Leaning against the cool stone, he fished in his pocket for a cigarette, lit it, and gazed out across the Bekaa Valley.

It was not the clearest of nights; high, ragged clouds crawled across the waning moon, obscuring its pale light completely from time to time. The shadows in the jumble of boulders and loose rock surrounding the house alternately faded and deepened as the light came and went. The craggy mountain that rose immediately behind the compound blotted out the lower stars to the north with its black mass.

Rajim exhaled a cloud of smoke and stared out into the night in total boredom. To the south and slightly below the elevation of the house, the Bekaa Valley stretched off to the horizon. Here and there the flickering lights of watch fires marked the locations of small encampments, but for the most part the local area was blacked out. Only three days earlier the Israeli jets had knifed in and bombed a cluster of houses into rubble at the north end of the valley.

Hamad, the other guard assigned to the gate, entered the archway and stood beside his comrade. He slipped the heavy machine gun from his shoulder and rotated his arm, grimacing.

"That damn thing is like a sack of rocks," he muttered. His voice was hoarse and guttural; six months earlier a rocket fragment had caught him in the throat and nearly killed him.

"You've seen nothing?" Rajim said disinterestedly. It was more of a statement than a question. He kicked absently at the hard ground.

"Of course I've seen nothing," Hamad growled, "because there's nothing to see. Nothing—"

A soft clattering of stones interrupted him, and they both glanced to the left to see a goat emerging from behind a large boulder. Two others followed it, hooves clicking on the rocks.

"Nothing," Hamad continued, "except these damn goats!" He picked up a stone and threw it at the lead billy, hitting it in the flank. The animal squalled and bolted off a few yards, then resumed its lazy meander through the rocks.

Rajim drew on the last of his cigarette and flicked the butt onto the ground. He ran a hand through his tangle of black hair.

"I don't mind being on Mudeen's personal guard," he said. "It's a lot safer guarding a Shiite holy man than doing penetrations and assaults on the coast. And we get fed decently. I'm tired of being shot at. Let some other fool get killed; I'm content to be bored here for a while."

Hamad snorted. "The smell of goat dung is making me sick. I can't eat with it around me all the time. I was born in the city. Give me exhaust fumes anytime."

They walked back to the archway and sat on the stone steps. Two more goats ambled by, nosing at the ground. One of them lifted its tail and defecated noisily. Hamad swore in disgust.

"You see?" he said, the cigarette clamped between his lips, eyes squinting against the smoke. "They just—"

He lay back suddenly, gently, on the stone of the top step. Rajim looked down at him in mild surprise. The cigarette was still clamped in his mouth, and his eyes were wide open. There seemed to be a dirty mark in the center of his forehead. Beneath his head, a dark, wet pool was spreading rapidly . . .

Alarm began to register in Rajim's mind. It was the last thought he ever had. The dumdum slug from the silenced 9mm pistol tore through his right eye and blew off the back of his head, spraying blood and brains on the wall of the archway. He slumped back beside Hamad without a sound.

Four black figures fanned out from behind a huge boulder thirty feet from the steps, moving fast. All wore black knit hoods and carried compact submachine guns. The lead figure also held a silenced automatic pistol in one hand. He and the man immediately behind him reached the wall first and flattened themselves on either side of the archway, weapons trained into the compound. The last two went straight on through, split left and right when they entered the courtyard, crouched, and covered the first two as they followed.

Without a word the four sprinted to the front door of the house. Two took up positions on either side of the door, and two continued along the wall of the house, ducking under windows as they worked their way around to the back.

The two raiders at the front eyed their watches. The one who held the silenced pistol slid it back into its shoulder holster, then raised his hand, fingers spread. He counted the final five seconds silently by dropping his fingers. As his fist balled on the last second, his companion leaped to his feet, faced the door, and fired a long burst from his submachine gun into the lock.

Almost simultaneously the sound of more machine-gun fire came from the back of the house, followed by two quick explosions. In the stillness of the night, the sounds were shattering.

The two raiders crashed through the front door almost on top of four stunned guards who were just beginning to reach for their weapons. Four well-placed bursts later they were all dead.

Well rehearsed, the two entered the single hallway of the small dwelling. There were only four doors leading off it: two toward the front and two at the back. The other pair of raiders who had gone around to the rear of the house appeared at the far end of the hall. The four acknowledged each other with nods, lined up on one door apiece, and simultaneously kicked them in.

Each man sprayed a short burst into his room, tossed a fragmentation grenade inside, then backed out quickly and flattened himself against the wall. There was an odd pause in the cacophony for a heartbeat or two, except for some muffled yelling in one of the back rooms.

The four grenades went off like a quick string of giant firecrackers, blowing out every pane of glass in the house and filling the hall with dust and wood splinters. The raiders ducked into their respective rooms, firing fast.

The two front rooms were empty, but those toward the rear held eight people, two in one and six in the other. The concussion had killed only one person outright in the six-man room, but the black-clad raider eliminated the wounded by carefully emptying the magazine of his submachine gun into the tangle of broken bodies. He jerked open the single closet door, checked inside, and finding it empty, hurried back out into the hall.

The other three raiders were in the opposite room. Two people, a man and a woman, lay crumpled on the floor. They were bleeding from the ears as a result of the grenade's concussion, but both had been killed by the first burst the raider had fired into the room after kicking in the door.

They had apparently been in bed, and were groping for clothing when the machine-gun fire had caught each of them cleanly across the chest. The grenade had been unnecessary insurance.

The woman was naked, about twenty-five, with heavy breasts and hips. Her long black hair was splayed about her head, and her eyes stared sightlessly up at the ceiling. She was very dark, with exotic features that were almost East Indian. One slug had hit her in the sternum, killing her instantly.

The man was wearing a long white sleeping robe. He was in his late fifties, with a coarse, graying beard, balding head, and an excessive amount of black body hair. He had strong features, hawk-like, with an arching nose above a wide mouth that now grimaced in death. Five slugs in the chest had nearly torn him in two.

The lead raider knelt over the man, turning the dead face in the dim light with a black-gloved hand. He looked up at the other three. They all nodded. One extracted a small camera from an inner pocket, bent over, and took six quick flash pictures of the corpse's features.

The three turned toward the door, but the leader hissed for them to wait. Still kneeling, he slid a thin, six-inch stiletto from his boot and fumbled inside his breast pocket for something else. He extracted a playing card and slapped it onto the dead man's forehead.

It was the ace of spades. The raider positioned himself directly over the dead face, placed the needlelike tip of the stiletto in the center of the card, gripped the hilt with both hands, and thrust violently downward with all his body weight.

There was a wet crunching sound, and then the leader rose and waved his men out of the room. The knife had penetrated the dead man's skull to the hilt, pinning the playing card in place.

The raiders trotted down the hall toward the front door. Outside, there was the faint sound of shouting. The leader glanced at his watch, then held up three fingers. Three minutes.

The team made its way from the front door to the archway, crossing the courtyard using the same staggered running pattern by which they'd entered: two covering, two moving. Once again, they positioned themselves on either side of the archway along the inner wall.

Machine-gun fire from outside raked the stone of the archway, sending chips and dust flying. Two men dressed in khaki jackets and street pants and carrying AK-47s came through on the run. They got ten feet inside the courtyard when all four raiders opened up on them. Their bodies jinked crazily as the high volume of fire impacted. They were dead before they hit the ground.

The leader glanced at his watch again, clapped his hands together once, and pointed through the archway. The four raiders rose and dashed through as a unit, firing random bursts in the direction of the valley as they went. Some sporadic return fire from the darkness to the south sent slugs ricocheting and whining off the rocks. The team scrambled for cover behind the same large boulder that had hidden them from the unlucky gate sentries.

The deep chugging sound of a heavier machine gun drowned out the popping of small-arms fire. The team crouched behind the boulder, covering faces as the heavy slugs slammed into the rocks around them, sending more stone shrapnel flying.

The sound of a revving engine started low and quickly grew louder. The lead raider took a quick look around the boulder, ducked back, and mimed his hands on a steering wheel. The others quickly palmed fragmentation grenades.

From the direction of the valley, a car came bouncing up over the rocky ground, headlights on. The engine was screaming in low gear as the driver powered up the slight rise, kicking up a cloud of dust and exhaust. It was a battered old Volvo station wagon with the roof over the wagon bed cut off. A heavy machine gun was mounted on the remaining forward roof, manned by a gunner who was expending most of his energy trying not to be thrown out of the vehicle.

As the old car roared up to the archway, the machine gunner cut loose in the general direction of the boulder. Green tracers mixed with regular ammunition churned the ground and smacked into rock around the team. The driver ground the gears and jerked the car violently to the right, throwing the gunner off balance. The firing paused.

As one, three raiders rose and hurled grenades at the station wagon; the leader raised his submachine gun to eye level and fired a long, carefully aimed burst at the gunner. The man screamed, clawed at his chest, and flopped over limply.

One grenade exploded five feet to the side of the car. Another went off under a rear tire, lifting the vehicle up on its front bumper. As it jolted back down, the third grenade, which had gone through the cracked windshield, detonated and ignited the gas tank. The entire car blew up in a fifty-foot-high sheet of flame.

Green tracers shot out from the burning wreckage in all directions. Behind the boulder each member of the team extracted a stainless-steel snap hook from a shoulder pocket. Each hook was attached to a short length of eighth-inch cable, which in turn was secured to a body harness, worn beneath the outer clothing, at a point between the shoulder blades. The leader checked his watch again and looked up toward the northeast.

A large black shape rose up over the ridge of rock above the house. It made almost no sound, and but for blocking out the stars and moonlit clouds was virtually invisible in the night sky. It descended rapidly toward the team's position.

The fierce downdraft from the big helicopter's main rotor kicked up a whirlwind of dust and flattened the guttering flames of the burning station wagon. The team emerged from behind the boulder in a tight group, weapons ready, and moved directly under the chopper. Fifty feet above them there came a deep chattering sound as the door gunner opened fire on movement he'd spotted to the south of the house.

A red dot of light dropped rapidly from the helicopter: a heavy cable with a chemical illumination stick attached to the steel ring at its end. The door gunner kept firing.

The lead raider grabbed the cable as it swung past, snapping his harness hook into the ring and holding it still as the other followed suit. Secured to the cable, the team closed into a tight circle, back to back, facing outward. Two more sets of headlights were jolting up the rise toward the house.

One of the raiders opened fire in the direction of the headlights as the chopper suddenly rose straight up. The cable went taut, and the team was snatched into the air. In five seconds they were invisible in the night sky. The helicopter accelerated up and over the ridge behind the house, disappearing from view.

On the ground two trucks slid to a halt beside the

smoking wreckage of the station wagon. Armed men spilled out, shouting to each other in Arabic. Some hurried toward the archway, while others fanned out toward the jumbled boulders, hunting.

But it was much too late.

The command bunker was seventy-five feet underground, hollowed out of solid mountain rock. Located six miles inside Syria, its upper observation post provided a panoramic view of the Lebanese border to the west. Colonel Rashid Assir drew deeply on his clove cigarette, and gazed out of the concrete-reinforced viewing port at the jagged foothills and the hot brown plain beyond. He let the harsh smoke trickle from his mouth and rubbed his eyes.

It was the shrieking, he decided. The informant had extraordinarily robust vocal cords. Fourteen hours of interrogation and still in excellent voice. He shook his head. It was unprecedented.

He ground out the cigarette butt under the heel of his boot and sighed. The sustained interrogation was necessary, of course—simply a matter of procedure— but the screaming was becoming intolerable. Perhaps it was because only a few days earlier he had celebrated his eldest daughter's fifteenth birthday at home in Damascus. He wasn't in the right frame of mind for this kind of work . . .

Or perhaps, he thought, it was that demon Gradak. He started down the concrete spiral staircase to the level below. Ojim Gradak. What was the name he had fed to the western press after the Naples hotel bombing? The Revenger—no, the *Avenger* of the Tribes. That was it. True to form, they'd gobbled it up like vultures on carrion—the most reliable allies Gradak had ever had. He had been front-page news worldwide for six months after that one bombing.

Colonel Assir grimaced unconsciously as he reached

the lower hallway. Gradak achieved results, no doubt, but to have to deal with him on a personal level was . . . objectionable. The man was sociopathic. Being in the same room with him for any length of time made Assir's skin crawl.

A high-pitched wail emanating from the level below startled him as he reached the main office. That damned screaming again. He'd already figured out that the sound traveled from level to level through the air ducts, but knowing that didn't diminish the chilling effect.

He opened the door and entered the office. Ojim Gradak sat in a gray velour office chair behind the central desk, smoking.

"Ah, Colonel," he said smoothly, "did you enjoy the fresh air up there?" He grinned, showing teeth stained dark red from chewing betel nuts.

"Yes," Assir replied. "I find it clears the head."

"My head is always clear," Gradak said, drawing on his cigarette.

How wonderful for you, Assir thought. But he smiled tightly and sat down behind the next desk, swiveling his chair to face the other man.

"Our guest," the colonel inquired, changing the subject, "how is he at this point in time?"

"Conscious," Gradak replied. "Unfortunately for him, however, we're not quite satisfied that he's told us everything. We're going to put him through the cycle at least once, possibly twice." His eyes narrowed. "We have to be sure."

"Naturally."

Gradak rose to his feet. "I believe the first session is nearly over, Colonel. Care to join me for a quick inspection?"

Assir studied the man in front of him. Six feet tall with a heavy build; short legs, long arms, thick midriff, and powerful shoulders. The face was broad and heavy-featured, with a large nose and thick, arching brows. The sparse head of hair and beard were very black. He was clad in a German-made red-and-white track suit and running shoes. The sports clothes looked vaguely ludicrous on his menacing figure.

His eyes were startling; an impossibly pale shade of amber that contrasted sharply with his dark face. They had the unnerving quality of seeming to look right through you, Assir observed, for the hundredth time that week.

The colonel stirred uncomfortably in his chair.

"I see no point in involving myself in this procedure," he stated. "I've seen it many times." He waved a hand in the air. "This is your project. I was instructed to make this facility available to you and your people until further notice; I've done so. When you require tangible assistance, I'll be glad to see that you get it. Until then, my regular duties require my full attention." He stood up and walked over to the main desk that Gradak had just vacated.

Gradak stood for a moment, then grinned and bowed slightly from the waist, cocking his head in Assir's direction.

"Thank you, Colonel. I'll keep you up-to-date. As a courtesy," he added pointedly.

He exited the room, leaving Assir rubbing his eyes.

Gradak stared at the prisoner coldly as he listened to the chief interrogator's report. No new information during the last two hours; the subject was alive, but threatening to slip into shock.

The prisoner was about twenty-five, slightly built, with dark, wavy hair. He was completely nude, his hands bound to his ankles. A steel rod had been inserted under his knees, and he had been lifted, swinging upside down and helpless, to a supporting framework in the center of the room. There was blood and water on the tile floor beneath him.

He had been systematically beaten with a cane stick on the buttocks and the bottoms of the feet over a fourteen-hour period. Vicious welts, some bleeding freely, covered those parts of his body. Several toes were clearly broken. His feet had swollen into red, lumpy masses.

Periodically, he had been hosed down with icy water, partly to revive him and partly to increase his shock and confusion. His face, purple and swollen from brutal blows, was covered with traces of vomit. His eyes were closed, and he was making a wet, sobbing sound.

Gradak considered for a moment, then nodded to the interrogator. Enough for now.

The interrogator pushed a button on the wall. Three men dressed in medical whites and carrying a collapsible stretcher came through the door and immediately began ministering to the prisoner, lowering him to the floor and cutting his bonds. He continued to sob unintelligibly.

Gradak turned away and walked toward a darkened corner of the room where a dim figure sat silently in an armchair. He was old, white-bearded, and wore the black robes and turban of a Shiite Muslim cleric. The eyes in the wrinkled face seemed to glow with a light of their own. He raised a few fingers of one hand as Gradak approached; the gesture was like a benediction.

"Salaam, Ojim Gradak." The deep voice was almost a whisper.

"Salaam, Holiness," Gradak replied, nodding politely. "Some tea, perhaps? In my quarters, of course . . . the smell in here—" He waved his hand.

"Where there is the stench of fear there is often the fragrance of truth," the old man intoned, offering his arm to Gradak. The younger man took it and helped the cleric to his feet.

They left the room, avoiding the blood-slippery tile near the support framework.

Gradak dimmed the lights in his quarters; the old man had sensitive eyes. An ornate silver-and-glass tea service with a huge spiraled pot sat on the low central table. A stick of incense burned in a small brass holder. The cleric accepted the small cup and saucer that Gradak offered and indicated for him to sit down.

He remained silent while Gradak poured himself some tea, contemplating the curling stream of fragrant smoke as it rose toward the ceiling. Only the clink of glass and silver disturbed the quiet. His eyes were very bright and far away, as though looking across a great distance.

"It would appear," he said suddenly, "that your people have obtained all the relevant information held by that misguided soul." He indicated toward the door with his chin.

"I believe that is safe to say," Gradak agreed, "but of course we cannot be sure until we have run him well into the second cycle."

"Regardless of what else you may extract," the cleric stated, "he has already provided us with the essential details. One: he betrayed Mudeen's location to a member of Israeli intelligence in return for a large number of American dollars and safe passage to Athens. Two: he went on to provide a precise drawing of the house to an unidentified man with an American accent. Three: he also provided this operative with an accurate estimate of the strength of Mudeen's bodyguard."

The old man paused to sip some tea. Gradak remained deferentially silent. The cleric coughed and continued.

"An American operative. American dollars. Is this not evidence enough of who is responsible? And yet there is more: the manner in which my holy brother's body was defiled by his assassins." The deep, raspy voice began to shake. "A dagger driven through his forehead, pinning a gaming card above his eyes."

He gripped the arms of his chair. The frail, aged body was trembling.

"He was a member of our inner council of elders! A holy man of wisdom and compassion! A shepherd of Allah's children in their times of trial!" His grip on the chair loosened as he regained control of himself. "A gaming card. It is unmistakable American insolence, one of the filthy symbols of their immorality." He shook his head slowly. "Ojim Gradak, this outrage will not stand unpunished. They must learn that their blasphemous arrogance has a price."

There was silence for a moment, then Gradak spoke:

"Am I to understand, then, Holiness, that I have your full support for the operation I described to you?"

He found himself hardly daring to breathe as the old man leaned forward.

"You understand correctly. You have my support."

Gradak felt his body flood with elation. The betel-stained grin spread across his face. It was going to happen!

He reached up, took the old man's right hand in his, and kissed it. Head bowed, he touched his forehead to the gnarled fingers repeatedly as he spoke:

"I am blessed by your indulgence, Holiness. I will not fail you. I promise you a day the Americans will never forget."

The old cleric leaned closer. His voice was a hoarse whisper; his eyes glittered like black diamonds.

"It must be close, Ojim Gradak." He gripped the

younger man's hand with surprising strength. "It must be close enough to make them taste the same fear that our people endure every day of their lives."

Gradak nodded.

"It will be close, Holiness," he said.

Chapter One

Ben Gannon identified himself to the security guard at the gates of the MacKintosh Offshore Drilling Fluids yard, and pulled the truck around the main warehouse to the docks. A large oilfield workboat was tied up to the bollards under the main cargo crane. Parked beside the boat was a flatbed truck loaded with deep-diving gear, painted in Universal Diving Services' familiar navy gray and international orange. Two MacKintosh dockworkers were hooking up the crane line to a rack of helium-oxygen breathing gas. As Ben watched, the crane picked it off the truck, swung it around, and set it down carefully on the long, open back deck of the oilfield workboat *Crimson Tide*.

He pulled around to the opposite side of the crane, toward the bow of the boat, where two U.D.S. vans were parked. Eight or nine people were pulling duffel bags and diving helmets from the vehicles, passing them along a human chain to the rail of the boat. Two of the *Crimson Tide*'s crewmen were hauling the gear aboard and setting it up against the bulwarks.

Ben Gannon was thirty-seven. Six feet tall, uncommonly broad in the shoulders, he carried his one hundred and eighty pounds with athletic ease. His forearms were thickly muscled and roped with veins, his hands rough and scarred from years of hard physical work.

He had thick auburn-brown hair that was always on

the long side; he kept forgetting to cut it. His face was clean-shaven with a high forehead, strong jaw, and wide mouth that seemed fixed in a wry smile. The eyes were gray-green and set well apart, with crow's-feet at their outer corners from a lifetime of squinting into the sun. His brows were even and somewhat arched. Along with his smile, they lent his face a permanent expression of mild amusement.

Leaning against the front of one of the vans and going over a sheaf of paperwork was the familiar figure of Joe Talbot, one of U.D.S.' job supervisors. Tall and long-legged, still slender at fifty-five except for a small whiskey paunch, Talbot was an ex-navy diver who'd begun doing oilfield work in the early sixties. He'd only stopped diving himself five years ago, and still passed his annual physical with flying colors. Whenever someone asked him why he'd quit voluntarily at age fifty, he'd spit a long stream of brown tobacco juice into the styrofoam cup he always seemed to have in his hand, and explain in his slow Texas drawl that he considered it undignified to be jumping into cold water at midnight at his age.

Ben parked the truck and got out, stretching his cramped legs. Talbot looked up from his sheaf of papers, grinned, and ambled over.

"Hey there, partner," he said, "how you been doin'?"

"Pretty fair, Joey. Yourself?"

"Cain't rightly complain. Workin' too much is all." Talbot turned his head and sent a stream of tobacco juice into the gravel. "You been offshore a lot?"

Ben nodded. "Sure have. Just finished a two-week job with Marine Services, for Conoco out of Galveston, and before that I did ten days with Imperial Divers in the Mississippi Delta off Delacroix. It's been busy for April."

"I heard that," Talbot replied. "Imperial Divers? Are they that new outfit out of Belle Chasse?"

"That's right."

"How'd they treat you, pretty good?"

"Yeah," Ben said. "Pay scale's a little lower than U.D.S., but they work safely. They had their own boat, too, and it was pretty comfortable. The food was excellent. Nice bunch of guys. I think I'll get some more work out of them in the future."

Ben was a commercial diver by trade, one of the small number of professionals who provided underwater services for the multitude of offshore oil rigs and production platforms scattered throughout the Gulf of Mexico off Texas, Louisiana, Mississippi, and Alabama. Modern-day descendants of the old hardhat divers, commercial oilfield divers worked routinely at depths up to three hundred feet, breathing mixtures of helium and oxygen and executing welding repairs, inspections, and construction tasks on the oil platforms' massive underwater support structures, or jackets.

There were a half-dozen large dive companies that serviced the Gulf oilfields. Ben freelanced among them on a call-out basis, preferring to sacrifice the security of full-time employment by a single company for the independence of being his own boss. His abilities as a jack-of-all-trades, combined with an engaging, laid-back personality, kept him well-liked and respected among his peers. He was rarely out of work.

Talbot dug in his jacket pocket and pulled out a crumpled package of chewing tobacco. He spat once more and then carefully jammed another wad of longleaf into his right cheek with a forefinger.

"Well," he mumbled, "I'm glad to see you been workin'. Gotta make hay while the sun shines. You know this crazy business, Ben. We could all be beggin' for jobs a month from now."

"Feast or famine," Ben agreed.

"Although," Talbot continued, somewhat ruefully, "I could sure do without this particular job here. Mike told you about it, huh?"

"Oh, yeah," answered Ben. "Sounds like a real good time."

"The best," said Talbot. "Look, lemme give you a hand with your gear. We'll get our sleepin' quarters sorted out, and then I'll give you a rundown of the gory details."

"Okay." Ben went around to open the rear door of his pickup's camper shell, smiling as Talbot began to yell at a couple of the junior members of the dive crew, chewing them out for working under the cargo crane without hard hats.

He thought back to the conversation he'd had the night before with Mike Hawkin, operations manager for Universal Diving Services out of Morgan City, Louisiana. The call had come just after supper. He'd been changing the plugs in his truck.

"Hello, this is Ben."

"Hiya, Ben. Mike Hawkin here." The ops manager's voice sounded like gravel in a gearbox.

"Hey, Mike. What can I do for you?"

"Well," Hawkin rasped, "sorry to say that an oilfield chopper went down off Pascagoula two days ago. Big one. Big shuttle Sikorsky."

Ben whistled through his teeth. "Nasty. What company?"

"O.H.I."

Oilfield Helicopters Incorporated. World's largest helicopter company. O.H.I. flew more helicopter flights, was under contract to more oil corporations, and employed more pilots, mechanics, and ground-support personnel worldwide than all other chopper companies combined. Seventh crash this year, thought

Ben. He shook his head. Oil prices had slumped during the past ten months. It was always the same thing.

Like all oilfield service companies, when times were good for the petroleum industry, times were good for O.H.I. However, when oil prices sagged it was another story. Maintenance budgets were curtailed and choppers went down. Statistically, the crashes weren't significant; O.H.I. flew over ten thousand flights a month worldwide. The company could still boast of an excellent safety record. But the fact remained: when maintenance was deferred, helicopters crashed. And working men, the men who pulled the two-week shifts on the giant offshore production platforms, got killed.

"How many on board?" Ben asked.

Hawkin sighed. "Seventeen. Including the two pilots."

"Anybody get out?"

"Nope. It went straight in. Witnesses on the nearby rigs said it just dove suddenly for no apparent reason, and that was all she wrote."

"Damn. Poor guys never had a chance." Like most people who worked in the oilfield, Ben hated to hear about any fatal accident; it was too close to home. "Anybody we know?"

"Don't think so. Just seventeen guys who won't have to worry about making mortgage payments anymore." Hawkin coughed; Ben heard him rustling for a cigarette over the phone. "Funny thing. This chopper was coming from that new big floating oil rig out in Green Canyon: the NAOC-X. Had some civilians on it, supposedly. Couple of aides to that Mississippi state senator—what's his name? Latham, ain't it?— who's been all over the TV news lately crowing about American oil independence from the Middle East, and how this new rig's the key to achieving it, and how we need to militarize the thing against possible Arab terrorist attacks, blah blah blah. God, the guy sounds like a broken record.

"Anyway, these two aides of his: I'm told they were out there trying to set up the dog and pony show for a presidential visit to the rig." The operations manager let out a hoarse chuckle. "Guess they won't be reporting back anytime soon."

"They're sure making a big deal out of that new rig these days," Ben commented.

"Hey, the thought of us not needing any more Arab oil makes most of the voting public real happy, and that NAOC rig's got the technology to make it happen. The senator's no fool." Hawken cleared his throat. "So, Ben—can you do this body snatch for us? We're low on personnel, and it's over in your neck of the woods, anyway."

Ben thought for a moment. "Yeah. Yeah, I can do it. By the way, how deep is it?"

"Chopper went down in two hundred and sixty feet of water, about forty miles directly south of Pascagoula. All you need to do is show up at the MacKintosh Offshore Drilling Fluids dock in Pascagoula at ten a.m. tomorrow. We'll send the gear out with the other divers and tenders from Morgan City at around three tomorrow morning. You can all meet at the dock. You'll be working off a boat called the *Crimson Tide*; it should be at the dock when you arrive."

An hour later Ben and Talbot were standing on the aft bridge outside the wheelhouse, looking down on the gear-crowded deck below as the *Crimson Tide* slid away from the dock, her screws churning the water astern into a brown froth. The captain revved the big twin diesels and took her into the main channel, heading seaward.

As oilfield workboats went, the *Crimson Tide* was fairly large—a hundred and ninety feet in length. Constructed entirely of thick steel plate, the aft three quar-

ters of her length consisted of a long, low work deck
with an open stern. Forward, her hull rose two stories
to a high, sharp bow with the superstructure—accommodations, galley, and wheelhouse—reaching another
thirty feet above that. Two immense engine and generator exhausts, known as North Sea stacks, were built
port and starboard into the superstructure and towered fifteen feet above the wheelhouse. Fast and
strong, expensive to run, she was built to work in bad
weather in the open sea.

On the open deck below Ben and Talbot, U.D.S.
tenders and divers worked to set up the dive station.
It consisted of a central command van—a steel cargo
container modified into a combination office and dive-
control facility—and three large diesel-driven compressors. The station had to be secured to the deck
and then plumbed up—its various components inter-
connected with flexible high-pressure hoses.

Gas diving was a fairly complex business. The main
gas manifold, located inside the dive-control van, was
at the heart of the operation. A bewildering bank of
pipes, valves, regulators, and gauges, the manifold delivered the necessary quantity of air or heliox breathing gas to the diver in the water through his dive hose.
In addition, a special gauge on the manifold, known
as a pneumo-fathometer, showed the diver's exact
depth at all times. The deepest depth of the dive,
along with the precise length of time spent in the
water, was crucial in the selection of the appropriate
decompression schedule. This was the rate at which
the diver could be brought back to sea-level pressure
without suffering an attack of decompression sickness—the "bends."

Along with the gas and air supplies, the other vital
component of the dive station was the decompression
chamber. A cylindrical vessel about twelve feet long
by four feet wide, constructed of heavy steel with

viewing ports set in its side, the chamber could be sealed with the diver inside, the internal pressure controlled by an outside tender. After making a series of in-water decompression stops, working up to shallower and shallower depths, the diver would be pulled up quickly from his last stop and hustled immediately into the decompression chamber. The chamber would be sealed and "blown down," or pressurized with air, to the equivalent of forty feet of water depth. Lying on a mattress in the chamber, the diver would breathe pure oxygen through a face mask for up to four hours, depending on the length and depth of the working dive. When at long last he was brought back to surface pressure and allowed to leave the chamber, he would hopefully remain free of the bends.

Sparks erupted from a blue flash as one of the divers struck an arc and began welding the dive-control van to the deck. Tenders wearing greasy U.D.S. coveralls turned away quickly, shielding their eyes from the ultraviolet rays.

The dive crew consisted of Talbot, the overall supervisor; Ben, the senior diver and alternate supervisor; four divers with less seniority than Ben; and five tenders. The divers performed all the underwater work, in addition to running the gas manifold and radios in the dive-control shack. The tenders, usually fairly young and new to the company, handled all the deck labor—setting up gear, feeding out and recovering the diver's hoses, running the chambers, and fixing the multitude of things that could break, burst, leak, or otherwise malfunction, usually at the worst possible moment.

As she passed the end of the long stone breakwater and headed toward the sea-buoy at the far end of the channel, the *Crimson Tide* began to ride over a five-foot swell that was running north in the open waters of the Gulf. Rhythmically, she rose and fell, the mo-

tion both massive and gentle, her steel bow slicing the
waves into twin torrents of foam. Gulls wheeled and
dove just behind the stern, picking up shrimp and bait
fish from the churning wake.

She passed the sea-buoy just before noon and
turned directly south, heading for the crash location
at a steady sixteen knots.

The *Crimson Tide* reached the designated site at
fourteen hundred hours—two in the afternoon. She
spent the next hour running anchors; positioning her
four big hooks on the ocean bottom in an X-pattern
that spanned a quarter mile. The tightly winched anchor cables held her in place in the center of the X,
exactly over the crash site.

A team of surveyors from yet another service company contracted by Oilfield Helicopters dropped a
Mesotech unit over the side on a three-hundred-foot
umbilical cable. Consisting of a small revolving sonar
unit mounted on a four-foot tripod, the Mesotech produced a three hundred and sixty degree sound-wave
picture of the area around itself. Like a kind of sonic
radar, any object within its range would reflect the
sound waves back to the tripod unit, producing an
image on a computer monitor aboard the *Crimson
Tide*. In this way, the surveyors could pinpoint the
location of whatever they happened to be looking for.
The device made life easier for a diver on the ocean
floor, too. In the event of poor visibility on bottom,
the Mesotech could be utilized to help talk the man
in the water over to the target.

Ben and Talbot stood in the darkened survey van,
looking over the shoulders of the lead surveyor as he
sat hunched over the keyboard in front of the flickering computer monitor. A wizened little man with a
pinched face and thin, greasy hair, he chain-smoked
furiously as he fiddled with the screen's gain and

brightness control, the green light glinting off his Coke-bottle glasses.

"Shee-it!" he said suddenly. "There it is!" He sat back, smiling triumphantly, pointing with a nicotine-stained finger at a glowing green blob in the lower right-hand corner of the screen. " 'Bout forty feet northeast of the tripod . . . dead under the stern, I'd say." He puffed vigorously on his cigarette, filling the small van with acrid smoke.

"All right. Good job," Talbot said, clapping a hand on the surveyor's shoulder. "Can you get an exact lat-long reading for the F.A.A. records?"

"Shee-it, yeah!" the little man said, punching keys rapidly. "Just need to feed the Mesotech coordinates into the linkage with the Sat-Nav, cross-check the accuracy parameters with the Loran, and calculate the . . ."

His voice trailed off into a mumble as he worked, the stub of his cigarette bobbling in his mouth, dropping ash onto the keyboard.

"Done!" he said abruptly, sitting back again. "In the records!" He reached for another smoke from a crumpled pack on the table.

"Good enough," said Talbot, smiling. "Well, it sure looks like you've got it all under control. How about jumpin' down there on the end of a dive hose and baggin' up those bodies for us?" He nudged Ben. "We'll letcha."

"Shee-it, no!" exclaimed the surveyor. "Diving's for crazy people. Besides, I don't want to run into whatever *that* is."

He pointed at the screen again. An elongated green blob about one quarter the size of the helicopter indication was moving in a slow circle around the crash site.

"We can probably figure out what it is," the surveyor continued. "Lessee, it's likely about eight, maybe ten feet long—"

"Never mind," Ben said. "I don't really want to know. I can imagine just fine." He grinned and looked at Talbot. "I'll just keep my eyes closed. If I can't see him, he's not there, right?"

Talbot gave him a knowing wink. "Right. That's how it works, partner."

They left the van laughing. The little surveyor swiveled his office chair around and stared after them, thinking that anyone who'd go to the bottom of that ocean after seeing something ten feet long swimming around down there must be a certifiable lunatic.

Chapter Two

Ben stood at the open stern of the *Crimson Tide,* fully dressed to make his dive. He wore a three-eighths-inch neoprene wet suit, a fifteen-pound weight belt, heavy-soled rubber boots, and a sturdy chest harness of thick canvas webbing. A folding stainless-steel knife and a small crowbar on a lanyard hung from D-rings on the harness. Thick, flexible fish-handler's gloves protected his hands.

He was closing the cam-lock on his diving helmet, securing it onto his head. A molded fiberglass shell with a Lexan faceplate, it enclosed the diver's head completely in foam-cushioned comfort. Built-in mouth and ear speakers provided two-way radio communications with the dive-control van via a cable married into the dive hose. Air or heliox gas was supplied according to Ben's needs through a demand regulator built into the front of the helmet; additional valves gave him the option of free-flowing breathing gas into it as well. Another valve controlled a reserve supply of gas contained in a large scuba tank that Ben wore on his back—a bailout bottle. It was for use in the event that breathing gas could not be delivered down the dive hose.

The helmet locked onto a neck-dam; a fiberglass-and-rubber yoke that the diver wore around his neck to prevent water from filling the helmet. It would only leak slightly even when he was upside-down. As long as the helmet was locked to the neck-dam, it could not come off the diver's head. The dive-helmet, or "hat," as it was commonly called, was every diver's most prized piece of personal equipment; it kept him alive while he was doing his job.

A small crane had been welded to the back deck of the boat off to one side of the stern. A large steel-grating basket was suspended from it, with black vinyl body bags rolled up and lashed along its lip. Two tenders held tag lines attached to the basket to prevent it from swinging too much as the boat surged gently up and down in the light swell.

"Hey, Joey, how do you hear me?" Ben asked, his voice muffled to his own ears by the oral-nasal mask covering the lower part of his face.

"Real good, Ben, real good," came the answer. Talbot's voice sounded thin and disembodied in the hat's ear speakers. "You ready to do it to it, partner?"

"Sure." Ben looked up through his faceplate at the hanging basket. "Tell that crane operator to put the basket in the water, willya? Have him lower it to about twenty feet and stop."

"Okay. You're gonna ride it down, huh?"

"Roj-o."

Ben saw the crane operator concentrate as Talbot's instructions came through his headset. He slipped the brake on the crane and lowered the basket into the clear blue water. Salty foam hissed as it hit the surface and continued on down, stopping at twenty feet.

It was about a six-foot drop to the water from the back deck. The crane cable hung some eight feet out from the stern. Ben steadied himself with a hand on his tender's shoulder, poised to jump.

"I'm going in," he said.

"Roger that," Talbot answered. "Be lucky." He always said that.

"Only way to be," Ben quipped.

He put a hand firmly on top of his hat and leaped off the stern toward the cable, plunging through the surface of the water in a welter of silvery-blue bubbles. The visibility was excellent. All around and below him the ocean stretched away into vast blue emptiness. He shivered a little as cold water seeped into his wet suit, and swam down to stand on the lip of the basket, one hand holding the crane cable.

"All right, Joey," he said, reaching up and cracking his free-flow valve slightly, "come on down on the basket." Air hissed through the diffusion bar that ran across the top of the faceplate inside the hat, cooling Ben's face.

"Comin' down," came Talbot's reply. There was a crackling noise in Ben's ear speakers as the supervisor adjusted the radio's volume controls. "Gonna stop you around one hundred feet for the gas switch, okay?"

"Sounds good," Ben acknowledged. The exchange of information was merely a procedural formality; both men knew the routine by heart.

The basket dropped smoothly, the surrounding water losing its intense blue color as the ambient light decreased with depth. A school of two-foot-long blackfin tuna shot by like a salvo of small silver missiles, disappearing in the distant blue gloom. Ben looked at his bright orange fish-handler's gloves; they were a dull purple. He was thinking he must be getting close when the basket halted abruptly.

"You're there," Talbot said. "Ventilate for gas."

"Ventilating," Ben replied. He cracked the free-flow valve on his hat wide open. Simultaneously, the diver operating the gas rack topside in the dive-control van shut off the air to Ben's hose and opened a series of valves that delivered pressurized heliox instead. The check valves on the rack squealed as the thin gas rushed through them. The rack operator monitored the switch intently, never taking his eyes off the supply gauges.

Commercial divers breathe gas when working at depths greater than two hundred and twenty feet for one primary reason: the presence of nitrogen in the bloodstream—the inert gas that makes up seventy-eight percent of breathable air—has a narcotic effect on the human brain at depths greater than one hundred and forty feet or so, an effect that intensifies and becomes more disabling as the depth increases. An experienced diver can—and often does—work under nitrogen narcosis to a certain extent, but at extreme depths it becomes impossible to function.

Ben ventilated until all the air had been pushed out of the hose. When the sound of rushing air changed to the higher-pitched whine of rushing gas and he sensed the cold taste of helium in his mouth, he shut off the free-flow valve and adjusted his demand regulator. It delivered the expensive heliox to him breath by breath.

"I've got it," he said hoarsely into his mouth speaker. "One, two, three, four, five, six . . . Okay?"

Topside, Talbot heard the sudden voice change that indicated the diver was on gas; Ben sounded like Donald Duck on a bad long-distance line. Helium distorts the human voice, making speech high, thin, and almost unintelligible. The slow count gave Talbot an opportunity to adjust his radio's helium voice-descrambler, which artificially modified the diver's tones into some semblance of normality.

"Okay," Talbot said. "Go. You've got thirty-six minutes left."

"Roj-o. Come down fast on the basket."

The basket started moving again, dropping swiftly into the depths. At one hundred and twenty feet, Ben felt a sudden chill as he passed through a thermocline, or temperature layer, into much colder water. By one hundred and ninety feet the bright, sunlit blue of the surface had given way to a dark, shadowy gray-green, and visibility had reduced to thirty feet.

"Gettin' close," came Talbot's faraway voice. The open end of Ben's pneumo-fathometer hose spurted a small gust of bubbles. The rack operator was checking the depth. "Looks to be about two-forty," the supervisor reported.

"Roj-o," Ben said. "Come down a little more slowly, now . . ."

The basket's rate of descent slackened as it dropped into a layer of suspended sediment. All remaining ambient light was effectively blacked out. Ben felt the chill of another thermocline as he snapped on his hat light. Looking down at the basket under his feet, he found that he had about four feet of visibility. Not good, but better than nothing.

There was a sudden clunk, and the basket tilted sharply under Ben's feet.

"All stop, all stop," he said quickly, dropping down to see what the basket had hit.

The white-painted aluminum skin of the helicopter loomed in the beam of the light. Ben put a hand on the fuselage, scattering a small storm of sediment particles.

"Pretty good shot," he said. "The basket came down right on top of the chopper." He planted his feet against the helicopter and pushed the basket out five feet or so. "Slack the basket some more."

"Comin' down," Talbot acknowledged.

Ben walked the basket down the side of the aircraft and set it in the soft mud of the bottom.

"All stop on the basket," he directed. The cable stopped moving. "Slack the diver." He pulled about fifteen feet of dive hose to himself. "All stop on the diver."

Sinking to his knees in the soft gray ooze, Ben

began to inspect the ruined helicopter, following the fuselage to the tail and around the opposite side. He tried not to stir up the bottom too much, but it was difficult; clouds of mud boiled up around him as he moved. His visibility shrank to less than two feet.

"Okay, Joey," Ben said as he felt his way along, "here's what we've got: the chopper's right-side-up on the bottom, leaning to port a little. About a quarter of it's sunk in the mud. As far as I can tell, the fuselage seems to be intact . . . no, wait a minute . . . belay that. A large chunk of the aluminum skin is gone from the starboard side." He explored some more, running his hands carefully over the ripped metal. "I guess this is where the big sliding door used to be."

"Roger that," Talbot answered. "Can you see it lyin' around down there, anywhere? Probably not, huh?"

"Nah," Ben said. "Too murky. Lousy viz. Maybe we can tie off a search line and make a sweep for it later."

"Yeah," Talbot mused. "It'd make the F.A.A. happy if we found it. But that door could've drifted away in the current as it sank . . . could be halfway to Cuba by now. Can you see inside?"

"Not yet," Ben replied. He followed his hose back around to the other side of the helicopter. "I need to move this basket closer to the door."

Giving curt directions, he guided the basket up over the top of the chopper and set it in the mud beside the opening.

"Okay," he said. "I'm going inside." He took a deep breath. This was going to be fun.

"Roger," Talbot acknowledged. "Be careful. Watch your hose on them sharp edges." There was a slight pause as he checked the elapsed time. "You've got twenty-nine minutes left."

"Roj-o."

Ben stepped gingerly through the opening, feeling for the aircraft's seats. Sediment swirled in the glare of his hat light, illuminated like a swarm of fireflies against the shadowy black background. He held his hand up in front of his faceplate; he could barely see eighteen inches.

As Ben turned his head this way and that, a small amount of seawater leaked up around his neoprene neck-seal. A smell began to permeate his hat: the sickly sweet odor of decaying flesh. In spite of the intense cold a trickle of perspiration ran down into his eye. He blinked it away. Steeling himself for what he knew he was about to see, he moved farther into the helicopter's interior.

His hand touched something soft and cloth-covered. He drifted in closer, trying not to stir up the light dusting of sediment that covered everything.

Abruptly, the face of a dead man loomed up in the light, impossibly pale and swollen. Ben grimaced and hesitated, then felt for the corpse's shoulder. The sickly sweet smell was almost overpowering.

The man was still belted into his seat, his head sagging off to one side. A small crab was crawling through his short blond hair, and a half-dozen minnows were picking at his empty eye sockets. Ben brushed the crab away, trying not to look at the man's face.

"I got one here," he said. "Young guy, looks like. Wearing red coveralls."

"Roger that," Talbot came back. "All in one piece?"

"Roj-o. As far as I can tell."

"Yeah. Ain't been down there long enough to really soften up, y'know?"

"Jesus, Joey . . ."

"Sorry, sorry," the supervisor said hastily. "Kinda nasty, huh?"

"It's not real pretty," Ben said. "Got some critters gnawing on him. Hell, at least this one's not all torn up. Hang on a minute while I get a body bag."

He backed out to the basket, cut off one of the bags, and returned to the first seat. Carefully, he worked the unzipped bag up around the corpse's knees, then cut the seat belt with his dive knife and gently pulled the body forward. It hung suspended in the murky water as Ben unfolded the black vinyl, enclosing the arms and finally the pale face. He zipped the bag shut, breathing a sigh of relief, and pulled it slowly out of the chopper onto the ocean floor.

"I've got him bagged," he said, "and I'm putting him into the basket."

"Roger that. You're gonna tie him off, huh?"

"Roj-o."

Repositioning himself, Ben lifted the body bag and deposited it in the bottom of the basket. Using a length of manila that had been attached to the steel mesh, he lashed the corpse securely in place. More than one body had been lost in the past by being washed out of a lifting container during recovery.

"Okay, Joey," Ben said, "I'm going back in for another one right now."

"Roger that," Talbot replied. "You've got sixteen minutes."

Ben cut off another bag, turned back toward the helicopter, and froze in his tracks.

Swimming leisurely through the six-foot gap between the basket and the chopper, huge and dark against the paleness of the fuselage, was an immense shark. At least, it looked immense to Ben, who could have reached out and touched its mottled gray-brown skin with ease. He watched transfixed as the great animal cruised on past, propelling itself with unhurried sweeps of its asymmetrically lobed tail. It disappeared into the black murk.

"Ben? Ben, you all right?" Talbot's voice came crackling through the ear speakers.

"Yeah," Ben said. "I'm okay."

"I couldn't hear your breathin' for a minute." One of the ways Talbot monitored his diver was to keep an ear attuned to the sound of his regulator exhalations. "Maybe there's something wrong with the radio or the com cable . . ."

"I don't think so," Ben replied. "I don't think I was breathing for a few seconds, there . . ."

"Oh, yeah? Problem?"

"No," Ben said. "I just got a good look at the Meso-tech Monster, is all. He startled me."

"Really? What is it?"

"Sand tiger. Big guy."

"How big?"

"About fifty feet," Ben said, laughing. "No—right around eight or ten feet, I guess. Took me by surprise. He's still around here somewhere."

"No doubt," Talbot agreed. "Sand tiger, huh? Could be worse. He actin' crazy or anything?"

"Nope. Just cruising the neighborhood."

"He probably likes the smell."

"Please," Ben said. "Don't remind me."

He made his way back to the opening in the fuse-lage and ducked inside. Feeling a slithering sensation around his left ankle, he looked down in time to see a three-foot conger eel dart out into the mud cloud. The creatures of the ocean floor never missed a free banquet.

"Hey, Ben." Talbot's voice crackled through the speakers again.

"Yeah?"

"Coast Guard officer's here in the dive shack with me. Wants me to remind you that the senator's office made an official request that bodies of the two aides be given special priority during the recovery. Since they were out on that high-profile NAOC rig, this crash has a few politicians worked up, seems like." Talbot couldn't keep the irritation out of his voice.

Ben bit off the expletive that rose to his lips and said, "You tell Slick Rick up there that those political aides aren't any more important than any *one* of these regular working men down here. *All* these boys are coming home, not just the ones who managed to earn a living without getting their fingernails dirty."

"Know what you mean, Ben," Talbot said. "But I don't guess I'll tell him that." He chuckled. "Good thing I got these headphones on . . ."

Nearly gagging on the smell that pervaded his hat, Ben worked his way up to the cockpit. He pulled back the small curtain that separated pilots from passengers and trained his hat light around the interior.

The port pilot's seat was completely gone, as was the large Plexiglas windscreen and supporting framework on that side. Mud had silted in through the open nose, partially covering the cockpit floor. Torn wiring and broken electronic units dangled from the ceiling. Incredibly, a digital clock on one of the mangled radios, likely powered by an independent lithium battery, still displayed the correct time in glowing red numbers.

The starboard pilot was still in his seat, strapped in place by an over-the-shoulder harness. Ben drifted in behind him in the cramped space and put a hand softly on his upper arm. Dust puffed up from the short-sleeved white shirt, the black-and-gold epaulet gleaming a little in the light. The body moved slightly in its harness, and the left arm, freed by Ben's touch, floated slowly upward in a ghoulish salute.

Ben stepped around the seat and unfolded the body bag. Intending to start at the feet and work up, as he'd done before, he ran a hand lightly down the corpse's leg. There was too much sediment stirred up near the floor to be able to see. Then Ben felt the leg end abruptly. His hand bumped into a large, jagged piece of metal.

Feeling around, seeing what he could, he discovered that the pilot's legs had both been severed just above the knees, probably when the piece of metal had come slicing across the cockpit upon impact with the water. Groping around some more, he thought he felt a shoe well back under the tangle of aluminum and steel, but couldn't get a firm grip on it.

Abandoning the attempt to recover the pilot's lower legs, he turned back to the torso and worked the bag over the thighs and buttocks up to waist level. Then he straightened up, preparing to cut away the seat harness at the shoulders. The beam of light caught the pilot's dead face momentarily.

Ben felt himself go numb. He knew the man. Blinking, he swore under his breath. Maybe he was wrong.

"You all right?" Talbot asked quickly, hearing the oath.

Ben didn't answer. He brushed the sediment from the gold name tag clipped to the pilot's shirt pocket. "Anthony D'Angelo" it read, "Senior Captain."

There was no mistake.

"Goddammit," Ben muttered. "God*dammit!*"

"Hey!" Talbot said. "You okay? Goddamn what?"

Ben cut the shoulder harness and began to roll the bag up over the rest of the body, trying to keep his eyes averted.

"I'm all right, Joey," he said. "I'm all right."

"What's with all the cussin', partner?"

Ben coughed, working the zipper closed.

"You remember Tony Angel? Used to have that big house up on Bayou Teche?"

"Used to have it before he got divorced," Talbot corrected. "Yeah, I know Tony."

"You used to know Tony," Ben replied. He finished zipping the bag closed. "He's down here with me."

"Oh, shit." There was a pause, then Talbot's voice came back. "Look, Ben, I know you guys were friends. Just forget about trying to recover any more bodies on this dive. Get out of there and come on up; you're almost out of time, anyway."

"I've got him in a bag," Ben said evenly. "One minute and I'll have him in the basket. No problem."

"Okay," Talbot responded. "I need you off bottom in three minutes."

"Roj-o. I'll make it."

Ben pulled the unwieldy bag over to the torn door and out onto the mud, glancing around quickly for any sign of the big shark. Nothing but black, particle-filled water. He dragged the bag over to the basket and, straining, heaved it slowly in. Working fast, he cut free some more manila and began to lash the body in place.

"Come up on the diver's hose," he instructed.

"Comin' up," Talbot repeated. "Fifty seconds, Ben."

"Roj-o," Ben said. He felt the dive hose tug upward where it was clipped to his safety harness. Looking up, he saw the hose disappearing into the blackness alongside the crane cable.

"All stop on the diver," he said. The strain eased up immediately.

"All stop on you," Talbot echoed. "Thirty seconds."

Ben finished the lashing and whirled around to grab the slack crane cable. He hopped up on the lip of the basket.

"Come up on the basket."

"Roger that. Comin' up."

The crane cable moved slowly upward, tightening and taking the weight of the basket. As it pulled free of the bottom, it drifted back toward the helicopter, and Ben fended it off with a foot. It cleared the top of the fuselage, scraping against a broken rotor blade, and ascended smoothly into open water.

"Leaving bottom," Ben said.

"Roger that," Talbot came back. "Just in time. Your first in-water stop's at one-seventy. We're pickin' you up at twenty-five feet per minute; it should take you four minutes to get there."

"Roj-o."

The ambient light and visibility suddenly increased as the basket rose out of the sediment layer. Ben glanced around three hundred and sixty degrees. The demarcation between the sediment layer and the clearer gray-green water above was sharp. It looked almost solid enough to walk on, like ground covered by dry-ice vapor in an old horror film.

A movement off to his left caught Ben's eye. It was the big sand tiger, planing slowly upward out of the murk like a zeppelin rising out of the clouds. The shark cruised around the basket as it rose, maintaining a radius of fifteen feet as it swam in a leisurely vertical spiral.

Ben regarded the animal, cautious but unalarmed. Any shark nearly ten feet long bore watching, but to a commercial diver it was just another fish in the sea. Far from being ravenous man-eaters, most species of sharks were wary of people, preferring—when they allowed themselves to be seen at all—to make one or two curious passes from a safe distance, and then leave. In Ben's long experience, the worst part of encountering a shark in the open sea was the primordial jolt to the nervous system the initial sighting caused; invariably, they showed up when they were least expected.

This one had become curious about the movement of the ascending basket and diver. It was not a particularly handsome species of shark, having a lumpy, prehistoric look to it. Unlike the streamlined, hydrodynamically clean blue or mako, the sand tiger was fat and heavy, with a small head, humped back, and bulging belly. It had loose gill slits, a bug-like white eye, and a jumble of ragged-looking teeth spilling out of a smallish, underslung mouth. It looked ugly and powerful.

The basket stopped suddenly, and Talbot's voice crackled over the com lines again.

"Looks like you're there, Ben. Let me get a pneumo on you."

"Roj-o," Ben said, holding the end of the pneumo-fathometer hose at his chest. It spurted bubbles again as the rack operator checked the depth.

"Perfect," Talbot said. "One hundred and ninety-five feet. Ventilate back to air."

"Ventilating," Ben replied, cracking open his free-flow valve once again. The cold gas was flushed out of the hat as air raced down the hose. Ben inhaled deeply as the warmer breathing medium hit his face. The familiar pleasant numbness of nitrogen narcosis quickly enveloped him—the unavoidable side effect of switching back to air from heliox on a deep gas dive. Old-time divers liked it—cheaper than booze, they said, and no hangover.

Ben switched off his free-flow and relaxed, closing his eyes. "One, two, three, four . . ." he counted.

"Gotcha," Talbot said. "Back on air. How do you feel? Are you buzzed?"

"I feel great," Ben murmured.

"I'll bet you do. Nothin' beats comin' back onto air at one-ninety-five, does it?"

"Nothing," Ben concurred, breathing deeply.

Talbot set about rechecking Ben's decompression schedule. It called for ninety minutes in the water, moving upward in ten-foot increments, with the last stop at forty feet. Then Ben would have to do three hours in the deck decompression chamber breathing pure oxygen.

Ben half dozed with his eyes closed for a couple of minutes, and when he opened them the big sand tiger was gone. In its place was a school of hardtails—small silver jacks about ten inches long—milling loosely around the basket. Ben looked down just in time to see the shark's bulky form disappear into the deep green shadows below.

He shifted his gaze to the body bag that held what was left of D'Angelo. The black vinyl undulated gently in its lashings. Anthony D'Angelo. Tony Angel to his friends. Three tours of Vietnam without a scratch. One wife, one ex-wife, and three kids; one stepson and two of his own.

Ben shifted on the edge of the basket. It would hit Tony's kids and his new wife Jill the hardest. He wondered if they already knew.

One of the lashings on D'Angelo's bag was loose. Ben bent down to retie it. As he did so, the slightly open flap of the bag shifted back, partially revealing the dead pilot's ear and neck. In the pale flesh just behind the ear, Ben noticed a small round hole, about a quarter-inch in diameter.

Just the sort of hole one would expect a bullet to make.

Nah. Couldn't be.

It was some kind of head trauma caused by the crash, Ben decided. Gently, he cradled his friend's head in one hand and drew the bag's flap up over it. He zipped the bag completely closed.

"Ciao, Tony," he whispered. "At least you didn't have long to think about it."

The basket began to move upward again, very slowly. Talbot's voice broke the silence.

"Comin' up twenty feet, partner," he said. "Ten feet per minute. You'll be stoppin' at one-fifty for four minutes. Okay?"

"Roj-o," Ben said.

The nitrogen narcosis cleared rapidly as the basket's depth decreased. At one hundred and fifty feet Ben had only the slightest sensation of dizziness; by one hundred and twenty, some fifteen minutes later, the narc had left him entirely.

"Hey, Ben, lemme talk to you now," Talbot said.

"Sure, go ahead," Ben replied.

"First of all," the supervisor began, "I want you to know that I had no idea whatsoever that Tony was flyin' this chopper. You know U.D.S. has a policy against lettin' friends recover friends . . . people tend to get upset."

"Tell me about it," Ben said.

"I wouldn't blame you for bein' pissed," Talbot went on, "but you know as well as I do that nobody would do something like this on purpose—change the policy without tellin' you ahead of time."

"I know that," Ben replied, "that's why I can't understand why Mike said no when I asked him if it was anybody we knew."

"Well, I just gave him a call on the cellular," Talbot said, "and told him about this little situation. He was apologetic as all hell; apparently he thought you were askin' him if there were any divers on board. It never occurred to him that you might know the pilot. You freelancers get around a lot more than us company men. Anyway, he says if you want to drag up off the job, he'll understand, with no hard feelin's."

Ben listened to the air hissing gently into his hat. A hardtail swam up as if to nip at his fingers, and he batted it away with the back of his hand.

"Nah," he said finally. "I'll stay. The big shock's

over now. There can't be anyone else down there I know."

"Great," Talbot said. "I need you around, anyhow. These other divers are kinda green. Know what I mean, partner?"

"I know what you mean," Ben answered. He laughed a little. "Right now I'm halfway wishing I'd turned out to be a stockbroker or insurance salesman. I'll bet they don't have days like this . . ."

"I'll bet you're right," Talbot returned.

They spoke very little as Ben did the rest of his in-water decompression; he didn't feel like talking, and Talbot didn't push it. Sitting on the edge of the basket, his elbows hooked around the support slings, Ben alternately dozed and watched the hardtails, stretching his limbs frequently to avoid cramps. At ninety feet his breathing mix was switched again, this time to a nitrogen-oxygen mix known as fifty-fifty, a designation that referred to the percentage of each gas in the blend. The high concentration of oxygen in this mix enabled Ben's body to rid itself of the helium retained during the dive more efficiently.

After nearly twenty minutes at forty feet, Talbot spoke again:

"Ventilate back to air, Ben. We're fixin' to pick you up."

Ben vented the fifty-fifty out of his hat in a blast of bubbles. Leaving the free-flow open, he checked to see that his hose was running straight up toward the stern of the boat, free of the crane cable. The *Crimson Tide* was a massive dark bullet above him, her big twin propellers glinting a dull bronze against the hull's shadow.

"Ten seconds, Ben," Talbot said. "You feelin' all right? No aches, no pains?"

"Feeling good," Ben responded.

"Okay. We're pickin' you up."

The dive hose went taut as the tender on the back deck began hauling it in. As it took his weight, Ben let himself drift off the basket into open water.

"Hanging free," he said.

"Roger that."

Topside, Talbot was watching the time, coaching the tender to recover the hose at a rate that would put Ben at the surface one minute after leaving forty feet. The next two minutes were critical; Ben had to be brought on deck, shed of his dive hat, bailout bottle, guided to the chamber, locked in, and repressurized to fifty feet.

Ben reached the bottom of the ladder at the stern in fifty seconds and climbed smartly up onto the deck. Two tenders were beside him instantly, helping him get out of his hat and shrug off his harness and bailout bottle, while two others manned the decompression chamber—one outside to run the blowdown valves, the other waiting to assist Ben inside the transfer lock. Talbot hovered nearby, clipboard in hand, watching the elapsed time.

"Let's go, let's go," he prodded.

At the chamber door, Ben unzipped his wet-suit jacket and held his arms back as the tenders stripped it off him. Grabbing a freshwater hose that lay on the deck, he gave himself a quick rinse, then ducked through the chamber's circular hatch into the transfer lock.

The heavy steel door clanged shut behind him, and the lock was filled instantly with the roar of high-pressure air. Kneeling in the cramped space, barely four feet long by four feet in diameter, Ben and the inside tender concentrated on clearing their ears as the internal pressure rapidly increased.

In thirty seconds their bodies were under an atmospheric pressure equivalent to that of fifty feet of seawater. The tender helped Ben get out of his wet-suit overalls and handed him a towel, then pushed open the hatch door to the inner lock. The heavy steel disk swung back on its hinges to reveal the seven-foot space where Ben would spend the next three hours, lying prone on a thin plastic mattress, breathing in pure oxygen through an oral-nasal mask.

He wrapped the towel around his hips and entered the inner lock, pushing the door closed behind him.

"Pick up the transfer lock" he said to a small speaker mounted beside the door.

There was a blast of air as the outside tender, wearing headphones and watching Ben through a small, thick Lexan port, sealed the inner-lock door and bled the pressure off the transfer lock. Thirty seconds later the inside tender stepped out of the chamber onto the back deck.

Ben strapped the rubber breathing mask over his face and turned on the oxygen-delivery valve.

"On O-2," he said to the outside tender, who nodded through the Lexan and jotted down the time on the decompression schedule.

Wrapping a blanket around himself, Ben stretched out flat on his back on the plastic mattress, his head resting on the single damp pillow.

Through the steel walls of the chamber, he heard the faint roar of the crane's diesel engine; they were picking up the basket containing the two body bags.

Ben stared up at the white-painted interior of the lock, breathing deeply and evenly, and tried hard not to think of Tony D'Angelo and his final, ill-fated flight from the NAOC-X.

Chapter Three

The sun had just dropped below the horizon, and the western sky above the barrier islands was aflame with orange and purple hues when Ben turned the pickup into the marina parking lot. He pulled into the spot marked "Gannon" by a faded wooden sign, hauled his duffel bag out of the cargo bed, slung it over his shoulder, and headed down the rickety stairs to the dock, his battered work boots clumping hollowly on the weathered wood. The gulls quarreled on the galvanized roof of the marina restaurant, gathering to roost for the night.

Wojeck's Marina was situated in a small, crescent-shaped inlet about five miles west of Fort Walton, Florida. The inlet was protected from the open waters of the Gulf of Mexico by the long stretch of barrier island that ran from Pensacola to Fort Walton/Destin, interrupted only by a small natural channel opposite the marina. Unlike the southern half of the state, the coastal areas of the Florida panhandle remained relatively undeveloped by big business, primarily because it got too cold in the winter for tourists. That was just fine with locals like Ben and his companion Sasha Wojeck; it kept their part of the Gulf uncrowded and unspoiled.

Ben shifted the bag on his shoulder as he started down the long pier, stretching his stiff neck. He hadn't stopped to sleep after the *Crimson Tide* had hit the dock in Pascagoula, the crashed chopper chained down on the back deck in several large, twisted pieces, but had said his good-byes and headed for home immediately. Much of the way he'd thought about Tony Angel.

The *Teresa Ann* rested gracefully in her slip, her dock lines slack in the calm air. Ben rubbed the back of his neck and cast an experienced eye over his boat. She was forty-four feet long, a Colin Archer-designed double-ender with a twin-masted ketch rig. Custom-built in the mid-1950s for a wealthy industrialist, she was one of the last boats Ben knew of that was constructed of solid teak—each plank was two inches thick and ran from stem to stern. A boat like the *Teresa Ann* couldn't be built in the 1990s. Even if someone had the money, there weren't enough teak trees left on the planet large enough to yield straight-grain planks of the necessary size.

The main hatch was open, a warm yellow light emanating from below. Ben could hear music playing softly—Miles Davis' "In a Silent Way." The lonely trumpet sang its clear melodic lines, putting a theme to the fiery abstract in the evening sky.

Ben clumped up the short gangplank and let the duffel bag slide off his shoulder to the cockpit bench. The *Teresa Ann* moved slightly with his weight, and there came a rattling, scuffling sound from the companionway. Ben turned around in time to see the massive, bearlike head of a jet-black rottweiler pop up over the hatch coaming, golden-brown eyes alert and searching.

"Hey, Caesar!" Ben exclaimed, catching the big dog by his floppy ears. "You're good-looking, but you're not the one I came to see! Where's your boss, huh? Where's your boss?"

Wagging his stub of a tail frantically and trying to back down the companionway ladder, Caesar slither-

thumped to the floor of the main cabin as Ben came down the steps. The dog stretched out his paws, head low and rump high, clawing at Ben's boots and whimpering with excitement.

"Caesar! Behave!" Sasha's voice, quiet but sharp, calmed the rottweiler instantly. His handsome head came up, and he trotted around the cabin sofa to his mistress. She got to her feet, pushing blonde hair out of her eyes, and smiled at Ben, her teeth white against her bronze tan.

"Hey, babe," she said, and stepped over the back of the sofa. At five-foot-nine and one hundred and thirty pounds, she moved with the easy grace of an athlete, fit yet feminine. She was barefoot, wearing old jeans and a faded denim shirt knotted around her midriff. Two fingers were bandaged and taped together, and there was a smudge of black grease at the corner of one eye.

She came up close, put the fingers of both hands in Ben's belt, and kissed him unhurriedly on the mouth. Ben rested his hands on her narrow waist and indulged himself in the warm taste of home. She smelled like Ivory soap and salt water.

He pulled back, licking his lips, and grasped her bandaged hand gently, holding it up between them.

"What's this, Sass?" he inquired softly. She put her forehead on his collarbone and nuzzled.

"Crazy Ed needed a hand pulling his diesel auxiliary this morning," she said, "so I gave him one." She grinned into his shirt.

Ben looked the fingers over. "Looks like he tried to keep it," he observed.

Sass straightened up and led him by the belt buckle over to the couch.

"Sit," she said, and headed for the refrigerator. Ben let himself flop down on the soft pillows.

"Ed couldn't do it himself," she continued, rummaging around for a beer. "You know him: he's seventy-seven and still won't pay a mechanic to do anything for him—not even pull an engine. He's nuts. As soon as I suggested it, he spent the next thirty minutes telling me . . . guess what?"

"That he was an engineer on a Dreadnought-class destroyer for twenty-five years, and he'd be pickled in diesel fuel before he let any landlubberly truck mechanic get within ten feet of his boat engine," Ben said flatly.

"You got it," Sass said. She tossed him a bottle of Guinness. "So, anyway—I helped him break loose the mounts and drop the prop shaft, then I phoned Hank Montgomery over at Destin Crane Rental and called in a few favors . . ."

"I don't think I like the sound of that," Ben said, feigning annoyance.

"Tough," Sass countered, throwing a balled-up paper towel at him. "Don't be stupid. Listen: Hank brought his small cherry picker over—the one with the really long boom—and we got Ed's boat under the main block. We had the engine hanging above the mounts free and clear—without breaking anything— and then wham!"

"Wham?" Ben echoed. "What? The engine fell on your hand?"

"No," Sass said, "Ed stepped on my fingers while I was picking up a wrench. Hurt like hell, too," she added. She burst into laughter. "Poor Ed nearly broke down on the spot! You'd have thought he'd murdered me. He wanted to take me down for X rays, but I told him to forget it. So he bandaged them all up, brought me back here, and made me promise to lie down for the rest of the day." She giggled. "I had to sneak up to the office to pay some contractor's bills. I think he would have hog-tied me and made me drink chicken soup if he'd caught me."

"Hog-tied you?" Ben said mildly. "Hmm. Sounds good to me . . ."

Sass came around the corner of the galley counter and jumped on top of him, pinning his wrists up by his head.

"Think you're man enough?" she teased. "Boy?"

Ben stayed limp, grinning up at her. "I refuse to take advantage of an injured female."

Sass squeezed his wrists hard, her long blonde hair falling down around her face. "You're a chauvinist pig, you know," she stated. Then she bent down and kissed him hard. "But I'm kinda partial to pork now and then.

"Anyway," she continued, sitting up and pushing hair out of her face, "that's how my hand got messed up. It's cut and bruised, but not broken." She shrugged, smiling. "No big deal. Good sex leaves more marks than that."

Ben grinned. "You're a bad one, youknowit?"

Sass put a finger in his chest. "When it comes to you, babe," she said softly, "I'm very good when I'm bad."

Ben pulled her down to him and held her very tightly. "You certainly are," he whispered into her hair.

They stayed locked together in silence for a few moments, listening to each other breathe, then Sass extricated herself from Ben's grasp and went back to the galley to pour a tumbler of cold white wine from the big jug in the refrigerator. Ben popped the cap off the bottle of Guinness with the back edge of his belt knife and drank, the dark stout bittersweet on his tongue. Sass came back and sat down beside him on the couch, sipping her wine. Ben smacked his lips and regarded the label on the beer bottle.

"Did you know," he mused, "that you can be drawn

and quartered in England for serving Guinness that isn't lukewarm?"

"No wonder Britain's a dying empire," Sass remarked. She looked Ben up and down briefly. "You know what?"

"What?"

"You've got something on your mind, Mr. Gannon. Wanna talk about it?"

Ben patted the hand that was roaming through his hair, swung his legs to the cabin sole, and hoisted himself to his feet. He pitched the empty beer bottle neatly into the swing-top garbage container and opened the refrigerator to find another Guinness. Turning and looking at Sass as he popped the cap, he decided on sudden impulse to come clean with her.

"The job turned out to be a little rough," he said. "A body snatch on a crashed chopper." He took a long swallow from the bottle. "Remember a guy I told you about, a friend from the old days named Tony Angel?"

"I think so," Sass said. "Sure, I remember. A helicopter pil—" Her voice trailed off, her face registering a sudden realization. "Oh, Ben . . ."

She put her hand over her mouth, shock in her eyes.

"I recovered his body," Ben continued slowly, "along with a number of others. It took awhile." He smiled ruefully.

Sass took her hand away from her mouth. She was frowning.

"You didn't tell me you were going on a body snatch," she said softly. Her eyes searched his, gentle yet accusing.

"I know."

"Why not?"

Ben sighed and looked at the countertop, absently sliding his beer bottle in little circles on the white Formica.

"I didn't want you to worry," he said. "I didn't see any point in two of us getting down in the dumps. I mean, it's part of my job to do this kind of thing once in a while . . . but I don't see that it's fair for you to have to hear about every unpleasant job I'm given. What's the point? What are you going to do except dwell on the fact that it might be me in one of those wrecked choppers someday? You don't need that." In addition, he decided, she didn't need to hear disturbing little details like D'Angelo's severed legs and the odd hole behind his ear.

He took a long draft from his beer, tipping his head back and closing his eyes, and when he was done he saw Sass standing right beside him, one hand on the counter and the other on her hip.

"It's my job to share everything with you," she said. "That's my choice. Bad as well as good. It's part of trusting the person you're with, remember? You're always telling me that." She crossed her arms and leaned closer to him, eyes steady on his. "Well, that works both ways, doesn't it?" Ben didn't say anything.

A ghost of a smile flickered across her face. "I'm not this sweet little girl you have to insulate from the big, bad world, Ben. I'm thirty-four years old, I run the marina my dad left me, and I do it well enough to keep things up and take a small profit out of the business.

"After ten or twelve years of near misses, I finally find a guy who's worth keeping around—that's you, by the way—but he's got this John Wayne, tough-guy thing about keeping bad news away from his hepless Southun flowuh."

She rolled the exaggerated Dixie accent off her tongue with a flourish. Ben cracked a smile.

"You see," she went on, "I wasn't kidding. You really are a chauvinist at heart." She paused. "But at least that heart's in the right place."

She turned and went back toward the couch, stopping to bend down and scratch Caesar behind the ears. The big dog yawned and rolled onto his side, eyes closed.

"Hey," Ben said.

She looked over her shoulder at him, still fondling the rottweiler's ears. "Yes?"

"How about if I never do that again?"

She continued to pet the dog. "Never do what again?" she prodded.

Ben sighed and drained the last of his beer, then came around the counter and stood with his palms open. "Permit me to elaborate," he said. "How about if I never patronize you by choosing to 'insulate' you from something that might be bothering me?" He was grinning now.

Sass came up and put her arms around his waist.

"Never, never?" she inquired, looking up at him.

"Never," he replied, and kissed her.

Ben lay on the couch, an old patchwork quilt over his legs, staring up through the open main skylight at the constellation Orion. It was a navigator's night, clear as a bell, the stars cold and white against a pure black sky. Antares, Betelgeuse, Polaris: Ben ran through the list of classic star shots, fixing them in a sextant mirror in his mind's eye. A night-flying gull drifted silently past the *Teresa Ann*'s mainmast like a small white ghost.

The brass chronometer on the cabin bulkhead chimed softly nine times. Over the faint sound of running water, Ben could hear Sass moving around in the shower, humming to herself. He felt wonderfully tired, the long hours of the past few days finally catching up to him, sheer fatigue soothing the nagging thoughts in his mind. He pulled the old quilt up around his chest and let his eyelids go heavy.

The phone rang with an abrupt metallic buzz. Ben stiffened, then sighed and sank back onto the couch, putting a hand over his eyes. He let it ring four times before reaching over and answering it.

"Gannon."

"Hey, Ben. Howya doin'? Ian Hodge here." Hodge was the operations manager of Challenge Diving out of New Orleans, an American subsidiary of Nautique Du Monde, a giant French subsea services company and the largest diving contractor in the world. A native Scot who'd worked as a saturation diver in the bitterly cold waters of the North Sea throughout the sixties and early seventies, Hodge had emigrated to the U.S. when Nautique Du Monde opened Challenge in 1979. Now, after more than twenty years in Louisiana, his accent was a curious blend of Cajun drawl and Scottish burr.

"I hope I didn't disturb you. I know it's getting late."

"No," Ben said slowly. "Not at all."

"I have a little work here for you if you're available," Hodge said. "I'm really hoping you are, because I'm in a bit of a spot, old fellow. I need a good underwater welder, and all my full-time people are either working on other projects or out of touch. It's not deep, but you should get in three or four days of long hours at top rates. You'd be in charge of a four-man crew, so you'd pick up the supervisor's bonus as well. What do you say? This is something of a sticky wicket for me . . ."

"What and where, Ian," Ben replied wearily. His enthusiasm was at a low ebb, and the little Scot was talking too fast.

"Well, it's on the NAOC-X," Hodge continued rapidly. "You've been out there a few times, haven't you?" Before Ben could confirm this, Hodge rolled on. "Yes, well, basically they dropped an entire rack of drill string from the upper deck into the water, the silly buggers. Apparently a lifting sling broke when they were off-loading the pipe from a workboat. Twenty-four sections of forty-foot, four-inch drill string fell more than a hundred feet and went straight in like spears. Three of them hit the port flotation pontoon—about sixty feet down—and punched three lovely little holes in it. They're still there, sticking out of the pontoon like quills on a bloody hedgehog."

"Sounds great," Ben said. "What's the plate thickness on that pontoon?"

"Three-quarter inch, where the drill string hit," Hodge replied. "Went through like haggis through me grandmum, it did." There was a faint clicking sound over the line, a pause, then Hodge came back. "Ben, lad, I've got Eugene Fontenot from NAOC on the other line—in a state of extreme agitation. Can I call you back in a few minutes?"

"Yeah, no problem," Ben said. He hung up the phone and put his hands over his eyes, exhaling loudly. His plans for the evening hadn't included a frenzied call from an operations manager. That NAOC-X rig again. He just couldn't seem to get clear of the damn thing lately. He ran over the details in his mind.

N.A.O.C. North American Oil Corporation. The Experimental, or X, as the engineers called it, was NAOC's showcase deepwater project in the Gulf of Mexico. Located approximately one hundred and fifty miles directly south of New Orleans in the offshore area known as Green Canyon—the site of the richest newly discovered subsea oilfield on earth—it was a high-tech attempt to establish a floating oil-production platform in more than four thousand feet of water.

And it had proven to be fantastically successful. In the three months since it had first begun drilling and pumping, its production and efficiency had surpassed

the wildest expectations of NAOC's engineers. It was
nothing less than the prototype of a class of rig that
could release the United States from its dependence
upon foreign oil, unlocking the huge domestic reserves
contained in the new Green Canyon field at a cost of
under four dollars a barrel. As the tireless Senator
Latham from Mississippi repeated at every sound bite
opportunity, it was potentially the key to American
energy-independence in the twenty-first century.

The platform itself was a giant semi-submersible
drilling rig, specially modified for deepwater production. Semi-submersibles were traditionally used for ex-
ploration, moving from location to location in the
offshore oilfields of the globe and drilling test wells in
search of oil reserves far beneath the ocean floor. The
NAOC-X, built in Japan in 1993 originally for the
Asian energy conglomerate Honsha Industries, was
one of the world's largest. The North American Oil
Corporation had acquired it for the X project in 1998
at an auction in Hong Kong, following a worldwide
slump in oil prices.

It resembled nothing so much as an immense, rectangular, eight-legged table, with four legs to a side.
The upper deck—the top of the table—measured eight
hundred feet long by four hundred wide, and supported the drilling tower, command superstructure,
power systems, and personnel accommodations. The
legs themselves were hollow tubes fifty feet in diameter and two hundred feet long. Their bottom ends
were joined by horizontal pontoons of a similar diameter and length, and the entire structure floated freely,
its draft controlled by the rig captain, who, by pumping out or flooding the pontoons, could raise or lower
the vessel in the water.

When working on location, the semi was ballasted
down for stability to a depth of one hundred and
twenty feet, putting the waterline about halfway up

the legs. Under tow, it was ballasted up to a depth of only thirty-five feet, the top third of each huge pontoon out of the water. It was one of these ballast pontoons that had been punctured by the dropped drill string. To the uninitiated, it might have sounded like serious damage. But to a twenty-year oilfield hand like Ben, it was nothing but a routine accident, requiring a routine repair. Minor damage was always occurring in the offshore oilfield. It was Ben's bread and butter.

Sass stuck her head out of the door to the shower, her wet hair bunched up in a towel.

"I thought I heard the phone," she said apprehensively.

"You did," Ben sighed.

"Ed McMahon telling us we won the sweepstakes?" she inquired.

"Ian Hodge."

Sass made a face and disappeared back into the shower, closing the door behind her. Ben heard the door of the medicine cabinet bang shut a moment later.

The phone rang again, and Ben picked up quickly. "Hey."

"Ian again, Ben. Sorry about that; Fontenot is spinning in place at about the speed of light. No doubt he thinks he's about to lose NAOC's pet project, and his career along with it. He wants an emergency team dispatched immediately to pull out the drill string and weld up the holes."

"Three little holes?" Ben said. "Ian, they've got ballast pumps on that rig that would keep a pontoon bone-dry if a torpedo hit it. The damn thing isn't going to sink in the next hour, or the next week. Sounds to me like the guy needs to calm down."

"You know that, and I know that," Hodge replied, "but try telling it to Fontenot. The bloke's a bloody desk jockey. All he knows is that something's wrong with the NAOC-X, and it's his overpaid ass in the grinder if anything slows up the project. You know how excited everyone in the country is about that rig." Hodge's voice took on a pleading tone. "I really need your help on this, Ben. NAOC's a priority customer, and I haven't got anybody to send out. I need to get people on the move to the dock right away . . ."

Ben heard the door to the shower click open and glanced up. Sass came out silently and leaned back slowly against the forward bulkhead of the main cabin, brushing her damp blonde hair back from her face. She was clad only in a bath towel wrapped around her breasts, covering her to the tops of her thighs. She looked unwaveringly at Ben as she brushed her hair, her legs and arms lithe and golden-brown in the soft light.

". . . And Duke Butler is on vacation in Montana, shooting antelope or moose or giraffe or something . . ." Hodge was still chattering in Ben's ear. "So you see, I'm really in a dreadful predicament, old man."

Sass put down the brush, slowly and deliberately, and picked up a bottle of skin lotion. Her eyes mysterious and locked on Ben's, her expression inscrutable, she put one brown leg up on a chair and began to smooth lotion into her calf and thigh with careful, unhurried strokes.

Ben let himself stare as he spoke into the phone:

"What time were you shooting for?" he asked Hodge.

"Well, I want to have the crew—that's you, one other wet-welder, and two tenders—at the NAOC dock in Fourchon by three a.m. Oh, and I need you to pick up Rolly Savard at his house in Morgan City, too. He's the other welder."

Sass extended a lean arm and rubbed lotion into it. Her hips shifted under the towel.

"Hang on a second, Ian," Ben said, "I need to

check something." He lowered the phone, a half smile playing about his lips.

Sass leaned back against the bulkhead again, put her head back against the teak, gazing at him, and slipped one round breast out of the towel. She cupped it in one hand and rubbed lotion into it with the other; the pale skin and nipple that rarely felt the sun, the tan line farther up . . .

"Too early," Ben said into the phone. "Can't make it."

"But if you left now, you could get there just in time . . ."

Sass let the towel fall from the other breast, frowning a little as she smoothed more lotion into it.

"Thirteen hundred," Ben said with finality. "I can be there by thirteen hundred hours."

She unwrapped the towel from her hips and draped it over the back of the chair. She came slowly across the cabin, the warm light playing over her flat stomach and dancer's legs, her firm breasts pale against her tan.

"One p.m.'s really the best you can do?" Hodge mourned at the other end of the line.

Sass moved up behind Ben, behind the couch, and put the fingers of both hands gently into his hair, caressing.

"Thirteen hundred," Ben said.

"Oh, all right, old man," Hodge acquiesced. "Thirteen hundred it is. NAOC dock in Fourchon."

Sass brought one long brown leg over Ben's shoulder and placed her foot between his legs, her inner thigh against his cheek. Her fingers continued to wander in his hair.

"Deal," Ben said, and hung up the phone.

He grasped her calf with both hands and turned his face into the soft skin of her thigh, biting gently. She gave a little gasp and tightened her fingers in his hair. Then he reached up, brought her mouth down on his

with a hand behind her neck, and pulled her gently
over the back of the couch into his arms.

Just before dawn Ben awoke. The cool breeze waft-
ing down into the main cabin through the skylight had
turned cold. Sass lay draped along his left side, one
leg over his, her head cradled in the hollow of his
shoulder. She stirred a little in her sleep and touched
her fingertips gently to his lips. He tightened his arm
around her shoulders.

"Hey," Ben said softly. "Hey. You awake?"

The blonde head that was nestled in the hollow of
his shoulder stirred.

"Mmmmm?"

Ben pushed the tangled strands of hair back from
Sass' cheek. Her eyes flickered open, heavy with sleep.

"Timeizzit?" she said thickly.

"Four-thirty in the morning," he answered.

She closed her eyes again and patted his chest absently. "Don't talk," she mumbled. "Sleep."

He worked his fingers gently at the nape of her
neck, chuckling deep in his throat.

"Come on, girl, wake up. I've gotta talk to you."

She groaned and lifted her head, hair haystack-wild
and face puffy.

"I hate your job," she said hoarsely. He squeezed
one firm buttock.

"At times like this, I hate it, too," he offered. "But
like the saying goes—'a man's gotta do ...'"

"... what a man's gotta do,'" Sass finished. "Yeah,
yeah. I know." She kissed him quickly. "Blecch!
Morning mouth!" She got a leg out from under the
quilt, reached over to the old armchair, and grabbed
one of Ben's sweaters off its back. "Freezin'," she
said, pulling it on. She groped her way across the cabin
toward the galley. "Coffee. I must have coffee ..."

Ben stifled a laugh. As long as he'd known her,

she'd never been a fast starter in the morning, no matter how much sleep she'd had. He watched her struggle with the lid of the coffee jar for a moment, then got up, took the jar away from her, opened it, and let her lean on him while he spooned coffee into the coffeemaker.

"Ohhh," Sass groaned. Ben poured water into the machine and flipped it on. He went back to the couch, and she followed, shuffling after him with her arms around his waist. Over by the foot of the companion-way ladder, Caesar lifted his big head to contemplate the action near the galley, then sneezed and settled back down.

"Okay," Ben said, propping Sass into a sitting position against the cushions, "when you open both eyes, I'm gonna tell you this great idea I have."

She made a limp-wristed gesture in the direction of the galley. "Coffee first . . ."

"Deal," said Ben, getting to his feet again. "Coming right up."

He fixed two mugs of dark roast and brought them back to the couch, sitting next to Sass and passing her the coffee. She held it in both hands and sipped, looking at him through the steam.

"Thanks, babe," she said, her eyes clearer. "Okay. I'm listening. What's the great idea?"

Ben cleared his throat. "Well, here's the thing: I'm going offshore today to do this repair on the NAOC-X, right? It'll probably take one to three days to weld up the holed ballast tank and pressure test it. Good weather is supposed to hold through the week, and the *Teresa Ann*'s ready for blue water right now." His eyes twinkled. "Isla Mujeres is nice this time of year . . .

"Why don't you top up the fuel and water tanks and pick me up out at the NAOC-X in about three days? Then we'll just slide straight on down to the

Yucatan Channel and pull in behind the island for a couple of weeks. Dinner on Isla Mujeres or across the bay in Cancun every night, snorkeling on the reefs during the day . . . What do you think?"

Sass was grinning. "Can we afford it?" she asked, looking at him mischievously over her coffee.

"Oh, I think so," Ben replied. "What's the exchange rate on pesos right now? About a million to the dollar?" He tweaked her toe. "Of course we can afford it."

Sass frowned suddenly. "Oh, Ben. It's a great idea, but I've got so much going on around the marina right now. I've got the building contractor coming around to check the ground for that addition to the restaurant, the EPA's wanting to inspect the fuel dock tanks . . . Who's going to take care of that stuff and make sure the place keeps running half decently?"

"Jimmy," Ben said without hesitation. "He's always done it before."

"But he's getting old," Sass complained, her sleep-puffed face hardening as she contemplated her business. "I hate to bother him with it."

"Then, there's Tom at the far end of the dock, and Carl in the fabrication shop, and Anna in the restaurant; you know perfectly well they can handle everything just fine. Jeez, they'll probably be overjoyed to get rid of you for a couple of weeks." He grinned.

She kicked at him with an outstretched toe. "Be nice, ya big galoot."

"Always," Ben said. "Come on, Sass, we go through this every time. You worry about the marina—which always runs like a top—and then come to your senses, do what I say, and we have a great vacation. Why don't you just skip the first part, obey me, and let the good times roll?" He was trying not to laugh.

"Dead," Sass said, setting down her coffee. "You're dead meat, pal." She scrambled across the couch, forcing him back with her weight on his chest. "Apologize, or I'll smother you." She grabbed his nose between her thumb and forefinger and crushed her mouth onto his in a deep kiss.

After about twenty seconds Ben began making gurgling noises, and Sass pulled back to let him breathe.

"I'm sorry you worry about nothing sometimes," he panted, eyes crinkling with amusement.

Sass smiled down at him. "Let me set it up with Jimmy," she said. "I really want to go, you know."

"I know," Ben said. "We could both use it." He sat back up and retrieved his coffee cup. "The marina'll be fine for a couple of weeks, really." He glanced up at a small framed chart of the Gulf of Mexico on the cabin wall. "With a southeast wind you could make it to the NAOC-X from here in two days, easy."

"Yup," she agreed, studying the chart. "Piece of cake. A beam reach the whole way." She frowned. "Those big floating rigs are pretty high, aren't they? How do I pick you up? Pull up to one of the legs or something?"

"That's right," Ben said. "They've all got boat landings about ten feet above the waterline. You just put the bow up close, and I'll step off, gear bags and all. No sweat."

"What if the weather's lousy?" Sass asked.

Ben looked at her. "Think positive," he replied with wry smile. "It won't be."

Over by the companionway ladder Caesar sneezed again and stood up. He shook his head, collar tags jingling, and padded over to the couch, resting his jaw on the back and nuzzling Sass' ear with a cold nose. She winced, shrank away, then scratched behind his ears.

"Can we take him?" she asked, looking at the big dog's loyal brown eyes. "I don't want some bandito with a badge deciding he's a health hazard."

"As long as he stays on the boat," Ben said, "the official gunslingers don't usually make too much fuss. They also don't tend to hang around on board too long during their customs inspections, either." He grinned. "Big dogs make them nervous."

He leaned over, said excuse me to Caesar, and kissed Sass. "You really shouldn't worry so much," he whispered into her lips. "Everything's going to be just fine."

Chapter Four

Jeremiah Sligo burped and reached for the bottle of pink antacid set on top of the tackle locker. He chugged down a few swallows of the thick liquid and licked his lips, blinking in the mid-afternoon sun.

The little fishing village of Bahia Cristobal lay postcard-picturesque in front of his eyes. Nestled at the foot of a large hill, protected from storms by an exposed offshore reef, the village boasted one of the best small natural harbors on the northwestern coast of Cuba. Only one hundred miles east of Havana, with its tall office buildings and city bustle, Bahia Cristobal looked as though it hadn't changed for three hundred years.

In fact, very little *had* changed. Castro had provided the village with a pumping station and water tower in the late sixties, along with a feed line from Havana's outlying electrical-power conduits. The village had celebrated enthusiastically when the projects were completed, with Cuban flags waving and Castro's stern portrait displayed everywhere.

And when the pumps stopped working for lack of replacement parts and the electrical feed line rotted through somewhere back in the jungle, the fishermen and their families shrugged and went back to collecting rainwater in roof cisterns and lighting their little homes with candles and lanterns, just as they'd done for centuries. They still kept their Cuban flags and pictures of Castro, however—just in case.

About the only thing truly modern in Bahia Cristobal was the fleet of sleek, white-hulled sportfishermen tied up in individual slips along a floating dock nearly two hundred yards long. They looked out of place against the background of dirt roads and thatched-roof dwellings. And they were truly a fleet; there were at least forty of them, all over fifty feet long.

They had names like *Robert E. Lee,* port of registry "Biloxi, Mississippi"; *Yankee Clipper,* from "Delaware"; *Miss Liberty,* from "Hilton Head, South Carolina"; and *Marlin Master,* out of "Fort Lauderdale, FL." But the names didn't mean much; they were often changed at sea.

These handsome yachts, traditionally the toys of millionaires, were part of Fidel Castro's marijuana-smuggling fleet. Dope grown in government fields in Cuba's fertile interior was harvested, baled, water-proofed, transported aboard military trucks to coastal locations like Bahia Cristobal, and loaded onto boats by soldiers. Then the yachts would cruise toward some American port, blending with the clutter of recreational boat traffic off the U.S. coast, and slip ashore to off-load. They were rarely caught; it was impossible to differentiate between the smuggling vessels and legitimate pleasure craft.

In the late seventies and early eighties, the Cuban smuggling program had kicked into high gear, utilizing planes and freighters for transport as well as small boats. The expansion included the use of freelancers—smugglers of other than Cuban nationality who would run loads of marijuana into the U.S. for a fat fee. Some would take the Cuban government's sportfishermen; others would use their own boats.

Jeremiah Sligo was one of the others.

A Canadian in his late forties, Sligo had drifted to

the States in his late teens, working odd jobs and hustling. Smart but lazy, and self-involved to the point of narcissism, he had little use for society's rules and conventions. As far as he was concerned, anyone who worked a forty-hour week and then turned over a huge chunk of his pay to the tax man was a fool. Drifting and barhopping his way down South Florida's Atlantic coast in the early seventies, he found a cadre of people who shared his views.

He liked the way they lived. They wore jeans and flip-flops instead of suits and ties. They slept late. They might have been hippies, but for one important difference: they had money.

Lots of money. Money enough to live in luxury beachfront apartments in Fort Lauderdale, or town homes on the Miami River. Money enough to drive high-ticket imported cars like Porches or Jaguars.

They went out every night, partying at trendy, casual indoor-outdoor clubs on the beaches or canals. They drank to their laid-back lifestyle and sang the praises of an up-and-coming songwriter named Jimmy Buffet, whom they'd christened their patron saint. And they did a lot of drugs: cocaine, pills, but mostly marijuana. Grass. Reefer. Ganja.

Sligo thought he'd died and gone to heaven. He was easy to be with, a good talker, and there was plenty of spillover for him to lap up if he just tagged along—nobody ever seemed to care about the money. But pretty soon he began to wonder where it all came from. He began to ask discreet questions, just wondering . . .

The answers were all the same: I've got an inheritance. I've got a trust fund. I got lucky on some stocks. I have a disability pension. I've got some investments. And then the subject would be changed, with a lingering look and a tight smile, and that would be that.

And then, one night in a tiki-bar in Pompano

Beach—as Richard Nixon was on television telling America he was not a crook—Jeremiah Sligo got an offer he couldn't refuse.

Fly to Ocho Rios, Jamaica, board a Grand Banks trawler at the yacht club, and take it through the Windward Passage and the Bahamas up to Daytona Beach in North Florida. Five or six days. Child's play for a guy with a little experience on the water. Park the boat at the Dawkins Marina and leave. Forty thousand dollars in cash. Five now, thirty-five later.

He'd done it, alone. He didn't sleep for the first four days, until his little vial of coke ran out and he had to pull into the lee of a small island just south of Grand Bahama. He dropped the hook, shut down the engines, and crashed on the floor of the wheelhouse for fifteen hours. When he awoke, with a raging headache and a severe case of coke paranoia, it was just after midnight. He fired up the engines, weighed anchor, and headed west toward the U.S. mainland, grinding the boat's bow over a hidden coral reef as he left the island.

Hoping desperately that he hadn't holed the hull, he passed the light at Settlement Point before dawn and set a course for Jupiter Inlet. By the time he got across the Gulf Stream, it had pushed him north to within fifty miles of Daytona. That evening he cruised in with the sportfishermen and day sailers, berthed the yacht, and went looking for a bottle of whiskey and more cocaine.

Two days later he had the rest of his money, plus a five-thousand-dollar bonus for pulling it off single-handedly and the knowledge that he'd found his true calling in life. He felt as though he'd just broken the bank in Vegas.

Five months later he was broke again. But he hustled his way onto another run as a crewman and made a quick twelve thousand. And so it went.

Over twenty years in the business, and he'd never been able to make a score last more than six months. And there'd been some big ones. But last year he'd wised up; one long run from Barranquilla, Colombia to Galveston and he was sitting pretty. Instead of cash, he'd taken the boat as payment. He was nearing fifty; he needed something that would last.

Now he sat on the bridge of the *Circe* and looked over his floating home and investment. She was a Bertram International Sportfish, fifty-six feet long, with twin Cummins diesels and a towering flybridge. She'd been equipped with Furuno radar and two expensive Loran-C units, as well as a costly Sat-Nav system. Though she was over fifteen years old, she had only one real flaw: the Colombians had ripped all the accommodations out of the forward staterooms so that they could be packed with one-kilo bricks of cocaine.

Sligo had pulled it off again, more by sheer dumb luck than any kind of superior seamanship or tactical cunning. He'd left Barranquilla, put the *Circe* on autopilot, and cruised north through the Yucatan Channel all the way to Galveston. He went right by the Fat Albert drug surveillance balloon at Roatan, and right by the U.S. Coast Guard cutter prowling the waters of the Channel off Isla Mujeres, Mexico. All the way to Texas he kept himself awake by sampling the finest cocaine he'd ever tasted.

He'd helped to offload the boat in Galveston, duffel bag by duffel bag, in broad daylight. It was ridiculous: men in dark glasses walking back and forth on the dock, loading dozens of bags into a parade of cars and trucks. It couldn't have been more obvious. But Sligo's luck had taken him through twenty years as a professional smuggler without a single bust, and his luck held. He sailed away cleanly with his payment: the *Circe* and two kilos of prime cocaine.

The coke hadn't lasted long. By the time he'd partied his way east along the Gulf Coast and then south to Key West, he and a parade of temporary acquaintances had snorted up one-and-a-quarter kilos. He'd managed to peddle off the remaining three quarters of a kilo, at a cut-rate price, to a health-club owner in Naples, but after filling the *Circe*'s long-range tanks with diesel and living it up for a month in Key West, he was running dangerously low on cash.

Asset-rich but cash-poor, he found a way to put his asset to work. A Mariel Cuban who sold coke by the gram in the tourist traps on Duval Street turned him on to what he claimed was a standing offer from the Cuban government: sail into one of three Cuban ports, identify yourself to the local police, and permit your boat to be inspected and then loaded with marijuana. Run the dope up to a pre-designated port on the U.S. mainland, off-load, be paid on the spot, and leave. See you next time.

Sligo had heard about this arrangement before through the drug-running grapevine. Now that he had his own boat, it sounded pretty good; Cuba was a mere ninety miles away. He'd partied with the Marielito until dawn, then slipped the *Circe*'s mooring lines and headed south toward Bahia Cristobal.

Pulling up to the little town's floating dock that evening—somewhat taken aback at the sight of forty U.S.-built sportfishermen lined up in their slips like thoroughbreds in the starting gate—he'd been met by the local customs officer and a chubby police sergeant with a pockmarked face. Stay here, they told him; don't move the boat. Enjoy the town—the food, the rum, the senoritas—but don't move the boat. Someone will be down to speak with you about business.

That had been eight days ago, and Sligo was out of patience. Three days earlier, half deranged by a vicious rum-and-cocaine hangover, he'd cornered the customs officer in Bahia Cristobal's waterfront main square and threatened to leave if he was kept waiting any longer. The officer had merely smiled politely, shaking his head, and gestured out toward the Gulf. A dark gray gunboat, long and low, was cruising through the indigo-blue water just outside the coral reef.

"Not a good idea, senor," the man had said simply.

So Sligo had had to content himself with sampling the local food, drink, and hookers, fueling his energies with a fast-dwindling supply of coke. He'd found that the younger girls were far more enthusiastic about sharing his company if there were a few lines of blow to be had; they'd put a serious dent in his stash.

Now he sat in the *Circe*'s captain's chair, head splitting, trying to decide if a rum punch or a couple of lines would make him feel better. He settled on the rum.

"Luis!" he shouted, reaching down and banging on the floor of the bridge with the antacid bottle. "Where the hell are you?"

There was a thumping sound from below, and Sligo heard the door to the main salon slide open. A moment later Luis Garcia's pudgy hands and face appeared at the top of the bridge ladder.

"Joo call me, Cap'n Jerry?" he panted.

"Yeah, dammit. Look, go down to the galley and blend me up a Redrum, willya? Lots of papaya juice and ice, and dump in some of that vitamin C powder that's behind the microwave." He felt a cold, sickly sweat building up in his armpits and on his forehead. His hands were shaking slightly. Jesus, he felt lousy. "Hurry up!"

"Hokay."

Luis' head dropped down the ladder out of sight. Sligo mopped his dripping face with the tail of his loose, gaudy Hawaiian shirt and cursed fluently. Damn greasy little spic. Maybe he'd been too hasty in asking him aboard as crew. Still, he admitted to himself, anybody as ugly as Luis who had the nerve to come up to a rich Americano and introduce himself as a "procurer of whores" couldn't be all bad. He'd availed himself of Luis' services the first five nights running, and after a memorable encounter on the fifth night with a thirteen-year-old girl of astonishing athleticism had, in a fit of uncharacteristic generosity, offered Luis a job as crewman aboard the *Circe*. The little hustler had accepted with tears in his eyes, "gracias, Cap'n"-ing Sligo until the smuggler had begun to feel uncomfortable and told him to go away.

Now he couldn't get the little bastard off the boat. But, he mused, it wasn't half bad having your own personal slave to order around. He grimaced as another bubble of gas worked its way up from his sour stomach. As he waited for it, he noticed a military jeep with four passengers driving slowly along the waterfront road on the far side of the little harbor. He belched, mildly curious about the jeep. There were almost no vehicles in Bahia Cristobal; everyone rode bicycles or walked.

There was a thump as the sliding door opened again, and then Luis appeared at the top of the ladder, hoisting his little Buddha-body up one rung at a time, a tall rum punch clutched in his fat hand. He gained the bridge, breathing heavily, and held out the drink.

"One Redrum, Cap'n Jerry!" he panted, his grin wide and gap-toothed. "Two ounce Cap'n Morgan, papaya juice, orange juice, grenadine, ice, vitamin C, and one *huevo*. Enjoy, enjoy!"

Sligo pursed his lips. "I didn't ask you to put any eggs in the goddamn thing!" he erupted. "Shit!"

Luis looked pained. "Is good for joo," he explained earnestly.

Sligo snorted and took a drink. Not bad, really. He

sipped again, Luis grinning and nodding in silent encouragement.

"Excuse me, Captain Sligo."

Sligo swallowed hard, startled, and sat up. The voice had come from below the bridge, on the dock. He slid from the captain's chair and peered over the side.

The customs officer, one Lieutenant Escobar, stood on the dock looking up at him, his eyes sharp and black under the low visor of his military cap. Sligo didn't like him; the man had a way of sounding insulting even when he was being perfectly polite—which was all the time. The way he enunciated and clipped off the word "captain" made the title ironic and patronizing. But Sligo was in Cuba to make money, so he played the game.

"Hey, Escobar," he called, saluting with his rum glass. "How're you doin' this morning?"

"It's four in the afternoon, and I am fine, thank you." Unlike Luis, Escobar spoke excellent English with only a trace of a Spanish accent. "Permission to come aboard? I would like to introduce you to these four gentlemen and have a brief talk about your upcoming, ah . . . project."

He gestured down the dock. Walking toward the *Circe* were the four men Sligo had seen driving through the main square in the jeep. They were all dressed in jeans and T-shirts, and all were black-haired and bearded. Sligo thought at first glance that they looked more Middle Eastern than Cuban.

"Yeah, yeah," the smuggler said, beckoning with his free hand. "Feel free, amigo." He went to the bridge ladder and started down to the aft deck.

Escobar stepped across to the boat's gunwale and jumped down lightly onto the white fiberglass deck, his black-soled shoes leaving tarry scuff marks with every step. Sligo winced inwardly but said nothing. He'd get that little greaseball Luis to buff up the deck after Escobar and company left. This bastard of a lieutenant knew better, too; he'd been on plenty of boats. He knew damn well you didn't walk on a clean white deck with street shoes.

Sligo forced himself to smile.

"So we're gonna talk turkey, huh, Escobar? About goddamn time. I thought you were gonna keep me here for the rest of my life!" He laughed good-naturedly. "A little pleasure with your business, maybe? How about a rum or a Johnny Black to cut the dust?"

"No, thank you," Escobar replied. He looked around. The four other men were stepping across onto the *Circe*'s gunwales.

Sligo sized them up quickly. They all looked pretty serious, but the oldest one—the one in the lead—was downright scary. He was ape-bodied, with short legs and long, powerful arms. His eyes, an unearthly pale amber, seemed to glow in his dark, hook-nosed face.

Sligo turned to Escobar. "Who're these guys?" he asked bluntly. "They gonna load me up or something?"

Escobar shook his head. "No, Captain. They are considerably more important than that. These gentlemen"—he indicated the four with a graceful movement of his hand—"are your cargo."

Sligo frowned. What the hell was going on now?

"Cargo? Look, amigo," he said, "I'm here to make money, not play bus driver. The cargo I came for comes with a lot of dollars attached, and I ain't into sharing. No offense, but I don't need these guys. I work alone, and if I do take on a crew, I do the choosing. Know what I mean?"

Escobar nodded patiently, waiting for Sligo to finish.

"Of course I know what you mean, Captain," he replied smoothly. "If you will just permit me to explain the situation, I think you will find that this project has definite appeal." He smiled. "But where are my manners? Allow me to introduce these gentlemen . . ."

He stepped back, gesturing first to Sligo and then to the heavyset man with the amber eyes.

"Captain Jerry Sligo, meet Carlos Rodriguez."

The man stepped forward, his face suddenly opening into a broad grin. Sligo noticed that his teeth seemed to be stained a purplish-red. He offered his hand, which the man grasped and shook vigorously.

"A pleasure to meet you, Captain," said Ojim Gradak.

Chapter Five

Sligo led Lieutenant Escobar and the four other men into the main salon of the *Circe*. He flopped down on one of the plush, pit-style couches that lined the interior.

"Have a seat, boys, have a seat," he offered loudly. "Make yourselves at home."

Escobar took a deck chair opposite Sligo, across a low glass coffee table. The other four sat on settees along the far bulkhead, saying nothing. Sligo looked at them blankly for a moment, then shook his head and turned back to Escobar.

"So, Lieutenant," he said, "think your silent buddies would like a drink? After all, if we're gonna be shipmates, we ought to get to know each other."

Escobar stirred uncomfortably and glanced over at the four men. Rodriguez/Gradak, sensing the wary mood overtaking Sligo, stood up quickly and approached, smiling, his open palms held up in a gesture of gracious refusal.

"Please, Captain," he said, "my friends and I do not drink. All of us have recently experienced a touch of, ah, dysentery, and we find that alcohol aggravates it. But thank you for your kind offer. Perhaps at a later time?"

Sligo smiled back and shrugged.

"Hey, I can relate," he said. "Last time I was in Mexico, I was down with the squirts for five days. Lost

ten pounds—best diet I was ever on." He slapped his
knee and laughed. Gradak and the others quickly
joined in, nodding and chuckling.

Sligo settled back on the couch and smiled agree-
ably at Escobar.

"So, Lieutenant E.," he said jovially, "let's hear it.
What's the deal, bud?"

Escobar cleared his throat and made a precise pyramid with his fingers. Gradak took a seat beside him.

"Well, Captain," he began, "first of all I would like
to thank you for your patience. You have been here
in Bahia Cristobal for—what is it now?—better than
a week, and it's quite understandable that you should
be feeling a little restless. I was wondering what I
might do to compensate you for your time, and it
occurred to me"—he reached into his breast pocket—
"that you might be able to use a little more of this."

He extracted a small brown pill vial and set it on
the glass coffee table in front of Sligo. "I understand
that this is your recreational drug of choice," he continued smoothly. "Please accept this as a token of ap-
preciation for your patience."

Sligo popped open the vial's safety cap and shook
some of the contents out onto the glass. The lumpy
white powder had a pink tinge in the salon's frosted
lights. Sligo picked up some with his forefinger,
touched it to his tongue, then rubbed the rest into his
upper gums.

"Hmm!" he exclaimed, smacking his lips. "Peruvian
flake, I do believe!" He glanced up, smirking at Escobar beneath his brows. "This goes a long way toward
settling accounts, Lieutenant E.," he said. "At least as
far as the past eight days go . . ."

"I'm very gratified that you feel that way," Escobar
replied. "After all, people who are about to do big
business together should trust each other, should they

not? Perhaps the best expression might be—mutual respect?"

"Hey, I'm all for mutual respect," Sligo agreed. He slipped a battered leather wallet from his shorts pocket and extracted a laminated driver's license from it. He pushed some of the cocaine back into the vial with the corner of the card, snapped the cap back on, and began cutting up the remainder. Gradak watched him detachedly, catching Escobar's eye once. As Sligo chopped up the coke, deftly pushing the grains around the glass tabletop and drawing out two long lines, it became apparent to the others that for him the process was a labor of love.

He sat back with a broad grin, admiring his handiwork, and pulled the gold chain that he wore around his neck out of his shirt. Dangling from it were a gold crucifix, a small gold skull with ruby eyes, and a thin gold tube about two inches long. Pulling the chain over his head, he offered the tube to the room in general.

"Anybody?" he asked, grinning from ear to ear.

Gradak studied him: an overfed, paunch-bellied man with thin arms and legs, wearing a ridiculous multicolored shirt, baggy shorts, and rubber sandals. His thinning, dirty-blond hair was sun-bleached and greasy, and his mustache was long and unkempt. He had a dark, rich tan, which made his jowly face seem narrower than it was. Set close together above a beaky nose, his eyes looked very blue against his brown skin. Gradak forced himself to smile and shook his head.

"Suit yourselves," Sligo shrugged, bending over the table. He snorted up the two lines, one in each nostril, and sat back, sniffing and wiping his nose with the back of his hand.

"Aaaahh," he said.

Escobar leaned forward. "The proposition is very similar to the one you were expecting, Captain," he said softly. "But instead of marijuana, you will be carrying a much less incriminating cargo—these four gentlemen." He indicated Gradak and his companions. "Mr. Rodriguez and his associates require discreet transportation to the U.S. mainland, specifically New Orleans or close by. Your, ah, line of work makes you—along with your excellent boat—particularly well suited to the task."

Sligo sniffed hard, his blue eyes very open, very bright.

"How much?" he asked, drumming his fingers on the back of the couch.

"Fifty thousand U.S. dollars," Escobar replied. "And you may have it in bearer bonds drawn on a bank in Georgetown, Grand Cayman, or in cash."

"Cash," Sligo said quickly. "How much do I get in advance?"

Escobar laughed lightly, shaking his head. "My dear Captain," he said, "this is not a standard arrangement. You get it all in advance."

Sligo's eyes widened. His face broke into a broad grin.

"No shit?" he declared incredulously.

"Quite," Escobar said. "You will receive the full amount in cash just before you leave. Don't worry, you'll have plenty of time to count it."

"Sounds like I can't complain," Sligo observed. He drummed his fingers on the back of the couch and tapped one foot rapidly. "Suppose," he said, glancing at Gradak, "I run into one of those Coast Guard cutters somewhere between here and New Orleans. They don't like my looks and search the boat. They don't find shit for drugs, but they want to know why I'm heading north with four . . . aliens. No offense," he added.

"These gentlemen are all carrying documentation indicating that they are resident aliens of the United

States," Escobar responded. "For example, Mr. Rodriguez possesses a valid British passport and a green card showing that he has been properly admitted to the U.S. He has a Florida driver's license, a social security card, and a business card from the state-licensed catering service he owns and operates in Orlando." He smiled. "You could call the business number right now and ask for Mr. Rodriguez, and his secretary would inform you that he is on a fishing vacation and will not be available for the next two weeks."

"Pretty impressive," Sligo said, sniffing.

There was an uncomfortable silence.

"Just being careful," the smuggler said at last. "I gotta watch my ass. I mean, nobody does it for me, y'know?"

"Of course, of course," Escobar agreed. Gradak and the other men nodded sympathetically. "In your business, caution is essential for survival. We can appreciate that."

Sligo fidgeted, gnawing at a hangnail. The others sat silently, watching him.

"How about fuel?" he asked. "That's a long way, and diesel ain't cheap."

"We will top off your tanks before you go," Escobar said, "and have a mechanic check your engines and fluid levels. Your boat will be completely serviced and refueled, at no expense to you."

"Good, good."

Sligo looked around, chewing his finger and tapping his foot. His wandering gaze fell on Gradak, who smiled politely.

"*Hablo Espanol,* Rodriguez?" the smuggler inquired.

Escobar stiffened. Gradak stared back at Sligo, still smiling, his amber eyes narrowing beneath his heavy brows. "I beg your pardon?" he said.

"What I said, 'Rodriguez,' " Sligo repeated, "was *'hablo Espanol.'* Don't you understand that?"

"I'm sorry, no," Gradak said.

Sligo got up abruptly, walked back into the galley area, and unlatched the refrigerator. He pulled out a beer, twisted off the cap, and took a long swallow. Then he leaned back on the counter, arms crossed, and looked hard at Escobar.

"Okay, Lieutenant," he said, "how about cutting the bullshit and telling me what the fuck is really going on."

Full of cocaine, adrenaline, and bravado, Sligo didn't notice the sudden effect his words had on Rodriguez's three silent companions across the salon. They were looking at him the way a pride of lions regards a fresh kill. Escobar's face was pale, his jaw set. Then Gradak suddenly laughed and shrugged.

"Ha! Well, Captain," he said, "I believe you've caught us. *'Hablo,'* whatever you said, is Spanish, I suppose. Very clever." He turned to Escobar, who remained pale with his mouth set in a thin line. "You didn't tell me you'd retained a captain possessed of such a penetrating intelligence, Lieutenant. But it's all for the best. I'm certain we'll reach the U.S. safely with this gentleman commanding the vessel."

He stood up and approached Sligo, clapping him on the shoulder and grinning broadly.

"I am relieved, my friend, that we will not be crossing all that water in the charge of a person of . . . low capacity. You deserve to know the truth. Ask me anything you wish, and I will answer it honestly."

Sligo glowed at the praise. Swigging his beer, he sat down on the couch again, pleased with himself. He'd shown them he was nobody to mess with.

"Okay, 'Carlos,' " he began, feeling well in control of the room, "let's start with some names." He nodded across the salon. "Who are these three?"

Gradak gestured at the man who sat nearest Sligo. "Introduce yourself to the captain," he said pleasantly.

The man held Gradak's eye for a moment, then rose to his feet. He was slender, of medium height, and had a boyish face that was lightly scarred by smallpox under a sparse beard. His black, wavy hair was cut short, and he regarded Sligo coolly with intelligent brown eyes. He appeared to be in his early twenties.

"I am Riad," he said in careful English. "I am glad to meet you." He looked at Gradak again, then sat down.

The next man stood up and nodded to Sligo. He was a bit shorter than Riad, but more thickly built. His swarthy face was heavily bearded, and he looked to be about thirty-five years of age. "Saeb," he said shortly, and sat back down.

The third man did not stand up, but sat staring at Sligo, unsmiling, with his massive arms folded across his broad chest. He was built like a decathlete, long-legged and powerful, with huge trapezius muscles that gave him a bullet-headed look. His black hair was cut short like Riad's and Saeb's, and his beard was carefully trimmed and shaped, coming to a neat point below his chin. He had the flat, soulless gaze of a reptile.

"Turgut," he said, his voice a gravelly baritone. He unfolded his arms and shifted in his seat, his shoulders rippling under the tight T-shirt. Even through his coke euphoria, Sligo caught the menace of the man. Not the type you'd want coming at you with a broken bottle.

Gradak nodded at Turgut and said, "What else, Captain, what else?"

Sligo looked around, pleased. This was more like it.

He studied the man who called himself Rodriguez. "I get the feeling that if I asked you exactly why you were going to the States, you wouldn't tell me."

Gradak smiled and cleared his throat. "And I have

the feeling, Captain, that you have not survived this long by meddling in the private affairs of others. Shall we leave it at that?"

"Whatever," Sligo shrugged, distractedly. He was beginning to get the familiar feeling that he was going to crawl out of his skin. It was time for another line or two. He fumbled in his shirt pocket for the vial.

Gradak bent close. "You *do* understand me, don't you?" he asked quietly.

Sligo was cutting up cocaine with his credit card again. It was a moment or two before he realized Gradak had stopped talking.

"Uh-huh, uh-huh," he grunted, nodding and glancing up.

Gradak stared at him briefly, fiddling with his little pile of white powder, then caught Escobar's watchful eye, shook his head, and sat down. He waited until Sligo had snorted up two more lines before he spoke.

"Do we have a working understanding now, 'Captain'?" He said the word the same way Escobar did, as though it tasted sour on his tongue. Sligo, however, was feeling too good to notice.

"Hell, I don't know," he said, stretching back on the couch. "I guess. As long as you ugly bastards don't crack every mirror on the boat with your faces." He threw his head back and roared with laughter, like it was the funniest thing he'd ever heard. The other five men stared at him, tight-lipped. Sligo finally got control of himself and looked around, red-faced and teary-eyed.

"Shee-it!" he exclaimed, giggling. "Sometimes I just *kill* myself!" He jumped up off the couch and headed for the refrigerator to get another beer, sniffing and wiping coke grains off his upper lip.

Without warning, Turgut got to his feet and advanced toward the galley. Instantly, Gradak fixed a steely gaze on him and raised a couple of fingers, motioning him back. The big man stopped where he was, pushing his balled fists into his pockets. He made a conscious effort to soften the expression on his face as Sligo turned back from the refrigerator, beer in hand.

After another uncomfortable silence, the Cuban officer spoke: "Well, Captain Sligo? Do you accept the proposal?"

Sligo took a long pull at his beer and lolled his head back, staring at the ceiling.

"W-e-e-e-l-l . . ." he intoned, tapping his beer bottle on the back of the couch. "Wellwellwell . . ."

Even Escobar's studied cool was beginning to weaken. The smuggler's manner was intolerable. Across the salon Turgut looked ready to explode.

"Sure," Sligo said finally. "Why not?"

The tension bled off the room as though released by a safety valve. Escobar relaxed perceptibly, his easy smile returning to his face.

"An excellent decision, Captain," he commented. "You're aiding in a just cause, whether you know it or not."

"If it's all the same to you," Sligo replied, sniffing hard, "I'll just take the money. And the free engine work," he added.

Gradak stood up and walked to the salon door, staring through the tinted glass at the sparkling waters of Bahia Cristobal's harbor. "We must leave by the day after tomorrow," he said softly, as though talking to himself. "We have a schedule to maintain."

"As soon as my engines are up to par, my tanks are full of diesel, and I've got fifty large in my hand, we're outta here," Sligo said, grinning.

"Your engine service and fueling will be done first thing in the morning," Escobar promised. Totally relaxed now, the lieutenant crossed his legs, pulled a thin black cigar from his shirt pocket, and lit it with a silver lighter.

"There will be a small amount of equipment to bring aboard," Gradak said, turning away from the door. "Nothing terribly substantial: two duffel bags per man."

"No problem, pal," Sligo responded. "Lotsa room." He turned to Escobar. "But most important of all: when do I see my cash?"

"I will hand it to you myself when you depart," Escobar answered. Sligo looked at him. "Yes, Captain. I will wait for you to count it and check its authenticity."

"Great," the smuggler said. He cast his gaze around the room. "Looks like everybody's happy!"

Escobar let cigar smoke trickle from his mouth and inhaled it into his nostrils. Rising to his feet, he extended a hand toward Sligo.

"Well, then, Captain," he said, "Thursday morning it is. Shall we say sunup? An early start is always best."

Sligo snuffled noisily and gave Escobar's hand a cursory shake.

"Whatever," he said. "You're paying the tab."

Gradak made a slight upward motion with his hand, and his three companions got to their feet as one. They moved over to the salon door behind their leader. Gradak smiled and opened the sliding glass panel, flooding the interior with hot late-afternoon sun.

"Until Thursday, Captain," he said, and stepped out onto the back deck, followed by Riad, Saeb, and Turgut. Escobar nodded, butted his cigar in the coffee table ashtray, and went out as well, sliding the tinted door closed behind him.

Sligo watched them step off the gunwales onto the dock, then flopped down on the couch, rolling back with his feet kicking in the air.

"Yes!" he exclaimed in a chortling whisper. "Yes, yes, yes!"

After a few minutes he pushed himself upright again, running his fingers through his greasy hair to smooth it behind his ears. He dug into his pocket, extracted the vial, and set it on the table. Then he threw his head back and yelled, "Hey, Luis! Get your lazy ass in here and make me a double Redrum! And goddammit, make one for yourself, too!"

Chapter Six

The *sayan* stood in the main lobby of Houston International Airport, nervously smoking a cigarette. The place was jammed with travelers, and his eyes darted over them incessantly, trying to pick out Mr. Calder, a man he'd never met and whose name he'd never heard before seven that morning.

He moved over to a large illuminated billboard and leaned back against the six-foot-tall image of a dancing raisin. Grinding the butt of the cigarette out under his toe, he went through the description of Mr. Calder again in his mind: five-ten, one-seventy, medium build, black hair, about thirty years old, wearing a black and gray Los Angeles Raiders team jacket and a tweed longshoreman's cap. Oh, and the briefcase. He'd be carrying a metallic silver briefcase. The *sayan* looked around anxiously again. People everywhere. There were so many.

The *sayan*'s name was Irving Koppelman, and most of the time his sole preoccupation in life was running the successful chain of specialty bakeries he owned in and around metropolitan Houston. He was forty years old, a prematurely balding little man running to fat, and had been an American citizen since 1962.

In the early fifties, his parents had emigrated from Israel with their only child and set up a bakery in the Bronx. They'd prospered, but had never forgotten their Jewish homeland. Fully twenty percent of the profits from their business and investments had, over the years, gone back to Israel to help fund the consolidation of the Jewish state.

This loyalty to Israel had been thoroughly ingrained in young Irving. And as he grew older, moved way, and became successful in his own right in Houston, he discovered that there were ways to serve the Israeli cause other than by merely sending money. One day he found the Mossad—or rather, he thought he'd found them. In reality, the Mossad—the Israeli secret service—found him.

He was recruited into the ranks of the *sayanim,* a worldwide corps of ordinary, law-abiding people of Jewish descent who could be counted on, if and when the situation arose, to provide logistical support for any Mossad operation in their area. A *sayan* doctor might treat a bullet wound and not report it, or a *sayan* banker might provide quick funds for an operative with no questions asked. Koppelman, as the owner of a small hotel and several modest apartment complexes, could provide discreet accommodations for any agents who might happen to need them, as well as a certain amount of financial and material aid. He could facilitate the acquisition of a rental car, for example, or the purchase of a certain type of camera.

The day he'd been officially recruited by a *katsa*— a Mossad officer from a regional bureau—Irving Koppelman, feeling rather James Bond-ish, had gone home to his fine house in West Houston and waited. And waited, and waited. The master-spy fantasy drifted away from him in time, and he went back to focusing his attention on his business and investments. But in the back of his mind he still waited. Once or twice a year the *katsa,* who served as his handling officer, would drop by for a quick cup of coffee and a gentle admonition never to forget the Jewish homeland—which would have been impossible for Koppel-

man, anyway—and then disappear, leaving him to wait
and wonder some more.

And then this morning the waiting had ended. A
curt phone call from the *katsa* had interrupted Koppelman's breakfast, the agent giving him instructions
to meet a Mr. Calder at noon in the lobby of Houston
International. With a pointed assurance that this was
indeed the real thing, the *katsa* had hung up, leaving
Koppelman with scrambled eggs in his mustache and
a dial tone buzzing in his ear.

He was digging in his breast pocket for another cigarette when he caught sight of his man: Raiders jacket,
tweed hat, and metallic briefcase, walking along at the
same pace as the majority of passengers traversing the
lobby. He wore black Wayfarer sunglasses and gray
corduroy pants, the casual mismatch of his clothes
making him look much like an aging college student.
Not really someone you'd pick out easily in a crowd,
which, Koppelman realized, was almost certainly the
point.

He resisted the urge to call out to Calder, and instead fell in behind him as he walked past, attempting
to overtake him unobtrusively. The younger man went
on to the far end of the lobby, then turned sharply
into the men's washroom.

Koppelman, somewhat flustered by this, stopped
outside the washroom entrance and, unsure of what
to do next, leaned up against the wall, trying to appear casual.

He nearly jumped out of his skin when the young
man stuck his head around the entranceway and said:

"Mr. Koppelman, I presume?"

"I, ah, yes." Koppelman could feel himself about to
break a sweat. He looked away, fidgeting. "Umm,
should we, er, acknowledge each other?" he whispered.

"Well, I don't know," Calder replied, coming
around in front of him. "Do you think the CIA has

us under surveillance? There may be a Delta team ready to jump out of this trash can at any second." He grinned and indicated one of the refuse containers standing near the washroom.

At this Koppelman looked up and saw Calder, an amused expression on his face, standing in front of him with his right hand extended. He relaxed slightly, feeling a little sheepish all of a sudden, and took the other man's hand.

"Mr. Calder?" he inquired timidly.

"Ari," the young man said. "Calder'll have to do for the last name, though, I'm afraid. Do you have a car?"

"A car? Oh, yes! Of course!"

"Well, then, let's go to your car," Ari said, "and I'll be glad to fill you in on a few details." He flashed his white-toothed grin again.

Koppelman got his feet moving. His heart felt as though it would beat right out of his chest.

"Yes, yes," he said breathlessly. "Down this way."

He was halted by Ari's firm grip on his arm.

"A little less haste," the young man admonished, "often results in a lot more progress." He turned Koppelman loose and patted his shoulder. "Calm down, Mr. Koppelman. You're doing fine."

"Yes, well, thank you," the *sayan* said. He composed himself. "Down this way, if you would."

They moved off down the wide corridor toward the parking level elevators, in no apparent hurry.

Forty minutes later Koppelman was maneuvering his burgundy Cadillac Seville through fast, heavy traffic westbound on the Houston 610 loop, Ari Calder in the passenger seat beside him. In an attempt to impress the agent, Koppelman was doing about ninety miles per hour, a look of casual unconcern cemented to his face. It wasn't easy to maintain; it took considerable force of will to suppress the urgent twitching that seized his jaw muscles every time he shot by another car with scant inches to spare.

"My, my," Ari said pleasantly, looking at Koppelman's white-knuckled grip on the steering wheel out of the corner of his eye, "you certainly know how to handle a car, Mr. Koppelman."

Koppelman felt his heart swell in his chest.

"Obviously you've done some racing," the agent continued. "Stock cars, right? Something with a standard wheelbase. A Charger, maybe, like Richard Petty?"

A rush of adrenaline burned from Koppelman's ears to his toes. "Well, ah . . ."

"You've got the feel, that's for sure." Ari was shaking his head in admiration. "Yes, sir. Just like King Richard." He smiled broadly at the *sayan*.

Koppelman steeled himself and swerved into the fast lane to pass a garbage truck, goosing the engine as he did so. "Well," he said, trying to sound like it was nothing, "I did have a Dodge once . . ."

"Charger?" Ari inquired.

"Er, no . . . Dart."

"But you raced it, of course," the agent continued smoothly.

"Yes," Koppelman lied, unwilling to lose the ground he'd apparently gained. "All the time."

"I thought so," Ari said, looking satisfied. "Damn!" He put a hand quickly on the dash as the Seville careened around a station wagon full of children at nearly a hundred miles per hour. "If the Israeli Defense Force had a few drivers like you, there wouldn't be a terrorist within fifty miles of the Golan Heights."

Koppelman thought he'd burst with pride. He felt as though he'd suddenly leaped to a higher plane. It was obvious that this agent considered him an equal, an ally indispensable to the success of his mission.

Koppelman felt giddy, but at the same time deserving. He'd always known, deep in his bones, that he was destined for great things. To actually be part of a Mossad operation! It was wonderful, wonderful.

"Watch out!" the agent shouted abruptly. Koppelman stood on the brake pedal with both feet, what was left of his hair standing on end, and the Cadillac shrieked to a halt just inches behind the Volkswagen bus that was stalled in the fast lane.

"Yaaaaaagh!" Koppelman screamed as the car stopped, heaving back on its shocks. His eyes were bulging and the sweat had popped out instantaneously all over his forehead. He looked over at his passenger fearfully. Ari had his hand on the dash, a tight smile grafted to his lips.

"Nice stop," he said through his teeth. "Excellent driving."

Feeling much more like a bakeshop owner again, Koppelman pulled out around the Volkswagen and continued on down the highway at fifty-five miles per hour.

"Will you be needing anything else?" Koppelman inquired anxiously, standing in the doorway of the small apartment. Located in one of his older buildings, it was unobtrusive and had a back entrance. Ari had said it was perfect.

"No, nothing more, Mr. Koppelman," the agent replied, ushering him out the door. "At least, not for a day or two. The accommodation is more than enough for now." He smiled broadly. "Oh, there is one thing . . ."

Koppelman leaned in like a dog expecting a biscuit.

"A gun," Ari said. "By noon tomorrow."

The *sayan* felt a thrill of fear shoot through his body. "A—gun," he repeated, trying not to stutter. "Any particular kind?"

"Yes," the agent continued casually, "a .380 Beretta automatic, flat black finish, with a hideaway boot holster. Two spare ammunition clips, and a box of fifty rounds." He looked hard suddenly at the wide-eyed little man. "Also .380," he added.

"Yes, ah, there may be a problem with—"

"Mr. Koppelman," Ari interrupted, "this is Houston, not Toronto. You are a respected member of the business community. Somewhere in this city you will find a gun shop or pawnshop owner who will sell you the handgun I require without a lot of questions or background checks." The hard look left his eyes, and he gave the *sayan* his most charming smile. "A man of your abilities can handle this assignment. I wouldn't ask if I thought otherwise. I'm depending on you to provide this important piece of equipment for me."

Koppelman squared his shoulders. "Shall I bring it here tomorrow?" he asked, jaw sticking out a little.

"Yes," Ari replied. "And I'll be here. I'll give you a call later, all right?"

"Oh, yes."

"Fine, then," the agent said. "Good afternoon, Mr. Koppelman." He ushered the *sayan* through the doorway. "Oh, and Mr. Koppelman . . ."

"Yes?"

"Try to act naturally when you come by, will you? Let's not be too obvious. Who knows; *they* might be watching."

Koppelman hunched his shoulders, glancing around nervously, and held a finger to his lips. "Shhhhh," he whispered, backing down the hallway. "Shhh."

Ari nodded and waved him on down the hall, then closed the door.

Rubbing his eyes, he went over to the television, turned it on with the volume low, and sank back onto the threadbare sofa. The *sayan* was an idiot; a gofer nursing a spy fantasy. Ari hoped he'd be able to buy the handgun without getting thrown in jail or shoot-ing himself.

He shook his head. The *sayanim* had their place. They were a tool of the trade, some better than others. Koppelman would simply have to be used within his limitations and watched carefully. At any rate, Ari re-assured himself, the *sayanim* involvement in this oper-ation was minimal; more a matter of convenience than necessity. If worse came to worse, Koppelman knew absolutely nothing of importance. Ari intended to keep it that way.

He reached down and pulled a flat gray object from the top of his sock. It was about the size and shape of a small pocket comb, perhaps slightly thicker. Ari flicked his wrist, and a spring-loaded stiletto blade some five inches in length snapped out of the handle. Made of carbon-fiber composite and hardened with special resins, the knife was nonmetallic and therefore undetectable by standard airport security screens. The Mossad also stocked a small-caliber handgun made of the same material in its arsenal of covert weapons, complete with carbon-fiber bullets. Ari had elected not to draw one from the Atlanta office; it seemed an unnecessary risk to carry a gun on a domestic flight within the United States, and he didn't care for the way the little pistols handled, anyway.

The heat wouldn't be on until much later, and the Mossad commando team was supposed to arrive with all the firearms needed for the operation. To have insisted on being armed might have seemed . . . suspi-cious. He'd had to be careful not to do anything out of the ordinary.

He cleaned his fingernails with the knife, then snapped it shut and tossed it onto the coffee table. Picking up a Houston phone book, he flipped through the Yellow Pages until he found the listing he wanted:

Helicopters—Charter/Rental.

Chapter Seven

Ben punched up the volume on the radio as he took the exit ramp off the interstate to the New Orleans 610 bypass, joining the fast-moving traffic that was shunting across the northern end of the city toward Baton Rouge. The Allman Brothers always sounded good.

He left the interstate via the New Orleans Airport exit and paralleled the runways to Highway 61, then took the first turn south for the Luling Bridge. Spanning the Mississippi on the western edge of New Orleans, the bridge fed down to Highway 90, the main route into the heart of southern Louisiana bayou country.

The cypress trees were thick on either side of the road, their gnarled roots partially submerged in the tea-colored water of the swamp. Here and there egrets stalked through the shallows, flashes of pure white against the green foliage and gray sphagnum moss. Nearly every snag or floating log visible from the highway had several large turtles basking on it, and once in a while the elongated head of a swimming alligator could be seen cutting a clean, rippled V across the water's quiet surface.

An hour later, Ben stopped at a small diner in the center of Morgan City and picked up two large black coffees to go. He tipped the pretty teenage girl behind the counter a dollar, making her smile and blush, and then proceeded through town and across the Earl Long Bridge, which spanned the main course of the Atchafalaya River.

He turned off on a side road near the little community of Berwick and followed it down to the levee that ran along the river. He drove another mile and a half past shotgun shacks and mobile homes on the right, oil dock after oil dock on the left. The whole area had a dilapidated feel to it; the buildings were rundown, and the vehicles parked beside them were battered and outdated.

Ben passed a sign that read "dead end," swerved around a rooster that had taken up residence in the center of the road, and turned into the last crushed-shell driveway on the right. The rusty mailbox bore the label "R. Savard" rendered in fluorescent orange spray paint.

The driveway led to a rickety mobile home nearly hidden among the trees, well back from the road. The roof consisted of corrugated galvanized steel sheeting, bright orange with rust. Orange stains ran down the sides of the trailer from the gutters, which were loose and choked with dead leaves. All the window blinds were drawn.

Ben pulled his truck up in front of the carport and killed the engine. Picking up the coffees and stepping out, he stretched his tight back muscles and walked up to the front door. Some kind of reptile slithered through the dried leaves beside the front step.

When no sound came from within, Ben knocked again, harder this time. A moment or two later there was a banging noise and a muffled curse. Then the door creaked open and a hand beckoned him to enter. Ben opened the rattletrap screen door and stepped inside.

He caught a glimpse of Rolly Savard's mottled

white buttocks disappearing down the short hall and into the back bedroom.

"Hey!" Ben called. "Where you going, bro?" He followed Rolly into the bedroom, where he lay sprawled facedown on the rumpled sheets of an expensive king-size water bed. He was making faint growling noises, like an injured animal.

"Hey, amigo, we're late," Ben prodded. "Up. I've got coffee. And aspirins, too, if you want 'em."

Rolly groaned into the sheets. "Ah need morphine," he mumbled weakly. "Ah need hard drugs."

"Can't help you there," Ben replied. "But I'll be in the living room with this coffee. C'mon, up. We gotta move."

He turned and went back up the hall, settling into an overstuffed old armchair in front of the television and popping the plastic lid off one of the coffees. He flicked on CNN news and sipped slowly, stretching the driving cramps out of his legs.

After a couple of minutes Rolly staggered into the living room and flopped onto the threadbare sofa, scratching his beer gut and belching. He was wearing a pair of boxer shorts with little Tweety Birds all over them. They contrasted sharply with the large blue tattoo over his heart, which read "Harley Fucking Davidson."

Wordlessly Ben held out the coffee. Rolly took it in one scarred hand, shook a Marlboro out of a crumpled pack lying on the arm of the sofa, lit it, and slumped back, the coffee resting on his stomach. He sipped at the cup and let smoke trickle from his mouth and nose, looking completely miserable.

Ben studied him in amusement. Erroll Baptiste Savard was a piece of work. At less than five-eight and one hundred and forty pounds, he could drink men twice his size under the table, name your poison. His skinny frame, paunch, and stringy muscles belied a

surprising strength and endurance, although Ben had
noticed him slowing down a little since turning forty-
seven the previous year. His curly black hair was
streaked with gray, as was the heavy stubble of his
beard. His face was wide and creased with wrinkles
from exposure to the sun, the dark eyes set far apart
and separated by a flat, twice-broken nose. Born and
raised in Cocodrie, Louisiana, he was one hundred
percent Cajun.

After lying still on the sofa for a few minutes, as
though mentally checking for serious damage, Rolly
heaved himself to his feet and wavered across the
room to a small wall cupboard. Pulling out a half-
empty bottle of Jack Daniel's, he leaned against the
wall and doctored the coffee with a healthy slug of
whiskey. He replaced the bottle, toasted Ben silently
with a bleary grin, and took a long sip.

"Little hair of the dog dat bit ya, Benjamin." he
chuckled in his sandpaper rasp, making his way back
to the sofa. "Just enough to lower de heat behind mah
eyes a bit. Whoo-ee!" He sat down weakly. "Goddamn, bro! Ah surely howled at de moon last night,
Ah guarontee! Man, Ah feel like shit!" He coughed
hoarsely, a wet hacking sound, then took a deep drag
off his cigarette.

"So where'd you go?" Ben asked, flicking the channels on the television.

"Oh, man . . ." Rolly coughed again, rubbing his
eyes with the heel of his smoking hand. "De devil
done captured me last night, cuz. Lured ol' Rolly, dat
poor fucker, right out into temptation, he did . . . as
mah ex-ol' lady Paula—goddamn her for a thievin',
black-hearted bitch—used to say."

Paula, thought Ben, remembering. That would be
the biker babe turned Holy Roller. The one with the
teardrop tattooed at the corner of her eye. Found the
Lord, but never quite got the hang of not stealing

everything she could get her hands on. Filled out those black biker leathers pretty nicely, though.

"Anyway," Rolly continued, sipping coffee. "Ah went down to de Deckhouse, just to hang out for a while and drink maybe two, three beers, tops." Ben shot a doubting glance at him, and he smiled sheepishly. "Well, maybe three or four. So, anyway, Ah'm shootin' pool, and here come Bullballs Thorsen through de front door wavin' a wad—and Ah mean a *wad*—of cash. Seems he went on a ride to Panama City with some ex-Banditos he knows, and ended up winnin' one of de Florida Lottery Quickpicks while he was in a gas station buyin' some smokes. Well, we-all had to help him drink up some of it. Jeezuz H. Christ on de cross, he won ten thousand dollars, de lucky fuck!"

Ben whistled. "That's a nice chunk of change. Personally, I'd settle for just getting back the money Sass has spent on those damn tickets over the years. I could probably retire." He shook his head sadly. "I think she won four dollars once . . ."

Rolly gave a hoarse laugh that degenerated into a wracking smoker's cough. He slapped his knee.

"Dat's de way, ain't it bro? You buy a couple of tickets every week for half a century, and don't win nothin'. Sumbitch rides into town on a three-day drunk, never played de damn game before, buys one ticket, and wins ten-goddamn-thousand bucks. Shee-it!"

He hoisted himself up off the sofa, broke wind noisily, and wandered back down the hall making pain noises. "Mah gear's all ready to go, Benjamin," he called over his shoulder. "Just lemme grab a quick shower, and we'll hit de road, bro. Ten minutes."

"Five," Ben corrected.

"Fuck you," Rolly replied cheerfully, closing the bathroom door behind him. Ben laughed and began flipping around the television channels with the remote.

Two hours later they were cruising south, following the state road that paralleled the wide bayou connecting the little shrimping town of LaRose with the Gulf of Mexico. The great coastal salt marsh of Louisiana opened up before them, a vast expanse of waving golden reeds and grasses infiltrated by innumerable small channels and bayous. One of America's great wetlands, it was home to a huge assortment of wildlife, particularly birds and fish.

The road was a thin ribbon of blacktop through the heart of the marsh, and while buildings were scarce, here and there power pylons and exposed pipelines reminded travelers that in addition to being a wildlife sanctuary, the marsh was home to Louisiana's offshore oil industry. Shuttle helicopters clattered through the clear blue sky overhead, running back and forth from oil company shore-based complexes to offshore production platforms, great noisy metal birds that sent the egrets and cranes spooking for cover among the reeds.

In the deepwater channels that meandered through the marsh to the east and west of the road, oilfield service boats were visible making the run to and from the Gulf. Because the landscape was so flat and the grasses so high, the waterways themselves were hidden from view, creating the startling illusion that the high-bowed vessels were sliding through the wheat-like vegetation on dry land.

An hour south of LaRose, Ben turned the truck onto a side road marked by a small billboard that read "PORT FOURCHON."

"What a shit hole," Rolly remarked, flicking cigarette ash out the window.

They drove toward a cluster of large metal warehouses about two miles distant. A few stilt houses were built alongside the road, some with access to dry land, others with small boats tied outside to ferry their owners to the bank. Near the entrance to the fenced-in docking area, an old Delta 88 was parked with a precarious tilt on the narrow shoulder. The trunk was open, and two men in T-shirts and baseball caps sat in lawn chairs beside it, drinking beer and fishing with cane poles in the little roadside bayou.

Ben and Rolly cruised down the dock access road and pulled into the NAOC facility at the end, pausing to identify themselves to the security guard at the gate. The yard consisted of a crane-equipped deepwater dock on Fourchon's main channel and several large corrugated-steel warehouses. A tall antennae tower stood at one end of the largest building, and a half-dozen sleek, narrow offshore crewboats in the seventy-foot range were backed down to the dock, their lines tied off to shore bollards. They were painted in NAOC colors: indigo-blue hulls and kelly-green topsides, with the ornate NAOC logo emblazoned on their bows.

Beside the boat closest to the dock's pedestal crane was a Challenge Diving flatbed truck, empty except for one decompression chamber. A rigger in a faded denim shirt and white hard hat was hooking up crane slings to the chamber's lifting padeyes. On the ground beside the truck, a stocky young man wearing a rose-colored muscle shirt and baggy camouflage pants gestured vigorously and shouted instructions.

As Ben pulled up to the flatbed, the young man turned and, seeing Ben and Rolly, spun back abruptly toward the rigger and hurled commands even more adamantly, loud enough for the two divers to hear.

". . . And make sure those shackle pins are in all the way, goddammit! I saw a guy get killed once 'cause someone didn't put a fucking pin in right! Gotta be safe!"

He turned and, acting like he'd just noticed Ben and Rolly's arrival, waved and swaggered over to the pickup, weight lifter's arms held out from his sides, his hands balled into fists.

"Hiya," he said cockily. "I'm Nelson Pinkham. Diver-tender. But everyone calls me Uzi—like the machine gun, y'know?" He extended his hand.

"I'll call you Nelson," Ben said, shaking his hand. "I'm Ben Gannon. This is Rolly Savard." He shot a glance over at his friend, who rolled his eyes and looked weary.

The kid stuck his head and shoulders through the open window and leaned over Ben to hold out his hand to Rolly. "Hiya," he repeated. "Nelson Pinkham. Call me Uzi."

"Hey," Rolly growled, ignoring the hand.

Unfazed, Pinkham withdrew from the window and stood up straight, puffing out his health-club pectorals. "Yeah," he said, shaking his head, "you know what these green tenders are like. Don't know their asses from a hole in the ground. I've gotta watch this one every minute—make sure she doesn't kill herself or anybody else." He laughed, an irritating, snickering sound. "Do you believe they're letting broads work offshore now? Shit, I've gotta do my job and theirs, too!"

Ben watched as the chamber was lifted off the flatbed, the rigger holding a tag line to control any swinging. He noticed for the first time the long brown hair curling out the back of the hard hat and the female curves under the baggy work clothes.

"Looks like she's doing fine right now," he remarked dryly.

"Well, yeah!" Pinkham blurted. "I told her how to do everything. I gotta stay on her all the time, man. Pain in the ass."

He turned and strode off suddenly, waving his arms

and shouting to be careful, goddammit, careful. Ben and Rolly saw the tender, who was handling the heavy load quite competently, glance over at Pinkham with a look of resigned patience.

"What an asshole," Rolly said flatly.

"Seems wired a little tight, doesn't he?" Ben mused. He shifted in his seat and pulled the door latch. "Oh, well. We've seen guys like him before. Looks like the type that hasn't been out of the military more than a year."

"Yup," Rolly replied. "In at eighteen, out at twenty-two, and brainwashed into thinkin' you can bully a man into doin' what you want by yellin' at him." He shook his head. "Probably thinks he's some kind of killin' machine, too." He looked over at Ben. "Ten bucks says he was in de marines."

"Hmm," Ben said, gazing at Pinkham through the windshield. "I'd say airborne. He looks like he'd probably enjoy jumping out of airplanes. With heavy weapons strapped to his body." He shook Rolly's outstretched hand. "Ten bucks it is."

They got out of the truck, donned hard hats, and walked over to the stern of the crewboat. The girl was just positioning the decompression chamber over the center of the boat's back deck. She stabilized it with her shoulder, then gave the "down-on-the-load" hand signal to the crane operator, who set it down on the deck boards.

"Okay, let's get a chain on that and get it bound down!" yelled Pinkham, who'd been standing on the edge of the dock with his hands on his hips. Ben looked the girl over as she paused to wipe the sweat off her forehead with the back of one dirty-gloved hand. Her denim shirt was soaked through and streaked with grease and dirt, as were the thighs and knees of her jeans. She was a marked contrast to Pinkham, Ben noted, whose clothes were clean and dry.

He frowned slightly. Loading and unloading gear, particularly when you were shorthanded, was shared work—even if the diver-tender *was* the senior tender in charge. He looked over at Pinkham again, who was running a clean hand over his crew cut blond hair.

He turned to Rolly, who hadn't missed the contrast between the two tenders, either, and patted him on the shoulder. "I'm going to go check in with the dispatcher," he said. "I need to get a few things signed. Back in a minute." He strode off toward the warehouse offices, his boots kicking up shell dust with every step.

Rolly extracted a Marlboro from his shirt pocket and lit it. He blew a cloud of smoke and looked from the girl on the boat's deck, struggling with a long length of tie-down chain, over to Nelson Pinkham standing casually on the edge of the dock, doing some clasped-hand shoulder stretches.

"Hey, Pinkham," Rolly rasped in his gravelly drawl. "C'mere."

The diver-tender marched over to him with his Hollywood-tough-guy swagger.

"What can I do for ya?" he asked briskly.

"Ben's and my dive gear's in de back of de pickup." Rolly's voice was a quiet growl. "Ah want you to move it onto de boat and stow it up inside de passenger section."

"No problem," came Pinkham's quick reply. He spun on his heel and began to shout at the girl on the boat. "Hurry up and get that bound down! You need to unload the gear from this truck. Make sure you put it all up in the passeng—"

"Hey." Pinkham went suddenly quiet as Rolly cut him off. The wiry Cajun diver moved directly in front of the diver-tender, his street-tough face inches from Pinkham's. "Ah asked *you* to do it." He punctuated the word "you" with a stab of his cigarette.

Pinkham blanched a little, then reddened with anger and embarrassment. He started to argue. "Hey, man, I'll get it done. I've got tenders I delegate that shit to—"

"You got one tender, boy." Rolly's gaze was searing. "And Ah need her for somethin'. So start movin' dat gear right now."

Pinkham colored again, but faltered under Rolly's withering stare and wisely decided to keep his mouth shut. He turned and started over to the trunk.

Rolly watched him for a moment, then stepped up on the stern of the crewboat. He walked up the deck to where the girl was struggling with a chain binder, stooped down, and helped her lock the heavy lever into place. She smiled shyly at the unexpected aid, puffing with effort, and stood up with a little groan.

"Tough, huh?" Rolly grinned, drawing on his smoke.

"Not too bad," the girl answered.

"Look," he said, "Ah need you to do somethin'."

The girl's face sagged a little. "Sure."

"Ah want you to go over to de waitin' room by de dispatcher's office and buy me some peanuts from de snack machine. Get yourself somethin', too. Then Ah want you to sit down in de air-conditionin' and take it easy until Ah or de other senior diver come and get you. Okay?"

He groped in his pocket, came up with a fistful of silver, and dumped it into her cupped hands. She smiled again, her face a portrait of relief, and trotted off toward the stern of the boat, passing Pinkham, who was lugging the first of the heavy gear bags up the deck.

Twenty minutes later Ben stepped up on the stern, a sheaf of papers in his hand, and went forward to the enclosed passenger cabin. He paused at the watertight entrance door, doing a double take at Pinkham. The diver-tender, stripped to the waist, was doing quick, close-hand push-ups beside the starboard rail. He was staring straight ahead, head up, his body rigidly at horizontal attention. His breathing was a series of taut exhalations: *chou . . . chou . . . chou . . .* one per repetition.

Shaking his head, Ben stepped inside and located Rolly, who was dozing in one of the Naugahyde seats with his arms folded and his hard hat pulled down over his eyes. Ben tapped him lightly on the shoulder with the bundle of papers and sat down on the arm of the seat across the center aisle.

Rolly tipped up the hard hat with one index finger and regarded Ben from beneath heavy lids, crossing his booted and blue-jeaned legs the other way on his gear bag.

"What say, Benjamin?"

"We're leaving in twenty minutes." Ben leafed through his papers. "Where's that girl tender? Whatsername . . . here it is: Marriot. Karen Marriot, tender third class. I didn't see her outside."

"Ah sent her over to de lounge to take a break. Ah'll get her." Rolly yawned and stretched. "Where's Izzy—Ozzie—whateverdehell."

"He's outside doing push-ups," Ben said.

"He's what?" Rolly blinked at his friend.

"Doing push-ups," Ben repeated.

Rolly looked stunned. "You mean, like, *exercise*?"

"That's what I mean," Ben replied. "He looks like a little piston engine out there."

"Jeezuz." Rolly shook out another cigarette and lit it. "It ain't like de old days, Ah tell you." He got to his feet. "Ah'll go get dat gal. Want a Coke or somethin' for de ride?"

"Why not?" Ben shrugged. "Coke'll be good. Thanks."

Rolly clumped down the aisle and out the door onto the back deck. As the heavy hatch swung closed, Ben could faintly hear him throw the inevitable dig at Pinkham:

"What de hell, boy. Get off your belly; de deck's dirty . . ."

Ben chuckled to himself, put his papers in his battered old briefcase, and went forward up the short flight of stairs that led to the crewboat's wheelhouse.

The large, upholstered pedestal chair that was bolted in place in front of the helm spun on its bearings as he entered. Sitting in it, regarding Ben severely with small, piggy eyes, was a large man with a full head of flowing gray hair tied back into a three-foot ponytail. His gray and white beard was untrimmed and bushy, and extended down to the center of his chest, the mustaches stained nicotine-yellow. Though tall, he was narrow-shouldered, and carried a huge belly that hung lumpily over his groin, straining against the faded blue cloth of his coveralls.

"Afternoon, Cap," Ben smiled, extending a hand. "Ben Gannon. I'm with Challenge Diving. Nice day for a ride, ain't it?" He slipped easily into the mandatory pleasantries that were the working language of the oilfield.

"Sho' is," the big man replied, shifting and re-wedging his immense lower torso in the chair. His bottom lip was bulging with tobacco, and like everyone who enjoyed a chew, he talked around the wad with his mouth all but closed. "I'm Bubba Dothan, the skippuh. Soon's they let us go, we gonna make good time out to the rig." He pronounced the last word *reeg*.

The Alabama accent was as thick as cane syrup, and coming from around the tobacco it would have sounded like Swahili to anyone who wasn't an old hand in the Gulf. Ben nodded, and unconsciously adopted some of the lazy meter of the man's speech as he spoke again:

"About twenty minutes, huh? Let me make sure I've got all my people, and we'll be ready to roll."

"Sho'," the captain agreed. "I'm just gonna warm her up now." He pressed first one, then another button on the helm panel. There were two successive dull roars as the engines came to life below decks, blending quickly into a single throbbing growl. The entire boat hummed with a slight vibration. "Sing to me, sweet thang," exclaimed Dothan, moving his chew around his gums with a pudgy index finger.

Eighteen minutes later, Ben and Rolly were standing on the back deck watching the dock slip away behind them as the crewboat moved out into the main channel, leaving a dirty smudge of black diesel smoke hanging in the calm air. A dolphin rolled in the swirling brown eddies of the prop wash, the sun glinting off its slick gray back and dorsal fin. Karen Marriot and Nelson Pinkham paused as they did their final walkaround check of the heavy equipment to watch the animal blow again at the starboard rail, then unexpectedly treat them to a high, tail-flipping jump. Then it was gone. Up in the wheelhouse Dothan bumped the twin throttles to one-quarter speed and the throb of the engines quickened, pushing the boat's narrow steel hull into a fast glide toward the Gulf of Mexico.

Chapter Eight

"Feel anything out of the ordinary?"

Ari nodded in response to the checkout pilot's query and adjusted the Bell 206 JetRanger's rpms up and down as he banked the helicopter around to the east and back toward Houston International Airport. A moment later he touched the small voice-activated headset microphone, positioning it directly in front of his lips, and answered the question directly:

"Sure do. Slight torquing vibration. Probably a sticky counterweight on the main rotor. Annoying, but not fatal unless it's left unattended to." Ari grinned over at the checkout pilot, and a moment of unspoken understanding passed between the two men.

The checkout pilot looked away, suppressing a grin of his own. He'd doctored a rotor counterweight slightly before takeoff just to see if the rental client had the experience to diagnose an inflight abnormality. Apparently this one did.

Ari palmed back the cyclic control stick to slow the forward speed of the chopper and cleared to land with the flight controller in the small tower at Grissom Aviation. He looked around in all directions, visually checking his airspace. It was a beautiful day, the blue sky cloudless except for some faraway afternoon thunderheads building to the south over the warm waters of the Gulf. Several miles ahead, a 747 and a smaller

DC-9 were taking off from runways at Houston International, vectoring off in opposite directions.

Picking out one of the Grissom landing pads—a blue X within a white circle painted on the tarmac—Ari brought the chopper in gently for a perfect landing, the skids straddling the center of the mark. He checked all the gauges, throttled down, slowing the main rotor gradually, then killed the engine.

"Okay," the checkout pilot drawled, extracting his lanky Texan frame from the helicopter, "you're good to go. Just c'mon into the office and we'll fill out your final rental paperwork."

"Sure," Ari agreed. His eyes wandered casually back down to the fuel gauges. Full. As he climbed out of the chopper on the side opposite the other pilot, he quickly slipped duplicate door and ignition keys off their ring and pocketed them.

One phone call with the location coordinates. That was all he needed.

Like many cities in the Middle East, Damascus, capital of Syria, was the site of a collision between the modern and ancient worlds. Tall, air-conditioned office buildings of steel and tinted glass gleamed in the hot sun, while only a block or two away goats roamed in and out of the open doors of low stone-slab dwellings that had stood since the time of the Crusades.

The El-Shabash coffeehouse—in a variety of different incarnations—had been serving customers from its location on a short side street in the heart of the old city for over three hundred years. It had a rather plain exterior, unadorned but for the black-painted Arabic letters proclaiming its name over the three tall entrance archways. Several wrought-iron tables and chairs were set up outside, close to the stone wall to catch the building's shade.

The interior of the coffeehouse was considerably

more ornate. The domed ceiling was decorated with spiraling patterns of hand-laid mosaic tile; the effect was that of looking up into a giant kaleidoscope. Beautifully woven tapestries of dark red and gold covered the whitewashed stone walls, more wrought-iron chairs and tables were set up around the single large room, and a long service bar of extremely dark, aged wood occupied one entire side. On it sat the wares of the coffeehouse: silver-and-glass coffee services, demitasses, and four massive, ornate coffee machines that looked as though they dated from the nineteenth century—and probably did. Four columns of heavy steam rose from them as they brewed the thick, potent coffee of the Middle East, filling the room with a dense, burnt aroma.

One table in a far corner of the coffeehouse was occupied by a lone man in a dark, sweat-rumpled suit who chain-smoked as he read a newspaper. He was somewhere in his mid-fifties and running to fat, with the slumped shoulders of someone who spends too much time hunched over a desk. His head was bald but for small patches of stringy hair above his ears, and he was sweating, drops of perspiration glistening on his forehead even in the relative cool of the coffeehouse's dark interior. Every time he turned the page of the newspaper, he took a long look around the room.

All at once he put the paper down on the table and plucked the cigarette from his mouth, exhaling a cloud of smoke. A man dressed in a cheap gray muslin suit and carrying a large brown paper bag had entered the coffeehouse and was making his way over to the corner table. A few moments later a second man walked through one of the tall archways and also approached. Both were around thirty, very fit, with dark, wavy hair and olive skin. The second man, in addition to a black suit coat, wore a red-and-white-checkered burnoose.

The two men seated themselves at the corner table and gestured to the proprietor to bring coffee. It was served Turkish-style, piping hot and poured over translucent lumps of hard sugar. All three men lit fresh cigarettes and waited until the proprietor had returned to the service bar before speaking.

The young man who had carried the paper bag, which now sat at his feet under the table, removed his sunglasses and regarded the fat man coolly.

"Well, Ghiz?" he inquired softly. "Have you got it?"

The fat man shifted in his seat uncomfortably and drew on his cigarette. Sweat trickled down one jowly cheek. Strangely enough, thought the young Mossad operative, his face was quite composed, the eyes downcast but unblinking.

"Yes," Ghiz said in a gravelly whisper. He looked up, and his dark eyes had the empty resignation of someone who has sold his soul to the devil. "I have the information you need."

The second agent wearing the burnoose leaned over casually, sipping his sweet coffee. "Any problems?" he asked.

Ghiz permitted himself a derisive smile. "An idiotic question," he said. "The entire endeavor was itself one immense problem."

There was an uncomfortable pause. It was clear that neither Ghiz nor the agents held the upper hand. After a few moments the man in the burnoose, whose face had hardened instantly upon Ghiz's retort, relaxed and sat back in his chair.

"I was simply hoping that things had gone smoothly for you," he said pleasantly.

"Your concern touches me," Ghiz muttered in a low monotone. He shook his head slowly from side to side and mopped the sweat from his upper lip with his jacket sleeve. "The Ministry of Foreign Affairs is not an office that gives up information easily, not even to a senior clerk such as myself. There was nothing smooth about it. However, I am certain that my acquisition of the information you seek remains undiscovered."

He glanced out through the archways to the sunbaked street. "At least, I am certain for the time being. Assad's secret police are extremely competent. I know—I've seen them operate. If they ever have a hint that I betrayed my office . . ."

He looked resignedly at the two agents. The bareheaded agent was thinking to himself again: this man believes he is already dead.

He tried to look reassuring. "You don't need to worry about us, Ghiz," he said. "We'd gain no advantage by giving you up. And it isn't the money"—he nudged the bag under the table with his toe—"not even the extra amount you demanded. Your information is far more valuable to us. Just stay calm, don't do anything stupid or out of the ordinary for a few months, then retire on schedule and fade gracefully away. Simple."

Ghiz looked at him with sudden vehemence. His mouth curled into a snarl as he spoke, but he kept his voice low. "Don't patronize me, Jew," he said, spitting out the last word. "You'll use me just as I use you— and we'll both get what we want. Though maybe not what we deserve." He sat back in his chair. "I am tired of being afraid, and I am already bored with you. The exchange. Now."

"In the bag, of course," the bareheaded agent said. The other man in the burnoose simply stared at Ghiz from behind his sunglasses, his face a mask.

The fat man hooked a finger into the top of the bag and slid it over beside his chair. He bent over to rummage in it for a few seconds, then straightened up, flushed but satisfied. "The currency and denominations appear to be correct," he said, breathing heavily, "as does the total amount."

He reached over and pushed the newspaper he had been reading across the table.

"An interesting article on page seven," he said. He rose, clutching the bag to his chest. "Good day."

He started toward the archway, but the hard-faced agent in the burnoose caught his sleeve as he went by.

"Never forget, Ghiz," he said evenly. "We can find you. Anywhere."

The fat man with the corpse's eyes laughed mirthlessly and pulled his arm away.

"Do you think I don't know that?" he inquired, as though talking to a small child. "Page seven," he repeated, and walked across the mosaic floor, through the archway, and out into the street.

The two agents sat for a few minutes, sipping their coffee and glancing casually around the room to see if their hushed exchange with Ghiz had attracted any attention. The proprietor was at the far end of the service bar, arguing prices with a woman who had come in to buy sweets. Several other tables were occupied, the patrons smoking and drinking coffee, but nobody appeared to be paying the slightest attention to the two Mossad men.

The bare-headed agent set his coffee down and nonchalantly reached for the newspaper Ghiz had left on the table. Opening it to page seven, he skimmed over the columns of Arabic type, finding nothing at first. He was beginning to feel alarmed when he noticed the almost imperceptibly small ballpoint printing in the bottom margin.

Straining his eyes in the coffeehouse's dim light, he was able to make out the first of two lines: three sets of two numbers each, followed by a letter. Underneath, the second line followed the same pattern as the first, but with a different letter and numbers.

A latitude and longitude.

The young agent stared at the two sequences for a full five minutes, committing the position to memory. Then he sat back and pushed the newspaper across to his companion, who removed his sunglasses, pushed back the hanging folds of his burnoose, and did the same.

When he had finished memorizing the printing, the agent fished another cigarette from his coat pocket and lit it with a wooden match. He dropped the match, still burning, into the table's ashtray, ripped the small section of newspaper containing the two lines from the bottom margin, and deposited it on top of the flame. It flared up briefly, and was gone. The agent crushed the remaining ashes to powder with his fingertip.

The two men finished their coffee and rose to leave, tossing a few coins onto the table. They made their way past the tables and chairs, nodding to the proprietor, and disappeared through an archway into the hot brilliance of the street.

Chapter Nine

At ten minutes to eight Ari was standing in a phone booth across the street from his temporary apartment, watching Koppelman's Cadillac Seville pull up to the opposite curb and park. The headlights winked off and Koppelman got out, carrying a leather briefcase. Ari stuck an arm outside the booth and waved to him, keeping the receiver pressed to his ear.

"Your order has been processed, sir. You should receive your software within the next seven working days. If you have any further inquiries, please don't hesitate to call. Please refer to the following dispatch number: G, C, dash, one, eight, six. Once again: G, C, dash, one, eight, six."

"I have it," Ari said, a rush of exhilaration seizing him.

"Thank you, sir," the voice acknowledged. "Good evening."

Ari hung up the phone and stood there for a full minute, repeating the letter-number combination over and over in his mind until it was etched into his memory. When he looked up he was almost startled to see Koppelman hovering by the door of the phone booth, looking unsure of himself.

Ari stepped out onto the sidewalk and smiled broadly. "Come with me," he said, and headed toward the apartment building. Koppelman followed at his heels.

Once they were inside the apartment, Ari motioned

Koppelman to sit down. The *sayan* did so, perching on the edge of the sofa with the briefcase across his knees and glancing at Ari nervously. The young Mossad agent seemed different to him; more intense and remote than he'd been in the airport.

Ari set his own metallic briefcase on the coffee table and sat down in an armchair facing Koppelman. "All right," he said. "Do you have that item we talked about?"

"Yes, yes," Koppelman replied, fiddling with the briefcase. "I have it right here . . ."

He got it open and extracted a small black handgun, which he put gingerly on the tabletop, followed by two extra clips and two boxes of .380 ammunition.

Ari picked up the little automatic and examined it, checking the slide and thumbing the hammer.

"It's not loaded," Koppelman offered. "I thought it would be safer to carry that way."

Ari glanced up at him and smiled. He pressed the magazine release and caught the clip in his other hand as it dropped out of the handle. Opening the box of shells, he quickly loaded the clip and reinserted it into the butt of the gun, smacking it home with the heel of his hand.

"Can you think of anything more useless than an empty gun?" he asked Koppelman casually.

The *sayan* fidgeted nervously, not sure what to say. Ari's face suddenly softened. Koppelman was way out of his element, and showing the strain.

"Take it easy, Mr. Koppelman," Ari said gently. "You've done well. There were no problems, I take it?"

"Oh, no," the *sayan* replied, "but I was just a little concerned, you know—if that gun should be linked to—an incident . . . Well, I could find myself in very serious trouble. It would be difficult to explain, you understand . . ."

"Mr. Koppelman," Ari interrupted, "calm yourself. No one will ever see this gun again, I assure you. You believe me, don't you?"

Koppelman looked at him, wide-eyed.

"Yes," he said, with a deep sigh. "Yes, I do."

"All right, then. Now, did you manage to get hold of an ankle holster as well?"

"Yes. Here you are." He handed Ari a small leather holster with velcro straps.

"Perfect," the agent said. "And now, sir, you'll probably be pleased to know that your assignment is at an end. Israel thanks you, and I thank you. We are lucky to have you, and I intend to report the same to my superiors."

Koppelman swelled a little at the praise, and got to his feet. Ari rose and ushered him toward the door.

"Don't hesitate to call me anytime," the *sayan* said. "It's been a pleasure to serve with you."

"Likewise, Mr. Koppelman," Ari said, smiling. "You will find the apartment empty tomorrow. Not a word, now. Remember: 'they' may be watching."

Koppelman nodded conspiratorially, then went out into the hall. Ari closed the door after him and walked back to the coffee table, rubbing his eyes.

He sat down in the armchair, opened the metallic briefcase, and withdrew a folded paper about the size of a typing tablet. Opening it out onto the coffee table, he smoothed the creases with his hand and began to study it intently.

It was a large nautical chart of the northern Gulf of Mexico, showing the U.S. coast from Corpus Christi, Texas to Mobile, Alabama. A fine checkerboard grid had been superimposed over it, with each tiny square of the grid having its own number designation. In addition, broad areas of the coastal and offshore waters were labeled with individual names. Ari began at the western edge of the map and moved slowly eastward.

"Mustang Island," he mused aloud, "West Cameron, South Timbalier, High Island . . . West Delta . . . Green Canyon."

He stopped abruptly.

"Green Canyon," he repeated. "G.C."

He took a ballpoint pen out of his shirt pocket and began searching the individual squares of the grid in the Green Canyon area. A moment later he put the tip of the pen down on block number one-eighty-six. He circled it.

"G.C. one-eight-six," he said.

He took a small blue registry book dated 1998 out of the briefcase and leafed through it. "Green Canyon Block One-Eighty-Six," he read. "Lease: North American Oil Corporation. Production facilities: One—NAOC-X; Experimental Floating Production Platform. Permit U.S. Mines and Minerals Service Number One-Three-Five-Seven-Two-Two."

He read a little farther, found the exact latitude and longitude of the rig, and wrote it down on a scrap of paper. Then he shut the registry book and put it back into the briefcase, followed by the chart, the spare ammunition clips, and the two boxes of shells.

Putting his right foot up on the coffee table, he secured the leg holster to the outside of his calf and inserted the pistol into it, snapping down the retaining strap. He pulled his pants leg down over the hideaway rig, got up, and began to collect the few items that were lying around the room.

Fifteen minutes later Ari was sitting in the back of a cab heading for Grissom Aviation. The evening traffic was slow, and what should have been a half-hour ride across Houston was showing all the signs of turning into a two-hour marathon. The cabbie, a quiet-mannered black man of about fifty, began turning off the meter whenever they got stopped cold in the crush of cars. Ari watched him reach out and pull down the flag a few times, then told him that it wasn't necessary, to leave the meter running.

"Just like to be fair, my man," the driver said. But he stopped turning off the meter.

As they inched across an overpass, Ari's mind began to wander. He put his head back against the seat and closed his eyes. Time for some mental file work.

Koppelman: gone. Good. One area of uncertainty removed. Hopefully he wouldn't turn out to be the type who babbled about his "covert exploits" at cocktail parties.

The Location: got it, at last. The offshore field, the block number, and the precise latitude and longitude. Not closer to the Mexican border, as the Mossad had hypothesized, but directly south of New Orleans. He'd flown into Houston expecting that a terrorist team would be inserted into the U.S. via Mexico, and would then hit an oil rig off the coast of Texas. Sensible guess, but wrong. They were going to strike at the very heart of the American offshore oil industry. At the rig that represented the West's potential future independence from Arab oil.

All that remained now was to get out ahead of the others.

Ari replayed the meeting in the Mossad's Manhattan safe house over in his mind. It was nearly a month ago now . . .

"All right, gentlemen, I'd like to let Mr. Stein enlighten you all a little more. . . . Sir?"

The tall blond man wearing the green polo shirt stepped back from the dining room table, ushering up the next speaker. The half-dozen men seated throughout the dining room jockeyed their chairs a little closer.

Stein was a small, sharp-faced man in his fifties with a resort tan and a full head of perfectly coifed silver hair. He was wearing the requisite old-boy's club attire: gray flannel pants, expensive Italian shoes, white shirt, and dark blue blazer.

"Good evening, gentlemen," he began. "My name is Karl Arlen Stein, and I am a critical-path engineer specializing in the offshore petroleum industry. I am the sole owner of OceanOil Consulting, Incorporated, and have a broad-based familiarity with the oil and gas production systems typically used on domestic American oil rigs."

He nodded to the blond man in the green shirt, who flicked off the overhead light and turned to a small carousel slide-projector sitting on the table.

"If you'll direct your attention to the far wall," Stein said, "we'll get started."

He switched on the projector and punched a button on his handheld remote. A color image of a four-leg oil production platform, its brilliant yellow paint job contrasting with a sparkling blue sea, came up on the kitchen wall.

"This is a typical Gulf of Mexico offshore oil rig," Stein recited smoothly. He'd done thousands of boardroom presentations and was utterly in his element. "This one happens to be about thirty miles southwest of Fourchon, on the coast of Louisiana, and stands in one hundred and thirty feet of water. It was built in 1969 and has been pumping oil steadily for over twenty-nine years.

"You will notice I said 'stands' in the water. The rig actually stands on the bottom, the upper decks supported by a huge underwater construction of legs and braces known as the 'jacket.' "

He flicked the remote, and a diagram of the rig showing the legs and support members came up. "These platforms stand in water depths ranging from five feet to nearly two thousand." There was a murmur of astonishment throughout the room. Stein let the numbers sink in for a moment, then continued. "That's right, gentlemen. Two thousand feet. And lest you doubt my word"—he punched the remote—"I'd like you to have a look at 'Bullwinkle.'"

An overhead view of a gigantic rig jacket lying on its side in a construction yard came up on the wall. It was difficult to appreciate the scale of the structure until Stein began pointing things out with a little red remote-control arrow.

"This is a full-sized container truck," he said, positioning the arrow on an ant-like white speck in the corner of the slide. "And this"—he moved the arrow—"is a large mobile home that was serving as a field office."

The truck and office were minuscule beside the jacket, which resembled a skyscraper laid on its side.

"This jacket was one of the largest movable structures ever made by man," Stein said emphatically. "It was floated out to its present location in the Gulf of Mexico and successfully erected on-site in the mid-eighties." He flicked the remote, showing the Bullwinkle rig fully complete, only the upper decks above water. The immense jacket was hidden, like the greater part of an iceberg, beneath the waves. "It is at the opposite end of the scale from the rig I first showed you.

"And of course," Stein lectured, "the celebrated NAOC-X floating deepwater production platform"—Stein flicked a picture of it up on the wall—"is the first of a new generation of modern rigs; rigs that will operate in over four thousand feet of water. Much more cost-effective and versatile than Bullwinkle. But a floater such as this is certainly not the norm—not yet. The great majority of rigs off the southern coast of the United States are jacket-supported, standing on the seabed.

"Statistically, it is likely that if a terrorist group was to target a domestic American oil rig, it would be one of these typical production platforms."

The cab hit a bump, and Ari shifted in his seat. Wrong, Stein, he thought. You were wrong. They've picked a floating, state-of-the-art, deepwater rig. The biggest and newest one of all. A prestige target.

His thoughts drifted back to another part of the lecture.

"I've been asked to address the question, 'What components of an oil rig would be particularly vulnerable to sabotage?' A better question might be 'What components are *not* vulnerable?' The list would be considerably shorter, gentlemen.

"The unfortunate truth is that an oil rig happens to be a collection of relatively delicate systems that are not designed to take abuse much beyond that inflicted by, say, a category two hurricane. The engineering parameters do not include tolerance to stresses of a military nature—"

"You mean," one of the listeners interrupted, an intense young operative with short-cropped red hair, "that they're easy to blow up?"

"Precisely," Stein smiled, looking at the redhead as though he was an ill-mannered schoolboy. "And let's take a look at why, shall we?" Another slide clicked up on the wall, showing a forest of valves and pipes running atop grated decking.

"These are wellheads," Stein said. "They are the heart of an offshore oil rig. These valves control the flow of oil from the seabed, up through the conductors—these huge vertical pipes you see extending down into the water underneath the decking—and into the lines that reroute it toward the beach. This entire area"—the shadow of his hand passed across the image on the wall—"would be extremely vulnerable to the smallest explosive charge. There is natural gas and oil flowing up from the ocean floor and through this piping system at as much as three thousand five hundred pounds per square inch,"—he paused for effect again—"all of it highly combustible, of course."

He clicked the remote. A picture of the rig's supporting legs between the bottom of the deck and the water's surface appeared. Stein moved the little pointer arrow and cleared his throat.

"Another vulnerable point would be these pipes running down the outsides of the legs and into the water," he continued. "They are called risers, and they are the actual conduits through which oil is pumped into larger main lines and onto the beach. A small charge placed on one of these would certainly cause a massive explosion and an accompanying firestorm fed by leaking gas or oil. If the proper valves could be accessed, it might be possible to shut down such a leak, but it would depend on the extent of the damage to the rig as a whole.

"All in all, gentlemen," Stein said, "the best way to destroy a rig and cause general havoc would be to blow up the wellheads. This would leave the wells running wild, probably on fire, with all the controlling mechanisms destroyed. There are down-hole shut-in valves that operate automatically if something goes wrong on the surface, but historically they do not always perform up to spec. It is the wellhead that controls the well; if something happens to it, the results are unpredictable in the extreme."

"So if we suspect that a rig's been mined," the redhead interjected, "the first place to check for explosives would be the wellheads and valve assemblies."

"That would follow, yes," Stein agreed, amiably superior. "But as I said, there are other locations in which to place charges that could result in damage nearly as severe. The entire platform would have to be checked, starting with the wellheads and moving on to other sites in decreasing order of damage potential. Explosives on the wellheads would be the worst scenario, gentlemen, but explosives anywhere on an oil rig would have the capacity to inflict catastrophic damage.

"Personally," he concluded, "I believe that the best way to prevent terrorists from blowing up oil platforms is to never let them gain access in the first place. Do you realize that any one of us could rent a boat in southern Louisiana, load it with weapons from the local sporting goods store, run out to a rig, tie up, walk up to the upper decks, and kill everyone in sight—completely unopposed?

"The only security the oil companies maintain is at their major supply docks, and that is only designed to prevent petty theft and drug or alcohol abuse by employees. There is no security on an oil rig. A few years ago all platforms in the Gulf of Mexico were equipped with special alarm signals, to be used in case of a military attack, but their effectiveness is unproven and they are easy to disable.

"I think it is a miracle that America's domestic oil platforms have not already been subjected to terrorist assaults. They are huge, costly, vital to the nation, and very photogenic when they catch fire or explode. In addition, they are isolated from the usual law-enforcement agencies by virtue of their location. They are physically inaccessible, and a large number of rigs stand near the edge of the federal limits, close to international waters.

"Delta Force, SEALs, and other much-vaunted American commando units notwithstanding, an oil rig could be raided, mined, and the terrorists taken off to detonate remote charges at their leisure long before

word of something amiss made it to Fort Bragg or
Norfolk. In an hour or two the terrorists could be
safely in the hold of an anonymous freighter heading
for Cuba or Panama, or airlifted south by a seaplane.

"The danger is very real, gentlemen."

The cab bounced over a pothole, shaking Ari out
of his thoughts again. He glanced out the window and
saw the light-flecked silhouettes of Houston's modern-
istic skyscrapers. They were still downtown, stuck in
traffic. He sat back with a sigh. In a moment he was
back in the meeting.

This time the slender blond man in the green shirt
was speaking again. He was Lev Solomon, one of the
Mossad's antiterrorism experts. Deemed too valuable
an intellectual to be risked in the field, he had been
pulled off an elite Mossad commando team and put
in charge of a think tank processing all intelligence
related to terrorist activity originating in the Middle
East.

"As I mentioned earlier," Solomon said, "several
weeks ago we received information suggesting that a
strike against a domestic American oil platform in the
Gulf of Mexico was imminent. Subsequent analysis of
additional intelligence linked this report to activity
centering around Ojim Gradak's organization in Syria."

There was a general intake of breath around the
room. Solomon smiled grimly and nodded.

"Yes. Gradak. It seems he is on the move again."
He paused and scratched his forehead. "However, the
picture is sketchy at this point. We have operatives
working our moles in Damascus, trying to come up
with some hard facts, but right now all we can do is
hypothesize about the nature of such an attack and
draw up a series of possible scenarios.

"Hopefully one of them will be right, and we'll
know it before the fact."

Ari watched a white stretch limousine with blacked-out windows slide past in the next lane. We've ended up knowing where, he thought. And we're ninety-nine percent sure we know who, when, and even why. But we still don't know how.

"There are any number of ways a terrorist team could gain access to an oil rig," Solomon went on. "We're relatively certain it would be a small group—perhaps a half-dozen men. They could be brought to the rig posing as contractors or new employees on the regular shift change.

"They might simply approach by boat and storm the platform, mine it, and escape the same way. Or they might come by helicopter—all oilfields support large volumes of helicopter traffic.

"There is also the possibility that they might not simply destroy the rig, but attempt to create a hostage situation and thereby a drawn-out media event. This would require a somewhat larger terrorist force, as they would have to run shifts to keep the hostages under control and American antiterrorist teams off the rig on a twenty-four-hour basis.

"Again, they might arrive by boat or helicopter, or perhaps even swim in underwater from a drop-off vessel. Some of the smaller, more tightly knit terrorist cells have actually received commando training that advanced.

"For example," Solomon continued, "we know for a fact that the core team of Ojim Gradak's cell received SpecWar—that's 'Special Warfare'—instruction over a five-month period from an individual named Malcolm Durant in a training camp in southern Libya. Durant is a disgruntled former SEAL who ran into trouble when he attempted to sell large amounts of U.S. Navy inventory to an arms dealer out the back door of a SEAL warehouse. He was indicted by a U.S. military tribunal in absentia, having avoided capture. His whereabouts were unknown until he turned up working as a technical adviser for Muammar Ghaddafi.

"By all accounts, he was a very good SEAL. Five months with him and presto!—a terrorist team with SEAL-level training."

Lev Solomon was a master analyst, thought Ari, as the cab drew near the airport. No wonder he ran his own think tank. A shame he was too conventional a *strategist* to realize when the Mossad was missing a good opportunity. Sometimes, a few visionary people had to break away from established authority in order to get the job done right.

The cab pulled up in front of Grissom Aviation, and the driver turned in his seat to look at Ari.

"Okay, buddy," he said. "This here's the place."

Ari handed him two folded twenties. "Thanks for the ride. That enough?"

"Hell, yeah. You sure 'bout this?" The cabbie's eyes were a little wider. "You overpayin' here, buddy."

"Keep it," said Ari. "It was a good ride."

The driver leaned over a little more. "You want me to wait for you?"

Ari smiled. "No, thanks."

He got out and shut the car door. The night breeze felt cool in his hair; he stretched his stiff neck and looked up at the black, star-studded sky. Off to the east a large passenger jet was coming in low on its final approach to Houston International, lit up like a Christmas tree.

Ari watched it drop below the skyline, then turned and strode up the broad walkway to the front door of Grissom Aviation.

Chapter Ten

"Let it go, let it go!" Sligo shouted from the flying bridge of the *Circe*. At the stern Luis fumbled with the last line, pried it loose from its cleat, and threw it awkwardly toward the dock. It made it halfway and fell limply into the water like a wet dishrag.

"Jesus Christ," Sligo muttered under his breath. He bumped both idling engines into gear, and the *Circe* slid forward, her twin stern exhausts growling wetly. The smuggler passed a hand over his damp forehead and blinked hard behind his mirrored sunglasses. His head was killing him. It had been a very late night. He took a sip of Bloody Mary from a quart-sized mayonnaise jar and spun the wheel slowly to turn the *Circe* north into the harbor's deepwater channel.

Gradak climbed the ladder from the back deck to join him on the flying bridge as the sportfisherman cruised swiftly toward the narrow pass through the exposed reef that protected the harbor. Riad, Turgut, Saeb, and Luis were all standing by the rails, gazing back at the spectacular scenery surrounding Bahia Cristobal. The *Circe*'s path down the channel was marked by her wake, a hissing white carpet of salt foam stretching back to the floating dock where the fleet of bandit yachts lay, their bright hulls shrinking in the distance.

Sligo bumped the throttles forward a little more to improve the boat's steerage as he centered her up on the narrow pass. On either side of the thirty-foot-wide cut the indigo-blue water seethed and churned green and white against the jagged yellow coral of the reef. Sligo whistled softly to himself between his teeth. Any boat that ever ran onto that would have no chance. He kept the *Circe* dead in the center of the pass.

The wind was blowing a good twenty knots from the southeast, pushing a strong seven-foot sea, and about a quarter of a mile outside the reef the dark gray silhouette of the gunboat nosed slowly forward between the deep blue swells and hurrying whitecaps. Gradak stared at it, holding onto the rails of the fly-bridge as the *Circe* cleared the reef and began to take the seas just aft of the starboard beam.

Sligo settled down into the helmsman's chair and pushed the throttles to three-quarter speed, fast enough to make good headway, but slow enough to keep a fair amount of the boat's hull in the water and smooth the ride, as well as save fuel. The smuggler sneaked a glance up at Gradak. It was the first time he had ever seen the man's face show the slightest sign of strain. He was already turning green around the gills. Sligo turned away to hide the smirk on his face. No sea dog, this one. He looked down at the back deck; it was empty except for Turgut, who was sitting amidships on the transom, his feet spread wide, weaving back and forth unsteadily.

May you be the first son of a bitch ever to die of seasickness, ape shape, thought Sligo to himself. He couldn't resist the temptation as Gradak made his way over to the ladder, handhold by handhold, and started down:

"Something wrong, Rodriguez?" he asked.

Gradak shot him a look of pure hatred and descended out of sight.

The smuggler turned back to the wheel and laughed out loud.

"Rock and roll, boys," he chortled, finishing the last of his Bloody Mary. He reached up to the Loran-C navigational unit that was mounted above his head and punched in a preset waypoint—a latitude/longitude position for New Orleans—and then engaged the Loran's interface to the *Circe*'s autopilot. Now the navigational computer would plot the boat's straight-line course to its destination—the waypoint—and tell the autopilot's computer which way to steer to remain on course. Sligo let go of the wheel and watched as the computers took over the *Circe*'s helm. There was a soft grinding sound as the autopilot's hydraulic actuator arm, coupled to the steering linkages under the bridge console, forced the rudders slowly to port and brought the boat around to a heading of 325 degrees. Her motion eased as the wind and seas moved around to her starboard stern quarter, and she began to surf down the faces of the swells as she overtook them.

Sligo listened to the grinding of the hydraulics for a few minutes, checking the feel of the boat as she settled onto her course. Satisfied, he got up and went down the ladder to the back deck.

He slid open the door to the main salon and stepped inside, standing with the easy surefootedness of someone accustomed to the rhythmic motions of the sea. Sliding the door closed behind him, he gazed around at the bodies sprawled on couches and chairs, faces the color of green chalk. The sound of someone retching violently in the forward head could be heard faintly over the muted thrum of the engines. He stepped over a pair of feet and headed across the salon toward the galley, grinning broadly.

"Yo ho ho and a bottle of—" He rummaged in a lower cabinet. "Vodka!" He stood up in triumph, brandishing a fifth of premium Stolichnaya. Then his face fell. "Nah," he muttered. "Doesn't rhyme . . ."

Saeb, sprawled prone on the port couch, looked

over at him with watery eyes. He stared at the bottle of vodka for a few seconds, licking his lips, then turned and vomited over the arm of the couch onto the carpeted floor.

"Hey!" Sligo shouted, stung into action. "Hey, goddammit! Hold up, there!" He grabbed a towel and a wastebasket from beneath the galley sink. "Here, ya jerk," he said, coming forward. "Puke in this, not on the floor of my house!" Saeb looked up at him weakly, spitting.

"Medication, Captain," Gradak said, sitting stiffly in one of the armchairs. His brow was shiny with sweat as he struggled to control his rebelling stomach. "I believe there is medication for this sickness."

Sligo was tempted to tell the man that he should have thought of that before leaving Bahia Cristobal, but something in Gradak's rheumy, pale eyes made him think better of it. He grinned innocently instead.

"What?" he asked. "You guys seasick?" He took a second to look around. "Jeez. Come to think of it, y'all do look a little pale . . ."

He went back into the galley, dug around in one of the drawers, and returned with a large brown-glass pill bottle. Unscrewing the top, he shook out three capsules and offered them to Gradak.

"Diphenhydramine hydrochloride," he drawled. "Twenty-five milligram capsules. Fix ya right up, Rodriguez, if you take 'em with a little water and lie down for an hour."

He went around to the other men and gave them each a dose, talking as he went.

"Yup. Diphenhydramine hydrochloride. It's a wonder drug, gents. Cures insomnia, motion sickness, and stuffy sinuses. Cheap as dirt. Drug companies in the U.S. sell it under fifty different names and charge a fortune for it, but it's all the same shit."

He stopped short in front of Luis, who was cringing

in a corner behind a fake potted ficus tree. He looked up at Sligo piteously. "Feelin' real bad, Cap'n Jerry," he moaned. "Sick . . ."

Sligo leaned down closer to him. "Got an old-fashioned cure for you, Zorro," he announced loudly. "Gonna get a big slice of that salt pork fatback outta the icebox, slap it cold on a piece of damp white bread, an' make you chew on it for a while. Sound good?"

Luis looked up at him in horror, then threw up all over the smuggler's deck shoes.

The wind and seas gained strength throughout the afternoon, boosting the *Circe*'s ground speed. When Sligo checked her position at three p.m., he found that she was averaging nearly twenty-five nautical miles per hour—theoretically just under six hundred miles per day. He'd figured the distance from Bahia Cristobal to New Orleans at slightly more than seven hundred miles, but knew that the *Circe* was bound to lose ground due to course variations caused by the effects of the Loop Current—an unpredictable pattern of water flow throughout the Gulf of Mexico that coalesced near South Florida into the Gulf Stream.

He looked over his shoulder, hearing someone coming up the ladder. Gradak stepped up into the bridge, followed by Riad. Both looked somewhat tousled, but their faces had returned to near-normal color. Gradak sat down in the chair opposite the helm while Riad propped himself into the port corner of the console.

"Feelin' better?" Sligo inquired with a grin.

"Considerably," Gradak replied, "although I feel quite fatigued." He smacked his lips. "My mouth is very dry."

"Side effect," the smuggler explained. "Those pills dry you out. Great for colds."

"I would rather have the dry mouth," Riad interjected ruefully, "than the seasickness."

Sligo lit a cigarette. "Well, you may not need the pills after today," he said. "You'll get your sea legs, y'know? Just try not to eat or drink too much until tomorrow." He paused to draw on his smoke. "That stuff makes you drowsy, too. That's why you're tired."

Gradak nodded. "Fortunately, the effect is not too strong." He smiled pleasantly. "Are we making good progress, Captain?"

Sligo looked up at the Loran. "Looks like it." He punched a few buttons, changing the display on the unit's backlit screen. "See this number? It tells you how far we've come over the ocean bottom since leaving Bahia Cristobal. The Loran constantly updates our position as we move. We left at ten o'clock this morning, and this says we've covered one hundred and forty-three point seven miles. What time is it?"

Gradak looked at his watch. "Ten minutes past four."

"Okay," Sligo continued, "six hours to go about a hundred and forty miles. What's six into one-forty?"

"About twenty-three, twenty-four," Riad said quickly.

"Okay." Sligo punched another button. "This number here," he said, pointing at the screen, "gives the exact average speed of the boat. Twenty-three point three one knots—that's nautical miles—per hour." He grinned at Gradak and Riad. "Modern technology, gents. It's a beautiful fucking thing.

"'Course, you can't always trust the Loran," he added. "That's why I've got other systems, too. Like the Sat-Nav there, and the RDF." Riad looked blankly at him. "Radio Direction Finder," clarified the smuggler. "An' of course, the ol' DR." He extracted a battered chart of the Gulf of Mexico from a drawer beneath the console. "Dead reckoning. Plotting the course gives you a seat-of-the-pants feel for where you're at. And you can tell if something changes between position checks by comparing the old positions with the new one—lets you know if your nav gear's fucking up."

He spread the chart out on top of the console, did some figuring with a pair of dividers, and made a pencil mark west of the tip of Florida.

"That's where we're at," he told Gradak, tapping the mark, "and that's where we're going." He moved his hand up to the top of the chart and tapped the Mississippi Delta. " 'Bout five hundred and fifty miles—twenty-four hours or so, if the weather stays good."

Gradak looked at his watch. "The date today is? . . ."

"July second," Sligo said.

Gradak looked at him without expression. "Mmm . . ."

An unusually large swell heaved up the *Circe*'s stern, causing the propellers to cavitate momentarily and triggering an extended burst of loud grinding from the steering hydraulics as the autopilot compensated for the sudden veering off course. Gradak and Riad reacted instinctively, clutching for support. Sligo merely wrapped a foot around the pedestal of his chair and leaned opposite the roll.

When the *Circe* settle back down, he rotated his chair to face astern and studied the oncoming seas and sky. A number of small squalls had appeared on the horizon like ragged gray mushrooms. Behind them loomed an unbroken front of darker gray cloud, very far off but expanding steadily. The blue sky overhead had gone hazy and dull, and the swells had taken on a metallic gray cast. The sea was littered with whitecaps, the tops of which were starting to blow off, streaking the dark water with foam trails.

"Lookin' shitty," Sligo muttered.

He swung the chair back around to face the console and began fiddling with one of the two VHF radios mounted overhead, changing channels and adjusting the volume and squelch controls.

"Maybe I can get the NOAA or Coast Guard weather bulletins from Key West or Naples . . ." he said, thinking aloud. He was also thinking that he should have kept an eye on the forecasts while he was in Cuba. The radio spat static on channel after channel.

"Come on, come on," Sligo prodded, dialing carefully. He was beginning to think it was futile when, abruptly, a faint but clear monotone voice broke through the crackling interference.

". . . Is Coast Guard Group—(crackle)—Key West Flor—(crackle)—area of counterclockwise circulation, one hundred and twenty miles southeast of Key West, Florida. Trop—(crackle)—storm formation expected. Movement is to the northwest at eighteen miles per hour, expected to gain momentum as circulation becomes more organized—" There was a long burst of static, then the voice returned. ". . . Small-craft advisory in effect for—(crackle)—and the Upper Keys. This is Coast Guard Group . . ."

The voice faded behind the white noise of static once again. Sligo played with the dials for a second, then turned the unit off and slumped back in his chair.

"A storm, Captain?" Riad inquired. He looked anxious.

"Yeah," the smuggler replied. "But it ain't really a big deal. Sounds like it's forming in the Old Bahama Channel, east of Cay Sal Bank." He waved a hand. "I know that don't mean anything to you. Sometimes these local things blow up all of a sudden in the heat of the summer. This one's moving in the same direction as us, but we're moving faster, and we've got a two-hundred-mile head start. We'll beat it."

He grinned at the other two, hoping he looked confident.

The *Circe* twisted down hard into a deep trough, nearly burying her flared bows. A sheet of frothy spray exploded upward, made a right-angled turn in midair as a random gust of wind caught it, and dashed into the bridge through the open side window, soaking Sligo's baggy shorts.

"Shit!" he exclaimed, jumping up. He slid the window shut, motioning Riad to do the same on the opposite side. Then he reached up and unrolled the canvas cover that, once snapped into place, would enclose the open aft portion of the bridge. With Riad and Gradak's help, he got it secured after a five-minute struggle. A small zippered door provided access to the back-deck ladder.

"Hell, I'm goin' below," he said, punching a button on the radar unit. "I've just enabled the gate. That means that anything solid coming within a thirty-six-mile radius of this boat will trigger an alarm below decks. That way we can't get run over by some Russky banana boat or tanker or something. Gives me lotsa time to get up here and check it out."

He glanced at the viewing scope. At the very bottom of the scale, directly astern, a band of rain squalls showed up as a dense cluster of glowing green dots. There were no other contacts.

The smuggler shrugged his shoulders, unzipped the door, and slid down the ladder to the back deck. Riad and Gradak followed. They ducked inside the salon door in time to avoid a sheet of spray that doused the aft section of the boat from rail to rail.

Sligo went straight to the galley and got himself two beers, pouring both into one of his immense mayonnaise jars. He chugged hard, wiped his mustache on the back of his hand, then slowly began to notice what was going on around the room.

Turgut and Saeb were sitting on the carpet, their backs to the port settee, with an incredible array of high-tech military equipment spread out around them. Turgut had broken the bolt out of a small and very deadly looking submachine gun with a flat black finish, and was going over it carefully with a soft cloth. He looked up at Sligo and grinned wolfishly.

"Skorpion," he said briefly. "Very good made." He waited until he saw the smuggler's Adam's apple bob before turning back to his task.

Saeb was checking a small pile of electrical devices, each about the size of a box of matches, with an ohmmeter. Stacked beside him against the salon bulkhead were eight rectangular black-fabric backpacks. As Sligo watched, intrigued, Saeb disconnected the meter from the device on which he was working and tucked it into a small pocket on one of the packs, making some kind of connection inside as he did so. Then he hooked up the meter's test leads to the next unit and repeated the process.

The *Circe* took a deep roll to port, her bows crashing through a wave. Riad waited until she settled down again, then quickly made his way over to the starboard settee and pulled a navy blue athletic bag out from between it and the bulkhead. Sitting down on the floor with the bag between his legs, he unzipped it and pulled out a roll of black duct tape and two long ammunition clips.

Turgut said something to him from across the room, holding up his hands about eighteen inches apart and speaking in a guttural language Sligo didn't recognize. Riad grunted assent and proceeded to tape the two clips together, the open ends opposite each other. Then he tossed them over to Turgut.

The big man caught the clips, checked to ensure that they were taped together securely, and inserted one end into the reassembled submachine gun, driving it home with a loud *snick*. Then he pointed it at the bug-eyed Sligo with a vicious leer.

"Tak-tak-tak-tak!" he growled.

Sligo felt little prickly bubbles of perspiration pop out on his forehead. He laughed weakly, pretending to share in the amusement of the other men, then ducked down into the passageway leading forward to the sleeping cabins.

He opened the door of his quarters to find Luis sprawled on his bed in a dirty white T-shirt and baggy undershorts, snoring. He kicked hard at one of the dangling legs, and the grubby little Cuban came awake instantly, howling.

Sligo kicked him several more times, driving him off the bed, then grabbed a belt and thrashed him screaming out the door with the buckle end. The pitiful yammering faded away quickly as Luis scuttled off to find a safe hiding place. Breathing hard, Sligo locked the door and sat down on the bed.

Too many guns. It looked like a scene from a Chuck Norris movie out there. He was beginning to get a bad feeling, like the surge of trapped desperation he felt when he was running a loaded boat and a Coast Guard cutter appeared on the horizon. Whatever these guys were going to do in the States, he was damn sure he wanted nothing to do with it.

He bent down and pulled the briefcase Escobar had given him just before leaving the dock out from beneath the bunk. Flipping the catches, he propped it open and stared at the neatly wrapped piles of American twenty-dollar bills lying inside. The smell of new money permeated the air of the cabin.

A small vial of cocaine lay on top of the bills. Sligo tooted up a modest hit in each nostril, using the little tube around his neck, then picked up a wad of cash. He waved it under his nose, inhaling deeply.

"Ah, freshly minted," he said aloud. He was feeling much better.

Then he thought about Luis and frowned. The little

weasel would be at the money in a heartbeat, given the chance. What the hell had he been doing in the captain's cabin, anyway? And you couldn't tell about the other guys, either. Who wouldn't like to get hold of fifty thousand bucks of free pocket money?

He had to hide it. Fortunately, hiding things on boats was his specialty. But he had to hurry; they were probably thinking about the money already.

He dug into the standing locker next to the door and came up with a roll of silver duct tape and a box of green garbage bags; tools of the trade for a drug smuggler. He put the briefcase in one of them, knotted it closed, and bound it with several wraps of tape. Then he placed this bundle inside another bag, repeating the process until the briefcase was tightly packaged inside three layers of plastic.

From beneath the bunk he produced a small exercise dumbbell with two ten-pound plates on it. He undogged one of them and taped it flat onto the side of the package with the remainder of the roll.

"Good ol' hippy-chrome," he whispered to himself, using the old smuggler's slang for silver duct tape.

Setting the package aside on the bunk, he bent down and peeled the carpet back from the wall, exposing a square, flush hatch cut in the teak-and-holly cabin sole. He pulled it up by a recessed finger ring and revealed in turn a round fiberglass tank-inspection hatch, its cover secured in place by twelve bolts around its circumference. Sligo rummaged in the closet again, coming out with a ratchet handle and a selection of sockets, and began to loosen the nuts holding the hatch cover.

He stopped once to give himself a bump from the coke vial, then spun off the last nuts and pried the hatch cover loose, tearing the old silicon-rubber sealing gasket in half in the process. The faint smell of

Chapter Eleven

Sass jumped nimbly off the stern rail of the *Teresa Ann* and walked down the dock toward the marina office, jingling her keys. There were a few thousand things going through her mind, and she didn't really see how she could justify leaving the marina when there was so much to do, but come hell or high water she was throwing off the lines and getting under way by noon. Ben had left that morning, slipping away as he always did without waking her, and she'd overslept.

She waved to Anna, the jovial, rotund old black cook who turned out the marina's excellent restaurant fare, who was shooing seagulls off the sill of the main building's kitchen window. Anna could keep the place running like a clock, whether Sass was there or not.

She walked around to the far side of the marina, to a small corner of the inlet where four slips lay in the lee of the western breakwater. Three of them were empty—they weren't the best berths in the place; the water was too shallow—but in the fourth floated an old navy launch of World War II vintage, some thirty-five feet in length.

She was truly a relic of another age. Her wood-plank hull was covered in multiple coats of regulation navy gray paint; a chipped area near her bow showed the buildup to be well over half an inch thick. Her topsides and cabin, high and bulky, with the rounded lines common to boats of the era, were sealed with paint-filled canvas—a waterproofing technique predating the use of fiberglass and modern resins. A long piece of three-inch woven nylon hawser had been secured around the boat's entire circumference at the hull-deck joint to serve as a rub-rail.

The roof of the pilothouse supported the only modern thing on the boat—twin VHF radio antennae. Potted plants dangled from the edges of the roof and lined the stern rail, forming a green barrier of foliage that hid the interior of the bridge and the small back deck from view. The transom bore the faded name *USS Solomon Sea*.

Sass walked out on the small access dock and was met with a piercing shriek.

"*Awwk!* Buy war bonds! Buy war bonds! *Awwwwk!*"

"Be quiet, will you, Sam?" Sass said. She leaned toward the boat. "Jimmy? You busy?"

A small green parrot, about six inches tall and incredibly dilapidated, came walking out on the rail from behind a plant. Its bill was stained a dark, blotchy yellow, its scaly feet were grayish and cracked, and it had only stubs for wings. Its emerald-green feathers were in total disarray, sticking out in all directions. Only its large black eyes looked clean; they were bright with that undeniable but alien intelligence birds such as parrots and owls seem to possess.

It marched slowly along the rail, picking up and putting down each foot with exquisite care, and stopped in front of Sass.

"Meeow," it said.

Sass stuck a finger out by the parrot's feet. "C'mon, Sam," she coaxed.

The parrot stepped carefully off the rail onto her finger, its powerful claws tightening firmly.

"Moo," it said.

Sass leaned toward the boat again and called out more loudly, "Jimmy! Jimmy, are you there?"

There was a thumping sound from inside the main cabin, and a moment later the main hatch swung open.

"Come aboard, madam, come aboard! Make your way below!" The rasping voice had a flourish to it—the hint of a stage actor speaking lines. It also had a distinctive edge that was pure Brooklyn.

Sass stepped onto the rail and hopped lightly to the back deck, picking her way through the wall of hanging plants.

"We keep you alive to serve this ship," Sam said. "Row well and live." He ducked his frizzled head and rubbed his bill on the back of Sass' hand.

She looked at the parrot in amazement, then shook her head and stepped through the hatchway, descending into the main salon.

"What have you been teaching this bird?" Sass demanded. "Did you hear what he just said to me?"

Old Jimmy appeared out of the galley from behind a stack of corned beef cans. He was a little man, two inches shorter than Sass, bent and stooped with age. His face was sharp and leprechaun-like, fair-skinned and rosy-cheeked, with innumerable tiny broken blood vessels on the nose. He was bald except for two patches of feathery white hair that stuck out above his ears, giving him a wizened look. He was wearing a pair of baggy khaki shorts, a plain white undershirt, and a pair of cheap slip-on canvas shoes.

"He's been watching *Ben-Hur* lately," he explained, gesturing toward a television set and VCR mounted in a corner. "A minimum of five times a day for the past three days. It's the only way I can keep him quiet." He looked at the bird in disgust. "I don't know why I put up with his nonsense."

Sam awwked quietly and began walking methodically up Sass' arm. She held it out straight so he wouldn't have to dig his claws into her bare skin. He paused on her shoulder and began to pick gently at her hair with his bill.

Jimmy poured two cups of coffee and handed one to Sass. "Java?"

"Thanks, Jimmy."

He opened the lid of a mahogany humidor that was fastened to the corner of the salon table and extracted a long, thin cigar. He smoked only hand-rolled Premiums, made by Cuban exiles who'd set up shop in Key West after the fall of Batista. One box arrived at the marina office by mail at the beginning of every month, like clockwork.

"Let's go outside," he suggested, lighting the stogie with a wooden match.

. They made their way up to the back deck and settled into a pair of old canvas lawnchairs. Sass let Sam hop off her shoulder onto a potted plant.

"So you're on your way to the oilfield, my dear," Jimmy said, smiling slyly at her.

She feigned annoyance. "How come everybody knows what I'm doing when I only decided to do it last night? You people are all mind readers."

"Actually, Ben left a note for Anna up at the restaurant early this morning. She told me about your trip when I went up for an egg around seven. You see, not everyone sleeps as late as you do." He grinned again, blowing a stream of smoke.

Sass made a face at him. "The one morning that I'm not up with the sun, and you give me a hard time." She passed her bandaged hand through her tied-back hair. "Well, I guess you know what I'm going to ask you."

"The answer, of course, is yes. And I have only two questions," Jimmy said. "How is your poor hand, and do you have the keys?"

"Oh, the hand is fine," she laughed, flexing the fingers for him, "and I've got all the marina keys right here." She unclipped the large ring from the belt loop of her jeans and held them out. "I'm not asking too much, am I Jimmy? This place can be a real headache to run sometimes . . ."

The old sailor shook his wrinkled head in mock irritation and took the keys. "Don't even think about it," he said. "You see, you don't know it, but you need to get away from your business once in a while. Of course, you don't believe me, because you're young; it's only when you get old like me that you realize it was all that racing around chasing the almighty dollar that made you old in the first place." He gave a theatrical sigh. "Youth, as they say, is truly wasted on the young . . ."

Sass raised her hands in capitulation. "I don't know how I got so lucky as to have people like you and Anna in my life," she said. "Thank you, Jimmy."

He shrugged, drawing on his cigar. "It's simple: you're your daddy's child. A finer man never drew breath, and you're a chip off the old block. I know he looks down from that big home port in the sky every day and feels real proud of his little girl."

Sass stirred in her chair. "I'm gonna get out of here before you make me cry. I think you do it on purpose, Jimmy."

"Go on, and be safe," he said, smiling paternally. "And don't worry your pretty head a bit about the marina."

"Ramming speed!" Sam squawked from behind a rhododendron. "Ramming speed!" He hopped onto the toe of Jimmy's canvas shoe.

"Thanks for the coffee," Sass said, setting her mug down on the rail. She got up, parted the hanging plants carefully, and stepped over to the access dock.

"Teach that bird some manners," she called, waving. Jimmy raised his hand.

"Ramming speed!" Sam said.

At eleven-thirty Sass uncleated the last line from the dock, leaned hard into the side of the *Teresa Ann* to start her moving away from the dock, and climbed aboard, taking up her position behind the wheel. Caesar stood on the foredeck, his stub of a tail wagging furiously. The wind carried the bow out far enough for her to slip the idling diesel auxiliary into gear, and the graceful old boat moved forward into the marina's central waterway. Two gulls that had been perched on the mainmast spreaders screamed in protest at their roost's sudden motion and swooped off toward the marina office.

Sass glanced up at the masts. The *Teresa Ann's* aluminum spars were heavily rigged for blue-water cruising with stainless-steel shrouds and turnbuckles. Her main and mizzen sails were neatly flaked and lashed to their booms; her staysail and jib were furled tightly in their roller-reefing gear. Sass smiled to herself. The boat was ready for any weather.

She started making her turn into the feeder channel that led out past the eastern breakwater, carefully judging the effect of the wind. To an onlooker it might have seemed as though she'd initiated the turn too soon, but the wind slowed the *Teresa Ann* and pushed her slightly to leeward so that she ended up perfectly centered in the narrow waterway. Sass had a good eye.

"*Solomon Sea* to *Teresa Ann,* come back." The cockpit VHF crackled to life. Sass picked up the microphone and held it to the corner of her mouth.

"*Teresa Ann* to *Solomon Sea*. Hey, Jimmy."

"Channel eighteen."

"Roger." She reached down and dialed in the new channel. "Come back, Jimmy."

"Roger that." Jimmy's voice kept its theatrical zest even over the airwaves. "I just wanted to tell you once more to be careful, especially crossing those shipping lanes near Gulfport and New Orleans. But you know that, don't you?"

"Yes, Jimmy," Sass said patiently, bumping the throttle up a bit. "I appreciate the concern, though. Thanks."

"And watch the weather. Something might be brewing down off Cuba. See you later dear. *Solomon Sea* going back to sixteen."

" 'Bye, Jimmy. *Teresa Ann* going back to sixteen." She dialed the VHF back to the standard mayday channel and hung the hand mike back on its clip.

According to the cockpit anemometer gauge, the southeast wind was steady at twelve knots; not quite enough to stir up more than the occasional whitecap on the waters of the sound. Sass took the *Teresa Ann* a hundred yards outside the marina breakwater, then rounded her up into the wind, idled down the engine, and becketed the wheel.

Stepping forward around the steering post to the mizzenmast, she reached up and quickly untied the three lashings that held the sail flaked down to the mizzen boom. Then she uncleated the halyard, took a wrap on the self-tailing winch mounted on the mast, and rapidly cranked the sail all the way up. It luffed noisily in the brisk wind, the boom dancing around like a mad thing. Sass cleated off the halyard, then hopped up on the cabin roof and hurried forward to the mainmast.

She repeated the procedure, raising the big mainsail and cleating it off securely. It flapped and shook in the breeze, powerless to propel the boat as long as she was pointing directly into the wind. Sass jumped back down into the cockpit as Caesar, excited by the commotion, cut loose with a series of sharp barks.

Uncleating the retraction line for the roller-furling jib, she threw a couple of wraps of jibsheet around one of the big winches mounted on the cockpit coaming and cranked furiously. The big jib unrolled from the special forestay like a window blind, shaking and slatting. The combined noise of the three luffing sails was deafening.

Sass slacked the jibsheet a little, cleated it off, and spun the wheel to starboard. The *Teresa Ann* bore off the wind rapidly—south, southwest, and finally west—heeling and picking up speed as her big sails filled out over the starboard rail. The water began to foam and hiss as the heavy hull cut through it, and the *Teresa Ann*'s solid wooden bones creaked happily from the strain of being under sail once again.

Sass let the boat settle onto her course for a minute or two, checking the feel and balance, and then began making small adjustments to the sails, gazing critically aloft and taking a half crank on the jibsheet here, easing off on the mainsheet there. When at last she was satisfied with the sails' trim, she killed the diesel engine, sealed the ignition lock with a watertight plastic cap, and stowed the key in a little compartment in the steering pedestal.

With the mechanical humming and vibration of the engine gone, the sounds of a little ship under sail filled Sass' ears: the rush and hiss of waves washing along the hull just below the leeward gunwale, the fluttering *wapwapwapwap* of the little yarn telltales tied into the shrouds and sails, and the stiff, deep creaking of strong wood as the *Teresa Ann* rose over the larger swells.

As she sat behind the wheel, Sass opened the hinged seat of one of the cockpit benches and extracted a light chest harness made of yellow nylon webbing. She slipped it on, secured it, and uncoiled the three-foot stainless-steel wire tether that was fastened to the harness' central D-ring. A small stainless-steel carabiner clip was attached to the free end. She hooked it into one of the belt loops of her jeans.

Caesar padded carefully along the windward rail and clambered down into the cockpit, assuming his customary cruising position, lying cradled along the leeward bench and coaming. Sass reached over and scratched his head, then locked the wheel again and went down the companionway to the main salon.

She gave the interior of the boat the once-over just to see if she'd forgotten to secure anything, then slid in behind the chart table at the navigation station. Glancing up at the bank of electronic nav units, she made sure that they were all cycling properly, then opened the *Teresa Ann*'s log and, checking her watch, made an entry.

"1100 hours—Left Wojeck's Marina," she wrote. "Underway to Pensacola Pass."

She shut the log and went back up through the main hatch to the cockpit. The wind had freshened, setting the *Teresa Ann* farther over on her starboard rail. Sass looked up at the sails, checking their trim, and took the wheel once more, getting comfortable. It was at least two hours to the pass.

In the locked wooden dock box beside the *Teresa Ann*'s empty slip, the yacht's combination telephone and answering machine began to ring, the sound too muffled for anyone nearby to hear. On the fourth ring, the answering machine greeted the caller, then beeped for a message.

"Ben? This is Mike Hawkin. Look: remember that chopper salvage you did for us a few days ago? I've got three FBI agents in my office who insist that they have to talk to you. Apparently at least five of the bodies you guys recovered had bullet wounds in them, the F.A.A. inspectors found an empty automatic pistol in the muck in the bottom of the fusilage, and one of the dead men wasn't even supposed to be there. Turns

Chapter Twelve

The change in the tempo of the crewboat's roaring engines woke Ben out of his doze. He struggled up onto an elbow, his damp shirt sticking to the Naughyde seats on which he'd stretched out. The boat's motion changed as well, from a forward bucking to more of a side roll. Across the aisle of the darkened passenger compartment, in the opposite set of seats, Rolly coughed and stirred.

The engines throttled way down, then back up again as Dothan worked the boat around with the screws. Ben got to his feet feeling rumpled and gritty—as usual after a crewboat ride—and went forward and up into the bridge, tapping Rolly on the toe of his boot as he went past.

Dothan was standing hunched over the wheel, both hands on the throttles, staring out through the bridge windows. His hulking body, long hair, and bushy beard were silhouetted by the dull red glow of the instruments' night-vision lights. He looked like some kind of demonic Santa Claus.

Careful not to crowd him, Ben peered through the salt-stained windshield. He saw one immense, brightly lit steel column sweep by in the pitch-darkness, and then Dothan was gunning the engines and working the screws again, spinning the boat around for another trial approach.

"Current runnin'," he growled, shifting his chew

from one side of his lower lip to the other. He swore softly under his breath. "Blowin' us into the rig when we try to get under the crane."

Ben glanced at his watch. "Must've fallen asleep," he said. "How'd a three-hour run turn into six? I thought we'd be out here way before sundown." He grinned ruefully at Dothan, just to let him know he wasn't blaming him directly. "Man, the toolpusher up on that rig's gonna chew my ass. This was an emergency callout."

Dothan regarded him for a moment with total lack of concern. "Well," he drawled, "you look like you been out here a few years. At least he ain't gonna get no virgin."

He turned the wheel a little and peered out the side window. A huge, incandescent mountain of lights came into view, suspended in the blackness, the lower half melting into wavering trails of liquid white and yellow and red on the otherwise invisible sea. From mid-range distance the NAOC-X resembled some ethereal fairy-tale castle floating in empty space.

"Starboard engine started to run hot," Dothan said. "I had to keep them rpms down. Maybe somethin' blockin' the coolin' water intake." He paused to spit tobacco juice into a styrofoam cup. "Took twice as long to get out here."

"Beautiful," Ben said. He squinted out at the massive rig again. "Well, at least it doesn't look like it's going down."

Dothan looked over at him in surprise, chewing slowly. "Boy, I hope not. That why they called y'all? To stop it from sinkin'?"

"Kinda," Ben replied. "It's got a couple of small holes in one of the underwater ballast tanks. If they didn't pump it for a hundred years, it might end up on the bottom. It's really no big deal. Just a small accident, and a standard, run-of-the-mill repair."

"But they's nervous, I bet," Dothan chuckled. He plucked the microphone off the VHF radio. "Well, lemme call that li'l ol' rig . . ."

Ben went back down the short flight of steps to the darkened passenger compartment. Pinkham and the girl were still lying flat out on the seats, their heads pillowed by life jackets. Rolly was sitting up against one of the ports, a dark shadow punctuated by the glowing red coal of a cigarette.

"Rise and shine, boys and girls," Ben said in a clear voice. "Time to fly like Superman."

Rolly snorted with laughter. "More like a gutshot goose," he growled.

Ben flicked on the overhead lights, donned his hard hat, and stepped out the aft hatch onto the back deck. As he dogged the door shut, an acrid blast of diesel exhaust whipped over him, stinging his eyes. Coughing, he walked across the deck to the windward rail and found some clear air. There was a chill in the wind, enough that he could see his breath. He turned up his collar and shoved his hands into his pockets.

The stern of the crewboat was pointed directly at the NAOC-X. Ben heard the bridge hatch slam and turned to see Dothan shamble out to the aft steering station, an outside wheel-and-throttle pedestal mounted behind the bridge on top of the passenger compartment. From here a skilled crewboat skipper could maneuver beneath cranes or into tight slips with an unhindered view of the vessel's position.

"They's sendin' down a couple of riggers," yelled Dothan over the engines, losing some of his chew down the front of his shirt. He gestured up at the rig. "Can you catch the basket?"

Ben nodded and gave him the thumbs-up sign.

Far above the boat's deck, one of the NAOC-X's eight swing cranes boomed around slowly with a personnel basket of orange netting—so high it looked no bigger than a thimble—dangling from its fast line. Ben strode down the back deck to the clear area near the stern, looking up.

The engines roared and poured out clouds of blue-white exhaust as Dothan worked the throttles to keep the crewboat in position under the crane. Spray flew up as the stern butted into the light oncoming swell. Ben steadied himself with a hand on the rail.

The basket began to descend rapidly, its circular base of orange canvas growing as it neared the deck. Ben could see the two life-jacketed riggers clinging to the netting on the outside of the basket, standing opposite each other to balance the load evenly.

About twenty feet above the deck, the basket stopped moving. Far above on the rig the crane operator had paused to allow Dothan to center the boat up for the landing. The hulking captain kicked his vessel sideways about five feet, threw the helm hard over, and shifted gears back the other way, holding his position.

Before Ben could grab the dangling tag line to guide the descent, the crane operator dropped the basket— too fast—down onto the deck with a wet *thunk,* sending the occupants sprawling across the slippery boards. Ben hopped out of the way, shaking his head. Just as quickly, the crane operator yanked the basket up off the deck again and into the night sky.

"Harley, you sum'bitch!" yelled one of the riggers, shaking his fist at the crane. He staggered to his feet, holding onto the frame of one of the air compressors. "Crazy sum'bitch," he repeated.

The other rigger was nursing a banged knee. He limped over toward Ben, muttering under his breath. "Sue them bastards," he kept saying. "Sue them bastards."

Ben gave the pair of them the once-over. They were both about twenty years of age, and least twice that many pounds overweight. Baby-faced and pallid, with receding chins and limp blond hair, their features had a barbecue-and-beer meatiness that looked decidedly unhealthy. They were probably brothers. In their insulated coveralls and life jackets they looked like dirty, khaki-colored Pillsbury doughboys.

"All this shit goin' up?" one of them asked, snuffling. He gestured at the compressors and decompression chamber.

"Yeah," Ben replied. "Everything on the back deck, including the bottle rack and equipment box. Want any help?"

"Naw," the talkative one said, scowling. "They don't let call-out contractors do any of their own riggin'. Liability, y'know?"

"Oh, yeah," Ben said. "I know. I suppose we have to wait inside until all the lifts are made, too, huh?"

"Yup. Liability."

Ben looked up and saw the personnel basket dangling about fifty feet over their heads. "How about if we load the basket up with personal gear and send it topside. The thing's still hanging there. Why waste the trip?"

"Cain't do 'er," the talker said. "Cain't send personal gear up without two contractors on the basket to mind it."

"Don't tell me," Ben said. "Liability."

He turned and started walking back up the deck to the passenger compartment. "Let me know when you're done," he called over his shoulder. "I'll be in here, sleeping."

He half expected the rigger to tell him that he couldn't do it because of liability, but instead the two look-alikes started to argue about who was going to give hand signals to the crane operator. Ben figured the point was moot; the operator was too high up to see them, and he was going to run the crane any damn way he pleased, anyhow. He'd already demonstrated that by his handling of the basket landing.

Ben hurried over to the rear hatch. The best way to deal with a crane operator who worked to the beat of his own drummer and ignored everyone else was to get the hell out of the way. Preferably under a heavy steel roof.

He ducked inside the passenger compartment and dogged the hatch behind him.

"What say, Benjamin?" Rolly drawled. "We goin' up?"

"Be a little while," Ben replied. "They want to off-load the dive package first."

"Shit," Rolly said, and lay back down on the seat, cocking his hard hat over his eyes, the cigarette in his mouth pointing straight up at the ceiling.

Ben looked at Pinkham. "That gear's ready to lift, right? Gearbox locked, bottles chained into the rack, etcetera, etcetera?"

"Yeah," the diver-tender said. "No problem."

"Good. You checked it yourself, right?"

"Oh, yeah," Pinkham said, looking quickly over at Karen, "I checked everything twice."

Ben looked hard at him for a moment, then went back to his seat, pulled a notebook from his hip pocket, and began to enter the details of the off-loading procedure.

"Hey, Ozzie," Rolly rumbled from beneath his hard hat.

"Uzi," Pinkham corrected, coloring slightly.

"Whatever," the grizzled diver continued. "You dog shut de inner-lock hatch of dat chamber so's it wouldn't bang around?"

"Uh—yeah."

"Dat's funny," Rolly mused, " 'cause Ah heard it bangin' around as we was passin' de sea buoy on de way out. So Ah went inside an' dogged it mahself."

Pinkham turned a deeper shade of red. "Yeah? Shit, it must've come undone by itself, man," he argued defensively.

Rolly tipped his head up suddenly and regarded Pinkham coldly from under the brim of his hard hat. "Never try to snow de snowman, boy," he said. "Them hatches don't undog themselves." He put his head back down.

Pinkham started to speak, but before he could Ben turned in his seat and made a cutting motion with the edge of his hand.

"Make sure next time," he said, putting a lid on the issue.

He glanced over at Karen Marriot, who'd been sitting quietly a few seats down. Her face was ashen, and she was swallowing reflexly. She saw Ben looking at her and attempted to smile.

"You all right?" Ben asked.

"Not really," she replied. The crewboat heaved up on a particularly large swell, and she swallowed hard, blinking.

"Go below into the lower compartment," Ben said, "and lie down on a bunk or a seat that runs fore and aft in the center of the boat. The motion's the least down there. You take any Dramamine before we left?"

She shook her head, looking miserable.

"Won't do any good now, then," he said. "Just hang on; it won't be too much longer, and we'll be off this boat. That rig stays as steady as a skyscraper. Once you're up there, you'll be fine."

"Thanks," Karen said weakly. She got up and disappeared unsteadily down the stairs to the lower compartment.

Pinkham snorted derisively and lay down on his seat.

Outside there was a thump-*bang* and some yelling

as the first piece of equipment was lifted off the deck.
Ben closed his notebook, glanced at his watch, and
lay back down. It would be another hour, anyway.

It was nearly midnight when Ben, Rolly, and the
two tenders finally donned life jackets and hard hats,
loaded their personal gear into the center of the basket, and climbed onto the outside. Ben waited until
he saw that the other three had locked their arms
through the netting, then waved to the crane operator
and quickly grabbed hold himself. With a sudden jerk
the basket lifted cleanly off the deck and ascended
into the night sky.

The basket rotated slowly as it rose, and the boat
below shrank into a narrow steel bullet heaving on
the black swells. Then Dothan gunned the engines, a
spurt of white foam churned out from the stern, and
the crewboat pulled rapidly away from the rig.

Karen was swiveling her head, looking around and
down, fascinated by the sensation of dangling so high
in the air. Pinkham, on the other hand, was staring
rigidly ahead, his face set. He was clutching the netting
so tightly the veins were bulging on the backs of his
hands.

Rolly looked at him, then caught Ben's eye and
grinned. It was obvious that he wanted to say something, but he was too professional to harass someone
who was apparently afraid of heights while they were
dangling several hundred feet in the air. He freed up
a hand and moved it over near the shoulder strap of
Pinkham's life jacket, ready to grab if the need arose.

"How you doing, Nelson?" Ben inquired lightly.

"Good, good," the diver-tender answered through
clenched teeth. He tried a nonchalant smile, which was
anything but.

"Okay," Ben said. "We'll be setting down in just a
few seconds." He kept watching Pinkham carefully.

"Just a few more feet . . . bend your knees a little, folks—touchdown."

The basket thumped heavily onto the steel deck.

Pinkham and Karen jumped off quickly, both looking relieved. A couple of roustabouts who'd been standing by the landing site helped Ben and Rolly pull the personal gear out of the center of the basket. Once empty, the crane operator lifted it out of the way and set it in its cradle on top of a utility building.

The two tenders stared around in awe. Neither of them had ever been aboard a semi-submersible of this size before. It wasn't much compared to Mount McKinley or the Grand Canyon, but as works of man went, it was pretty impressive.

The main deck of the NAOC-X stretched off into the distance, an expanse of plate steel and grating nearly three football fields in length. In the center of the rig, forty-nine fifteen-foot-high valve trees—one for each well—stood in seven rows of seven each, the various pressure-control and monitoring components color-coded with bright red, blue, or yellow paint. Endless runs of shiny half-inch stainless-steel tubing—hydraulic actuator lines—twisted though the wellheads, and gauges of every shape and size sprouted from valve housings and flow junctions. A half-dozen men in fluorescent-orange NAOC coveralls and hard hats were moving slowly through the forest of valve assemblies, jotting down pressures and flow rates on clipboards.

Swing cranes like the one that had just picked them up were mounted above each of the eight legs of the rig, supported and tied into the main structure with massive I-beams and gussets. At the far end of the main deck was a three-story control building with a large octagonal helideck mounted on top of it. A NAOC field chopper was perched near the helideck's edge, its main rotor, skids, and tail tied down with tensioning straps.

The drill tower, a huge movable derrick mounted on hydraulic skids, rose off to one side of the wellheads. The top of it reached one hundred and seventy-five feet into the air above the main deck. It could be positioned over any of the forty-nine wells in the event that down-hole work had to be performed. Specialized tools could be lowered on drill-string tubing to accomplish tasks many thousands of feet below the seafloor.

Rolly whistled softly through his teeth. "Lotta wells," he said, looking down through the grating of the main deck at the forty-nine large-diameter conductors, the black water turning to white foam as it washed against them far below.

"Hey!"

Ben spun around at the sound of the voice. A beefy man dressed in emerald-green coveralls and a white hard hat was striding across the deck toward them as fast as his belly and short legs would allow. He bore a remarkable facial resemblance to the movie actor Edward G. Robinson, right down to the well-chewed cigar clamped in the corner of his mouth. He had the waddle fat men can't avoid when they try to move too quickly. The embroidery above his chest pockets read "Emil Duplessis" and "Toolpusher." Ben braced himself inwardly.

"Goddammit, where y'all been? We gonna have to talk about a fee discount right from the word go, son! Ask for a quick callout, an' get the damn crew showin' up nearly twelve hours later! We coulda put this job up for bid if'n we knowed it was gonna take this long! Gonna be somethin' said to the front office 'bout this, for sure!"

Ben let the harangue wash around him. They were a couple or three hours late at most—an inconsequential delay by offshore oilfield standards, where you might wait days for delivery of a simple engine part. The toolpusher was using a common bullying tactic favored by oil companies in their dealings with contractors. Seizing on some grounds for complaint, no matter how flimsy, and riding it into the ground—making something out of nothing—often resulted in the creation of a negotiating point that could be used to reduce the contractor's bill once the job was completed.

It was an old ploy, and one that wearied Ben no end when it was pulled on him. Not every toolpusher used it, but once in a while he'd encounter some hard-assed old company creature who preferred ugly tactics as a matter of course. Like Duplessis. Ben sighed. It always made for a long job.

Rolly stood by Ben's shoulder, scowling and smoking. Pinkham and Karen had wisely moved off to check the dive gear.

When Duplessis finally paused and drew a breath, Ben calmly and politely asked where the damage to the pontoon was. The toolpusher puffed on his cigar and waddled swiftly off toward the port rail, motioning them to follow.

There was a piece of red plastic tape tied to the handrail, about forty feet aft of the port bow leg. Ben and Rolly peered over the side. Far below, illuminated by a crane spotlight, was a bubbling circle of froth about twenty feet in diameter, undulating on the black swells.

"That's where she fell at," Duplessis announced. "A whole load of drill-string. I need her fixed ASAP. Let's get on it, son. I cain't wait for Challenge Divin' to get around to it next week. Clock's runnin', boy."

Ben resisted the urge to get in the toolpusher's fat face.

"You got it," he said, and wheeled away, putting a hand on Rolly's shoulder as they walked back toward the dive gear.

"Line me up a crane, will you?" he asked his friend. "And a trash basket to use as a stage. The quicker we get in the water, the quicker Duplessis'll go find somebody else to bother. I'll get the tenders moving in the right direction and check out the welding machine." He glanced at his watch. "Let's shoot for being set up and ready to dive in, say, an hour and fifteen minutes. Okay?"

"Sho'," Rolly replied. "You divin' first?"

"Yeah," Ben said. "I want to see these holes, y'know?"

"Good," Rolly nodded. "Ah hate gettin' mah ass froze off before de sun even comes up."

An hour and a half later Ben was standing in the steel trash basket, fully dressed in to dive, with Pinkham and Karen hovering nearby tending his dive hose, burning-torch leads, and welding cables. He swiveled around, looking at Rolly through the Lexan faceplate of his hat, and gave the thumbs-up signal. The grizzled Cajun returned the gesture and leaned over the primary dive radio.

"Y'all set, Benjamin?" he asked.

"Yeah," Ben replied. "Let's do it."

Rolly checked the air pressure in the portable manifold box in front of him once more, then waved a finger skyward in the direction of the crane operator.

The crane cable to the basket slings went slowly taut, then picked the basket and Ben up off the deck, trailing leads and dive hose. The two tenders kept the cables and hose clear as Ben was swung over the rail, then lowered toward the dark water.

It was a long way down. Two full minutes elapsed before the first swell slapped the bottom of the trash basket, tilting it, and then Ben was underwater in a haze of silvery bubbles. He snapped on his hat light, checked the lay of his hose and the leads, and adjusted his breathing regulator.

"Keep coming down, Rolly," he said.

"Comin' down, bro," came the reply, and the basket jolted and descended farther. Ben held the open end of the pneumo hose up in front of his faceplate.

"Stop me at forty feet," he instructed.

A puff of bubbles erupted from the pneumo hose as Rolly checked Ben's depth. The basket rumbled down a few more feet, then jerked to a halt.

"You be there, bro," Rolly's voice crackled through Ben's ear speakers. "Four-oh."

Ben spun slowly around, three hundred and sixty degrees. Below the basket the beam of his hat light faded into empty blackness, and above him he could see the flickering gleam of the rig lights as they danced on the surface of the water. He turned off his light and waited.

After a moment his eyes became accustomed to the darkness, and he began to see shapes in the faint ambient light. As he watched, the massive horizontal pontoon took shape in the gloom, as did two of the immense vertical legs. On the opposite side of the pontoon, barely discernible in the distance, was the stand of well conductors, stretching down below the rig into the depths.

Ben estimated that the basket hung ten feet above and thirty feet out from the top of the pontoon.

"Boom up, hold the load, Rolly," Ben said.

"Roger that," came the reply. "Boomin' up, holdin' the load."

The basket jolted again, then started to move in the direction of the pontoon as the crane operator topside followed Rolly's hand signals. Ben cleared the mist of condensation from the inside of his faceplate with a blast of air from his free-flow and gauged his position.

When the basket was suspended about ten feet above the outer edge of the pontoon, he spoke again.

"All stop."

"All stop, bro," came the repeated command.

About twenty feet away Ben could now see a wavering column of bubbles rising to the surface from a point on the upper curve of the pontoon. There was something else there, too, some kind of oddly shaped shadow, too vague to identify.

"I can see the location of the damage, I believe," Ben said. "I'm gonna have you come down on the basket till it's just a couple of feet above the pontoon, then go over there and check it out."

"Yeah, okay," Rolly returned. Ben could hear him take a quick drag off a cigarette. "Ready?"

"Yeah," Ben said. "Come on down easy."

The basket descended jerkily until Ben gave the command to stop a foot above the steel plate of the pontoon. He glanced up, checking that his hose wasn't wrapped in the welding leads or crane cable, then swam out of the basket.

"Slack the diver," he said, dropping down on the pontoon.

A thick puff of pale paint dust rose off the steel plate as he put a gloved hand on it. He grimaced in distaste inside his hat, wary of having to touch the toxic anti-foulant coating.

About ten feet from the site of the damage he flicked his hat light back on, continuing to approach cautiously. Three lengths of drill-string tubing, heavy steel pipes thirty-three feet long and three inches in diameter, were sticking out of the pontoon's steel skin at different angles. All three had impacted within an area less than eighteen inches across, and had punched through the thick plate as though it were no more substantial than cardboard.

Air from the interior of the pontoon was bubbling

out around the tubing sections. The rig's giant compressors had been constantly repressurizing the holed compartment, displacing excess water out its bottom through an opening called a sea chest. Sensors inside the pontoon relayed information to the master buoyancy-control computer in the heart of the NAOC-X, which then analyzed the reading and tripped on either the air compressors or water pumps, depending on whether the internal water level needed to be raised or lowered.

Before getting dressed in, Ben had asked Duplessis if the holed compartment could be flooded completely without destabilizing the rig. The toolpusher had confirmed that it could; he would simply have to flood the corresponding compartment in the starboard pontoon. The operation would temporarily compromise the NAOC-X's optimum buoyancy, but with the weather expected to remain calm for at least the next twelve hours, the patch welds could likely be completed and the compartments repressurized before full buoyancy control was needed again.

The volume of air escaping from the pontoon was steadily decreasing. Ben moved up to within arm's reach of the punctures and examined them under the white glow of his hat light.

"Hey, Benjamin." Rolly's voice crackled over the ear speakers.

"Go ahead."

"Duplessis says both sides are pretty much flooded now. Ah can still see air comin' up to de surface. Them bubbles slackin' off any?"

"Sure are," Ben replied. "Getting down to a trickle now. Once the water level gets past this point— whoops . . ." He paused momentarily. "Well, I guess that's it. They've stopped completely."

"Good."

"Okay. First thing is to get these tubing sections out

of here. Send down that second crane line, willya? I'll sling up one of 'em and trim the hole with the torch before we pull on it.''

"Roger that."

Ben spent the next fifteen minutes giving crane directions, moving the basket over beside the work site and lining up the lifting cable with the first section of tubing. He climbed out on the protruding length and double-wrapped the lifting slings around it, shackling them back into themselves. Then he had Rolly come up on the crane until the cable began to take the weight of the tubing.

"All stop," he said. The lifting cable stopped moving.

He pulled the burning torch out of the basket, along with enough lead to work freely, and inserted an ultrathermic burning rod into the head.

"Make the torch hot," he instructed, flipping down his hat's welding shield.

At the topside dive station Rolly threw shut a large knife switch, sending one hundred and fifty volts of DC current to the torch head.

Ben hit the oxygen trigger, blowing a stream of O_2 out of the end of the rod. Seconds later it ignited on the damaged steel plate in a blue-white flash, and began burning through the pontoon's thick skin.

As Ben worked, oblivious to everything but the rod's molten tip, two male dolphins detached themselves from a pod that had been dozing near the rig and soared in to investigate the unusual activity that had disrupted the normal rhythms of the ocean. They kept their distance, cruising by no closer than twenty feet, seeing as much with their highly evolved sonar as with their eyes. Whatever the strange creature hunched over the flickering white light was doing, it seemed unaware of their presence and, more important, appeared to pose no threat to the females and young in the pod.

After making several passes the dolphins picked up something more ominous: the presence of a large shark shadowing the pod some two hundred feet below. Alert to this new danger, they veered off and hurtled silently back the way they had come like twin torpedoes, leaving the sluggish, crab-like creature curled over its light, very small in the cold vastness of the night sea.

Chapter Thirteen

The front door of the Grissom Aviation office was locked, and most of the interior lights were off. Ari rapped a few times on the plate glass to see if any security personnel were near the front lobby. When no one showed, he picked up his briefcase and walked around to the side of the building.

A high chain-link fence topped with three strands of angled barbed wire closed off the rear area of Grissom Aviation, with its landing pads and choppers, from the street. Ari leaned back against the building next to the fence, partially hidden in the shadows.

Traffic on the street was light, and the adjacent offices seemed deserted. He looked up at the barbed wire; the lower strand was about seven feet high. Not much of a problem, particularly with the side of the building to lean on. The briefcase he could pass through the gap between the bottom of the fence and the ground.

He was about to slide the briefcase under when a man ambled out from the rear of the building, smoking a cigarette. Ari froze. It was a uniformed security guard, his peaked cap pushed back on his graying head. He stopped, drew on his smoke, and looked up at the landing lights of an incoming 747 on approach to the main airport. As the noise of the big plane's engines grew louder, he turned and walked back behind the rear of the building without looking in the Mossad agent's direction.

Ari let out his breath, waited a few seconds, then shoved the briefcase under the chain-link. As the 747 roared overhead, he leapt up, grabbed the lower strand of barbed wire, and pulled himself easily to the top of the fence. He threw a leg over the top strand, grimacing as a barb dug into his calf, and scrambled over the wire, leaning back on the side of the building for support. When his feet were clear, he jumped free and dropped the eight feet to the asphalt on the opposite side, landing with athletic ease. He picked up his briefcase and flattened himself against the wall once again, invisible now from the street.

He moved quickly along to the rear of the building, expecting at any moment to see the guard step around the corner. When it didn't happen, he sneaked a glance around the edge of the wall. The man was sitting in a folding chair next to one of the building's rear doors, an open workman's lunch box on the ground beside him, eating a sandwich. White gospel music was coming from a cheap radio propped up on the sill of a rear window.

Ari looked over at the landing pads. Six Grissom helicopters—three Bell JetRangers, two Aerospatiale Astars, and a large Sikorsky S-76—were lined up neatly in a row, tied down to the ground with tensioning straps, including the one he'd piloted during the checkout flight. He felt in his pocket for the two keys he'd secreted away as he'd gotten out of the chopper, then straightened up, put a pleasant smile on his face, and walked around the corner of the building.

The guard swiveled his head to look at him in surprise, his cheeks bulging and smeared with mustard. The folding chair nearly tipped over backward as he jumped to his feet, still holding the sandwich.

"What the hell you doin' in here, mithta?" he exclaimed, spitting mustard and mayo. He chewed and swallowed furiously, putting the sandwich down on the chair. A greasy hand came to rest on the butt of his pistol.

Ari spread his hands. "Excuse me," he said innocently. "I apologize if I startled you. There was nobody up front, and I thought I might find someone back here who could help me. I was supposed to meet Frank Stone here"—he paused and glanced at his watch—"well . . . now." He smiled helplessly.

"Stone? The checkout pilot? He ain't never here this time of night." The guard's eyes narrowed. "What you need him for, anyhow?"

"Well, I rented that helicopter," Ari explained earnestly, pointing at the choppers, "and he was going to go over some charts with me tonight because I have to leave very early in the morning. You haven't seen him?"

"Nope," the guard declared. "Ain't seen nobody. Mister, you're gonna have to leave. Ain't nobody supposed to be back here now. Try the office in the mornin'." He popped the retaining strap off the hammer of his revolver.

"Well, hold on, hold on," Ari said. "You're not going to shoot me, are you? I just came in to meet Frank Stone. I can't imagine why he wouldn't be here." He edged up a little closer to the guard. "Please, firearms frighten me somewhat. I'd be happy to show you my identification, if you like."

"Well," the guard muttered, the rusty wheels in his head turning at full speed, "I don't guess I need to see any, if'n you know Mister Stone . . ." His back straightened. "But I'm ree-sponsible for security in this here area. An' I aim to do my job."

"Good," Ari said, and kicked him between the legs.

The guard's breath rushed out in a gasp, and he sagged forward, knees buckling. His eyes bugged out, and his fingers scrabbled ineffectively at his holster. Ari grabbed his hair, pulled his head forward and down, and broke his neck with one vicious downward punch. The man dropped as though poleaxed, drew one rattling breath, and lay still.

Ari knelt down and with two fingers calmly took the guard's pulse at the carotid artery. When the faint beating finally ebbed away to nothing, he stood up, retrieved his dropped briefcase, and began dragging the dead man by the collar across the tarmac toward the helicopters.

He stopped beside the Bell 206 JetRanger he'd flown during the checkout and, looking around quickly, unlocked both doors with his stolen key. Kneeling down, he got the guard draped over one shoulder and hefted him into the copilot's seat. He belted the corpse in securely, then stepped back and began to disconnect the tensioning straps that tied the chopper to the landing pad.

After trotting quickly around the entire aircraft once to ensure that nothing remained attached that could prevent liftoff, Ari climbed into the pilot's seat and dogged the doors shut on both sides. Switching the electrical systems on, he adjusted the independent throttle control on the collective pitch lever for start-up and cranked the engine over.

It fired immediately, and Ari adjusted the rpm for warm-up, then slowly disengaged the rotor brake. The blades of the main rotor began to turn, and he lowered the collective pitch lever to keep the lift they produced to a minimum. When the engine temperature and manifold pressure reached optimum levels, he centered up the cyclic control stick and increased the pitch of the main rotor blades until the chopper jogged slightly, then rose unsteadily into the air.

Adjusting the throttle upward, Ari palmed the cyclic control forward, and the helicopter dipped its nose and accelerated ahead, continuing to rise as it did so. Leaving all lights off, Ari banked the aircraft over the Grissom building and came around to an east-south-east heading of one hundred degrees. Beside him in the copilot's seat the dead guard's head lolled off to one side.

He leveled the chopper off at three hundred feet and continued forward at maximum airspeed, and five minutes later switched on all his external lights. Keeping a sharp eye out for electrical pylons and large smokestacks, he searched the glittering carpet of lights ahead and below for signs of the coast.

As he left Houston behind, the lights thinned out until eventually they were replaced by the flat black expanse of Galveston Bay. He lit a cigarette, flicked on the red cockpit lamp, and checked his chart. Crossing the bay, he'd continue on to the High Island area of southeastern Texas, then follow the coastline east to the Sabine River and the Louisiana border.

An hour later, the lights of Sabine Pass emerged out of the darkness ahead. As the JetRanger flew over the wide shipping channel, Ari picked up a weather report detailing the storm in the eastern Gulf. Weather was something he hadn't considered; he listened intently and checked the position of the disturbance on his chart. It was well to the south of the Florida panhandle, but beginning to drift to the northwest.

He drummed his fingers on his knee. Not good. In all likelihood the storm would end up off the coast of eastern Louisiana—right where he needed to be. He'd planned to refuel before morning at one of the numerous helicopter bases between Sabine Pass and Intercoastal City before heading out into the Gulf, but continuing on up the coast would waste valuable time while the weather deteriorated. He had to reach the NAOC-X before flying became impossible.

There was an alternative. He could plot a course directly out to Green Canyon 186 from Cameron, Louisiana, just ahead. The Gulf of Mexico in this area was dotted with oil rigs, all of which had helicopter facilities, including aviation fuel. He'd fly until the tanks got low, then set down on the nearest available rig and talk his way into getting the fuel he needed. And if they wouldn't give him the fuel willingly—he glanced over at the dead guard slumped in the copilot's seat—well, there were other ways.

He took out the chart again and with a small parallel rule calculated a straight-line course to Green Canyon 186. It came out at roughly one hundred and twenty degrees—imprecise, but by morning it wouldn't matter. He'd be able to check his exact position by dipping low enough to read the designations on the production platforms. Every rig in the Gulf was clearly marked with a large signboard showing its corporate owner and the number of the offshore block in which it was standing. A pilot or boat captain could literally hop across the oilfield from rig to rig, checking his position each time. It was impossible to get lost.

It was only forty miles by helicopter from Sabine Pass to Cameron, and in less than half an hour Ari could see Lake Calcasieu by moonlight to the northeast, and then the lights of Cameron shimmering beside Calcasieu Pass. As the JetRanger reached the little oilfield town he adjusted his heading to one hundred and twenty degrees and proceeded out over the Gulf.

He climbed gradually to an altitude of two thousand feet, then leveled off. The night sky was crystal clear, the black Gulf below rippling with silver moonlight. The tiny lights of oil rigs winked here and there on the vast expanse of water.

Ari flew into the Gulf for thirty minutes, then reached over and unbuckled the straps holding the dead guard in his seat. Scanning the sea far below, he saw no rig lights within a dozen miles or so of his position. He eased back on the cyclic control, checking the forward motion, until the helicopter began to hover in place nearly a half mile in the air.

With the slipstream outside the fuselage thus eliminated, he was able to open the door on the copilot's side, then tip the guard toward it. The body slumped over, half off the seat. The dead, surprised eyes stared up at Ari. He took a foot off the floor pedals and kicked the corpse the rest of the way out the door. It glanced off the landing skid as it fell, shaking the chopper slightly, and was gone.

Ari moved the stick forward, and the JetRanger cruised ahead, gathering speed rapidly. The slipstream banged the door shut again, and the agent reached over and dogged it. He looked down at the black water.

"Sorry, old man," he whispered, half smiling. "You'd have been a tough passenger to explain."

Two hours later, with the fuel tanks barely one-quarter full, Ari descended to five hundred feet and headed for a dense cluster of oil platforms just to the south of his course line. He was rehearsing the story he'd planned to use upon landing—that he'd been marooned on another rig by a trim-control malfunction and was now trying to outrun the coming storm—when a black shape loomed up on the water directly below the helicopter's nose, silhouetted by moonlight.

Ari slowed the aircraft to a hover, then banked around for a second look. As he approached, the shape resolved itself into a large platform, unlit and devoid of the usual buildings on its upper level. He worked the JetRanger in closer, fighting the slight head wind that had come up from the southeast, and switched on the landing spotlights.

The platform appeared abandoned. There was an old walking crane sitting at one end, its boom lowered and resting on the deck, and a cluster of fifty-five gallon oil drums around the north stairwell, but otherwise the top level was clear. The south end of it supported an octagonal helideck, painted white with a red X in the center. Beside it, next to the upper-deck handrailing, was a cylindrical steel tank about ten feet long and five feet in diameter, also painted white.

Ari hovered in closer, some twenty feet above the deck, until the spotlights illuminated the tank. The words "CAUTION! AVIATION FUEL" were stenciled on the side in large black letters.

Bringing the JetRanger directly over top of the red X, Ari gingerly decreased the pitch of the main rotor until the chopper began to descend, steadying the nose into the wind until the skids touched down. He feathered the blades and throttled back to an idle, then opened the door and stepped out, keeping his head low.

The night wind was heavy and damp, blowing steadily from the southeast, and the stars and moon were beginning to show coronas as a haze moved in. Ari trotted across the helipad, shaking the stiffness out of his body, and jumped down beside the big white fuel tank.

He rapped it with his knuckles and was disappointed to hear a hollow booming sound, but when he knocked on the lower half, he was rewarded with a solid thunk. The tank was about one-third full. He dragged out the coil of hose that was attached to the valve on the tank's underside, opened that valve, then cracked the operator's valve on the free end of the hose.

A spurt of gasoline shot out of it, and he closed it immediately. He sniffed the end of the valve nozzle—

high octane. Climbing up on the helideck, he began to drag the fuel line over to the chopper.

There was enough fuel to top up both of the Jet-Ranger's tanks. Ari hoped that it wasn't contaminated with rust or water; it had looked a little cloudy by flashlight. He pulled the hose back to the edge of the helideck and dumped it down beside the tank. Then he returned to the chopper and switched off all the lights.

Lighting a cigarette, he strolled down the empty deck to the north end of the platform. The grating under his feet was swollen with corrosion, crunching at every step. Once his foot went right through, tearing the cuff of his pants. The entire rig was covered with rust, and the fifty-five gallon drums beside the stairwell had long since rotted through and lost their contents into the Gulf.

There was a chain across the stairwell, and hanging from it a sign that read "ABANDONED PLATFORM: ALL AREAS UNSAFE." Ari gripped the handrail and tried his weight on the first stair. It crumpled almost immediately, chunks of rust and half-eaten metal tumbling down through the lower level to splash into the water below. He wouldn't be going down there.

Leaning back on the handrail, he glanced at his watch: three-thirty in the morning, July second. One day ahead of schedule. He decided to wait until just before dawn to take off. He wanted to have enough light to be able to start reading the signboards on the platforms. The helicopter had a small Loran-C unit in it. He'd punch in the NAOC-X's latitude and longitude and use that as well.

As he flicked the butt of his cigarette over the rail, he heard the JetRanger's engine suddenly falter, then rev back up to a fast idle. Then it happened again. He hurried back across the upper level toward the helicopter, wary of the rotten grating beneath his feet.

When he reached the handrail, the engine stuttered and died completely, the main and tail rotors coming to a halt. The big main blades bobbed limply under their own weight. Ari cursed and ran over to the aircraft.

Jumping into the pilot's seat, he set the rotor brake on full, choked the engine, and tried to start it. There was plenty of battery power to crank it over, but it refused to fire. Ari worked the choke and made a few more attempts, then shut down the electrical systems to conserve amperage.

He banged his fist hard on the Plexiglas door and passed a hand over his eyes. The fuel. It had to be the fucking fuel. Water wetting down the plugs, or dirt clogging one of the in-line filters, or both. He should have opened the inspection hatch in the top of the tank and siphoned off the clean fuel bucket by bucket, instead of using the hose and sucking up all the water and sediment that had collected on the bottom. Now it was too late, and he was going to have to bleed the fuel lines, clean the filters, and dry the plugs.

There was no way he could flush the chopper's tanks, all his available fuel was contaminated. He'd just have to hope it wasn't bad enough to stall the engine in flight. He propped open the side panel of the engine compartment and retrieved the small tool-box from beneath the copilot's seat.

He worked on the first fitting down the fuel line from the tanks, swearing softly under his breath. He'd been comfortably ahead of schedule. Now he was stranded on an abandoned platform hundreds of miles from his destination, with a helicopter that wouldn't fly and a severe storm approaching.

He had no time for this. No time.

Hundreds of miles away, in a fine, upscale house in one of Houston's tonier neighborhoods, Irving Koppelman was sitting straight up in his Ultra-Rest Extra-Kingsize bed, his red silk pajamas soaked with his own urine. He'd awakened suddenly to find his bedroom full of dark-clad, hard-faced, extremely agitated men. After losing his water, he'd begun to scream for help, forgetting that he was alone in the house. His wife Moira was visiting her parents in Palm Springs.

"Will you shut up, you idiot!" one of the men commanded, a young, intense redhead. Koppelman restricted himself to whimpering into the percale sheet he'd pulled up under his chin. The redhead grimaced, got control of himself, and continued:

"Look, Koppelman, just answer my question: I want to know where the man who initially contacted you is at this moment."

"I don't know!" Koppelman moaned, his eyes rolling. "Isn't he at the apartment?"

"Where? *Where?*"

The *sayan* told him, very quickly. The redhead waved a hand, and two of the men disappeared from the bedroom. "Where did he say he was going?" the man went on.

"He didn't say! That's the truth! He said he was going to have me commended for the fine job I did for him!" Koppelman was nearly hysterical. "I did my duty for the Mossad! I did—"

"Shut up! *Shut up!*" The redhead passed a hand quickly over his eyes and looked at the frightened little man intently. "The man you met was supposed to organize transport for this Mossad team . . . for a very important mission." He jabbed a finger into Koppelman's sheets. "We were supposed to rendezvous with him an hour ago at an aviation company. The place was closed, and he never showed up. *You* were the last person to see him. Now—*where is he?* He must have told you something."

"No, no!" Koppelman sobbed, his nose running. "He never told me anything!"

"God*damm* it!" The redhead looked at his watch and got abruptly to his feet. He turned to the unsmiling man at his shoulder, his face crimson with strain.

"Call Central, Moshe. Tell them we have a problem."

Chapter Fourteen

Riad paused at the foot of the bridge ladder, gripping the rungs tightly to keep from being pitched off the *Circe*'s back deck, the wind whipping the fabric of his black combat coveralls against his legs. The moon was a silver disk overhead, its face streaked with dirty cloud trails. Its surreal light glinted off rolling mountains of black water that raced along in the same direction as the boat, huge and alive and threatening.

The *Circe* took a fifty-degree roll to port as she slewed sideways down the steep face of a cresting wave, then buried her bows with a shuddering jar that checked her forward motion as though she'd hit a wall. The screws chattered in air momentarily, then bit deep into the water again as the stern settled, driving the boat forward.

Riad fought down a rush of panic, keeping a death grip on the slick stainless steel of the ladder. To him the towering waves and eerie sky were part of a panoramic nightmare, a scene for which his own experience left him totally unprepared. He had never been out of sight of land on a boat before, never been confronted by the malevolent power of a storm-lashed ocean.

He waited for a particularly nasty roll to subside, then climbed swiftly up the ladder and ducked through the zippered opening in the canvas spray shield protecting the bridge.

Sligo was stretched out in his helmsman's chair, his legs propped up on the console. He had an old Black Sabbath tape in the stereo, and the plodding, grungy music filled the bridge, overpowering even the howl of the wind. Coke vial clutched in one hand and a beer in the other, his head bobbed rhythmically in time to the brontosaurus beat of "Iron Man."

Riad went over to the opposite seat, sat down, and braced his legs against the console. Sligo waved his beer at him.

"Heyyy, amigo," he called, feeling no pain, "que pasa? Still got your pharmaceutical sea legs?" He broke out in high-pitched chortle. "Hooo! I'm a fine one to talk, huh? Got a drug-powered captain on this canoe—might as well have a drug-powered crew, too!" He bawled with laughter. "God, I just crack myself up sometimes . . ."

The *Circe* crashed down into a trough and softball-sized dollops of foam battered the transparent forward spray shield. Riad braced himself against the roll, hanging on like grim death, but Sligo just let his body move opposite the motion, his feet flying up in the air.

"Yeeeee-haaa!" he screamed, grinning from ear to ear. He took three deep chugs from his beer and wiped his mustache with the back of his hand.

What kind of madman is this? wondered Riad, staring across the bridge at the smuggler. He looked like some demented clown in his ridiculous beach shorts and loud shirt, his ample potbelly poking out above his waistband. Now he was holding his arms in a curious position and wiggling his fingers, stomping one foot and bobbing his head furiously.

"DAH-na-na-na-na-na-na DAW na-na!" Sligo glanced up suddenly, beaming. "Air guitar, pal," he said. "Or in your case, air sitar . . . no—wrong country. Ah, fuck it."

He bopped around in his chair a little longer, then sat back and drained the last of his beer. He seemed oblivious to the angry sea and the boat's violent motion. Riad burped and tasted seasickness pills. He'd eaten three more of them twenty minutes earlier. If the medication was unpalatable, it was at least better than retching every thirty seconds.

"Are we much closer?" he asked Sligo.

The smuggler glanced up at the backlit display on the overhead Loran unit.

"Yeah," he said. " 'Bout halfway now." He spun around in his chair, reached out, and pulled back one of the flaps of the rear spray shield, revealing the heaving seas chasing the *Circe*'s stern. A thin talon of lightning etched itself across the black sky far behind, briefly illuminating a horizon thick with storm clouds.

"Shit," the smuggler said, mildly. "Lookin' real funky out there, ain't it?" He closed the flap again. "Oh, well. It's the beauty of nature in maximum overdrive. Enjoyin' the spectacle, Riad?"

The young man smiled weakly. "Truthfully, I do not care for the situation. It makes me . . . nervous."

Sligo whooped and slapped his knee. "*Nervous*? Nervous of what? The weather?"

"Of course," Riad replied defensively. "Does it not concern you? Your ship is caught in a storm at sea."

"What," Sligo demanded incredulously, "this li'l ol' breeze? Son, lemme tell you somethin': this is barely enough air to dry laundry." The bump he'd taken from the coke vial just before Riad's arrival had put him in the mood to talk, his adrenaline pumping.

"Hell, I remember bein' caught in a waterspout on a thirty-bale run from Jamaica back in eighty-two. Talk about wind! Man, that sucker waffled us good." He settled back in his seat and put his feet up on the console.

"The boat was a piece of shit, a home-built ferrocement job with a wooden mainmast and an aluminum mizzen. 'Bout forty feet long, and as tubby as a Spanish galleon. God, what a pig!" He was too wired to notice that this information meant absolutely nothing to Riad, who sat and nodded politely. "It butted through the water like a fucking shoe box—could barely sail out of its own way.

"I'd partied away all my cash in Fort Lauderdale and needed a run bad, or I'd have never got aboard the thing. The guy who owned her was this hillbilly type from Arkansas—never sailed a boat on the ocean in his life. But he had a plan. Same plan as nearly every other swingin' dick in South Florida at the time, but it had worked for other people, so why not him?

"He was gonna build his boat, sail to Jamaica, load up with sensimilla, and bring it back to the States. Then he was gonna live rich and happy on his yacht for the rest of his life. Simple, huh?"

Riad nodded, looking both bewildered and fascinated.

"So we get aboard this tub he's just finished building and set sail for Jamaica. He didn't even have enough money to put food on the thing. We ate fish the whole way, and all we had to dress 'em up with was ketchup and peanut butter."

He opened his vial and took a small hit, snuffling the powder up carefully. The boat took another lurching dive into a deep trough, the bows slamming down on the water with a boom that shook the whole hull and rattled Riad's teeth. Sligo backed the throttles down just a hair and resumed his story.

"So we load up in Negril, see, and haul ass outta there. We came in through the Bahamas and the Windward Passage, and we're gonna get back to the States via the Yucatan Channel—makin' a big circle right around Cuba from east to west, okay?

"Well, we're about seventy-five miles west of the

Caymans, beautiful clear day with maybe ten knots of wind, with all the hatches open and the tunes on and porpoises playin' around the boat—all that good shit—and whammo!"

"Whammo?" Riad echoed.

"Whammo," Sligo repeated. "All of a sudden there's sheets of solid water flying everywhere, the boat's rockin' like the Jolly Green Giant's shaking it, and there's a roaring noise like a 747 taking off a foot over your head. I'm hangin' on for dear life going 'what the fuck,' right? I can't see shit and I can't breathe; it's like the air's being sucked right outta my lungs. It was hairy, man, hairy."

"Hairy?" Riad said uncertainly.

"Right. Then all of a sudden it stops—just like that. I pick my sorry ass up off the floor of the cockpit, which is full of water, and stand there like a drowned rat, tryin' to get some air back in me. I musta swallowed ten gallons of salt water; I feel like I bin keelhauled."

Riad shrugged his shoulders.

"You know—dragged under a ship with ropes . . . Ah, never mind. Anyway, I have a look around, and I just can't fucking believe it! The mainmast is gone—stays, spreaders, sails, everything. The mizzenmast is still there, but there ain't a shred of cloth on it bigger'n a playin' card; the whole sail's been blown out like a kiddie balloon.

"Billy Ray—that was the hillbilly's name—Billy Ray is fucking gone! He was layin' up on the foredeck catchin' some rays, and now he's history!

"Then I look off to starboard and right there, not more than a few hundred yards away, is this giant waterspout. Nice calm, blue water everywhere, hardly any clouds—and this great big sonofabitch!

"I figure it must've formed right on top of us, 'cause there was no warning at all. It got Billy Ray—probably sucked that poor fool up off the deck and drowned his ass a thousand feet up in the air! Those waterspouts are pretty much—guess what?—solid water! Kinda makes sense, huh?"

"That waterspouts would be full of water?" Riad commented. "Of course. But what happened next? Could you find your friend's body?" He had to admit to himself, as repulsive as Sligo was in his person and his habits, he could be entertaining when he was doing what he loved, which was to sit around drinking, snorting cocaine, and talking.

"Nope," Sligo said. "Didn't even try." He grinned like a gargoyle. "He might've been alive, and one hundred percent of a load's better'n fifty.

"I go below and the boat's full of water, a foot deep over the cabin sole. All the square groupers were stowed—"

"Square groupers?" Riad interrupted. "I don't understand this expression . . ."

"Dope. Grass. Marijuana," Sligo explained. "All the bales were stowed in the forepeak and forward cabin. The waterspout sent tons of water down the open hatches. Every bale in the forward cabin—more than twenty—had busted open when the boat got thrown around and was soaked with salt water.

"What a fucking mess. The whole place smelled like a Rastafarian funeral." He paused for a second, looking at Riad, then shook his head. "Never mind. It'd take too long to explain.

"Anyway, I ended up throwing all the ruined dope over the side, setting up a jury rig on the mizzenmast, and sailing on up to Tampa. Moored the boat at the municipal dock, took eight big bales of weed off one at a time in my seabag, sold 'em that weekend, sold the boat, and went to New Orleans. Got there in time for Mardi Gras, too."

Riad braced himself again as the boat took another

wild roll. When the motion diminished, he relaxed and gave Sligo a quizzical look. "This smuggling," he said. "You have had good success with it. Being caught does not worry you?"

Sligo laughed. "Hell, yeah, it worries me. But I'm good, pal. I've been doing this a long time. Had my share of luck, I gotta admit, but I know the angles, too. Like, for example, when to hit port with a load so's your chances of bein' stopped and searched are real low: make sure you come in on a nice weekend, maybe Saturday around three in the afternoon. The pleasure boat traffic's so heavy you can just blend right in.

"Really works well in a big boating town like Lauderdale or Miami. Ain't no way the narcs are gonna be able to single you out. Unless, of course, somebody rats."

"Rats?"

"Rats. Informs on you. That's the way most busts go down. The narcs wouldn't have a clue, except for that Jamaican cop you forgot to grease when you were on-loading the product. Or that ex-ol' lady you shit-canned a couple of months ago.

"Anyone who wants to do a number on you, all they gotta do is pick up the phone and call the DEA. That's why I always pay my loaders properly, don't have no steady ol' lady, and never talk about business until after it's done. And even then I don't give out a whole lotta details."

"Very wise," Riad nodded, noting that Sligo talked about himself and his affairs more than anyone he'd ever met. "It is easy to make money in America, it seems. You have never been arrested?"

"Not at sea," the smuggler said. "I got picked up in Tampa once with a quarter-ounce of weed in my pocket. You know—sell a little, smoke a little—just partying." Riad nodded as if he knew. "Judge let me off with a fine and a warning. Piece of cake."

"In my country," Riad said, "there are also people like you who move hashish and opium from east to west. However, they are much more cautious than you. When they are caught, the punishment is somewhat more severe."

"Oh, yeah?" Sligo responded. "What do they usually get?"

"One pistol shot to the back of the head. The lucky ones. If a man has caused the police much embarrassment, the pistol shot comes after several days of treatment that is quite—unpleasant." Riad grinned as he watched Sligo swallow hard.

"Remind me never to go to—what was it?"

Riad nearly answered him, but caught himself. "We didn't say."

"You can keep the whole mess, wherever it is, pal," Sligo stated, popping open another beer. "God bless America, that's all I gotta say. Here's to 'er." He tipped up the bottle and drank deeply. Riad eyed him coldly, then turned away and yawned.

"You don't sleep?" he inquired. "You will exhaust yourself."

"Nah," the smuggler said. He tapped the vial in his shirt pocket. "A little bump now and then, and I'm good for three days straight. I'll sleep when the job's done. Right now I wanna keep an eye on things. Wanna beat that storm center into New Orleans."

Like a scene from a bad movie, a clap of thunder punctuated Sligo's last sentence, the lightning flash illuminating the wild sea around them for a split second.

"Hoo!" Sligo exclaimed. "That was close." He peered out through the clear plastic of the starboard spray shield. "Gettin' worse all the time," he mused. "Oh, well. We just keep on keepin' on."

A high-pitched *beepbeepbeep* suddenly pulsed

through the bridge, and the green LCD display on the primary Loran unit began to flash. Sligo reached up and punched a couple of keys. The beeping stopped, and the display reorganized itself into new sets of backlit numbers.

"Halfway," Sligo announced. "Right at three hundred an' fifty miles." He glanced at his watch. "Fifteen hours. We're averaging around twenty-four knots at three-quarter throttle; that weather's pushin' us north real fast."

"That is good, then?" Riad asked, gripping the chair as the *Circe* rolled again.

Sligo toasted him with his beer bottle.

"It's groovy," he said, and put the bottle to his lips.

Below, Luis was creeping slowly along the narrow passageway connecting the forepeak—where he'd fled to hide from Sligo and his belt buckle—and the main salon. The ten diphenhydramine tablets he'd swallowed had virtually knocked him out and made him sick to his stomach instead of seasick. He felt able to make the distinction.

The Yankee captain was going to be sorry he'd ever beaten Luis with a belt. But not yet—not now. Luis would bide his time. He would let the crazy Yankee get them through the storm, let him deliver the four men to New Orleans. He would mop the decks, shine the brightwork, and carry drinks up to the bridge; and he would learn about maps and charts and the little electronic boxes that told you where you were.

He would learn about all these things, and say "yes, Cap'n Jerry" and "no, Cap'n Jerry," and work like a happy little peon. And then one day when the sun was high and the sea calm and sparkling blue, far from land, and the Yankee was leaning over the rail reeling in a fish or passing water, Luis would give him one good push, then climb up to the bridge and drive his new boat to Mexico, where the police and the senoritas knew how to treat a man of means.

Luis leaned against the bulkhead and giggled with pleasure at the thought. There was also the briefcase he had seen Escobar pass to Sligo at the dock in Bahia Cristobal. He knew from the way the Yankee had handled it that it contained something valuable; probably money or drugs—payment for taking the four passengers north. He would have that, too.

The *Circe* rolled and so did Luis's stomach, forcing a gassy burp. He swallowed hard, and as he looked up, he saw Gradak's short, powerful legs descending the steps from the main salon. Without a second thought he ducked into Sligo's cabin, quickly pushing the door shut behind him.

He heard Gradak pass by and enter another cabin, and sighed with relief. The four men frightened him— hard faces and too many guns. They reminded him of the military police from Havana, who could make people vanish off the face of the earth for no reason at all. He would be glad when they were gone.

He looked around, knowing that Sligo was on the bridge and would probably stay there most of the night. The briefcase. Just a quick look to see what was really inside it. It had been under the bed, and if the Yankee hadn't made so much noise coming down the passageway he'd have caught Luis fumbling with the latches instead of faking sleep.

He dropped onto all fours and felt around under the bed. Nothing. He cursed. The Yankee had moved it. Then he put his hand down on wet carpet.

For a moment he was afraid. Was water coming into the boat? No. The *Circe* was strong and free of leaks. This was only a small damp spot.

He pulled back the carpet, exposing the hatch in the cabin sole. It suddenly dawned on him where the briefcase was, and he giggled again. The Yankee was not as smart as he thought.

He lifted the cutout section of the sole to reveal the water tank's inspection hatch. Trying the nuts, he found that they were only finger-tight and quickly spun them off. When he pried up the hatch and peered down into the tank, he could faintly see the briefcase-sized package sitting under three feet of sloshing water.

It was too risky to fish the briefcase out and open it now; it was enough to know where it was. Luis was sure it contained money—why else would Sligo have taken such pains to hide it?

He replaced the tank hatch and began spinning the retaining nuts back down. The *Circe* and the briefcase were the answer to his dreams. He would bide his time.

Gradak emerged from his cabin dressed in black military-style coveralls and lightweight jump boots, a black balaclava hood stuffed into one of his breast pockets. He passed the door to Sligo's cabin and wondered briefly what the dirty little Cuban was stealing now; he'd noticed Luis pocketing various small articles since the boat had left the dock, like a rat secreting away buttons and bits of shiny foil.

Leaning hard on one side of the passageway, he made his way aft to the main salon as the boat heaved and pitched, water roaring against her hull. Turgut and Saeb were seated on the floor with their backs to the port bulkhead, also dressed in black coveralls. Each held between his knees one of the large black packsacks Saeb had been preparing earlier, as well as a Skorpion submachine gun. They wore automatic pistols strapped under their arms in shoulder holsters.

The door slid open, and Riad stepped inside in a gust of wind and rain, his hair damp and plastered to his forehead. He glanced at Gradak, checked his watch, nodded, and sat down on the starboard settee, another packsack and submachine gun beside him.

Gradak settled himself into the big lounge chair and picked up two automatics in shoulder holsters from the floor beside the coffee table. He passed one to Riad, then extracted the other and pulled back the slide, locking it open.

"Equipment check," he said in Arabic. "Pistols."

Four days earlier the captain of a small inter-island freighter that was making its way along the north coast of Cuba toward the Yucatan had finally lost patience with a frayed and sun-rotted two-inch polyethylene mooring hawser. Finding it brittle and impossible to splice yet again, he had roundly cursed the owners who were too cheap to buy him the mooring lines he needed, and ordered the entire three hundred feet thrown overboard.

Now the tangled hawser floated just beneath the surface of the heaving night sea like some immense black and yellow snake, directly in the path of the *Circe*. Even if anyone had been looking, it was impossible to see.

The *Circe* rose up on a great swell, her bows and the forward third of her hull clearing the water, then smashed down on the snarl of line that lurked in the trough. Instantly the whirling screws sucked up the hawser, wrapping it again and again around the shafts and blades.

As the line bound itself in more tightly, the friction of the spinning shafts began to melt the polyethylene, driving it into the cutlass bearings of the shaft struts and eating away at their rubber linings.

There was a sudden crack as the soft bronze of the port propeller's keyway yielded to the much harder stainless steel of the shaft, and the port engine raced as it was suddenly freed from its load. The shaft spun uselessly inside the bored-out body of the ruined prop.

The starboard shaft simply wrapped up yards of hawser until the ball of polyethylene bottomed out on the underside of the hull and stalled the other engine.

The entire event had taken less than five seconds.

On the bridge, Sligo heard and felt the rhythm of the engines change abruptly, followed by a loud cracking sound, and then he was thrown violently out of his captain's chair as the *Circe* slewed sideways in the driving seas and nearly rolled over in a broach, dipping her antennae in the water. The smuggler's head smashed down hard on the main console, shattering the glass of the port tachometer and opening a four-inch gash in his temple at the hairline.

Gradak and his men were hurled across the main salon, piling into one another against the starboard bulkhead in a crush of arms, legs, and equipment. Saeb howled as his left wrist bent back and broke with a sickening crack under the combined weight of Turgut and Riad.

Luis, just reaching for the door after smoothing the carpet back into place, was bowled over onto Sligo's bed, bounced once, and dropped forcefully into the foot-wide space between the bed and the bulkhead, his pudgy body wedged so tightly he could barely breathe. He struggled for air, found he was unable to move at all, panicked, and began to scream.

Sligo, blinded by the sticky blood running into his eyes, groped frantically at the console for the throttle levers, finally locating them and idling back the redlining port engine. The hydraulics of the autopilot moaned in a futile effort to swing the *Circe* back on course. Swearing at the top of his lungs, Sligo hit the disengage switch and grabbed the wheel, wiping blood out of his eyes, and tried to bring the boat around. With no steerage way on, there was no response.

A great wave broke full on the *Circe*'s port side, driving her over and down again into the trough, ninety degrees onto her starboard rail. Solid water poured into the bridge, washing Sligo away from the console and slamming him into the pedestal of the opposite chair.

The *Circe* staggered upright again, heavy with water, every drain streaming, and wallowed helplessly, side-sea to the driving swells.

Chapter Fifteen

Gradak and his men scrambled to find handholds as the *Circe* rolled ninety degrees again, laying down her starboard rail for the fifth time in two minutes. Saeb was braced between the armchair and the bulkhead, clutching his smashed wrist to his chest and moaning. Water roared against the hull, hammering it until the whole boat shook with the impact.

The main salon door slid open with a bang as the *Circe* wallowed upright again, and Sligo stood there wild-eyed, his face running with water and blood, fingers gripping the door frame like claws.

"Help me get the sea anchor out!" he screamed. "Or we're all fucking dead!"

Turgut and Riad looked at each other, faces drawn and pale, then started for the door. At that moment a huge graybeard wave broke full on the back deck, filling it to the gunwales with a lather of white foam and green water. The *Circe* rolled hard onto her starboard rail yet again, and Sligo lost his grip and disappeared.

When the boat shuddered upright, Turgut and Riad staggered to the door and looked out. Sligo was on his knees fumbling with the latch of the starboard deck locker, waist-deep in seething foam. He threw open the lid, then noticed the two men standing in the doorway.

"Come on!" he yelled hoarsely. Then his eyes widened, and he seized the edge of the locker in a death grip.

The giant rogue wave broke over the port stern quarter of the boat, driving the transom below the surface. A five-foot wall of water rushed up the deck and slammed into the back of the cabin, burying Sligo completely.

White foam and green water exploded through the open door of the main salon, knocking Turgut and Riad back inside. Gradak yelled something in Arabic and fell facedown into eighteen inches of salt water.

The *Circe* found her feet once more, wallowing heavily in the trough. A small tidal wave of water, gear bags, weapons, paper, cushions, and galley utensils washed back and forth in the salon from wall to wall. More water poured down the steps to the forward cabins, and out the rear door to the back deck.

Gradak shouted again in Arabic as he struggled to his knees and pointed frantically at the door. Riad and Turgut fought their way outside, then together slid the glass panel closed. Gradak locked it from within.

Sligo had jammed open the lid of the deck locker and was tugging feverishly at a large bundle of heavy canvas. Riad and Turgut leapt to help him, and the three of them were able to free the bundle from its lashings.

"Don't take it out yet! Don't take it out!" Sligo bellowed over the howling wind. "I gotta get it secured to the bow first, or the next big wave'll wash it outta the boat!" He grabbed the end of a large coil of one-inch yacht braid and held it up. "Feed me this line! I'm goin' for'ard!"

He scrambled around the corner of the cabin and up onto the starboard rail, clawing his way along on his belly from stanchion to stanchion.

"Slack the bitch! Slack it!" he screamed over his

shoulder, yanking on the line. Riad fed him more rope, Turgut steadying him with a hand on his belt.

Sligo disappeared from view as he moved up onto the foredeck, and twice the *Circe* rolled so hard that Riad was sure the smuggler must have been washed over the side, but each time the tugging on the rope resumed as the boat stabilized.

Finally, Sligo came slipping and sliding on his belly back down the starboard rail, tumbling with a wet thump onto the back deck. Immediately he turned to the locker and began hauling on the canvas bundle.

"Pull it out!" he gasped, half drowned.

They rolled the bundle out of the locker and let it drop onto the sodden deck. Sligo shook free the bridle assembly of the sea anchor and locked together the two crosspieces that held its mouth open. He gestured frantically at the rectangle of heavy fabric.

"Stretch the fucker out! We gotta unfold it so it'll open!"

Fighting for balance, Riad and Turgut yanked the tail of the anchor out and pulled it down the deck. It was a conical canvas sock some ten feet in length and four feet in diameter at its open end. The bridle was secured to the heavy crosspieces and in turn to the thick yacht braid, which now ran up to the bow.

"Throw it over the side!" Sligo yelled, and together they tipped the sea anchor over the starboard rail. It disappeared under the boat immediately, the line trailing behind. As it passed beneath the hull, it hung up briefly on the tangle of rotten hawser balled up in the screws, then dropped away and began to fill out as the *Circe* drifted downwind of it.

The last of the line payed out, then tightened, and the boat's bow turned slowly into the seas, forced around by the drag of the anchor. The *Circe* began a controlled drift stern-first, her sharp stem parting the oncoming waves. No longer side-on to the weather, her motion calmed into a rhythmic pitching.

Sligo staggered to the salon door, tried to open it, and finding it locked began to pound on the glass with the flat of his hand. Gradak appeared and clicked up the latch, sliding the panel open. The smuggler fell inside onto the soaked carpet, sucking in air with great wheezing gulps, the gash in his forehead leaking blood. Riad and Turgut struggled through the door on his heels, breathing hard, and Gradak slid it closed behind them.

"Jesus Christ," Sligo groaned, getting to his knees. He looked around slowly at the ruined salon, then put a hand gingerly to his head. "Aaagh," he said, wincing and gritting his teeth. He grabbed a beer can as it rolled by, and popped the top. It erupted in a spray of foam. Sligo just jammed it against his lips and gulped, letting half the contents run down his chin.

Gradak lashed out with his foot and kicked the can away, splitting the smuggler's lip in the process. The Canadian reeled back in pain and shock, one hand to his mouth.

"—Th' fuck you do that for?" he screeched, his voice a strangled bleat.

His face very pale, Gradak dropped to one knee and seized Sligo by the front of his baggy Hawaiian shirt. His eyes seemed to emit a light of their own.

"You will not drink now, 'Captain,'" he hissed through his teeth. "I have need of you."

He accentuated the word "need" by lifting Sligo off the carpet and shaking him so that his head bobbled on his shoulders. Then Gradak released him, and the smuggler slumped back against the settee. He had enough sense left to keep his mouth shut.

"What has happened?" Gradak demanded. He stared down at Sligo, the muscles of his jaw working.

The smuggler, sprawled against the settee like a

drowned rat, swallowed several times before speaking. "We musta hit somethin'," he muttered, his eyes darting furtively around the salon. Like Gradak, the other three men were staring fixedly at him. He began to get that familiar feeling again—like he was the bait goat at a lion hunt.

"What the hell's that?" he said abruptly. There was a faint wailing sound audible above the rush of water against the hull.

Gradak cocked his head and listened for a moment, then looked over at Turgut and jerked a thumb in the direction of the cabins. The big man got to his feet and went down into the forward passageway. Sligo leaned over to get a better view and saw him enter the captain's cabin.

Thirty seconds later there was a burst of high-pitched screaming, and Turgut emerged from the cabin pushing Luis ahead of him, one ham-like fist gripping the Cuban's hair. The little man was waving his arms helplessly and making a continuous blubbering noise, his chubby face beet-red.

Turgut guided him roughly up the stairs, then turned him loose and shoved him into the salon. Instantly, Sligo jumped to his feet and began slapping Luis about the head and face with his open hands.

"What the fuck you doin' back in my cabin?" he yelled, his fear of Gradak forgotten. "You after my money, you greasy little spic? You think you can steal from me, you dirty—" He landed a stinging blow on one of Luis' ears.

Suddenly the little Cuban went berserk, screaming incoherently in Spanish, his arms windmilling at Sligo, eyes popping out of his head. The Canadian covered his head with his hands and fell back, trying to kick blindly at Luis from a half crouch. They reeled back and forth across the salon in an absurd slapstick battle as the boat pitched and rolled.

Gradak let them flail at each other for the better part of a minute, then nodded again to Turgut. The big man stepped forward and snatched Luis by the hair and the back of his waistband, lifting him off the floor and pinning him across the galley countertop. He squirmed at first, squalling in Spanish, then gave up and lay still.

Sligo leaned against the settee, breathing heavily, alternately glaring at Luis and eyeing Gradak. The Arab regarded Luis with disgust, then stepped across the salon and sat down in the armchair, waving Sligo to do the same. The smuggler dropped down onto the settee with a weary sigh, shivering.

"Now," Gradak said, his tone regaining some of its usual smoothness, "what were you saying? We've hit something?"

Sligo nodded unhappily. "I think so. And whatever it was, it messed up the screws bad. I heard somethin' break: a blade, a shaft, a strut—fuck, who knows? One engine ran wild and the other stalled. I don't even hafta look to tell you there's one unholy mess down there."

"It must be fixed immediately," Gradak said.

Sligo gave a snort of laughter. "You obviously don't know much about boats, pal," he replied. "Ain't no 'immediately' about this kinda damage. I can't even check it out until the seas calm down. Most I can do is pull up the floorboards and have a look at the engines." He pointed at the carpet. "Maybe see if the stuffin' boxes are leakin' from the shafts getting yanked around. But that's it."

Gradak's face was a mask. "We must be near New Orleans by tonight," he stated.

"Tonight," Sligo said, "we're gonna be driftin' on this sea anchor in the middle of a storm, makin' sure the boat stays watertight. There's no way you're seein'

New Orleans tonight, tomorrow night, and probably the night after that. Just forget about it."

There was a sharp, metallic *click-clack* as Riad pulled back the slide of his automatic pistol. He touched Sligo's ear with the barrel. The smuggler froze.

Gradak leaned forward, his unearthly eyes locked on Sligo's. "The damage must be fixed immediately," he said softly. "And we must be within fifty miles of New Orleans by tonight."

Sligo felt his insides wilt. The sheer malevolence Gradak projected was overwhelming. He looked away, unable to meet the terrorist leader's demonic gaze.

"You don't get it, man," he said, his voice cracking. "There's nothin' I can do right now."

"Yes there is," Gradak said. "You can die with a bullet in your ear. I promise you, you can do that." Riad pressed the barrel of his automatic into the side of Sligo's head.

"Whoa, whoa! Hang on, now! Just a fuckin' minute!" The smuggler grimaced and tried to turn his head away from the pressure. "*Aagh!* Okay, okay! Lighten up, willya?"

Gradak nodded at Riad, who removed the pistol and stepped back, letting the hammer down with the edge of his hand.

"Shit!" Sligo exclaimed, holding his ear.

"You will fix the damage to the boat," Gradak outlined tonelessly, "and then resume a course for New Orleans." He looked at his watch. "You will have the necessary repairs completed by noon today. We will assist you in any way we can."

"But, but—" Sligo stuttered. "You don't understand! Someone has to get into the water in scuba gear and check out the props under the hull! I just can't do it in a storm! I'll get my brains beaten out on the bottom of the boat!"

"If you don't do it," Gradak said simply, "we will kill you where you sit."

"You'll be in a tropical storm in a fucked-up boat without a captain!" Sligo shouted desperately.

"Choose!" Gradak barked suddenly. "The water or a bullet!"

Riad aimed his automatic at the smuggler's head and thumbed back the hammer.

Sligo's shoulders sagged, and he looked around at the ring of hostile faces in defeat. "Some choice," he muttered. "Guess I'm goin' swimmin' . . ."

Forty-five minutes later Sligo was sitting on the *Circe*'s transom dressed in a one-piece wet suit and fins. A face mask was tilted up on his forehead, and he was cinching up the chest strap of a set of fifty-cubic-foot scuba tanks he wore on his back. Riad and Turgut stood on either side of him, their knees braced against the gunwale, steadying him with a hand on each shoulder. Gradak sat in the big fighting chair, an open box of tools braced between his feet.

Even though she was being driven backward by the storm, the boat was riding well, her bow held into the weather by the sea anchor. Her side-to-side rolling had dampened considerably—the seas were no longer boarding over the gunwales—but her fore-and-aft motion was a roller-coaster ride. She'd climb up the face of an oncoming swell at a forty-five degree angle, then pitch forward over the crest, her stern kicking high in the air, and slide down into the trough at the same angle. Then she'd do it again.

On the back deck the effect was stomach-churning, like being jerked up and down in an elevator every fifteen seconds. Several times Riad and Turgut felt their feet leave the deck as the stern lifted, then dropped away beneath them.

Sligo knotted a length of one-inch yacht braid to

his chest strap, then turned to Riad, holding up a bight of the line.

"Keep hold of this," he shouted over the wind. "It's the only thing attachin' me to the boat." His face was pallid, and the crude bandage wrapped around his forehead was already soaked with spray and blood. He looked over at Gradak. "Gimme that hacksaw for starters, Rodriguez." He gestured at the tangle of black and yellow hawser snaking up from beneath the stern. "If this shit is real rotten, it might come off pretty easy . . . depends how much there is. And if I can get under there at all."

"You have considerable motivation to do so," Gradak replied impassively, holding out the hacksaw.

Sligo swallowed hard, then grasped the saw and positioned the face mask over his eyes and nose, the mouthpiece of his regulator clamped between his teeth. He hesitated, then slid off the stern as the boat bottomed out in the next trough, disappearing immediately beneath the waving tentacles of the hawser. Riad slacked off the safety line.

The *Circe* rose and fell over the next swell, then Sligo popped up some fifteen feet astern, flailing his arms and kicking. Riad and Turgut hauled him back to the boat, then reached down, grabbed him by the tanks, and yanked him up onto the transom. He gasped for air, pulling the mask off his face.

"I can't see!" he blurted. "I need a light!" He flapped a hand at Gradak. "In the toolbox. There's a small waterproof flashlight in the bottom."

"Could you tell how bad it is?" Riad asked.

"Well," Sligo said, spitting out salt water, "I got a hand on the starboard screw, so it's still there. But there's so much fuckin' rope everywhere, I couldn't get real close. I dunno about the port side." He repositioned the mask over his face, then took the flashlight from Gradak and held it up alongside the strap on the right side of his head. "There's duct tape in the tool-box. Tape the light right here."

When the light was in position, Sligo jammed the regulator back into his mouth and dropped into the foaming black water again.

He clawed his way along the web of rotten polyethylene, trying to keep his head low to avoid being brained by the underside of the hull. The water surged up and down past him as the *Circe* rose and fell, the hawser wrapping up his legs and tanks like a nest of boa constrictors. He kicked free and fought his way farther into the mess, nearly passing out from the exertion, until he could feel the blades of the starboard propeller.

The strut and screw looked intact, but the hawser had taken multiple wraps around the shaft, cinched tightly by the power of the starboard diesel. Sligo jammed his legs and left arm up around the strut and shaft, and began to saw with his right. Every time the boat rode over a swell, it felt like a giant hand was first tearing him away from the hull, then slamming him face-first back into it. The cut on his head stung from the salt water.

He sawed for twenty minutes, clearing most of the shaft, then rested briefly before tackling the hardest part: cutting off the half-inch-thick layer of polyethylene that had melted against the shaft as it spun. It took another twenty minutes to remove, the water having quenched it into case-hardened plastic.

Sligo's head was spinning as he clawed his way over to the port side through the remaining hawser. There was less rope on the shaft on this side, but he couldn't find the propeller at all. It was buried inside a huge ball of polyethylene. Hanging on grimly, he began to saw again.

Fifteen minutes later, with his tanks running low, the last shred of hawser floated away from the stern.

Sligo checked the prop and strut. The prop was bored out, and the cutlass bearing ruined. Even if he'd had another propeller, it was impossible to replace the bearing without dropping the shaft.

The *Circe* would have to run on one engine, if she ran at all. He let the hacksaw fall from his numb hand and with one last effort kicked his way out from under the stern.

When he surfaced, Riad and Turgut pulled him up to the transom, then lifted him roughly into the boat. He tore off his mask, lay back against his tanks, and had a two-minute coughing fit.

When he'd finished, he looked up at Gradak, who was still sitting in the fighting chair.

"Well?" the Arab demanded.

"The shafts are clear," Sligo panted, "but we can't use the port engine. The cutlass bearing's fucked, and it can't be replaced without hauling the boat. You can shoot me if you like," he added, too tired to care, "but it won't change a thing."

"And the other engine?"

"I think it'll work," the smuggler said. "But I won't know until I give it a try." He shrugged off the tank straps. "It looks lighter out here now. What time is it, anyway?"

Gradak glanced at his watch. "Six o'clock."

"Six," Sligo repeated. "Huh. Felt like I was down there longer than that." He unzipped the front of his wet suit and began to waddle up the deck, dripping. "I'm gonna fire up the starboard engine."

He climbed the ladder to the flybridge, followed by Gradak, Riad, and Turgut. The sky had lightened to a dark gray color, full of low, boiling clouds and rain squalls. Thunder cracked and rolled continuously over the angry sea, and the wind whipped off the tops of the waves, creating long, floating streamers of foam.

Sligo sat down heavily in the captain's chair,

reached over, manipulated the throttle back and forth several times, then turned the starboard ignition key.

There was a throaty roar as the engine caught instantly. Sligo revved it up, checking the tachometer, oil pressure, and temperature, then slipped it back into a fast idle.

Turgut smiled thinly at the sound. "Good. Is good," he said.

Sligo threw a skeptical glance at him over his shoulder. "Don't count your chickens yet, pal," he said. "I figured the engine'd be okay. It's the shaft and the screw I'm worried about. If I can't put the thing in gear, it can run like an Indy race car and we won't be goin' anywhere."

Turgut's face fell.

"What the fuck," Sligo said. "Here goes . . ."

He slipped the engine gently into gear. A faint vibration began under his feet, but it disappeared when he throttled up slightly. The *Circe* began to move up on her sea anchor line.

Sligo throttled back before the line got enough slack in it to be sucked up by the prop, and took the engine out of gear.

"Okay," he said, breathing a sigh of relief. "Here's what we gotta do."

It took Riad and Turgut more than half an hour to pull in the sea anchor, both of them nearly going overboard in the process, but after a terrific struggle they managed to drag it up onto the back deck. Sligo made them stuff it back into the deck locker before bringing the *Circe* around onto her original course.

"We ain't gonna make the same speed we had before," he said nervously to Gradak, who was hovering by his shoulder, "but the storm pushed us way to the north, so we ain't that far behind schedule. We'll make it." He adjusted the light intensity of the Loran display.

Gradak studied the little unit for a moment, then sat down in the unoccupied flybridge chair. "You can tell the boat which way to steer automatically by using that little device?" he inquired.

Sligo nodded. "Yeah. Like I said, I just punch in the destination and away she goes."

Gradak took a piece of damp paper out of his pocket and held it out.

"There will be a slight change of plans, Captain," he said. "I want you to adjust the steering computer so that the boat automatically takes us to these coordinates."

Sligo took the paper. "Where's this?"

"Very close to New Orleans," Gradak replied. "You will drop us off at this location, then go about your business."

It couldn't be soon enough, thought the smuggler. He shrugged and nodded.

"Okay. No problem. I'm just the bus driver."

He reached up and began to punch in the lat/long coordinates of the NAOC-X.

Chapter Sixteen

Forty miles south-southwest of Mobile Bay, the *Teresa Ann* surged along on a fast reach, the wind dead on her port beam. The sun had set an hour earlier, and now its final fading rays colored the sky to the west a glimmering magenta.

Sass was sitting on the threshold of the open companionway, poring over a folded chart by the dim light emanating from below. She'd caught a weather report some hours earlier while passing Gulf Shores, Alabama, and had plotted the last known position of the tropical storm that was building to the south. Now the topside VHF radio was buzzing with an updated Coast Guard advisory; she jotted down the storm's new latitude and longitude and rapidly marked the position on the chart, along with the time at which the NOAA spotter plane had determined those coordinates.

She sat back, running numbers in her head, and chewed her lip. The storm was coalescing rapidly into a tight circulation, racing northward as it did so. The tighter it got the slower it would travel, but it would also strengthen as it sat spinning and drawing heat and moisture from the warm waters of the Gulf. It was possible—even probable—that it would attain hurricane strength before reaching the coast.

Sass looked around at her little ship, at the heavy stainless-steel turnbuckles on the stays and the massive teak construction of the cockpit coaming and rails.

She felt the weight and strength of the *Teresa Ann* as she effortlessly parted the swells and drove onward. Her vessel was stout, built to last, and it gave her confidence.

She checked the wind-speed indicator. A steady eighteen knots. Three more than an hour ago, and five more than the hour before that. She looked up at the broad expanse of the mainsail, thought a moment, then made her decision: she'd haul down the main, secure it, and continue under a reefed jib and mizzen. Clipping her safety-harness' carabiner into the wire jack line that ran from the bow pulpit to the cockpit, she disengaged the self-steering gear, took the becket off the wheel, and spun it to port.

It took her fifteen minutes to round up into the wind, drop the mainsail into its lazy jacks and secure it, take a single reef in the mizzen and the jib, and then resume her heading westward. She played with the two remaining sails for another half hour before she was satisfied with the *Teresa Ann*'s balance, then reengaged the self-steering vane.

Upon returning to the cockpit, she also started the auxiliary engine and let it idle in neutral for ten minutes, once again remembering her father's advice: "Engines don't like to sit, Sass. Run 'em a little bit every day, if you can."

After she shut down the engine, she sat back on the helm seat and drummed her fingers on the cockpit coaming. The storm was going to change things considerably. It was standard practice for the oil companies to evacuate all offshore personnel whenever a hurricane entered the Gulf of Mexico; they'd been hit with enough wrongful death lawsuits in the past to have learned their lesson. But this wasn't quite a hurricane. More than likely, Ben would simply shut down his job on the NAOC-X and ride out the weather for a day. All boat and helicopter traffic to the rig would be halted until conditions improved, virtually isolating it from the mainland.

He might not get his repair work done, either, in which case he'd have to remain on the rig in order to complete the job once the storm had passed. She sucked at her teeth; already their plans were getting screwed up. She'd have to take the *Teresa Ann* into port, too. There was no way she was going to bob around in the oilfield in a severe, all-night storm, with no one to share the watch and no end of platforms to crash into.

Several miles dead ahead a freighter was cutting across the *Teresa Ann*'s bows, bound for Gulfport. She stared at its running lights for a long time, trying to let her feelings of apprehension ebb away. Caesar let his mistress simmer for a while, then finally whined, raised his big head, and nosed up under her arm.

"Had enough of the bad vibes, huh, Ceaz?" Sass said. "Okay. No more. You're right; no sense worrying about what you can't change."

She turned the wheel and set course for Gulfport, less than an hour away. There was a safe storm anchorage in the city's harbor. As soon as the eye of the storm passed inland, she'd be able to resume her voyage out to the NAOC-X, regardless of how bumpy the seas were. She'd lose half a day, at most.

She got up and stepped across the cockpit. "Help me take this jib in a little, will you?"

Caesar whined and rolled over on his back.

"Okay," Sass said, laughing and picking up a winch handle. "Fine. You just lie around and eat. I'll do it myself."

She locked the handle into the top of the winch drum and began to crank in the sail.

Ben sipped coffee as he sat by the dive radio and listened to the sound of Rolly's exhalations. The wiry

Cajun had been in the water for over two hours, and was in the process of welding small steel patches over the holes in the pontoon. It was work that had to be done right, and it was slow going.

He looked at the horizon to the southeast. It was mid-morning now, and the sky had become overcast very quickly, dulling the sun's light to a steely silver. The wind had picked up suddenly as well: Ben estimated it at about twenty knots and increasing, along with the height of the seas.

He waved Pinkham over to the dive station. "Listen to the radio for a few minutes," he said, and stood up.

He walked over to the handrail, took a last drag on the cigarette, and flipped the butt over the side. It fell ten feet before the wind caught it and whipped it horizontally out of sight. Leaning on his elbows on the top rail, Ben studied the seas below.

Blown-out streamers of salt foam were beginning to form on the surface of the water, and every swell was topped by a whitecap. Rolly's dive hose danced and twisted in the wind, and the heavy welding cables snapped back and forth as the waves washed past them. Thirty feet beneath Ben's feet a gull appeared, its wings pumping rapidly as it tried to make headway into the wind. He watched it fly vainly in one place for nearly two minutes before it gave up and sheared off, soaring back to its roost somewhere under the main deck.

The port bow leg had a depth scale—used for confirming ballasting ranges visually—painted on it like a giant ruler. Ben checked the height of the surge against it as the seas rose and fell from mark to mark. After watching for a while he estimated that the swell was running over ten feet, with fourteen-footers rolling through frequently.

Working off a boat, he'd have shut the operation down. It would have been too difficult for the diver to climb out of the water on a ladder, and too easy for a tender moving around on a pitching deck to take a fall and get hurt. However, it was possible to continue working in poor conditions, to a certain extent, off a big, stable platform like the NAOC-X.

There were limits, though, and it was up to the dive supervisor to make a judgment call as to when to cease operations. Ben worked by one axiom: a man's safety was worth more than any amount of oil company money.

Duplessis was going to squawk if Ben pulled Rolly out before the patch was welded in place, but it didn't matter. If he insisted that a diver continue working on a task in unsafe conditions, he could hire some other crew to do it: Ben and company would "drag up" and go home.

Ben went back to the radio and keyed it. "Hey, amigo."

"Yeah, cuz."

"Talk to me about the conditions down there. You think it's getting a little rough?"

"Well, Ah was wonderin' when you was gonna ask me dat," Rolly said. "Matter of fact, Ah'm bouncin' around like a goddamn beach ball. De surge is getting real strong. It'd be all right if Ah was just tightenin' some bolts or somethin', but it's startin' to move me around so's Ah cain't make a good weld. Y'know-whuttamean, cuz?"

"Yeah," Ben replied. "I gotcha." He thought a moment, then keyed the radio again. "You think you can finish that patch with quality welds, or is it gonna turn out shitty?"

"Shitty," Rolly said without hesitation. "Ah already ground out part of one bead 'cause de surge threw me and made me fuck it up. It's just gettin' too rough, bro."

"Okay," Ben said. He thought a moment, then

made his decision. "Shut it down; we're picking you and the gear up. It's gonna get worse before it gets better."

"Roj-o," Rolly acknowledged. "Dis oughta make Duplessis happy."

"Screw Duplessis," Ben said. "He's gonna have to live with it. The patch can't be put on properly, and it's getting too rough for the diver to work safely. End of story."

"Ah heard dat, cuz."

Ben turned to Pinkham. "Stand by to recover those welding cables," he instructed. "Then we'll pick Rolly up. We're shutting down for weather."

Ten minutes later, Ben and Rolly were standing by the rail, talking in low tones. Pinkham and Karen were busy coiling cables and hoses, rinsing off Rolly's dive hat and bailout bottle, and generally securing the dive station. Duplessis was on the opposite side of the rig, dressing down a couple of roustabouts who'd done something not to his liking. When Pinkham pushed the kill switches on the two air compressors, the sound of their dying diesels drew the little toolpusher's attention over to the dive station. Seeing Rolly standing by the handrail, dripping, he stared for a few seconds, then started across the deck at a fast waddle.

"Well, cuz," Rolly growled. "Here it comes." He scowled and spat over the side. Ben put his hands in his pockets, leaned back against the top rail, and composed himself.

Duplessis came stomping past the compressors like a little green polyester boar, chewing furiously on the stub of his cigar. He halted in front of Ben.

"You ain't got no diver in the water," he observed keenly, his hands on his hips.

"Right," Ben said. "I'm shutting it down."

Duplessis' mouth continued to work around his

cigar. "Shuttin' it down? You done? Patch is welded on?"

"No," Ben answered evenly, "it's only partly welded. There's about another—" He looked over at Rolly.

"Hour," the Cajun rasped, giving Duplessis a black look.

"Another hour of welding," Ben finished.

Duplessis turned a slightly darker shade of purple, and his jaw began to stick out. "Well, hell, son; you ain't done. You gots to get that thing put on right quick. Clock's runnin', an' bad weather's comin'."

Ben looked around mildly. "Bad weather's here, Emil. It's not safe to dive, and the diver's not able to hold his position down there well enough to weld properly. We'll have to finish up as soon as the seas lie down a bit."

"Look, goddammit," the toolpusher argued, "you an' me both know that if you quit now, I'll have to pay y'all just for layin' around out here. Could be maybe three, four days before the weather settles down again. That don't make me real happy."

"Well," Ben replied, "you can always put us on a boat or a chopper and send us to the beach for a few days. Then all NAOC'll get billed for will be a small day rate on the heavy gear we leave out here."

"My district supervisor gave me orders not to let the dive crew go until the hole was patched," Duplessis stated, his voice rising. "Y'all are stayin' here until the work is done. I think you can work just fine"—he stabbed a finger in Ben's face—"in this here weather."

Ben's expression hardened. "I don't think so," he said bluntly. "And since I'm the only dive supervisor I see on this rig, it only matters what *I* think. And I think it's unsafe to dive."

"You're tryin' to hold me up!" Duplessis exploded.

"You're milkin' the job, son! Ain't no reason you cain't jump down there an' finish that plate! I know how this goes with you damn divers. Y'all are turnin' a one-day job into one *week*! Y'all show up late, work too slow, then shut down before the project's done. You think I just fell off the melon truck, boy?"

Ben's face was a cool blank as the torrent of invective lashed him. He let Duplessis exhaust himself, then said quietly, "I'm sorry you feel that way, Emil. If you're unhappy with Challenge Diving's services, we'll just offload our gear and drag up. But I can't—I won't—put the safety of my crew in question. You can take it up with the head office in New Orleans, if you like."

"Oh, now you're tryin' to make me the bad guy!" Duplessis exclaimed defensively. "Well, it ain't gonna work. Y'all are stayin' here till the project's finished! An' you better hope this rig don't have no ballastin' problems durin' the storm, 'cause it'll be on y'all's heads for not completin' the repair!"

He glared at Ben, then stomped off through the valve trees, yelling at someone else.

Rolly, who'd barely been able to contain himself throughout the argument, moved back closer to Ben and angrily shook a cigarette out of his pack, then offered one to his friend. Ben took it and let Rolly light it for him.

"Is there anything left of my ass?" he asked. "Or did he chew it all off?"

"Dat little motherfucker," Rolly snarled. "He needs to accidentally fall over de side some night." He looked as though he'd have seen to it without a second thought.

"Down, boy," Ben said. "Just a little more oilfield bullshit; nothing we haven't seen plenty of before. Five minutes from now he probably won't even remember what he said."

"You see why Ah don't let dem make me a supervisor?" Rolly remarked. "First sumbitch talked to me like dat'd be suckin' his meals through a straw for six months—and Ah'd be back in jail."

Ben laughed. "It goes with the territory, partner. They've been bitchin' me out for years now, and I haven't died of it yet. Forget it; it doesn't matter."

"Ah'd still like to kick dat dickhead's ass," Rolly grumbled as he moved away, toweling his wet hair. "Ozzie! Where's mah regulator at? You rinse it off? . . ."

Ben sighed and took a drag on the cigarette, watching Rolly tramp around collecting his wet dive gear. He thought about Sass and wondered where she was. They weren't going to be able to keep to their original schedule, that was certain. He couldn't help feeling a little worried. Sass was more than capable of getting the *Teresa Ann* to a safe anchorage if necessary, but he really hoped she'd heard of the sudden storm in time and hadn't left the marina. It was unlikely, though. She'd already have started out before it had begun to grow and track northward.

There was nothing he could do about it, one way or the other. He'd probably find out something from Hodge, if he could get a call through. Sass would probably try to leave a message with him. In the meantime, there was gear to be secured, daily reports to fill out, and a job log to be updated. Ben crushed the cigarette out under his boot and began to walk slowly through the dive station, checking for loose equipment.

The wind moaned through the NAOC-X's valve trees, and he leaned into it to keep his balance. The eerie sound rose in pitch steadily.

It was going to blow hard.

Chapter Seventeen

The *Circe* had been running well on her one functional engine for nearly twelve hours, though at greatly reduced speed. The big sportfish hull no longer cruised along on a near plane, but mushed through the water like a workboat. It was a good thing they were going with the seas, thought Sligo, sitting on the flybridge drinking coffee. If they'd been running the opposite way their progress would have been nil.

He was feeling better. Although the *Circe* had lost an engine and taken a sustained beating while she'd wallowed around side-sea, most of the onboard systems remained undamaged. Sligo had been able to take a quick hot shower and change into dry jeans and a sweatshirt. He'd also been able to do two long, leisurely lines of cocaine from the spare vial he kept hidden in his cabin locker. Nothin' like blowin' the blues away, he thought to himself, his gums still buzzing from the powder he'd rubbed into them.

He began to whistle, swiveling the captain's chair to look astern. It had stopped raining, so he'd unzipped one side of the canvas-and-plastic spray shield that covered the aft portion of the flybridge and furled it up. The gray following seas rolling in the *Circe*'s wake looked even larger than they had the previous night, but the boat was holding her course well on the thrust of her single screw.

He gazed out toward the west. Somewhere behind

that boiling wall of black clouds was another beautiful gold and purple sunset, but he wasn't going to see it from where he was sitting. No problem, though; in another few hours he'd be rid of Rodriguez and his crew of psychos and be sitting pretty with cash, coke, and all of New Orleans to party in. There was a nice little canal on the south shore of Lake Ponchartrain that was lined with upscale bars and restaurants, overflowing with college girls . . .

He frowned suddenly. There was a problem: what to do with Luis. The little spic had gone loco on him and couldn't be trusted any longer. Not that Sligo ever had, but at least their relationship had been amiable. Now things were different.

Sipping his coffee, he contemplated simply turning Luis over to the INS upon docking in New Orleans. He dismissed the thought almost immediately: the little Cuban knew too much about the *Circe* and her owner, and would certainly spill his guts if he thought he was going to be deported. Scratch that idea.

If he gave Luis a few thousand dollars and a little coke, then sneaked out of port and headed for Florida, there was still no guarantee that the Cuban wouldn't get picked up eventually by immigration and talk too much. Luis wasn't very bright; he'd probably attract more attention with money in his pocket than if he was dead broke. Besides, the thought of parting with any of his fifty thousand ran totally against Sligo's grain.

He stared astern again at the huge, dark swells chasing the *Circe*. There was another alternative, simpler and cleaner. They were still far out to sea, and as the saying went, it was a great, big ocean.

Even if the body was found eventually, there would be no way to identify it. Cuban and Mexican fishermen were always drowning and turning up in U.S. waters,

half eaten by sharks. One more wouldn't raise any
eyebrows.

He finished his coffee and set the cup in a gimballed
holder attached to the console. It was kind of a shame,
really. He'd taken an initial liking to Luis back in
Bahia Cristobal. He'd been the sort of happy-go-lucky
boob who was always eager to please and provided
ongoing comic relief. Sligo had actually intended to let
him walk with a few bucks in his pocket. But not now.

He braced himself as the *Circe* slewed down the
faced of a large wave. The automatic pilot let out a
hydraulic groan as it corrected the course. It was
working overtime now, in the absence of the steerage
way two engines would have provided. Sligo hoped
the damn thing wouldn't burn out; that was all he
needed under the present circumstances.

It occurred to him that he was going to have to
spend a sizable amount of money to have the *Circe*
hauled and repaired. He only hoped that there was
no structural damage to the hull. If he had to have
glasswork done around the shaft through-hulls, it was
going to cost a fortune. The thought of it made him
ill. Fifty grand wasn't really all that much cash.

After checking the temperature of the starboard engine he climbed down the ladder to the back deck and
went into the main salon. It was empty. Soaked as it
was, everyone had gone forward into the cabins, which
were relatively dry. The air was heavy with humidity
and the musty smell of mildew, and the carpet
squished under his feet, full of salt water. Sligo swore
under his breath; it would cost more money to refur-
bish the boat's interior. He'd be lucky if he had the
price of a beer left after it was all done.

He padded on up the passageway past the cabins to
the forecastle. Luis was lying on one of the side berths
staring listlessly into space, a sheet pulled over his
pudgy body. At the sight of Sligo, he paled and shrank

back like a spooked animal. Resisting the urge to kick
the Cuban around the room just for the sheer satisfaction of it, Sligo smiled and spread his hands in a con-
ciliatory gesture, sitting down on the opposite bunk.
Luis' face regained some of its color.

"So, Luis, amigo," the smuggler said. "How you
feelin'?"

Puzzled and wary, Luis hesitated before answering. "Hokay."

"Good, good," Sligo continued. "I've been a bit
worried about you, y' know?" He forced his expression to turn sheepish and a little sad. "Ever since we,
well, had our, ah, disagreement, I've been feelin'
pretty lousy. I don't like that kinda thing, and I really
hate that it happened between you and me. After all,
we're buddies, ain't we? I—I just wanted to ask you
if maybe we could put it all behind us."

Luis was up on one elbow, looking bewildered. Sligo
went on, oozing apologetic sincerity.

"I don't know what came over me," he said re-
morsefully. "Those other guys—they freak me out, y'
know? And there was all that damage to the boat . . .
Shit, man, I'm sorry. Really."

Luis' mouth trembled, and his eyes went moist.
Christ, thought Sligo; this was going to be too easy.
He held out his hand.

"Whaddya say, amigo? Friends again?"

Luis seized his hand in both of his and pumped it
vigorously, tears running down his cheeks. "Cap'n
Jerry, me amigo," he exclaimed over and over, grinning from ear to ear. "Cap'n Jerry, me amigo . . ."

Sligo smiled back, clapping him on the shoulder.
"Yeah, buddy, yeah. All right, all right." Stupid little
spic.

After a full minute of backslapping and glad-hand-
ing, they sat back on their bunks, drained by the flood
of goodwill. Sligo was having trouble keeping a

straight face. He pulled out his vial of coke, took a bump, then held it out to Luis. The little Cuban was awestruck. This was unprecedented. He took the vial reverentially and snorted up a politely modest amount.

"Thank you, Cap'n Jerry," he panted. *"Muchas gracias."*

Sligo waved him off. "Oh, hell, it ain't nothin'. What's a little toot between friends, huh?" He paused while he returned the vial to his jeans pocket. "Look, Luis, I hate to ask you right now, but I need a little help out on deck. The latch on the stern gate got broken and the damn thing keeps swinging open. I'm afraid it'll get ripped clean off if the right wave hits it. I need you to hold it shut while I put a bolt in it. Can you handle doin' that right now?"

Luis swung his chubby legs to the deck. "Jes, jes," he nodded. "No problem, Cap'n Jerry."

"All right," Sligo said, slapping him on the upper arm. "Won't take long." He had to look away to keep Luis from seeing the involuntary smirk that crossed his face.

They walked quietly back down the passageway to the main salon. Sligo flicked on the galley light and rummaged through one of the utility drawers, finally coming up with a small stainless-steel bolt. The *Circe* took a couple of hard rail-to-rail rolls as a set of big swells overtook her, then settled down again. As the water drained off the back deck, Sligo slid open the glass door and stepped out. Luis followed.

"We'll go back along the starboard rail," the smuggler shouted over the engine noise. "Then you just hold the gate while I stick the bolt in."

Luis bobbed his head, grinning.

Sligo moved over to the rail, groping for handholds. His feet skidded on the wet deck, and he crouched down to lower his center of gravity. He began to work his way toward the stern, picturing what he was going to do.

The stern gate was a hinged door in the *Circe*'s transom, used for boating large game fish like marlin or tuna. There was nothing wrong with its latch, but Luis didn't know that. All Sligo had to do was get the Cuban leaning over the rail, his weight over the gate, then move around behind him, hook his legs, and tip him up over the transom. There was nothing to grab hold of but slick fiberglass and teak. He'd be in the water and a dozen yards astern before he realized what had happened. And there was no way he'd last the night in this storm . . .

Without warning, something hit Sligo in the lower back, propelling him down the deck. The tops of his thighs struck the transom rail, and he pitched forward over the churning water of the wake. In one sickening instant he knew he was going overboard, and in a spasm of terror he threw his arms backward to find a handhold—anything.

His left hand smacked into the side of Luis' head and closed on a fistful of wet hair. The Cuban shrieked and tried to scramble backward, but Sligo hung on like grim death and managed to stop his forward momentum. Gasping with fear, he twisted around and threw himself back into the boat, dragging Luis to the deck with him. In an adrenaline frenzy he smashed his right fist again and again into the Cuban's face, screaming obscenities. He was aware of Luis' fingers clawing at his eyes but felt nothing. All that mattered was to crush his assailant into a bloody pulp . . .

A rogue wave broke full on the *Circe*'s transom, dashing the flailing pair apart. They ended up jammed into the scuppers on opposite sides of the boat, choking and half drowned. Salt foam stinging his lungs, Sligo gulped in air in huge, racking gasps. He scrambled to his knees, gripping the rail for support.

That bastard Luis had tried to push him overboard! He could hardly believe it—the ungrateful little scumbag! The hell with this: there was a loaded .357 revolver under the seat cushion of the recliner in the main salon. Sligo began to grope his way up the deck. He was going to blow the little greaseball's fucking head off . . .

He stopped suddenly. Gradak, Riad, Turgut, and Saeb, all dressed in black coveralls, were standing silently outside the salon door, bracing themselves against the *Circe*'s motion. Sligo blinked, wiping water out of this eyes, and then they started toward him, two moving down each rail, hand over hand.

Luis began to slide backward on the seat of his pants, kicking weakly, until his shoulders hit the transom. He raised himself up slowly until he was sitting on the stern rail, his eyes wide with fear. Sligo backed into the starboard corner of the deck near the transom gate, his mind racing. He pointed suddenly at Luis.

"Thank Christ you came out here," he shouted desperately. "That little bastard tried to kill me! He tried to push me over the side!"

Gradak regarded him coolly. "Indeed?" he said. He looked over at Luis. "A serious offense. As you mentioned, a boat in a storm cannot afford to be without a captain." He smiled, showing his teeth. "We'll handle it for you." He nodded to Turgut.

The big man stepped in close to Luis and grabbed him by the hair with one hand. The Cuban's scream of alarm was cut off by the vicious slash of the double-edged killing knife that opened his throat from larynx to vertebrae. Turgut released his grip, and the dying man toppled slowly backward into the surging water. He bobbed up once in the hissing foam of the wake, and was gone.

Sligo stared astern in horror. When he looked back around, Gradak was settling himself into the fighting chair, a pleasantly benign expression on his face. Turgut stooped down, grinning like a death's head, and rinsed his knife off in the water sluicing across the deck.

Sligo licked his salty lips nervously. "Hey, he had to go," he said, trying to sound nonchalant. "Thanks for savin' me the trouble. I don't know what he was thinkin', but it's a good thing he didn't get me over the side. You guys wou—woulda been in deep shit with no captain on board." He smiled weakly. "No, sir. A boat in a storm this bad wouldn't stand a chance without an experienced sailor in charge. She'd go down like a rock."

"Really?" Gradak replied. "Why? From what I've seen, this boat controls itself automatically. I watched you enter the correct destination coordinates into the computer. We have less than forty miles to go, by my calculations. Unless we hit something else, which I think is unlikely, we should arrive without further difficulty."

"Well, you never know," Sligo said hastily. "Anything can happen out here. Maybe an electrical malfunction, or an engine problem. It don't take much."

Gradak made a pyramid with his hands and nodded. "I defer to your experience, of course."

Sligo stared at him. The man was braced in a fighting chair on the back deck of a pitching boat in the middle of a howling gale, but he talked as though he were sitting in a quiet office. Like the calm in the eye of the storm.

A large breaking wave slopped water over the port gunwale. Turgut and Riad retreated up the deck a few steps to avoid being soaked, while Saeb steadied himself with his good hand on the back of the fighting chair. Gradak watched the water drain off the deck through the scuppers, then fixed his pale eyes on Sligo again.

"You have probably concluded by now that we are not merely thieves such as yourself," he said. "That is correct: money and drugs do not interest us. We are what you might call . . . propagandists. We generate propaganda, but not with words or pictures. We create actual events that focus the attention of the world's news media on our cause." He laughed unpleasantly. "And whether you like it or not, Captain Sligo, this time you are an essential part of the operation. You are quite right: we do need you. We need you to land us safely on the oil—'rig,' I believe it is called in English—that sits on the coordinates I gave you."

To Sligo's horror, he suddenly pulled his automatic pistol from its shoulder holster and cradled it in his lap with both hands, the barrel pointing at the smuggler's stomach. Behind the chair, Saeb grinned at him happily.

"Hey, man—what—hey!" Sligo exclaimed, holding out an open palm toward the gun and flinching back.

The pistol barked twice in rapid succession, and Sligo screamed an obscenity as the slugs splintered the fiberglass of the transom an inch wide of either hip. He slumped down into a sitting position on the wet deck, staring at Gradak with eyes the size of saucers.

"Rodriguez," he said weakly, "don't—don't . . ."

Gradak set the pistol on his knee and aimed it carefully at Sligo's head.

"My name is Ojim Gradak," he announced, raising his voice over the roar of a large cresting swell. "You will remember that, won't you?"

"Yeah!" the smuggler shouted, looking down the gun's barrel. "Fuck, yeah!" He felt like he was going to vomit.

"Good," Gradak said, and replaced the pistol in its holster. "Now, listen carefully to me, 'Captain': you are going to see to it that my associates and I land safely on this oil rig. Am I correct in assuming that it is likely to be a somewhat difficult business in this bad weather?"

Sligo nodded, unable to speak for perhaps the first time in his life. He was starting to shake uncontrollably. Gradak smiled down at him patronizingly.

"In that case," he said, "I think you need to get inside and conserve your strength for the task ahead, don't you agree?"

Sligo found his voice at last. "I think that'd be a real good idea," he said hoarsely.

Gradak stepped down out of the chair, still smiling, and gestured up the deck toward the salon.

"After you, Captain Sligo," he said with mocking politeness.

Chapter Eighteen

Ari tightened down the last fitting on the engine's fuel line, wiped up the remaining high-octane he'd spilled while bleeding the system and flushing the filters, and tossed his wrenches back into the small aircraft toolbox. Leaving the helicopter's engine cowling propped open, he walked to the handrail of the abandoned oil platform, stretching his legs and giving the volatile gas fumes a few minutes to dissipate before attempting a start-up. He blotted the sweat off his forehead with his shirtsleeve. God, it was humid.

He looked up at the sky. It was just after three in the afternoon, and the clear air of the previous night had been completely replaced by a high gray haze. The southeast wind was so damp that he felt almost as though he was breathing underwater. He could smell the faint, metallic tang of lightning.

It was time to go. He went back to the chopper and dogged shut the engine cowling, then climbed into the pilot's seat. Strapping himself in, he checked all the control settings, fingered the choke, and hit the ignition.

The engine turned over, coughed once, and died. Ari swore, gave it a moment, then attempted to start it again. This time it sputtered into life, faded briefly, then revved up and began to idle smoothly as he manipulated the choke. He let the engine warm up for ten minutes, listening for any hesitancy that could mean a fuel problem. There was none.

Sweat was running into his eyes, and it wasn't all from the heat. He blinked it away, unconsciously gritting his teeth, and pulled the chopper a few feet into the air. There was no loss of power or any break in the engine's rhythm, and after hovering for two minutes, he palmed the stick forward and accelerated the aircraft out over the water.

Coming around on his original heading of one hundred and twenty degrees, he climbed gradually to six hundred feet and throttled up to maximum rpm. The head wind was much stronger than it had been, and the chopper was subjected to constant buffeting, but that worried Ari less than the accompanying loss of airspeed. The longer he was in the air, the greater the chance the engine would suffer additional fuel problems in flight, and the more likely it was he would find himself flying at night in severe weather.

Conditions were deteriorating rapidly. The Gulf below was dotted with whitecaps, and the cloud ceiling was descending with every mile of progress he made toward the southeast. Ari could not see it yet, but he knew that somewhere over the horizon must be a black band of thunderheads and squalls marking the outer fringes of the main storm. He needed to be much closer to his destination before it appeared.

An hour later, Ari brought the chopper in low past a close-set formation of three oil platforms connected by long catwalks. The signboard told him that he was in one of the outer blocks of the South Marsh Island field—somewhat less than halfway from Cameron to the Mississippi Delta. He was going in the right direction, but the head wind was drastically slowing his rate of travel.

Just as he began a gradual climb back to cruising altitude, the engine faltered, the change in its normal sound and vibration sending a thrill of panic through him. Eyes flitting over the instruments, he arrested his climb and leveled out, gently manipulating the throttle. The rpm rose and fell irregularly, followed by corresponding losses of power. Ari looked down at the whipped-up water below. There would be no safe landing in those angry seas.

For a nerve-racking five minutes, the chopper lost altitude a few feet at a time, never regaining steady engine power long enough for Ari to make up the difference. He worked the throttle and choke constantly, bathed in a cold sweat. It was nearly six o'clock, and daylight was fading quickly from the overcast sky. The darkening waves below appeared close enough to reach down and touch.

Finally, a bare fifty feet above the whitecaps, the engine stuttered violently and began to run smoothly again, maintaining full power and consistent rpm. Not daring to risk trying to gain altitude immediately, Ari continued to fly level, all his concentration focused on the sound and feel of the aircraft's power plant.

He was in the small rain squall before he realized what was happening. Droplets of water battered the windshield and fuselage and were instantly swept away by the slipstream. Visibility dropped to nothing, and Ari checked the altimeter to make sure he didn't lose his orientation and fly straight into the ocean.

He was too low, flying blind, but the engine seemed to have cleared itself, temporarily anyway, of whatever had been blocking its fuel feed. The squall had to be quite small; he'd have seen it ahead of time otherwise. As soon as he passed through, he'd attempt to regain a comfortable cruising altitude.

The rain thinned out after a couple of minutes, and the surging water below reappeared. Feeling better, Ari glanced down to pick up his cigarettes off the copilot's seat. He looked back up just in time to see the massive, yellow-painted steel leg of an oil platform suddenly materialize dead ahead of the helicopter's windshield.

Instinctive reaction saved him from smashing head-long into the leg; the JetRanger stood on its tail rotor, engine screaming, as Ari pulled the aircraft up with every ounce of power it had. For a split second the windshield was full of bright rig lights, followed by dark clouds, and then there was a heart-stopping crash as one of the skids clipped the edge of the platform's upper deck.

The chopper tumbled through the air over the rig like a wounded albatross, narrowly missing the crane boom, and disappeared into the misty haze of rain on the other side. The well technician who'd been sitting near the leg having a last cup of coffee before taking the evening pressure readings picked himself up off the deck grating, suddenly aware that a change of trousers was in order.

Ari wrestled the helicopter back under control just as it emerged from the far side of the squall. There was a metallic banging noise coming from beneath the fuselage, but otherwise the aircraft seemed to be flying normally. Heart pounding like a jackhammer, he slowed the JetRanger to a hover. The noise stopped. That was good; it wasn't a mechanical problem.

He opened the pilot-side door and looked down. The port skid had torn loose, and was dangling verti-cally from what remained of its rear support strut. At maximum airspeed the slipstream was making it kick up into the fuselage.

Slamming the door, he put the chopper back on course. The banging resumed. There was little he could do about it, aside from setting down on a plat-form and cutting the skid loose. But landing on faulty undercarriage might damage the aircraft further, perhaps marooning him, and he couldn't risk that. He had to keep pressing on toward the NAOC-X.

Cursing the luck that had let him run into a platform during the only five minutes he'd been flying low on the whole journey, Ari worked the chopper up to an altitude of four hundred feet and flew on toward the southeast. It was too dark now to see very well, but he thought that the horizon was much blacker than it should have been, given the time of day.

He switched on the Loran-C unit. Up until now he'd been ignoring it, but he hadn't planned on having to locate the NAOC-X in the dark, and in bad weather. Dipping low to read signboards was fine during the day, but it would be difficult and dangerous at night.

The chopper bucked as it hit yet another pocket of increasingly violent turbulence; Ari felt his stomach press up hard against his diaphragm as the aircraft lost fifteen feet of altitude in less than a second. The loose skid banged and scraped on the underside of the fuselage.

Over the next hour, the weather deteriorated into a series of heavy squalls driven by a southeast wind that was approaching forty knots. By eight p.m. Ari was flying almost entirely by instruments, deafened by he constant whine of the engine, his shoulders aching from the pressure of the seat straps.

The windshield of the chopper was nothing but a black blur of driven rain, illuminated periodically by flashes of lightning, the strikes so close Ari could feel the electricity in his hands and feet. Earsplitting cracks of thunder followed, and as the chopper lurched through the fractured air, he had vivid recollections of World War II film footage he had seen—bombers flying through gauntlets of antiaircraft fire at night over Germany. It must have been something like this. Only worse.

He peered out the side window, looking for some kind of sign—a rig light, a glimpse of the water—that could help him regain his visual orientation, but there was only impenetrable blackness and streaming rain. He was stuck with instrument flight.

The altimeter was never still enough to give a single reading, but the aircraft seemed to be maintaining an altitude of three hundred and fifty feet—give or take thirty feet up or down—depending on which way it was being thrown. The Loran display showed an average speed of one hundred and nine knots. The chopper was literally clawing its way forward into the teeth of the storm.

Ari had become so accustomed to the engine hesitancy caused by the contaminated fuel that it didn't alarm him any more; he simply flew with two fingers on the choke. Mile after mile, minute by minute, he nursed the helicopter along, using every bit of flying skill he possessed, praying that the engine wouldn't suddenly ingest too much contaminant and die.

Finally, just after nine p.m., with the Loran display showing a distance-to-destination reading of less than ten miles, the black sheets of rain parted to reveal a storm-torn seascape eerily lit by a cold moon. As the helicopter twisted and bucked through a particularly nasty pocket of turbulence, Ari caught a glimpse, far off, of a cluster of glimmering lights. Relief flooding through his tired body like a warm wave, he headed the aircraft in that direction.

Bobby Lee Peltier was not a happy man. As if sitting in the cab of a crane for six hours doing absolutely nothing while the divers worked wasn't bad enough, after they'd shut down for weather that little bastard Duplessis hadn't given him time to draw breath before sticking him with a whole afternoon's worth of meaningless lifts. He'd spent three more hours moving generators and pipe racks from one end of the deck to the other, repositioning skids full of oxygen and acetylene—all for some mysterious purpose known only to the toolpusher. As far as Bobby Lee could see, it made about as much sense as digging one hole and filling it with dirt from another; everything had been fine just where it was, but you could count on Duplessis to make work even if there was none to do.

And now, instead of being stretched out on the big, tattered sofa in the rec room, warm and dry with a cup of fresh coffee in his hand and a porno movie on the VCR, he was stuck inside the leaking cab of the starboard stern crane, soaked to the skin, swinging bits of steel in to the two welders who were repairing an air duct just below the helideck. Why in hell Duplessis had decided that the duct, which had been broken for three months, had to be fixed now, in a storm, was beyond him. All he knew was that he'd been on shift for more than fifteen hours, and he wanted off.

One of the welders tipped his hood back and signaled him to swing the crane slightly to the right. Bobby Lee nudged the boom over a foot, wearily spitting tobacco juice on the floor of the cab. The welder dropped his hood back in front of his eyes and struck an arc, the shower of blue sparks whipping away in the wind.

He could feel the heavy crane boom bobbing as the gusts hit it, the metal creaking under the strain. The end of it extended a good forty feet above the level of the helideck, the cable hard up against the edge, supporting the steel duct framework that the welders were installing ten feet below.

A sudden splattering of rain obscured his view of the boom momentarily, and he lowered his eyes to gaze distractedly around the inside of the cab. Bored silly, he began to scratch the word "shit" in the peeled paint of the dashboard with the tip of his pocketknife.

He thought he was hearing things when the faint,

familiar *wapwapwapwap* of an approaching helicopter became noticeable. Wishful thinkin', Bobby Lee, he thought; ain't nobody comin' to take you off'n here tonight. But the noise grew louder, until it shook him out of his lethargy. He set the knife down on the dashboard and peered up at the welders and the crane boom.

He was stunned to see the huge white underbelly of a helicopter hovering unsteadily above the edge of the helideck, its main rotor blades only inches from the crane cable. Ten feet below, the welders were scattering, dropping tools and hoods in their haste to get out of harm's way. The chopper rocked wildly in the high wind and dipped toward the boom.

Bobby Lee never saw what happened next; he'd already hit the deck running.

As Ari brought the chopper down toward the white octagon of the helideck, fighting to keep the nose directed into the fierce wind, the fuel line sucked up a small piece of rotted rubber, part of a torn gasket from the refueling hose he'd used earlier on the abandoned platform. Less than half the size of a dime, it shot through the stainless-steel tubing of the line and flattened itself over the intake of the primary filter, cutting the flow of gasoline to the engine by two-thirds.

The engine began to lose power and die. Ari worked the choke desperately, trying to keep the chopper centered up over the helideck. But there wasn't enough power to counter the wind, and it began to sideslip rapidly toward the crane boom, out of control.

There was no time to think. Ari took the only chance he had. Hitting the release on his seat harness, he jerked open the pilot's door and threw himself out.

He fell eight feet to the helideck, landing hard on

his left side and cracking his lowest rib. As he lost consciousness the helicopter's main rotor blades hit the crane cable.

With a sound like a thousand oil drums falling on a steel floor, the aircraft flipped over on its side. The twisted rotor blades hammered into the deck, carving out great gashes and sending sparks and shards of metal flying.

The chopper bounced once on the edge of the heli-deck, hurtled into the crane boom, and exploded.

A fiery sheet of aviation fuel erupted from the shattered fuselage as it tumbled toward the base of the crane, dousing a collection of half-empty oil drums chained into the starboard stern corner of the main deck. The fumes inside two of them ignited instantly, producing explosions that shook the rig and sent the drums rocketing skyward like giant flares.

The fuselage smashed down onto the crane cab, crushing it, then caught on the edge of the aft deck and hung there, burning. Pieces of flaming Plexiglas and insulation whirled off into the darkness.

Down below in the galley Nelson Pinkham jumped and blew orange soda out of his nose at the sound of the first impact. It was like being inside a kettle drum. Plates and cups rattled off the shelves and smashed onto the floor. One of the cooks dropped a steaming cauldron of gumbo, scalding his lower legs.

In the two-man room they shared, Ben and Rolly dropped the books they'd been reading and leaped out of their bunks. Two doors down the hall Karen Marriot sat bolt upright in her bunk, dazed and disoriented in the dark. As an oil drum exploded on the deck directly above her head, she gave an involuntary shriek and covered her ears.

Emil Duplessis bit clean through his cigar as the fiery wreckage of the JetRanger crashed onto the top of the crane cab just outside his office window. The toolpusher stared at the inferno in shock, then whirled and hit the fire/muster alarm on the wall. A rapid clanging immediately began to sound throughout the NAOC-X.

Men began to pour out of the rec room and sleeping quarters, pulling on boots and coats. Ben hammered on the tender's door and threw it open, Rolly at his shoulder carrying two life jackets. Karen was sitting on the edge of her bunk, her hair down in her face, struggling to get her boots on.

"Where's Pinkham," Ben demanded, panting.

"I—I dunno," Karen replied, still half asleep. "I laid down as soon as we got off deck. I haven't seen him."

"Okay. Life jacket on and properly secured. You remember where your muster station is?"

"Uh—yeah. Forward starboard lifeboat."

"Right. Get down there ASAP." Ben turned to Rolly, who handed him a life jacket. "See if Pinkham's in the rec room, willya? I'll check the galley."

"Sho'," the Cajun said.

Ben hurried down the hallway, bumping shoulders with the men who were running in the opposite direction. He paused at the galley door to let two of the cooks carry out a third whose white pants were wet and steaming with hot gumbo. He was moaning and cursing through gritted teeth.

Ben slipped inside and was amazed to see Pinkham sitting calmly at one of the tables over a bowl of soup, stuffing crackers into his mouth. He waved a hand at Ben.

"Hi, boss," he mumbled, his cheeks bulging.

"What the hell are you doing?" Ben exclaimed.

Pinkham looked down at his bowl. "Havin' a bowl of soup, man," he said.

"Do you hear that bell?" Ben shouted.

"Yeah," the diver-tender replied. "They're havin' another one of their stupid drills. Fuck it; my soup'll get cold. Let those NAOC guys run around in the rain like idiots."

Ben couldn't believe his ears, but now wasn't the time to straighten Pinkham out.

"Get up!" he yelled. "Get a life jacket, and get down to the forward starboard lifeboat right fucking now! Move your ass!"

Pinkham blanched, scrambled up, and fled through the galley door toward the sleeping quarters. Ben walked swiftly after him down the passageway, turning the corner to see Rolly waiting for him outside the tenders' room. Pinkham came through the door a second later, pulling on his life jacket, and ran down the hall toward the stairs to the lifeboat decks.

Rolly grinned. "Found de boy, eh?"

"Yeah," Ben muttered, exasperated. "Where's the girl?"

"She gone along already."

"Good. Let's go."

They trotted along the hallway and down the metal stairs to the lifeboat stations, a series of sub-decks under the main level that accessed the rig's four forty-man survival craft. The international-orange fiberglass capsules swayed in their launching slings as the men boarded them, in single file, through the main hatches.

As Ben and Rolly mounted the access dais to the forward starboard lifeboat, a sudden screech of metal made them look up, and a cloud of incandescent sparks whirled off into the darkness from the main deck above. The gusting wind blew in the dirty smell of burning oil and charred metal, then quickly carried it away again. For the first time Ben noticed a dull orange glow flickering off the support beams of the rig's starboard stern quarter.

He was about to climb into the lifeboat when the clanging of the fire alarm stopped. It was immediately replaced by a softer, pulsing hum. The lifeboat's muster captain spoke into his walkie-talkie, then leaned into the hatch of the capsule and rapped sharply on its roof.

"Awright, listen up!" he called. "We just got the all-clear to return to normal stations, but Emil wants everybody up on the main deck in five minutes. That's all NAOC personnel. The contractors"—he looked briefly at Ben and Rolly—"don't have to show."

"What the hell happened, Bo?" came a voice from the rear of the crowded capsule.

"Helicopter crash," Bo said shortly. "Let's go, people. One customer at a time."

Ben and Rolly climbed down off the ramp, undoing the fasteners of their life jackets, and moved off to one side, clearing the way for the stream of men disembarking the survival capsule. The buzz of conversation filled the air as everyone began to speculate about the crash.

Rolly lit a cigarette and offered the pack to Ben, who shook his head. He gazed toward the stern at the flickering glow on the support beams.

"This we gotta see," Ben said, and the two divers headed for a nearby access stairway to the upper deck.

Chapter Nineteen

Ben and Rolly stood by the first row of valve trees, well out of the way, watching the spectacle at the stern of the rig. Men dressed head to toe in flameproof silver coveralls, their faces protected by bulky hoods, were shooting fire-retardant liquid chemical into the blazing oil barrels in the starboard stern quarter. They looked ungainly, like B-movie robots, silhouetted by the orange glare as they tugged on the retardant hoses and maneuvered for position.

The wreckage of the helicopter had burned itself out; it lay twisted and smoking on top of the crushed crane cab. Another team of firemen was soaking it down with chemical, making sure there were no smoldering hot spots that could reignite. The sound of the fire crews yelling to each other was nearly drowned out by the banshee howl of the wind. It was blowing so hard that men kept losing their footing on the wet deck as they leaned into the gale.

Ben and Rolly huddled back into the lee of the nearest valve tree as a sudden torrent of rain beat its way across the deck, the wind-driven drops stinging like air gun pellets when they hit exposed skin. Rolly swore and stuffed his hands into his pockets to protect them, hunching down behind the valve tree's steel body. The fire crews continued their work, slipping and scrambling on the wet, oil-slicked deck grating.

"Ah'm wondrin' what happened to de pilot," Rolly

shouted in Ben's ear, the wind and hammering rain nearly drowning him out. "Ah don't see no body."

By way of reply, Ben pointed up at the staircase that provided access to the helideck. Working their way slowly down it were a half-dozen men in hard hats and foul-weather gear. Between them they were supporting a collapsible stretcher. A man lay on it, strapped in place, with an inflatable collar immobilizing his neck.

The rain was letting up. Keeping their backs to the wind, the two divers circled around the perimeter of the firefighting activity until they reached the foot of the helideck staircase. Ascending to the first level above the bridge offices, they met the stretcher team struggling to maneuver their burden around the corner of the catwalk. Rolly stepped in to help support one of the stretcher's leading corners; Ben moved back along the narrow landing and held open the door to the rig infirmary.

Alternately encouraging and cautioning each other, the stretcher bearers carried the injured man gingerly through the door and set him on an examining table inside. Ben got a good look at him as he went by: a strong-featured young guy, about his age, with dark, wavy hair. The left side of his face around the eye and temple was swollen and purple, and he was breathing in short, shallow gasps.

Rolly and several of the stretcher bearers came out, and Ben shut the door. The Cajun was shaking his head. "Dat ol' boy don't look so good," he muttered.

"Seems like he's having trouble breathing," Ben said. "That's a bad sign."

"Probably all busted up inside," Rolly agreed. He tapped one of the stretcher bearers on the arm. "Hey, cuz, what happened up dere, anyway?"

"He said he was comin' in," the man shrugged, wiping at the grime on his face, "an' just lost power. He went out the door one way, an' the chopper went the other. Figgers he fell about ten feet down onto the deck." He sighed wearily. "The medical tech thinks he's got one or two broke ribs, an' maybe a concussion."

"That why he's having so much trouble breathing?" Ben asked.

"Med tech thinks so," the man nodded. "He ain't spittin' up no blood or nothin'. Seems like he just walloped the shit outta hisself when he hit the helideck. If'n his head ain't too broke, he oughta be okay."

"He's gonna have to be," Rolly growled. "Dere ain't no way he's gettin' evacked outta here tonight."

"An' maybe tomorrow, an' the day after that, too," the stretcher bearer remarked. He pointed at the helideck and the charred side of the bridge superstructure. "The crash cut all the conduits to the communications aerials. Gonna be at least a day before we can sort it all out. Till then, we cain't talk to nobody. Hell, even the field boat's done took off. We cain't even raise nobody by handheld VHF to relay a message." He wiped his face again. "I gotta get cleaned up. See y'all around."

"Later," Ben nodded. He turned to Rolly. "Can you believe this? What a mess."

"Back in 'Nam," the Cajun said, lighting a cigarette, "we used to call it 'SNAFU.' You heard of dat, huh?"

" 'Situation Normal: All Fucked Up,' " Ben recited. "Yeah, I've heard of it. It describes this little party to a tee. By the way: have you noticed Duplessis around anywhere? I haven't seen him."

Rolly shook his head. "Don't recall. Maybe near de fire."

They walked along the landing to the starboard side and edged out as far as they dared on the buckled grating. Below, the firefighters had extinguished the burning oil drums and were now pulling them apart, showering them with water from the primary fire hoses to cool off the hot steel. Waddling back and forth from man to man, waving his arms and yelling, was Duplessis. It occurred to Ben that this was the only time he'd ever seen the little toolpusher without his cigar. He looked naked without it. Then, almost as if Ben's thought had cued him, he reached into his pocket, produced a short cigar stub, and jammed it into his mouth.

"He seems upset," Ben deadpanned.

"You think so, cuz?" Rolly laughed. "Could be."

A half-dozen roustabouts were securing a network of slings and chains over the burned-out fuselage. Extensive official investigations always followed offshore crashes, and it wouldn't be looked upon kindly if the wreckage ended up blowing into the sea during the storm. Other roustabouts roamed the deck picking up small pieces of rotor blades and shards of Plexiglas— any remains of the chopper that could be found.

Ben and Rolly looked up at the smashed helideck overhead, its torn metal and wiring vibrating in the wind. Below, the crane boom was sticking straight out off the stern, the last twenty feet of it dangling vertically like a broken finger. The crane cab had been crushed into a pile of crumpled sheet metal, blackened and distorted by heat. The stern handrails had all been ripped off, and smoke and steam still billowed from the burned oil drums. The entire starboard stern quarter looked as though it had been the target of a kamikaze attack.

The two divers backed carefully away from the damaged section of landing and paused again outside the infirmary door. Another heavy sheet of rain swept across the rig, completely obscuring its far end and sending billows of steam up from the hot oil drums. Two roustabouts, soot-caked and soaked to the bone, came pounding up the stairs from the main deck.

"Lord have mercy," one of them panted, a gaunt

six-footer with lank, graying hair. "That chopper done spread itself from bow to stern. We found part of one rotor blade clear up by the number six wellhead." He took off his safety glasses, revealing two patches of white skin around his eyes in an otherwise soot-blackened face. "Damn good thing it didn't shear off any of that high-pressure tubin'."

"I heard that," his companion said, stifling a sneeze.

"Y'all are the divers, ain't you?" the first man inquired, leaning back on the bulkhead. "Y'all been up here awhile? What happened to the pilot?"

Rolly jerked his thumb at the infirmary door. "In dere, bro," he growled. "He got maybe some broken ribs, plus a crack on de head dat might be a concussion."

"He the only man in the chopper?"

Ben nodded. "Seems so. Unless you found any arms or legs down there. I didn't hear him say one way or the other, though."

The gaunt man smiled grimly and spat between his teeth. "I tell you: if'n there was anybody else in that crate, he ain't nothin' but a little pile of burned burger now. The heat from that chopper done melted the thin steel in the crane cab. Shee-it, even after the fire was out we couldn't get within ten feet of it until the rain cooled it off some."

"I heard that," said the second man. "Malice, I'm freezin'. We gonna get changed before Emil figgers we's gone, or what?"

"Tatum!" came a hoarse bellow from the main deck.

"Oh, shee-it," Malice grumbled, spitting again. As he turned, Ben noticed the embroidered "M. Tatum" over the breast pocket of his dirty coveralls. "He done caught us."

He put his safety glasses back on and stepped up to

the handrail. "What say, Mister Duplessis?" he yelled, cupping an ear with one filthy glove.

The little toolpusher came storming up the stairs in a fury, paused at the top to catch his breath, then proceeded on down the landing toward the four men. The second roustabout began to cower noticeably, but Malice Tatum stood his ground, an expression of quiet patience on his thin, seamed face.

"What the hell you doin' up here, Tatum?" Duplessis shouted. "How I'm supposed to keep them crews workin' proper when my lead hand's done disappeared on me?"

"Well, suh," Tatum replied in an imperturbable drawl, "I asked Danny Joe to keep the boys workin' while me an' Everett"—he nodded toward the second man—"come up to get some dry clothes an' rain gear."

"Danny Joe ain't got the brains God give a catfish," Duplessis bitched. "I need all them helicopter pieces picked up before they blow away. Get your asses back down there an' keep lookin' until I tell y'all to stop."

Just for an instant Tatum's eyes hardened, and then his calm, respectful expression returned. He nodded at Duplessis. "Yessuh," he said, putting a hand on Everett's arm. "Come on, partner. Let's go get it done."

The two of them shambled off down the landing and descended the stairs. Duplessis snatched the sodden stub of his cigar from his lips, looked at it in disgust, and threw it down at the remains of the crane cab. Pulling another from inside his jacket and sticking it in the corner of his mouth, he eyed the two divers up and down.

"What you two doin' up here?" he demanded, looking belligerent. "I don't want none o' my men trippin' over no contractors while they's tryin' to work."

"We were helping your guys get that injured pilot

into the infirmary," Ben said, his voice level. "He's pretty beat up."

"Goddamn flyboy," Duplessis complained. "He done half destroyed my rig. There's gonna be some heads rollin' over this shit, I guarontee. Main office ain't gonna like this—no suh. Man cain't fly proper, he shouldn't even be in the helicopter. He just cost his company some real big money." He shifted his cigar to the other side of his mouth. "What outfit that chopper's from, anyway? The markin's is all burned off it."

"He didn't say," Ben said. "He was too busy trying to breathe."

"Ain't he wearin' no uniform?"

"Not that I noticed. Just a plain white shirt."

"Ah, bullshit," Duplessis snarled. "He's in here, right?" He gestured at the infirmary door.

Ben nodded. "I don't think he feels much like talking right now, Emil."

"Aagh," the toolpusher scowled, and pushed open the door.

Ari tried to open his eyes, but the white light surrounding him made his head hurt, and he squeezed them shut again.

"Light," he groaned weakly. "Light's too bright. Hurts."

There was a click, and the painful brilliance disappeared. Ari's head swam; he could feel himself fading in and out of consciousness. Maybe if he sat up, his head would clear . . .

He began to struggle up feebly, then felt a firm pressure on his chest pushing him back down.

"Hey, hey," a man's voice said. "Take it easy."

Giving up and sinking back, Ari forced his aching eyes open. It took him a moment to focus, but he managed it and saw that he was lying on a table in a white-walled room, dimly lit now by a single desk lamp.

"Easy," the voice repeated. "We turned the lights down for you. That helping your eyes any?"

Ari exhaled a long breath and nodded. The ribs of his left side hurt like fury. He looked up at the owner of the voice.

The med tech was a military-looking type with chiseled features and a crew cut. Steel-rimmed glasses framed his face, giving him a severe, intellectual appearance. He squeezed a rubber bulb he held in his hand several times, and the blood-pressure cuff encircling Ari's upper arm swelled and tightened. The tech looked at his watch, counting silently.

"Pulse is slowing down some," he said, "and your blood pressure's stable. That's good. Hopefully you aren't bleeding internally." He peered down like a mechanic examining an engine. "You going to stay awake for good this time?"

"You tell me," Ari mumbled. "I didn't even know I was out."

"You've been coming and going," the tech said. "This hurt?"

Ari flinched as a searing pain shot through his right shoulder.

"Guess so," the tech mused calmly. "It ought to. You've got small third-degree burns over most of your right shoulder and right upper back. When the chopper exploded some of the fuel must have sprayed onto you."

"Lucky me," Ari said.

The tech looked at him. "I'll say. You landed right on the edge of the helideck. Another two feet to the south, and you'd have missed it completely. Nice night for a swim." He probed Ari's stomach and groin with two fingers. "Hurt? Stop me if it does."

"Everything hurts," Ari groaned, "but no; not like you mean. It's just my ribs—and my head."

"Uh-huh. One rib's gone for sure." The tech put a hand gently on Ari's side. "Bet you can feel that."

"*Ugh.* Yeah."

The tech sat back on his stool. "Look," he said, "I'm going to give you a shot. Demerol. You allergic to it?"

"No," Ari said, "but I don't want it. I want to stay awake."

"Make you feel better," the tech said. "But if you can do without it, it's probably a good idea. With a possible concussion I'd rather keep you awake for monitoring. Don't want you passing out and not waking up."

"Fine," Ari said. "No drugs."

The tech shrugged and pumped up the blood-pressure cuff again, watching the gauge.

The door swung open suddenly, letting a blast of warm, wet air into the infirmary, and Duplessis stood there, dripping. He kicked it closed with the heel of his boot and waddled up to the head of the examining table, glaring down at Ari. The med tech gave him the same critical look a librarian gives a noisy student.

"How he's doin'?" the toolpusher demanded, taking a plastic lighter from his pocket and firing up his cigar.

The tech grimaced, wrinkling his nose. "This is a hospital room, Emil."

"Wrong," Duplessis stated. "This is *my* hospital room. Just like everything else on this rig." He blew a cloud of smoke. "How he's doin'?" he repeated.

The tech sighed. "He's resting. A broken rib and a crack on the head. I'm going to be monitoring him for a while to see how severe a concussion he may have. If his vital signs remain stable, he should be fine. He needs to be evacuated to an onshore hospital for precautionary X rays as soon as possible, though."

"Merriweather," the toolpusher said, "like I've told you before—you sho' do talk funny."

Wearily, Merriweather pushed his glasses up on his forehead and rubbed his eyes. Sometimes Duplessis was more than he could bear. For the hundredth time he hoped fleetingly that the job offer from the private ambulance service in San Antonio would pan out.

"Whatever you say, Emil," he sighed. "Anyway— this man's hurt and needs to be monitored, at least until we can release him to a LifeFlight helicopter medical team for transport to the beach. Right now, he's resting."

"Yeah, but he's awake, ain't he?" Duplessis said. "He can answer some questions." He leaned over Ari. "Hey, boy. What company you fly for?"

Ari's eyes flickered open and focused on the thing that was looming over him. It appeared to be some sort of aged homunculus, breathing out great wafts of smoke. Ari shut his eyes hoping the apparition would go away, but when he reopened them, it was still there.

"What?" he said weakly.

"Your company," repeated Duplessis. "What company you fly for?"

Ari shook his head. "I don't remember."

"You don't remember?" Duplessis said incredulously. "It ain't that hard a question, boy."

Ari's eyes opened. He looked steadily up at the toolpusher for a long moment.

"Fuck off," he said, and closed his eyes again.

Duplessis came unglued.

"What?" he roared. "What you said to me, boy? By Jesus, nobody talks to me like dat! I don't care if he is all busted up! I'm gonna have your sumbitchin' job, son, an' no mistake!"

Merriweather rose off his stool and got in front of the toolpusher, maneuvering him toward the door.

"The man doesn't know what he's saying, Emil," he insisted. "You need to leave him be for now." He put a hand on Duplessis' shoulder and pushed him back hard. "If you keep shouting, I'm going to have to put in my report that you interfered with this man's medical care. NAOC'll probably be extremely pleased that your treatment of him generated a lawsuit."

That calmed Duplessis down to a slow boil. He yanked the door open, smoke billowing from his cigar. "I ain't done with that sumbitch," he snarled, backing out of the room. "He gots to answer my questions sooner or later!"

He turned on his heel and closed the door with a bang that shook the walls of the infirmary. Merriweather let out a long breath and sat back down on his stool. Outside, the wind's howl rose in pitch, and another deluge of rain began to beat on the steel skin of the bridge complex.

"Thanks for getting that guy off my back," Ari said quietly. "Who the hell is he?"

"Emil Duplessis," Merriweather said. "Toolpusher in charge of the rig. Also known variously as 'The Ego That Walks,' 'Emil The Terrible,' and 'Asshole.' "

"Nice man," Ari muttered. "Not a friend of yours, I take it?"

Merriweather smiled. "We've been known to have our differences. Generally, though, we get along. I'm not about to let him browbeat you when you're hurt, however." He paused. "Can you really not remember who you fly for?" he asked. "That can be a symptom of a more severe head injury."

Ari looked at him. "No. I'm a little disoriented, but I don't think I've got any memory loss." He chuckled, wincing slightly. "I just decided that I wasn't telling that loudmouthed pig anything."

"I see." Merriweather laughed with him, then cleared his throat. "So: who *do* you work for?"

Ari's eyes searched his face. "Does it matter that much?"

The med tech returned his gaze momentarily, then learned over and retrieved something from the shelf under the examining table.

"It matters somewhat," he said, "when I find things like this on an injured man." He held up the little Beretta automatic in its ankle holster. "Not something most oilfield pilots carry."

There was a lengthy silence, then Ari spoke. "Does anybody else know I was wearing that?"

Merriweather shook his head, returning the gun to the shelf. "I was in here by myself when I found it." He grinned. "Don't worry, I'm not going to say anything. If you want to carry a little extra protection, that's fine with me. Hell, a third of the guys in the oil patch are probably packing. I'm just wondering if maybe you're a cop, or a bounty hunter, or something like that."

Ari shook his head. "Just a guy who doesn't like to be helpless on a back road late at night."

The tech nodded. "I can appreciate that. I keep a Magnum hidden in my van, myself. You never can tell what might happen in these little oilfield towns after dark, and we're always getting rotated in to the beach at midnight. I like to be prepared."

"Exactly," Ari said. "You can't be too careful."

"Your piece is under here," Merriweather said, "wrapped up in a towel. You can take it with you when you go to the hospital in a day or two. It'll be okay here in the meantime."

"Good," Ari nodded. "Thanks."

Merriweather continued to look at him expectantly, so finally Ari mumbled something about working for International Helicopters in Houston, a new firm that was entering the oilfield chopper business. The story seemed to satisfy the med tech. He removed the blood-pressure cuff from Ari's upper arm, took his pulse once more, and jotted down something on his clipboard.

"Rest," he instructed, and slid his stool across the room to the small desk.

Ari stared at the ceiling. "Tell me something," he said.

"Sure."

"What day is it?"

Merriweather looked at his watch. "In thirty-two minutes it'll be Sunday, July fourth," he said. "Happy Birthday, Uncle Sam."

At that moment, half a world away in Damascus, Senior Ministry of Foreign Affairs Clerk Abrahim Ghiz put the barrel of a Russian Tokarev automatic pistol in his mouth and blew off the back of his head. As he slumped to the floor of his apartment, the door burst open and two Syrian secret police operatives leapt into the room, compact submachine guns at the ready. Four others poured from a van parked on the street two stories below and raced up the main stairs of the building.

One of the operatives prodded Ghiz with a toe, then knelt and turned his head faceup with the barrel of his weapon.

"Agh," he growled in disgust, looking up at his companion. "Dead."

Ghiz's sweat-stained shirt had come untucked, revealing thin stacks of American money taped to his pale belly. More bills were scattered on the floor where they'd fallen from a paper bag lying on the kitchen table.

The Syrian agent got to his feet and stared down at the pool of blood spreading slowly from the back of Ghiz's shattered head.

"A pity," he said, tight-lipped. "That really is a pity . . ."

Chapter Twenty

Sligo lay on his bed in the captain's cabin, staring at the ceiling. He'd changed into his last set of dry clothes—some old sweatpants and a plaid work shirt—and replaced the loose, sodden bandage around his forehead with a fresh one. Outside, the storm was at its height, the *Circe* twisting and slewing crazily through the ferocious seas.

But the smuggler barely noticed. The image of Luis, eyes boggling out of his head with fear, face contorting horribly as the knife slashed and a gout of blood erupted from his torn throat, played itself over and over again in his mind's eye. It was one thing to trip someone over the side and sail away; it was quite another to commit violent, bloody murder with a knife. The way Turgut had done it was perhaps the most terrifying thing of all: without hesitation, and with no more emotion than if he'd been tying his bootlace.

There was no doubt in Sligo's mind that these people would just as soon kill him as look at him. And yet they needed him; that was plain. If they hadn't, he would have been dead already, bobbing in the boat's wake with a cut throat alongside Luis. No, they wouldn't kill him. They really did need someone to maneuver the boat up to the rig so they could disembark.

One thing he knew for sure: the very second the last man was off the *Circe*, he was pulling away and heading north at top speed without looking back. Whatever Gradak and his lunatics had in mind for the rig, they were going to have to go about it without any further help from Jeremiah Sligo.

Of course, they would prefer to have him dead after he'd outlived his usefulness. They weren't the kind to leave any loose ends lying around. But the more he thought about it, the more he realized that they were stuck: they needed him to pilot the boat until the last man was off. What could they do? Machine-gun the flying bridge hoping to hit him? Toss grenades? They were going to be so busy trying not to end up in the water that they weren't going to be able to do anything else, and once he put the *Circe*'s engine in reverse and backed away downwind, he'd be out of range in seconds.

Stay cool, Sligo, he thought; you're going to slide out of another one. Just play along and cooperate until they get off the boat, then—*hasta la vista*.

He chortled, thinking about the celebration he was going to have in New Orleans. With Luis permanently out of the way, he wasn't going to have a worry in the world. Things were working out to his advantage after all.

Feeling a nasty wave of coke paranoia coming on, he tapped a fingernail full of powder out of the dwindling vial and snorted it up. A fresh burst of euphoria flooded through him, chasing the ugly feeling away. He knew from countless prior binges that the paranoia would recur more often as the hours went by, but he could usually beat it back—as long as he didn't run out of coke—for up to three days. After that, his way of avoiding a horrible day and a half of trembling withdrawal was to pop two or three Thorazines and sleep for forty-eight hours straight while his body sorted itself out. He could last at least another day—

plenty of time to dock the *Circe* in New Orleans and settle himself in for a rest.

He glanced at his watch. It was nearly eleven p.m. The rig should be no more than an hour away. It was time to head up to the bridge for the last leg of the journey.

He slipped his feet into a pair of cheap rubber thongs, and out of habitual vanity paused to gaze at himself in the mirror. He thought he looked pretty good, with his wrapped-up head, long hair, and dark tan. A real pirate.

"Cool runnin's," he said to his reflection, and went out into the passageway.

They were all in the main salon: Gradak, Riad, Turgut, and Saeb, talking in low tones in Arabic. Upon seeing Sligo they fell silent and moved apart, taking up positions around the room next to their backpacks. Turgut and Riad began checking their submachine guns again, but Saeb—his wrist splinted with a ruler and several strips of cloth—just leaned back against the bulkhead and stared at Sligo with an odd expression on his face. The smuggler found it disconcerting; the injured man was almost smiling.

Sligo averted his eyes and turned to Gradak, who was adjusting what looked like a small wire-framed headset. "I'm goin' up to the bridge," he said. "That rig oughta be real close now."

"There are eight legs," Gradak said, putting down the headset, "all of which are equipped with landing platforms ten feet above the waterline. You will set us off on one of the four corner legs."

"Ten feet?" Sligo tried to look confident; he wanted them off the *Circe* at any cost. "Well, it's gonna require pretty good boat handling, but I can do it." He didn't see any point in mentioning the fact that a ten-foot landing in fifteen-to-twenty-foot seas was going to be under a lot of water for thirty seconds out of every minute.

"Now, then, Captain Sligo," Gradak continued. "This is the point at which we must place ourselves in your capable hands. How do you plan to land us at the base of the chosen leg?"

"Well, there's only one way to do it that I can see," the smuggler replied. "We need to go on past the rig, circle around, and approach one of the north legs with the bow pointin' into the seas. You guys all need to be up forward near the bow pulpit, ready to go. I'll nose up just short of hittin' the landing—get you in as close as I can.

"You'll have to time it yourselves; you'll be ridin' up and down like you were on a goddamn roller coaster. Wait till I'm real close, and when you decide to jump, don't hesitate. Go as hard as you can for that landing. If you do it half assed, or change your mind in midair, you'll end up in the drink—and there ain't no pickin' you up in these seas.

"Hell," he said, nodding at Gradak's backpack, "if you fall in wearin' all that shit, you'll go to the bottom like a fuckin' cannonball." The thought warmed his heart considerably.

At that, Riad looked up, a shadow of apprehension flitting across his face. Then his expression went blank again. Gone was the accommodating young man of the first day at sea who'd attempted to make idle conversation with Sligo on the bridge. In his place was a cold-eyed assassin.

"If you put this boat in close enough," he said softly, "there will be no problems."

Gradak smiled. "I believe that Captain Sligo will be only too glad to see us safely off; I think we may have outstayed our welcome." He stared at the smuggler, his leopard eyes gleaming. Christ, thought Sligo, he's enjoying himself.

"Outstayed your welcome?" he said hastily. "Oh, no. Hey, it was a hard trip, but it all worked out okay, huh? You're where you wanna be, I got my money— everybody's happy, right?" He contemplated thanking them for getting rid of Luis, but thought better of it. He didn't want to bring up the subject of killing.

Gradak just kept staring at him, a demented smile frozen on his face. Sligo stole a glance over at Saeb, who was doing the same thing. The feeling that he was standing in a den of lions returned.

"Well, I gotta go topside," he said matter-of-factly, suppressing a shiver. "That rig ain't far away."

He stepped out onto the back deck and closed the sliding door, hopping quickly up on the bridge ladder to avoid a boarding sea. The wind tore at his clothes as he climbed the rungs, droplets of spray smacking into his head like small stones, and he nearly lost his grip as the Circe took a huge roll to port, dipping her rail in a partial broach.

Fuckin' great, he thought, as he clawed his way into the captain's chair. With any luck all four of those A-rab bastards would be washed off the bow and never bother him or anyone else again. He toyed with the idea of ramming the rig leg while they were all up forward and throwing them off, but there was no way to be sure he'd get them all, and the ones who were left would probably come back shooting. Scratch that plan.

The Loran readout showed thirteen nautical miles to destination waypoint. He peered into the radar scope, which was set at twelve-mile range, and adjusted it to twenty-four. A large contact began to glow green exactly thirteen miles dead ahead. Relieved, Sligo slumped back into the chair. At least he wasn't going to have to explain to a gang of bloodthirsty assassins that he couldn't find their rig. Thank Christ for modern technology.

Faintly, he heard the sliding door to the salon bang open, then close again. They came up the ladder, all four of them, fully geared up with backpacks, pistols in shoulder holsters, and submachine guns strapped horizontally across their chests. They wore black balaclava hoods, pulled up off their faces for the moment, and headsets like the one he'd seen Gradak handling in the galley, the tiny microphone support rods emerging from holes in the hoods' sides.

"You look like you're ready," Sligo said, for want of anything better to say. "About twelve miles to go."

"Can you see it?" Gradak asked, right next to the smuggler's ear. Sligo could feel the tension coming off the man like steam.

He tapped the radar unit. "On here."

While the terrorist leader gazed into the scope, Sligo pulled a pair of high-powered binoculars from the console locker and loosened one corner of the forward spray shield. He stood up, bracing himself, poked the lenses through the small opening, and began searching the darkness ahead.

It was hopeless. Between the sheeting rain, boiling black clouds, and flying spray, he could barely see six swells in front of the bow. They were going to have to get a lot closer. He snapped the spray shield back into place and sat down.

"So?" Gradak inquired.

"I can't see nothin' yet," Sligo said, trying to keep his voice steady, "but that don't matter. Between the Loran and the radar we can get right up on top of it. It's gonna have lights all over it, an' from the looks of this contact"—he flicked his finger against the screen—"it's about the size of a skyscraper. We can't miss it."

"It would be unfortunate for you if we did," Riad said.

Sligo pretended he hadn't heard, and gestured

toward the *Circe*'s foredeck. "You think that bow's movin' around pretty good now," he said, loud enough for all of them to hear, "wait 'til we come around and start headin' straight into the seas. I'm gonna try to get into the lee of the rig legs before I turn, but it ain't gonna help much. When that bow ain't under water, it's gonna be twenty feet in the air tryin' to buck you off. You're gonna have to hold onto the pulpit railing like your lives depended on it—'cause they do. Ain't nothin' I can do about that," he added quickly, looking at Gradak. "I can't change the fuckin' weather."

He turned back to the radar. The contact was now eleven miles dead ahead. He switched the unit back to twelve-mile range. Instantly, the contact vanished, then reappeared at the top of the screen, doubled in size. Sligo could see its rectangular configuration now. He gave a low whistle. He'd seen big rigs before, but this one was truly enormous. He assumed it was a floater—a semi-submersible—since the water was four thousand feet deep in this part of the Gulf.

He was starting to feel the paranoid shakes returning, so he took a little bump from his vial, not caring that Gradak was watching him. The terrorist leader wasn't going to bother him now. Reenergized, he reached over and turned off the autopilot, taking manual control of the steering.

"Look!" Riad called out suddenly. He reached up and jerked the forward spray shield off a half dozen of its upper snaps. Sligo got to his feet, and they stared out into the black gale, straining their eyes. Far in the distance, at the end of a lightning-lit corridor of storm clouds, a faint yellow glow appeared and disappeared at regular intervals.

"That's it!" Sligo shouted. "That's your rig!"

Gradak began talking in rapid-fire Arabic to his

team, then batted Sligo on the upper arm. "How long?" he asked tersely.

The smuggler glanced into the radar scope again. "Just under ten miles—maybe thirty minutes."

Sligo kept the *Circe* headed directly for the diminishing light until the clouds and rain closed in and visibility deteriorated once more. He began piloting by radar, keeping the big contact at the top of the scope. As the green rectangle neared the five-mile marker, he switched the range to six miles. The image doubled in size again, and now he was able to make out the eight circular shapes of the legs. He searched the darkness ahead, but all he could see were gust-driven sheets of spray and rain.

At three miles he began to let the contact slide off to the left of the scope's centerline. He didn't want to run up on the rig in near-zero visibility and have the seas drive him into the legs. With only one engine the *Circe* didn't have the power to claw her way out of trouble against the weather.

"Look for it," he called. "It'll be over there somewhere." He waved a hand in the direction of the port bow.

A sudden deluge of rain, as heavy as if it had been poured out of the sky from a giant bucket, enveloped the boat. Sligo let loose a muttered stream of profanity as the bow disappeared from view. He turned to Gradak.

"I'll have to move up on it in between squalls," he said. "I've gotta be able to see where I'm goin'."

Gradak nodded. "But the rain will reduce the chances of our being seen as we approach. We will not wait too long."

"The thing is—" Sligo began.

"There!" Riad called, pointing off the port bow.

The rain halted as though shut off from a tap, and the storm-torn panorama opened up before them once again. Like a giant steel fortress encrusted with lights, the NAOC-X rose up out of the wild sea, stark and immobile against the black clouds swirling behind its high-tech ramparts.

"Jesus," Sligo muttered. "That thing's big."

They stared as the semi-submersible slid by, barely a half mile off the port beam. There seemed to be a great deal of mist or smoke coming off its upper deck, haloing the top lights and partially obscuring the boxy superstructure that occupied one end. The rig faded to a vague, luminescent shape as another squall line passed between it and the *Circe*.

As the NAOC-X slid aft of the beam, Sligo began to bring the boat around to port. The *Circe* began to roll wildly as the seas started to hit her port side at ninety degrees, and she went rail to rail in the trough for five minutes until Sligo had maneuvered her directly downwind of the semi's north end.

Turning the boat into the seas, he gave her all the throttle he dared. At first he wasn't sure if she was moving forward, backward, or standing still, but after a few minutes the radar showed that the distance to the rig was decreasing slowly.

The pounding was incredible. With the engine pushing the *Circe* forward, each great wave became a twenty-foot-high jump ramp. She'd stand back on her transom, her bow pointing at the sky, but instead of pitching forward over the crest and sliding down the back side as she'd done while riding on the sea anchor, the wave would roll out from underneath the hull and she'd drop flat on her keel into the bottom of the trough with a bone-jarring crash. There would be no time for her to rise again before the next wave rolled over her, burying her in green water from bow to stern. Then she would recover just in time to catapult off the wave after that.

Gradak looked at Sligo, his eyes wild. "We cannot

go up there!" he shouted, his voice cracking. "What man could hold on through even one wave? There must be another way!"

Sligo flexed his knees and gritted his teeth as the *Circe* smashed down into another trough. "It'll be better behind the leg!" he yelled hoarsely. "The motion'll ease up once I stop tryin' to move ahead!" He hoped to hell he was right.

Gradak shouted something else, but Sligo lost his words in the roar of water that swept down the deck. Riad, Turgut, and Saeb clutched desperately at handholds around the bridge, their faces white with strain. The rig towered up in front of the *Circe,* barely four hundred yards ahead.

"I'm goin' to the port leg!" Sligo shouted. "Looks like there's more of a lee on that side!" He knew it was wishful thinking. The swells were monstrous at both legs.

Saeb, with only one good hand left, lost his grip as the *Circe* bucked over the next crest and became airborne, cracking his head on the bridge roof. He landed hard on his knees, swearing in Arabic, and was saved from tumbling down onto the back deck only by Turgut's hand on his collar. Sligo glanced down at him, feeling a rush of satisfaction at seeing him flounder on the deck. There was an excellent chance that a man with only one good hand would end up drowning himself during the transfer. At the very least, Saeb wasn't going to be able to hold onto the leg and shoot at him, too.

They were close enough now to hear the faint, high-pitched whine of the rig's generators. The leg Sligo had selected rose up in front of the *Circe* like a smooth, cylindrical skyscraper, dwarfing her. The narrow boat landing at its base was visible for only a few seconds at a time, streaming with water, as the waves rolled over it. A series of long steel ladders ran up the outside of the leg, connecting small rest platforms installed every forty feet or so, all the way to the top.

Riad watched in disbelief as wave after wave surged over the top of the boat-landing, burying it in white foam. He turned to Sligo.

"We have to jump onto that?" he shouted desperately. "How?"

"Timing!" the smuggler yelled, wrestling with the wheel. "You have to time it properly. Wait for your best moment, just as one of the smaller swells drops away, and go—if we're close enough! Then grab that ladder and climb like a bitch before the next wave picks you off the landing!" He looked quickly at Riad. "There ain't no other way, man."

They were a mere fifty feet from the leg now, and Sligo throttled back just enough to halt the *Circe*'s forward motion. The violent pitching diminished, but only slightly. The bow still buried itself in one wave out of every three.

"Well, guys," Sligo shouted. "It's been real. You need to get up forward, if you're gonna go."

Gradak barked some instructions to the other team members, then slid up beside Sligo. The smuggler was about to turn to him when he felt the cold barrel of the terrorist leader's automatic jam hard into the soft spot beneath the hinge of his jaw. He froze, and then Gradak's breath was in his ear.

"Do a good job, 'Captain,' " he hissed. "I will be the last to leave. Until the other three are off, I am going to stay here with you so there will be no—unfortunate mistakes." He clamped a hand on the smuggler's throat. "If one man goes into the water, I will put a bullet through your foul brain. Do you understand?"

Sligo swallowed hard and nodded. Gradak released his grip, holstered his automatic, then positioned the headset microphone in front of his lips and said something in a low voice. A moment later, Turgut appeared below the bridge, working his way along the starboard rail toward the bow.

Trying to stay within the slight lee provided by the giant leg, Sligo brought the *Circe* up to within fifteen feet of the boat landing. Three times the foredeck was completely swept by huge swells, burying the black figure clinging to the rails of the bow pulpit. The smuggler was certain Turgut would lose his grip, but each time he reappeared as the boat rose, drenched and gasping.

The biggest waves were coming through in sets of four, separated by six to ten smaller swells. Even these, Sligo noted, roared over the landing at least three feet deep—but that was as good as it was going to get. He waited until a large set rolled away beneath the boat, then throttled up and began to creep forward.

"Tell him to go in the next five swells," Sligo hollered, "or he's gonna get hit with the next big set! Tell him!"

Gradak was speaking rapidly into his microphone, watching Turgut intently. Sligo saw the man's leg move slightly, but that was all. The bow pulpit rose and fell a mere three feet from the landing. Behind the leg, rolling out of the blackness, Sligo could see the next set of huge waves approaching.

"What the fuck's he waitin' for?" the smuggler screamed, spinning the wheel and gunning the engine. "He's gonna miss it—"

It was too late. The first of the massive waves broke around the leg and crashed onto the bow of the *Circe,* driving her under, shuddering. Frantically, Sligo shifted gears and backed down, trying to get the boat to ride over the swells, but the stern dug in and green water poured over the transom. Sligo shifted to neutral, then forward, and held the bow into the seas as the *Circe* was driven backward. He felt panic rise in his chest. Turgut had to be gone, torn away from the railing by the tons of water that had battered the foredeck.

"It wasn't my fault!" he shouted hoarsely out of the side of his mouth. "The sonofabitch just froze! He had a perfect chance to make it and—"

"Be quiet, you fool!" Gradak cut him off angrily. "He is still there!"

Sligo blinked in amazement. Sure enough, the black-clad terrorist was still clinging to the bow pulpit. Gradak rattled off a string of commands into his microphone, then cuffed Sligo on the shoulder.

"Approach the leg again," he instructed.

Sligo shook his head in bewilderment and throttled up, trying to time his arrival at the boat landing to coincide with the first wave of a small set. This time, he noticed, Turgut was crouching at the very end of the bow pulpit, his feet under him, his hands gripping the railing on either side.

The *Circe* crashed into the trough following the fourth wave of a large set, and Sligo gunned the engine to bring her within five feet of the landing. As the bow rose, Turgut straightened up, put one foot up on the railing, and as the pulpit reached its maximum height launched himself in a wild, sprawling leap toward the leg.

He overestimated the distance and smacked into the steel plate some five feet above the boat landing. A split second later he dropped on his hip into a foot of boiling foam that was draining from the landing's grating. Badly shaken, he scrambled to his feet and managed to claw his way a short distance up the ladder before the next wave surged through, tearing at his thighs.

Sligo let the boat fall back from the leg, breathing a sigh of relief. Turgut was twenty feet up the ladder now, well above the swells, and heading for the first rest plaform.

"That's one," the smuggler said, grinning weakly. Gradak just looked at him.

"Approach the leg again," he said icily. He began to rattle off instructions into his microphone once more.

As he brought the boat in close again, Sligo noticed that Turgut had taken a coil of rope from his backpack and was securing it to the railing of the rest platform at the top of the first ladder. When the bow came within ten feet of the boat landing, both Riad and Saeb made their way up to the pulpit and crouched there as Turgut had, hanging on with all their strength as a welter of foam and water swirled around them.

Turgut threw the coil of line down onto the bow. The wind very nearly blew it away, but by sheer luck Riad managed to snare a couple of the loops with one arm. He took up as much of the slack as the boat's pitching would allow, then crouched off to one side of the pulpit, holding the rope in front of him. Saeb moved up into the same position Turgut had occupied just before leaping across to the leg.

As the *Circe* reached the height of a crest, Saeb rose quickly and made a rapid circling motion with his good arm, wrapping three or four loops of line around his wrist. The boat dropped into the trough, and he was plucked out of the pulpit. He swung in toward the leg, hanging by one arm, twisting and kicking.

Like Turgut, he hit the leg well above the boat landing, but backward, slamming into the steel plate with great force. Sligo could see the grimace of pain on his face as he dangled from the transfer line. The loops had taken locking wraps around his wrist, and he was unable to let go. He hung like a broken puppet by one arm some three feet above the landing, his legs thrashing.

To Sligo's amazement, Turgut seized the line and began to haul Saeb up hand over hand to the rest platform, a dead lift of nearly forty feet. Soaking wet and loaded with gear, the smaller man must have weighed well over two hundred pounds, but Turgut reeled him in as easily as if he had been a child. The man was incredibly strong. He got a hand on Saeb's backpack and pulled him over the handrail.

On the bow of the *Circe,* Riad still held the trailing end of the rope. When Saeb got his wrist free and payed out the slack, he pulled it in and glanced up at the bridge. The next large set was still several waves away. Sligo revved the engine and brought the boat to within five feet of the leg again.

At the high point of the next crest, Riad stepped nimbly up on the pulpit railing, grabbed the rope as high as he could, and swung in a perfectly controlled arc to the leg. He hit the steel column feet first, at least six feet above the boat landing, his knees flexing deeply to absorb the shock, and climbed swiftly up the line to join Turgut and Saeb.

Sligo let the boat fall back as the first wave of another huge set roared around the leg and heaved the bow skyward. Gardak kept talking rapidly, one hand cupped around his headset microphone. Another sudden deluge of rain beat a tattoo on the *Circe*'s decks and spray shield, obscuring the men on the landing.

Gradak braced himself as the boat crashed into the trough behind the fourth large wave, then turned to Sligo. "One more, Captain," he said. "One more, and you are on your way."

Not fucking soon enough, thought the smuggler, throttling up slightly.

The rain abated after a few minutes, and Sligo began to work the boat forward. As the rig drew nearer, he noticed that all three men on the rest platform were kneeling. He squinted into the swirling haze of mist and spray, then realized with alarm that they were steadying their submachine guns on the handrail, carefully keeping him in their sights. He suddenly became aware of just how little protection the thin fiberglass of the bridge afforded.

"I am going up there," Gradak stated, pointing at the bow. "You will move the boat up as before. I will catch the rope, and swing over. If I do not reach the leg safely, my men will cut this bridge in half, and you along with it. If I do cross over successfully"—he grinned like a werewolf—"then you, Captain Sligo, are free to go."

"How do I know you aren't goin' to try to waste me once you reach the leg?" Sligo protested.

Gradak shook his head. "You lack faith in your fellow man, Captain," he said mockingly. "We are not going to use up ammunition trying to kill you, provided you do your job. Once we are all on the leg, I have no further interest in you."

Sligo didn't believe a word of it, but he nodded anyway. "Okay," he said. "I'll get you real close—don't worry."

"I'm sure you will," Gradak replied, and went down the ladder to the back deck.

The boat corkscrewed its way forward through two more large sets, burying the bow pulpit and Gradak a half-dozen times before he was close enough to the leg to receive the rope. Mindful of the guns trained on him, Sligo tried to move the *Circe* even closer to the boat-landing, but Gradak didn't wait. With an awkward lunge he half fell out of the pulpit, the rope slipping through his fingers, and swung toward the leg.

He was far too low. His hips banged into the front edge of the boat landing, and he slipped down the rope another three feet, stopping himself just before he went into the water.

That's it, Sligo thought wildly. He's gone. In one

motion he shifted the engine into reverse and dived under the console.

The hail of bullets he was expecting never came. After a few seconds he poked his head up cautiously and looked forward. Already there was a good fifty feet between the *Circe* and the leg. The boat-landing was hidden beneath a froth of white water, and the swing rope of the rest platform was stretched out at a forty-five degree angle. Turgut and Riad were hauling on it furiously, and as the wave passed, Sligo saw Gradak's head and shoulders emerge from the foam. Somehow he had managed to hang on. As the smuggler watched, a lesser swell lifted the terrorist leader up level with the boat landing, and with a monumental heave Turgut and Riad yanked him onto the grating. He scrambled for the ladder and climbed several rungs before the next wave swept through.

Exhilarated, Sligo leapt to his feet. He was in the clear! The rig leg was fading into the darkness, and he was out of range. The men on the rest platform were so busy rescuing Gradak that they'd had no opportunity to shoot. Too bad the son of a bitch hadn't drowned.

Sligo couldn't resist. He leaned out from behind the spray shield and threw them the finger. "Get killed, assholes!" he yelled, knowing but not caring that they couldn't hear him over the tearing wind. He pumped the air with his fist and shuffled his feet in a demented little jig. "Yeah!" he exclaimed. "Yeah!"

Spinning the wheel and throttling up, he turned the *Circe* downwind and began running north on a heading for New Orleans, leaving the lights of the NAOC-X dwindling behind him.

Gradak paused, panting for breath, as he reached the top of the third ladder above the boat landing. Stepping to one side of the small rest platform, he

made room for the other three: Riad, Saeb, then Turgut. Saeb climbed awkwardly with his bad wrist, Turgut aiding him from time to time. As he leaned on
the platform's handrail he looked at Gradak, who nodded his head.

"Now," he said.

Saeb shrugged off his backpack and extracted a
small electronic box, about the size and shape of a
cigarette pack, from one of the waterproof pockets.
He extended a two-foot antennae from one end, and
pushed a switch. It emitted three beeps and several
red LEDs began to glow.

Turning northward, he lowered the antennae to a
horizontal position and pushed a button.

On the bridge of the *Circe,* there was a sudden flash
of white light and heat, and Sligo was aware of the
sensation of being lifted straight up into the sky.

What's in this coke? was the final thought that shot
through his head before he hit the water and everything went black.

Blown cleanly in two by the satchel charges Saeb
had placed beneath the bunks in the port and starboard cabins, the *Circe* sank in less than thirty seconds, the slick of flaming fuel dissipating rapidly in
the driving seas.

High up on the leg, Gradak grunted in approval as
a spurt of reddish-white light flared up far off in the
darkness, followed by a faint boom. The light died
quickly, and when it was gone, he turned and began
to climb the final ladder up to the top of the leg.

Three quarters of a mile away, as more bands of
rain swept across the Gulf, the storm winds and relentless seas began to scatter the last few floating remnants of the *Circe.*

Chapter Twenty-One

Ben sat slumped in his chair in the galley, idly playing with a saltshaker. Opposite him on the other side of the table, Rolly was stuffing soda crackers spread with potted meat into his mouth. Ben picked up the small can and gazed at the label.

"Beef," he read aloud, "beef fat, partially hydrogenated fatty beef by-products, salt, sorbital, sodium triphosphate—my God." He slid the can back over to his friend. "How can you eat that shit?"

"Ah'm like a car built before de catalytic converter," Rolly replied, munching away happily. "Ah run best on full-lead fuel. Y'all can keep dat diet crap; Ah'd just as soon eat wood chips an' grass clippin's as dat granola stuff you like. What you tryin' to do, anyway? Live forever?"

"No, but I wouldn't mind seeing sixty-five," Ben said, taking up the banter. It was a classic way to kill downtime offshore—hang out in the galley and harass one another. "Besides, I don't want to end up looking like *you*."

"What?" Rolly exclaimed through a mouthful of crackers. "What you talkin' about? All these gray hairs an' dis gut"—he slapped his belly—"come from years of livin' right. An' Ah enjoyed every beer an' pizza it took to get 'em, too. When de Good Lord decides it's time for you to go, you go, son. An' not before. Look at everything you miss out on, runnin' an' liftin' weights an' swimmin' laps when you're on de beach.'' He grimaced in mock disgust, piling another cracker high with reddish-brown meat paste. "Cuts into valuable drinkin' time, bro.''

"All I'm saying,'' Ben countered, "is that your body runs like a car. If somebody gives you a new Corvette, are you gonna fuel it up with clean gas or ditch water? You want to keep it working for as long as you can, right?''

"Yeah,'' Rolly argued, "but you don't wanna keep it parked in de garage 'cause you're scared it'll get a few nicks on de highway.'' He stuffed the last cracker into his mouth. "Ah'm tellin' you, cuz. You healthy types are gonna feel real stupid one of these days, layin' in de hospital dyin' of nothin'.''

Ben was about to retort when the intercom crackled and the preannouncement tone rang twice. "Attention, all hands,'' a thin, metallic voice said. "Attention, all hands. All rig personnel and contractors will report to the galley immediately for a general meeting. Attendance is compulsory. I repeat: all rig personnel and contractors will report to the galley immediately for a compulsory general meeting.''

There was a loud click as the intercom system disengaged. Ben looked over at Rolly, who shrugged, wiping his mouth with a paper napkin.

"Well,'' the Cajun drawled, settling back in his chair, "at least we're in de right place.''

"Pinkham and Karen still up?'' Ben asked.

"Yeah, I saw them both in de TV room.''

Men began drifting in to the galley two and three at a time, many of them grimy and soot-blackened from fighting the fires. Malice Tatum shuffled in, nodded to Ben and Rolly, and sat down at their table with a tired sigh. The two tenders showed up when the room was nearly full. All the seats were taken, so they leaned back against the wall by the door.

Conversation was muted; most of the men were too tired to talk. The room quickly became heavy with the odor of perspiration and wet clothing. Someone grumbled about not being able to smoke in the galley.

They sat for more than five minutes, and were starting to become restless when the side door swung open and Duplessis appeared. He didn't enter the room, but stood in the doorway stiffly. His face was very white.

"Everybody just stay right where they're at," the toolpusher said hoarsely. "Don't nobody do nothin' stupid . . ."

With that, he was propelled into the galley by Riad's knee in the small of his back. There was a collective gasp of shock from the seated men as the young terrorist strode into the room, his balaclava hood pulled down over his face, and leveled his Skorpion submachine gun at the nearest table. Turgut appeared at the main door, also hooded, and slid the bolt of his weapon back with a loud, telling click. Noticing Pinkham and Karen standing dumbfounded beside him, he snarled something unintelligible and pointed at the floor. They both sank down the wall to a sitting position, wide-eyed.

Gradak entered a few seconds later, his submachine gun strapped across his chest, his automatic in his hand. He turned, facing the men, his feet wide apart, and quickly fired four shots—two into the ceiling and a couple more into the far walls, barely a foot over the crowd of flinching heads.

"Quiet!" he shouted. "Hands on top of heads! Everyone!"

Bumping elbows with Tatum, Ben locked his fingers and put his hands on his head, catching Rolly's eye as he did so. The Cajun looked back at him, his mouth set in a grim line.

Gradak began pacing back and forth in measured strides, his gun arm cocked at the elbow, the pistol pointing casually up at the ceiling. He pulled the bottom of his hood up to expose his mouth.

"As of now," he said, "I am in charge of this installation. You will obey every command you are given without hesitation. If you do as you are told, you will not be harmed. If you do not, you will be shot dead."

His gaze roamed around the room as he spoke, finally resting on a tough-looking young man wearing a sleeveless work shirt who sat at one of the front tables. He was chewing steadily on a wad of tobacco, jaws pumping, and staring belligerently at the terrorist leader.

"You," Gradak said. "Come here."

Keeping his hands clasped on top of his head, the young man rose to his feet. His long brown hair hung in a loose ponytail down his back, and his tanned, tattooed arms were heavily muscled. With a poorly healed broken nose dominating his lean face, he had the aura of a street fighter.

"You want to be a hero," Gradak stated. "I can see it in your eyes." He thumbed the hammer of his pistol down and then back up. "You are trying to decide what your chances are of disarming me. And you are not the only one—just one of the most obvious." He pointed the automatic at the young man's face suddenly. "I am going to demonstrate to you why you do not want to be a hero."

As the young man's eyes widened in horrified realization, Gradak began to squeeze the trigger, then at the last second shifted his aim three feet to the left and shot Emil Duplessis straight through the forehead. The fat little man collapsed without a sound, his cigar still in his mouth. He twitched a few times as he lay on the floor, blood and pale tissue bubbling from his shattered skull.

"Heroes get other people killed," Gradak remarked, his amber eyes locking onto the young man's again. "Go sit down."

The other man stumbled back a few steps and took his seat unsteadily, staring at the toolpusher's lifeless body. The crotch of Duplessis' green coveralls darkened with urine as the abdominal muscles relaxed in death.

"Oh, Jeezus," someone said weakly.

"A minor prophet," Gradak said, "who isn't likely to appear here and perform magic tricks." He waved the pistol again. "I will kill the next man who speaks, and the two men on either side of him."

Even the sound of breathing in the room became muted. Gradak walked slowly back and forth, his wet boots creaking. When Saeb appeared at the side door, he conferred with him briefly, then turned back to face his unwilling audience.

"You six," he commanded, gesturing at Ben and Rolly's table. "Stand up. You will go with these men. Single file, hands on top of heads." Riad and Saeb moved up on either side of Gradak, submachine guns at the ready.

Malice Tatum went first, shuffling forward like a great, shambling skeleton, his eyes downcast. Ben followed him, then Rolly, and the other three who'd been sitting at their table. They were ushered out the side door, Riad leading the way, Saeb a few steps behind the last man.

They were marched down to the end of the hallway and up the staircase to the main deck. Outside, the storm was still raging, and they leaned into the tearing wind as they filed across the expanse of grating to a large corrugated-steel utility shed next to the wellheads.

Riad pulled open the heavy steel door and waved his submachine gun. "In!" he shouted over the wind.

One by one, they stepped over the threshold into

near-total darkness. Ben banged his elbow on something metallic and swore under his breath. He groped
his way along to the rear of the shed, finally coming up
against what felt like a couple of acetylene cylinders.
Someone brushed against him in the dark, and as he
turned and stepped aside, the door slammed shut with
a hollow, reverberating boom.

They stood in pitch-blackness for several minutes,
unsure if it was safe to speak aloud. Then there was
a quick scraping sound, and a small flame erupted in
the center of the shed at eye level. Rolly held his
Zippo lighter at arm's length, slowly panning it
around, his swarthy features illuminated by the guttering light.

Ben moved over beside his friend and glanced
around the shed's interior. It appeared to be used primarily for the storage of paint. There were hundreds
of one-gallon cans stacked on metal shelves that ran
down one wall from floor to ceiling. Along the rear
wall were a half-dozen oxygen bottles, secured upright
by a single loose chain, and an assortment of high-
pressure valves, some of which were stripped down to
empty housings. The acetylene cylinders Ben had run
into were standing free in the corner, and a tangled
coil of rotted oxyacetylene torch hose was piled up
on the floor plates next to them. An eight-foot-tall
equipment locker nearly hid the only window, a four-
teen-inch square of greasy glass that had been barred
inside and out to prevent tool theft. Virtually no external light penetrated the filthy, opaque pane.

Ben walked carefully up to the door and tried it. It
was locked. He counted his steps as he returned to
the rear of the shed. Twelve. The temporary cell was
about forty feet long, and maybe twenty wide. Unlike
most of the rig's upper level, which was decked over
with grating, the floor in here was solid steel plate,
devoid of hatches. The door was the only way out.

The wind rose to a scream outside, and the shed's walls and roof flexed, creaking and rattling in tinny protest. Ben reached up and tugged on the bars covering the window. They were absolutely solid, without a hint of give. After yanking on them several more times, he let go with an exasperated sigh and turned to face Rolly, who was still holding up the lighter.

"You look like the goddamn Statue of Liberty," he muttered, at a loss for anything better to say.

"Ah wish Ah was de goddamn Statue of Liberty," Rolly grumbled in reply. "If Ah was, Ah'd be standin' in New York, an' not here."

The lighter flame flickered and went out, leaving them in total darkness again. Rolly sparked the flint several times, unsuccessfully trying to relight it.

"Let's leave it out," Ben suggested. "We may need it later. There's no point in burning up all the fluid just so we can stare at each other."

One of the rig hands finally found his voice. "Who the fuck are them guys?" he asked in a shaky whisper. "How'd they get aboard?"

"Who cares how they got aboard?" cut in another man. "They's here. What I wanna know is what they's gonna do. Christ, did y'all see that bastard blow away Duplessis? I nearly pissed my pants when he done that!" His voice was rising, panicky. "We all gonna end up the same way? How come they picked us six to come up here? What are we, special? We—"

Ben cut him off. Panic was contagious. "Hey, cool down!" he said. "Getting all wired up isn't going to change anything. I have a feeling there are going to be a lot more people in this shed pretty soon, and we don't need a crowd of men jammed in here in the dark, all losing it." The frightened rig hand's hyperventilating slowed somewhat. "All right," Ben continued. "This is the way I see it:

"These guys look like terrorists to me—you know:

the *Achille Lauro,* the Munich Olympics—that kind of thing. I can't be sure, because I saw the one who was doing all the talking only for a moment, but when he pulled the hood he was wearing up off his mouth, I noticed that his teeth were stained red. I worked a pipeline job in Bahrain a couple of years back and saw a lot of the locals chewing betel nuts; they turn your mouth that red color.

"So, my guess is that they belong to some Arab terrorist group that wants to make a statement in the U.S." He paused. "You know: take hostages, blow something up."

"Man," somebody said, "I thought that shit only happened on airplanes."

"Guess it's our turn," Ben said. "Can you think of anything that makes a more vulnerable target than an offshore oil rig? No customs or immigration to get past; no cops or soldiers; a wide-open escape route in almost every direction . . ."

"An' a whole lotta stuff dat explodes with a big bang," Rolly concluded. The Zippo flashed on and off as he lit a cigarette. "Mother Mary," he said slowly. "Dis damn rig ain't nothin' but a giant firecracker."

"Oh, God," the spooked rig hand moaned, hyperventilating again, "oh, God . . ."

"Shut up, Duane!" snapped the crewman who'd spoken first. "You ain't helpin' none actin' like a scairt fuckin' woman!"

"Fuck you right back, Texas!" Duane sobbed. "You ain't got no wife, an' kids, an' a mortgage, an' a payment on a new bass boat—"

"Oh, Christ!" Texas fumed in exasperation. "Bass boat? We're out here about to get our asses shot away or blowed up, an' you're frettin' over a goddamn toy boat! You on the same planet as the rest of us, or what?"

Rolly flicked on the lighter, scowling, and Ben

moved over in front in Texas, taking him by the shoulders. Malice Tatum restrained the teary Duane, talking to him in a low, rumbling drawl. The third rig hand stayed where he was, slumped against the paint shelves, looking blankly from man to man. He appeared semi-paralyzed.

"Great fuckin' party," Rolly muttered, to no one in particular.

The latch on the door rattled suddenly, drawing everyone's attention. Rolly snuffed the lighter. The door flew open with a bang, pushed by the gusting wind, and men began to enter the shed in single file, hands clasped on top of heads. They walked with uncertain, shuffling steps, blinking into the darkness. Ben counted twelve new bodies before the door slammed shut again, cutting off the dim light. The latest arrivals groped around in fearful silence, trying to orient themselves.

Malice's slow, lazy drawl sounded much louder than usual within the confines of the shed:

"Howdy, boys. Once y'all get settled in, I'd sure appreciate the loan of a cheekful o' chew."

A half hour later, Riad locked the shed door behind the last of the men who'd assembled in the galley. Saeb took up a guard position in the lee of the nearest wellhead, sitting on an inverted five-gallon bucket with his Skorpion across his knees. Nodding to him, Riad trotted over to the lower-deck access stairwell and ducked inside.

He descended the stairs and ran down the hallway to the galley. Gradak and Turgut were leaning over one of the tables, studying a small blueprint. The terrorist leader was pointing to piping locations circled in red ink.

"Here," he said. "Here. And here. On the upstream side of these check valves." He turned the blueprint over, revealing another diagram on its opposite side. "And in these three locations, on the fuel-storage tanks for the main generators. One satchel per target point, as planned. Triggering sensors turned on and checked." He looked up at Riad. "You will take locations one through four. I will take five and six, and you," he said, turning to Turgut, "will mine seven through ten.

"We regroup outside the hostage building as soon as all charges are set. Questions?" Riad and Turgut shook their heads. "Go now."

Riad slung his and Saeb's backpacks over his shoulder and disappeared out the door, followed by Turgut. Gradak folded the blueprint, stuffed it inside his coveralls, and picked up his own backpack and submachine gun. Crossing the galley to the opposite door, he headed off down the hallway toward the toolpusher's quarters, located directly beneath the bridge superstructure.

Passing Duplessis' room, he climbed the narrow staircase to the bridge and glanced inside. It was empty. He continued on up to the next level and turned down the hallway toward the north exit.

As he passed the infirmary, he heard a thump. Instantly, he whipped up his machine gun and flattened himself against the wall beside the door. Again it came: *Thump. Thump.*

Taking hold of the knob, he steadied himself, then abruptly twisted and shouldered the door open, ready to fire.

The small, lamp-lit room was empty, save for a narrow hospital bed with rumpled sheets. As he watched, the heavy steel door that opened out onto the exterior catwalk swung closed in the wind. *Thump.* A towel lying across the threshold was keeping it ajar. *Thump.*

Gradak crossed the room, kicked the towel out of the way, and pulled the door shut. Looking out through the single small window, he could see Saeb sitting by one of the wellheads, watching the hostage shed. Far off to the southeast, the angry clouds were beginning to lighten as dawn approached. Gradak glanced at his watch, looked around the room once more, and then walked out into the hallway. His footsteps echoed loudly as he proceeded along to the north exit, pushed the door open, and went out onto the catwalk.

After two or three minutes of silence, one of the stainless-steel doors to the infirmary linen cabinet slid open, and a hand clutching a small-caliber pistol emerged, the fingers groping for the floor. Gasping with pain and effort, Ari uncurled himself from the impossibly tight confines of the cabinet and rolled out onto the cold tile.

He lay there for a moment, then slowly got to his feet, favoring his bad side, and padded cautiously out the infirmary door into the hallway.

Gradak followed the outside catwalk around to the northwest side of the superstructure and ascended to the level above, just below the helideck. Here, sheltered from the direct force of the storm, he opened his backpack and removed a compact, powerful transmitter about the size and shape of a large shoe box.

Quickly erecting the triangular antennae composed of thin, interlocking metal rods, he disconnected his headset from the small, short-range power pack in his breast pocket, and plugged it into a jack on the transmitter's front panel. With a flip of a switch, the unit came on, several red LEDs lighting up as it activated.

Kneeling and holding the antennae upright with one hand, its butt end jammed into the catwalk grating, Gradak grounded the unit to the rig by attaching a short length of wire terminating in an alligator clip to an unpainted bolt head protruding from the wall. A flash of lightning, very near, made him glance up apprehensively. Holding the antennae with the transmitter on, he knew, turned him into a human lightning rod.

Manipulating the dials gingerly, he searched for the required frequency, rotating the antennae as he did so. Finding nothing but static, he flipped on the unit's power-boost switch and kept trying, his frustration growing. Another flash of lighting illuminated the angry sky.

Gradak cursed in Arabic and shifted the antennae again. The weather had hindered his operation from the beginning, and it continued to do so. Unless he made radio contact on the designated frequency, there would be no private helicopter arriving, as prearranged, to pick up the team once the charges were set. He looked up again. The wind seemed to be marginally less powerful, overall, than it had been upon their midnight arrival. Perhaps just after dawn, when the storm—

The lightning bolt did not hit Gradak or the antennae he was holding, but simultaneously struck the only three blue landing lights, of the ten ringing the helideck, that had survived the helicopter crash. They disintegrated instantly as the huge electrical charge raced through the bridge superstructure.

The weatherproof battle lanterns lighting the catwalk exploded over Gradak's head, and his body jerked in sudden spasm as the diffused current shot through him. When he regained his senses five seconds later, he was flat on his back with a searing pain in the palm of the hand that had held the antennae, and a similar pain in the leg on which he'd been kneeling. Dazed, he held up his open hand in front of his face. There was a smoking, charred hole burned into the center of his palm.

The antennae lay blackened and twisted on the catwalk. Beside it was the overturned chassis of the ruined transmitter, every circuit within it fused or blown.

Gradak stared around blankly for a few seconds more, the smell of burned metal and ozone sharp in his nostrils, then began to drag himself painfully to his feet.

In a private study of the sprawling Pass Christian, Mississippi mansion of millionaire carpet-importer Ahmet Daoud, senior Pan-Am pilot Samir Sharif lit yet another Turkish cigarette and rattled the melting ice cubes in his water glass. He looked around wearily as the ornate mahogany door opened and Daoud entered, yawning, wearing pajamas and a robe of deep purple silk. The millionaire padded over to the antique desk that dominated the room and patted the elaborate radio transmitter/receiver sitting on top of it.

"Nothing yet?" he inquired, scratching his overnight growth of black stubble. Sharif shook his head. "Well, then," Daoud said inconclusively. He went over to a small rolling bar and poured a splash of scotch into a rocks glass from an intricately cut crystal decanter. "Mmm?" he suggested, lifting the container toward Sharif.

"As I said before," the pilot muttered, "I do not drink. First of all as a Muslim, and secondly as a professional flyer." He regarded Daoud disapprovingly. "As a Muslim yourself, you know perfectly well that you are poisoning yourself body and mind with that filthy beverage. You surprise me."

"I prefer to think of it as a concession necessary to doing business in the west," Daoud replied. "Who ever heard of an American closing a deal without having a drink on it? They get uncomfortable if you refuse, you know. Bad for future business."

Sharif looked at him sideways. "Oh. I see."

"Cheers, old boy," Daoud said. He raised the glass

to his lips and took a long, slow drink. "Ahhh. There is nothing like a single-malt scotch. Are you sure you won't join me?"

"By the Prophet, Ahmet, no!" Sharif waved his hand in irritation. "You've been asking me that for five days now. The Americans are rubbing off on you. You're becoming as annoying as any of them."

"Careful, brother-in-law," Daoud cautioned, a black look passing across his round face. "We all have our duties to perform, in the ways we deem most appropriate." He smiled again. "Besides, I'm rather of the opinion that when Mohammed forbade the devout to take wine and spirits, he hadn't tasted Glenlivet."

Sharif's expression twisted. "Don't lecture me about duty. I'd like to point out that it was *your* idiot nephew who nearly ruined Gradak's operation, sneaking out to the NAOC rig on a rented boat in an insane—and unauthorized—attempt to kill that jingoistic fool Senator Latham." He laughed hollowly. "Latham wasn't even *on* that helicopter. All your overzealous relative managed to do was kill two worthless aides, more than a dozen other nobodies, and himself. Oh, and attract the attention of the FBI to the main target. Did I mention that, Ahmet?"

Daoud's pleasant demeanor crumbled only slightly. "Let's not insult the dead, Samir. Granted, he was too anxious to impress Gradak, to make a name for himself, and went about it the wrong way. But he was my sister's son. Leave it alone. He's gone."

Sharif grunted, exasperated, and exhaled a lungful of smoke. "He should have stayed in classes at Tulane University where he belonged, instead of indulging himself in some harebrained kamikazi mission that had no purpose and, incidentally, has left a trail that leads right back to you. That doesn't concern you, either, I suppose."

Daoud smiled. "You worry too much. No connection can be proven."

Outside, the branches of a huge willow tree flailed in the wind and rain, scraping across the glass of the study's French windows like thin, hard fingers.

"It seems to be letting up a bit," Daoud offered hopefully, watching the rain stream down the glass. "Perhaps the electrical interference—"

"Of course that's what it is!" Sharif cut in, the strain of hours—days—spent in waiting for a single radio contact etched into his face. "I can't believe that we have no contingency arrangement for bad weather. Without this communication, we don't even know if they're on the rig or not, much less have the ability to set up a rendezvous time. And message or not, I certainly can't fly in this . . ." He waved a hand at the windows.

"That's probably what it is," Daoud said. "They know you can't fly into the storm, so they've delayed the operation, and the radio message, to allow conditions to improve. Be patient, Samir. You were always too high-strung." He smiled indulgently.

"I am not high-strung!" the pilot snapped, shifting in his seat agitatedly. "It isn't you who has to fly out into a storm—or what's left of it—pick up a military team and hostages, and take them all the way to Cuba under the noses of the U.S. Navy and Air Force. There are F-16s and F-18s in Biloxi, Pensacola, Guantanamo Bay, and a half-dozen other bases around the Gulf of Mexico. Suppose they pinpoint us en route and decide that hostages or no hostages, they aren't going to let Gradak get away again? One air-to-air missile and we're all dead. They can always claim that the helicopter crashed due to unknown causes, killing all aboard.

"You think they care one iota about a few oilfield workers? It'll be reported to the media as 'regretta-

ble,' 'unavoidable,' or 'shocking tragedy,' blamed entirely on the 'vicious terrorists,' and put on the shelf.
And that same evening the generals up at the Penta-
gon will be congratulating each other over cocktails
for finally having gotten rid of Ojim Gradak, at the
cost of only one small air-to-air missile and a few rig
workers nobody knows. Don't think for a second they
wouldn't do it, Ahmet."

"You must have considered the risks before agreeing to take part in this affair," Daoud pointed out, no
longer smiling. "If you had such doubts all along, perhaps you should have admitted them and disqualified
yourself. You seem to be suffering an attack of dou-
ble-vision, Samir. Such lack of focus puts the whole
operation in jeopardy."

"I intend to do my part," Sharif retorted. "Don't
jump to conclusions, Ahmet, you don't know me that
well. I'm voicing legitimate criticisms about the planning and execution of this operation. There is room
for improvement, that's all.

"Besides," he added gloomily, gazing out at the willow branches flogging the window in the driving rain,
"at the moment it looks as though whether I want to
go or not is a moot point. If there is no call, I don't
leave the ground." He butted his cigarette in a silver
ashtray. "It's absurd. For all we know, they could have
drowned in this storm days ago."

He got to his feet. "I want a shower," he said. "Will
you listen to the radio for a few minutes? Not that
anything's likely to come through."

"Of course," Daoud replied, pulling up an antique
chair. "Maybe freshening up will improve your
outlook."

"I doubt it," the pilot grumbled, and walked out of
the study.

Chapter Twenty-Two

"Abe, move your fat ass outta my way! Damn, son, you take up more room than a full-growed Brahma bull!"

"Well, you got yourself spread out over half the fuckin' floor! What you want me to do—float like a damn balloon?"

"You're more like the Goodyear blimp than a balloon . . ."

Ben and Rolly sat silently in a rear corner of the shed, their backs against the acetylene bottles, listening to the nervous bickering that had commenced soon after the last of the rig personnel from the galley had been herded into the makeshift cell. After five minutes of jostling and stumbling around in the dark, it had been decided that the best thing everyone could do would be to sit down, and some men were still trying to claim their space in the cramped quarters. A dozen cigarette lighters were burning, providing a flickering yellow light that revealed a crush of wet, haggard, frightened faces.

Malice Tatum sat beside Rolly, head back and eyes closed, leisurely chewing the wad of tobacco he'd bummed. He looked as calm as an old bull working his cud. Ben wished some of his outward steadiness would rub off on the more excitable types in the group.

A figure rose at the far end of the shed and began

to pick its way through the crowd of bodies, amid much protest. As it drew nearer, Ben saw that it was Pinkham. The diver-tender bulled his way to the rear of the shed and knelt down in front of Ben, forcing him to shift his legs over on top of Rolly's.

"Nelson," Ben said with weary patience, "why don't you just stay still, instead of being the only man in here who has to climb over the top of people? I seem to recall everyone agreeing that it would be best if we all sat in one place."

Pinkham ignored the question. "Look," he said, "I know about this stuff. I'm a specialist."

Ben blinked at him. "What? What're you talking about?"

The diver-tender leaned in closer, his eyes wide with excitement. "I just spent four years in the marines," he said. "I'm a heavy-weapons specialist."

"Dat's great," Rolly cut in. "If we had any heavy weapons with us, you'd be just de boy we need. By de way," he added, turning to Ben, "you owe me ten bucks. Ah wuz right: it's marines, not airborne."

"See me on payday," Ben said with a rueful smile.

Pinkham shifted on his haunches. "Hey, man, I'm serious. I had a lot of commando training, too, y'know. I'm an expert at dealing with situations like this."

Ben rubbed his eyes slowly. "I see."

"I've been puttin' together a plan in my head. We can take these guys. Everybody's just got to follow my orders."

"Ozzie," Rolly interrupted again, "how'd you get to be such an expert at takin' on terrorists?"

"Training, man," the diver-tender answered. "I'm a marine. The Corps turns its men into the best killing machines on earth. Semper Fi, Do or Die. We're all heart-breakers, life-takers, and widow-makers."

"Oh, Jeezus," Rolly muttered.

"Nelson," Ben said patiently, "have you ever been

on a real operation? I mean, with a real enemy trying to kill you?"

"Well, no," Pinkham replied. "But the training missions we went on were just like the real thing."

"Ever been shot at?"

"Hell, yeah!" the diver-tender beamed. "We used live ammo on lots of obstacle courses and field exercises. The instructors used to fire live AK rounds over our heads, set off smoke grenades—"

"Thanks," Ben said flatly. "That's all I needed to know." He tipped his head back against the acetylene bottle and closed his eyes with a sigh. "How about a smoke, Rolly?" he inquired.

"Sure." The Cajun's lighter flared as Ben drew on the cigarette.

"Look, Nelson," he said finally, "we appreciate the offer, but you gotta understand that there's a big difference between playing cowboys and Indians at Camp LeJeune—or wherever—and actually having the experience to handle these guys. You—"

"Hey, man," Pinkham protested, "we weren't playin' games! You could get your ass killed doing that training. It was just like combat!"

"Just like it," came Malice Tatum's slow drawl from out of the darkness, "but not the real thing." He paused to spit tobacco juice between his knees. "Ain't nothin' like the real thing, boy."

The tone of his voice was sobering, and a long silence passed before Rolly finally growled " 'Nam?"

"Yup," Tatum said. "Three tours."

"Dat's plenty," the Cajun rasped. "One was more'n enough for me." He drew on his smoke. "Marines?"

"Nope," Tatum replied. "Army. Long Range Reconnaissance Patrol."

"Huh!" Rolly grunted. "A Lurp. Officer?"

"Sergeant."

"Whew." The Cajun looked over at Ben. "Three

tours as a Lurp sergeant." He waved his cigarette in Tatum's direction. "This here's de real article, Benjamin."

Realizing he was no longer the center of attention, Pinkham moved off toward the front of the shed again, muttering under his breath. A stream of threats and curses followed him as he floundered over the tangle of limbs.

"Three tours," Rolly repeated slowly. "How come you ain't dead, cuz?"

Tatum spat tobacco juice over his shoulder into the corner. "Dumb luck," he said. There was a pause, then he cleared his throat softly. "All them other boys did the dyin' for me."

"You sound like a career soldier," Ben said. "What're you doing out here? You retire?"

Tatum let out a thin chuckle. "Retired?" he said. "Yeah. Yeah, that's right. I'm retired." He looked down at the floor between his knees, saying nothing more.

Ben and Rolly gazed at him for a moment, then settled back against the acetylene tanks. Outside, the wind was still blowing with a rising howl, flexing and rattling the corrugated metal walls of the shed. Another sudden downpour of rain swept across the NAOC-X, sounding like a bucket of marbles flung against the roof. The din rose until it was nearly impossible to talk, then ceased as abruptly as it had begun.

Rolly butted out his cigarette on the sole of his boot and tipped his head back against the acetylene tank, closing his eyes. "Well, Benjamin," he muttered out of corner of his mouth. "What we gonna do?"

"Aghh," Ben growled. "Fucked if I know." He stared around grimly at the flickering lighters and huddled bodies. "If we just stay cool and cooperate, we all might come out of this thing okay. On the other hand, they could just open those doors and start shooting. Who knows?

"If we try to do something heroic and it doesn't work, then a bunch of us—maybe most of us—are going to wind up getting killed for sure." He looked over at his friend. "You did plenty of fighting in Vietnam, and so did Malice and maybe a few other guys in here. But personally, I'm no Rambo. A little boxing, a few bar brawls; that's all the fighting experience I've got. I'd probably just get myself and a whole lot of other people killed if I tried to take on those guys. Hell, they're armed to the teeth."

He paused. Rolly lit another of his ever present Marlboros and blew smoke out between his teeth. The seconds ticked past with interminable slowness.

"Okay, cuz," he said finally. "We do nothin'."

Ben shifted his legs. "I guess it's the best thing."

"Sho'. No doubt."

They sat in silence for a few minutes, listening to the storm outside. Up by the front door a man coughed, a wet, hollow sound. Another beat or two passed, and then Ben and Rolly turned abruptly to each other.

"Screw that," Ben said. "We're getting out of here."

Ari leaned against the wall and shook his head, trying to clear his blurred vision. There was a throbbing ache behind his eyes, and each breath triggered a knifelike pain from his broken rib. He focused on one of the floor tiles in the hallway and tried to breathe slowly.

When the announcement of a compulsory meeting in the rig's galley had crackled over the infirmary intercom, Merriweather had checked Ari's vital signs, told him he'd be back in five minutes, and gone down to the lower levels. The Mossad agent had just been dozing off when the muted crack of pistol shots came through the hospital room's air-conditioning vents.

He'd rolled off the bed to his feet, grabbed his pistol from the pile of towels, and fallen flat on his face. Coming to a few seconds later, he'd killed the desk lamp and climbed back onto the mattress until the excruciating headache subsided.

How long he'd lain there in the dark he had no way of knowing, but when the sound of lone footsteps coming up from the lower levels had begun to echo faintly in the hallway, all his instincts had told him to make himself scarce. He'd just had time to jam the outer door open with a towel, then crawl inside the stainless-steel cabinet before Gradak had entered the room. Curled into the cramped space, his broken rib feeling as though it was coming through the skin, he'd barely managed to stay motionless until the terrorist left the infirmary.

Now he gritted his teeth and tried to stand up straight, planting his feet on the floor. The ache behind his eyes was making him light-headed, but his balance seemed fairly good. He took a few tentative steps without steadying himself against the wall.

For the hundredth time, he thought about his reason for being on board the NAOC-X and had to quell a surge of disgust with himself. Some entrance. The whole point had been to land on the rig with a more or less routine mechanical problem, then blend in quietly with the crew. The weather had derailed that plan. Now he was separated from the other personnel, conspicuous to them by his absence, half crippled, and without a means of getting off the rig.

He reached the end of the hall and paused beside the heavy crash-bar door leading to the outside catwalk, slumping against the wall. Lightning flickered through the small rain-spattered window set in the door at eye level. Ari held the cool steel slide of the

Beretta up against one throbbing temple. He had to think, do something to salvage the mission. If he could just find out what was going on, and stay out of sight . . .

The door opened with a crash, and Gradak lurched over the threshold, limping and clutching one hand in the other, accompanied by a hard gust of wind and rain. Both men froze in stunned shock at the sight of each other, eye to eye in the doorway.

Ari reacted first. He swung the Beretta in a vicious backhand that connected with the bridge of Gradak's nose, breaking it and knocking him flat on his back on the catwalk grating. Then, his head reeling, he sprinted along the hallway to the stairwell and leaped down toward the first landing just as the terrorist leader made it up onto one elbow, clawed his pistol out of its shoulder holster, and got off a snap shot.

Ari heard the Formica of the wall behind his head splinter under the bullet's impact as he hurtled down the stairs. He landed off balance in an ugly, sprawling crash that felt like it drove his broken rib through a lung, rolled to his feet, and kept on going, propelled by blind instinct and adrenaline. He could hear Gradak pounding down the hallway in pursuit.

Careening off walls from landing to landing, Ari descended to the fourth level, bypassing the galley and living quarters and ending up at the entrance to the main generator room. He burst through the door and dodged through layer after layer of piping and conduit, losing himself in the maze of heavy machinery.

The high-pitched whine of the diesel-powered generators was deafening, almost painful. Crouching behind one of the immense electrical armatures, trying to catch his breath, Ari spotted a set of protective headphones hanging on a pressure gauge. He slipped them on, instantly muting the sound of the generators to a dull hum. Trying to keep the stairwell door in sight, the Beretta at eye level, he backed farther into the room's labyrinthine interior.

Gradak paused at the first level just long enough to kick open the door and bellow for assistance. Having finished planting his first load of explosives, Turgut was returning to the galley to pick up a second back-pack. He reacted instantly to his leader's shout, dashing down the hallway to the stairwell.

"Down here," Gradak gasped over his shoulder as he descended the stairs. "One of them is free, and he's armed!"

Turgut snapped the safety off the Skorpion hanging across his chest and followed on his leader's heels. They reached the last landing in seconds and flattened themselves against the wall on either side of the generator-room door.

For the first time Turgut got a good look at Gradak's face. He stared in amazement. The prominent nose was clearly broken, the bridge smashed flat between two rapidly purpling eyes. Blood streamed from the man's nostrils, over his mouth and chin, and was clotting stickily in his tangled black beard.

Gradak toed the door open a couple of inches and peered through. The roar of the big power plants flooded into the stairwell. There was little to see beyond the broad, yellow-painted side of the nearest generator's engine block. With a quick nod to Turgut, the terrorist leader crouched low and charged through the door.

He took cover behind a large circuit box, expecting gunfire. When it didn't come, he looked around cautiously, then waved Turgut in. The big man leaped into the room and ducked behind a pump assembly, scanning for signs of movement over the barrel of his submachine gun.

Gradak waited another minute, then started to step out from behind the circuit box. The first shot from

Ari's Beretta skinned his left shoulder, making him jink back out of the line of fire. The next two slugs smacked into the wall. Turgut responded by opening up with his Skorpion, blindly hosing down the entire right side of the room with one long burst. Sparks and paint dust filled the air as the bullets ricocheted off pipes and engine blocks and tore through thin metal panels and wiring. A small electrical fire started in one of the transformer control boxes, spitting blue-white sparks, then sputtered and went out.

The ventilation blowers sucked away the faint haze of cordite fumes as Turgut shucked the empty clip from the submachine gun and banged home a fresh one. Realizing he'd probably hit nothing, he glared over at Gradak, seething with frustration. There was too much steel, and no target to pinpoint.

Gradak's face was screwed up in pain and fury, his amber eyes maniacal. Ari's first shot had just taken the skin off his right shoulder, doing no damage, but it served to drive him into a complete rage. He was literally foaming at the mouth as he screamed at Turgut to advance into the narrow walkway between the generators.

Turgut hesitated, then set his jaw and darted over to the first armature. A second later Gradak joined him, pistol in hand. Nearly deafened by the whine of the engines, they began to work their way farther into the machinery-crowded compartment.

From his vantage point between a series of parallel cooling-water pipes, Ari had let both of his pursuers enter the room, waited until they'd attempted to move, then loosed off three quick shots. He thought he'd seen Gradak take a hit, but he couldn't be sure. The hail of fire from Turgut's submachine gun had forced him to dive to the deckplates behind a support girder.

Now he scrambled along on his belly beneath an assortment of horizontal pipes, frantically trying to find either an exit or somewhere to hide. He fetched up against a wall, spun to his left to follow it, and ran into another one. With a cold throb of panic, he realized that he was trapped in one of the far corners of the generator room.

He got to his knees and glanced over the tops of the pipe runs. There was no door in sight, no ladder or stairway to climb. If he tried to go back the way he'd come, he'd certainly run into his heavily armed opponents.

He was about to lie down beneath the pipes again and prepare for a brief gun battle that could only end one way when he noticed that one of the cooling-water pipes emerging from the wall was missing a six-foot section. Twenty-four inches in diameter, the pipe had been roughly cut with an acetylene torch, perhaps to remove some obstruction. From back among the generators, ten or fifteen feet away, it would not be obvious.

Ignoring his aching ribs, Ari slid the lower half of his body into the opening, twisted around onto his stomach, and wormed his way into the pipe until he was completely inside, his arms jammed up around his ears. He didn't bother to try to keep his pistol aimed forward—if they found him, he was dead.

His shoulders ached in their cramped position. It occurred to him that he might end up getting stuck. The thought of coming to such a ludicrous end almost made him laugh out loud.

The impulse to laugh vanished instantly as Ari felt the faint vibration of footfalls through the walls of the pipe.

Turgut was walking across the numerous cooling-water pipes that ran horizontally across the aft third of the generator room about two feet off the deckplates. Gradak moved forward with him, taking a route along the side of one of the main transformer boxes.

Stepping onto the pipe in which Ari was hiding barely twenty feet away, Turgut paused. It occurred to him that his quarry might have crawled beneath the pipe runs, and he gestured to Gradak to take a look. The terrorist leader stooped down, saw nothing but bare deckplates all the way to the rear wall, and got up, shaking his head angrily. Turgut stepped onto the next pipe, continuing the hunt.

They completely traversed the generator room and, seeing nothing, turned their search pattern toward the forward circuit banks, away from the cooling-water pipes. Turgut jumped down to the deckplates, falling in behind Gradak as he led off in the point position.

Gradak's eyes were beginning to swell shut, impairing his vision, and the pain of his smashed nose and lightning-burned hand and leg was making it difficult to concentrate. He'd never taken the slightest wound in more than fifteen operations, but this time, with much still to do, he was close to being incapacitated. He let the face of the elusive rig crewman with the fast backhand burn itself into his mind's eye, drawing energy from it like heat from a furnace.

Sooner or later, the American would run out of places to hide.

Chapter Twenty-Three

The grimy glass of the utility shed's single window was brightening, and here and there thin shafts of sunlight streamed into the dark interior through rivet holes in the walls. The wind, though still strong, had subsided to the point where the little steel building no longer rattled like a tin can at every gust. Ben looked at his watch: nine-forty in the morning.

He banged the heel of his boot lightly on the steel deckplates. There was a faint, hollow, booming sound. He turned to Malice Tatum, who was stretched out beside him calmly working on a fresh cheekful of Redman.

"What's under here?" he asked.

Tatum thought a moment. "Water tank," he said. "Potable."

"You don't say." Ben kicked the deckplate again. "It sounds like it's partly empty. Or at least has some kind of air gap at the top. You know how deep it is?"

"I'd say 'bout twenty feet. It extends down to the next level—where the sub-deck valving for the conductor trees is at—an' forms one of the bulkheads near the secondary pump room."

Ben coughed slightly and swallowed. "Damn cigarettes. You know if this tank has any inspection hatches, Malice?"

The gaunt man smiled slowly. "Not in here."

"I mean anywhere," Ben persisted.

"Mmmm . . ." Tatum furrowed his brows. "Yeah. Yeah, it sure do. 'Bout three feet up from the bottom on the . . . starboard side, I recollect. You don't never see it unless you get to workin' way back in the secondary pump system. Hard to get in there, what with the tubin' an' all."

"The hatch has gotta be big enough for a man to get through, right?"

"Sure," Tatum nodded. "But I don't think the cover been broke open in a month o' Sundays. Ain't nobody interested in messin' with it."

Ben drummed his fingers on his knee. "You remember if the hatch cover is bolted to a flange on the outside, or dogged in place?"

"I could be wrong," Tatum answered, "but I believe it's dogged."

"Good. That's good."

Rolly looked at his friend. "What you got in mind, cuz? Ah can hear dem gears turnin' in your head like they was in overdrive."

Ben gave him a tight grin. "Why don't we see if we can get out through that inspection hatch?"

Rolly and Tatum exchanged glances. "What you gonna do?" the Cajun asked. "Chew through dat steel deck?"

"Nope," Ben said. "I'm just gonna open the door." He pointed behind Rolly's head. "You're leaning on the key."

The acetylene bottles rattled slightly as Rolly shifted his weight and glanced around. A smile broke across his face. "We got a torch an' hoses?" he rasped.

Ben pulled up a handful of the old hose sections. "Right here. Hoses, torch, and cutting tip. All we've got to find now is a bottle of oxygen and the two regulators, and we've got it licked."

"There's regulators on that shelf over there," Tatum said, pointing. "For acetylene an' oxygen both. Got some box-end wrenches the right size, too." He untangled his long legs and got to his feet. "Oughta be a bottle of oxygen back in this here corner . . ." Grunting, he dragged a five-foot-high cylinder out next to the acetylene tanks.

"Damn," Rolly said. "If de hoses ain't too ate up an' de regs an' torch work, we got us a cuttin' rig."

"Hell, let's put it together and find out," Ben exclaimed, "before the new bosses pay us another visit."

It took less than two minutes to attach the regulators and hoses to the gas cylinders. Ben pressed the thumb lever on the torch and was rewarded with a small hiss of oxygen.

"Crank it up a little more, Rolly," he said. "About forty psi."

The Cajun dialed in the regulator's flow control. "Howzat?"

"Good. How much acetylene we got?"

"Dis bottle's full. Ah got six psi comin' through de hose."

"That'll work." Ben knelt down and brushed the dust off a four-foot-square area of deckplate, then held up the torch toward Rolly. "Light me," he said, turning on the gas-control knob.

The grizzled diver snapped his cigarette lighter just under the torch's tip, and a foot-long orange flame roared into life. Ben adjusted the acetylene and oxygen controls until he'd reduced the flame to a tight blue cutting cone about two inches in length, then took a pair of dark safety glasses out of his shirt pocket and slipped them on. He looked up at Rolly and Tatum, smiled briefly, and bent down over the area he'd cleaned.

Molten slag and sparks erupted from the deckplate, sending nearby men shuffling back, then died down as the flame punched all the way through. Ben began moving the torch slowly along, leaving behind a clean, straight cut about an eighth of an inch wide.

"Deckplates are three-eighths thick," he said without looking up. "Maybe half inch."

"Hit any stringers or support beams?" Tatum asked.

"Not yet."

He continued his cut for another two feet, then stopped suddenly. "Stringer," he said. "I'll burn alongside it." He resumed cutting at a ninety-degree angle to his original line.

Rolly glanced over at Tatum. "Ah hope dem boys outside don't see no smoke leaking out nowheres."

The tall man nodded. "I was thinkin' that. But the wind's probably still strong enough to blow it away purty quick." He coughed. "I'm more worried 'bout chokin' in here than anything else."

"Well, he ain't got far to go," Rolly observed. "Just hold your breath, cuz."

Tatum gave his weary smile and nodded, working on his chew.

Ben had about a foot to go on his final cut, outlining a three-by-four-foot rectangle in the deckplate. Shifting position and clearing the torch hoses out of the way, he burned the last twelve inches and let the cut section drop cleanly away into the water tank with a muted splash.

He shut the torch off and stood up, removing his glasses. "That's it," he said.

The men crowded around, peering down into the black hole.

"Great," somebody said. "We got water. So what?"

Ben was peeling off his heavy work shirt. "What's the water level look like, Rolly? How far down?"

The Cajun knelt down, carefully avoiding the smoking-hot edges of the hole, and flicked on his lighter. "Looks to be 'bout four feet," he said, squinting. "Maybe five."

"Good. That's close enough for you guys to reach me and help me get out."

Tatum stepped forward with a five-gallon bucket. "Lemme dip up some o' that water," he said, tying a short length of manila rope to the bucket's handle. "Cool them edges down."

He dropped the container into the hole, pulled it up half full, and began dousing the hot steel, working his way around the cuts amid small clouds of hissing steam.

When the metal was finally cool enough to touch, Ben sat down on the edge of the opening, his bare feet dangling, wearing only his T-shirt and jeans. He began to breathe deeply and evenly, closing his eyes.

Rolly put a hand on his shoulder. "How 'bout if Ah go?" he suggested. "You ain't gotta do every fuckin' thing, cuz."

Ben flashed his wry smile. "No offense, pal," he said, "but you don't have the wind for it." He cleared his throat. "And if you keep giving me cigarettes every time I want to bum them, pretty soon I won't, either." He slapped his old friend on the knee. "Just get me out of here when I've had enough."

Placing his hands flat on either side of the opening, he heaved himself off the edge, stabilized himself in the center, his elbows locked, then abruptly snapped his arms over his head and dropped through the hole. There was a loud splash.

Rolly got down flat on the deck immediately and peered into the water tank. "You all right?" he called softly.

There was no answer.

"Ben?" he called again.

With a sudden gurgling sound Ben's head broke the surface. Rolly could just make him out about four feet below, treading water and puffing.

"Cold," he said. "Took my breath away."

"You wanna come out?"

"Nah. I'll get used to it." Ben panted some more. "Let me get my wind back, and then we'll see about this hatch."

"Take your time, cuz."

Nodding, Ben hyperventilated for another thirty seconds, then ducked beneath the surface. Though he kept his eyes open, he could see nothing. Not surprisingly, the interior of the tank was completely devoid of light. He stroked hard in what he felt was a downward direction, and felt the pressure on his eardrums steadily increase, confirming his orientation.

The heel of his hand smacked into something, and he halted his descent. Groping around in the dark, he identified it as a horizontal pipe about six inches in diameter. From the way his ears felt, he estimated it to be at least twelve feet from the surface. Cracking his jaw, he equalized the pressure on his eardrums, then pulled himself rapidly along the pipe, feeling his lungs beginning to burn. He ran into the side of the tank after traveling about fifteen feet, and began to work his way back up to the surface.

He narrowly avoided banging his head on some kind of large intake fitting, and then he was gulping moist air and treading water by the tank wall. He could see the tiny flame from Rolly's lighter suspended in the air gap some distance away, silhouetting his friend's head.

"Jeezus Christ." The gravelly voice echoed slightly within the confines of the tank. "You bin down nearly a minute an' a half. Ah thought you done drownded yourself, cuz."

"No such luck," Ben panted.

"Where you at?" The lighter flame moved a few feet in the darkness.

"By the wall, over to your right, I think." The lighter stopped moving.

"Ah cain't see you. You okay?"

"Yeah, fine." Ben began filling his lungs slowly and rhythmically once again. "I ran into some intake pipes down there," he said. "Hope there aren't too many. Or any grating to get caught under. Who knows how much shit's welded to the walls of this thing?"

"Be careful. Don't try to stay down so damn long."

"Roger that." Sucking up one last lungful of air, Ben inverted himself and began feeling his way swiftly back down the wall. Upon reaching the horizontal pipe, he maneuvered himself underneath it and stretched a foot down for the bottom. He found that he could stand on the floor of the tank while pushing on the underside of the pipe with his hands extended over his head.

He made a quick mental calculation and estimated the depth of the water to be at least eighteen feet—deep enough to exhaust a man attempting to perform work while holding his breath in short order.

He groped around on the wall as his air began to run out, hoping to encounter anything that might be an inspection hatch, but found only smooth steel plate. Abandoning the search, he began to ascend again, his head and heart pounding. He passed the horizontal pipe and intake fitting, and broke the surface with a loud gasp.

"Man," came Rolly's voice, "you better come outta dere an' rest. You pushin' it way too hard, cuz. You gonna end up with a shallow-water blackout an' drown like a goddamn rat. You got someplace to grab ahold of over dere?"

"Nope," Ben said, between great gulps of air. "How about giving me a hand so I can rest for a moment?"

"Come on," Rolly replied, stretching an arm down into the tank.

Ben breast-stroked slowly over to the opening and

grasped Rolly's hand, letting his body relax. "Thanks," he said, still panting.

"You find de hatch?"

"Not yet."

Ben floated limply for several minutes, letting his head loll back, eyes closed. He shivered a little. Without the exertion of swimming, the chill of the water was very apparent. Hopefully, it wouldn't sap his strength too quickly.

"Okay," he said at last. "Let me go."

Rolly relinquished his grip, and Ben dove again, quickly locating the horizontal pipe and orienting himself. This time he followed it to the opposite wall. Dropping to the bottom, he began feeling his way along in a counterclockwise direction.

He found the sump assembly—a collection of small-diameter pipes near the wall/floor seam, but nothing resembling a hatch. Impatient, he forced himself along another ten feet before giving up and kicking for the surface.

It was fortunate that he habitually kept one hand over his head when ascending. Otherwise, he'd probably have opened up his scalp when he ran into the rusty grating that blocked his route to the surface. In clear water, with some kind of visibility, detouring around it would have been simple. In pitch-blackness, bone-tired and desperately short of air, having his ascent suddenly blocked was terrifying.

Fighting off the unconsciousness that was rapidly overcoming him, he clawed his way horizontally along the underside of the grating. As the black tunnel in his mind's eye began to close in and the pain in his lungs faded away, he found the edge and gave one final frenzied thrash upward.

He bobbed up through the surface, coughing and spluttering, sucking the life-giving air into his lungs like a bellows.

"Ben!" came Rolly's urgent voice. "Ben! Over here, boy! Grab ahold of dis!"

Half drowning, Ben floundered weakly toward the flickering lighter flame. His hands fell on a mass of wet, buoyant fabric. Whatever it was, it provided support, and he clung to it with all his strength.

As the pounding in his head died away, Ben saw that he was holding onto a small raft made up of three or four old, oil-stained life jackets, tied into a bundle with several wraps of small-gauge wire. A length of manila rope leading up through the opening kept them from drifting off into a corner.

"Thought you might need something to rest on," Rolly said. "Guess Ah was right."

"I ran into a—grating on my—way up," Ben wheezed. "Fucking thing nearly—drowned me."

Rolly shook his head. "Man, you better come outta dere. Let someone else go."

Ben shook his head. "What? Now that I know— where everything is—we should start over from scratch? I don't think so. Just let me—rest a few more minutes. I'll find that—hatch this time." He laid his head down on the soggy orange fabric of the life jackets.

"Okay, okay," Rolly relented. "Just give yourself time to rest up enough."

After a few minutes Ben slipped free of the raft and side-stroked to the wall, conserving his energy. He figured he still had about three quarters of the tank to search. Taking a deep breath, he swam down to the bottom again.

He found the horizontal pipe immediately and set off in a clockwise direction, feeling his way along the slimy wall plates. It occurred to him that if the rig hands ever saw firsthand how nasty the insides of their drinking-water tanks became, they'd probably never put the stuff to their lips, filters or no filters.

Then he found the hatchway. It was a circular opening in the wall about three feet in diameter, with a
short trunk that extended outward some eighteen
inches and culminated in a flat steel plate—the hatch
itself. Ben continued to grope around, and to his great
relief found that the hatch was indeed secured not
by exterior—and unreachable—bolts, but by a single
threaded bar of one-inch steel, extending from its center back into the tank and through a cross brace that
spanned the trunk opening. It was a typical dogging
arrangement.

Ben felt a thrill of excitement pass through him as
he pushed off for the surface, this time with air to
spare. Unless the hatch had additional bolts securing it
on the outside, which was possible but unlikely, simply
cutting the threaded bar would result in it being blown
open by water pressure. The tank would drain to the
level of the hatch bottom, and the escape route into
the sub-decks would be open. There was always the
chance that the terrorists would spot the thousands of
gallons of water draining through the deck grating into
the sea below, but there was an equal or better chance
that they'd be otherwise occupied on the upper levels.

Ben exhaled hard as he broke the surface and took
in two deep breaths before attempting to speak.
"Rolly," he panted, blinking water out of his eyes, "I
found it! And I think we can cut it loose!"

There was no answer. The blackness was total; there
was no lighter flame, or even the slightest hint of illumination from the utility shed.

The access hole had disappeared.

"Quick, goddammit! Get dat plywood over here!"
Rolly beckoned frantically as the lock on the utility
shed door rattled. Stumbling in their hurry, two rig
hands dragged the four-by-eight sheet of marine ply
through the crowd and dropped it over the hole in

the deckplate. Several men stepped back onto it, while others crowded in front of them.

The door flew open with a bang, letting sunlight stream in. Saeb entered, menacing those closest to him with his Skorpion, followed by Turgut, and finally Gradak. The men flinched backward, shuffling into each other, blinded by the glare.

Far in the back, Rolly squinted into the brightness. He wasn't sure, but there was something odd about the terrorist leader; the man who'd shot Duplessis in the galley. There was something wrong with his face . . .

"You!" Gradak shouted, lunging forward and grabbing one of the roustabouts by the shirtfront. "And you, and you!" He shoved and kicked the three men up against the front wall of the shed. They hovered together like a clutch of scarecrows: dazed, bewildered, and terrified. Rolly noticed that one of them was Bo, the muster captain from the forward starboard lifeboat. A murmur began to rise from the milling hostages.

"Quiet!" Gradak shrieked, his face contorting. He brandished his automatic. There was immediate silence.

"Somewhere on this structure," he shouted, "one of you is hiding—armed with a pistol. I do not know what he hopes to accomplish, but I will show you what he has accomplished so far." He raised his left hand.

Turgut whirled and fired one long burst from his submachine gun into the three men huddled by the front wall. Their bodies slammed into the corrugated steel, writhing horribly. One let out a brief, choking scream, then all three slumped to the deckplates, facedown.

As a great pool of dark blood spread beneath them, Turgut stepped forward, ejected the empty clip, inverted it, slammed the fresh load back into his weapon with the heel of his hand, and standing over the bodies fired three short bursts across the backs of the victims' heads. Then he spun around and faced the crowd of horrified men again, grinning like a death's head.

"If I do not find the escaped man within the hour," Gradak shouted, "I will kill three more! And three more every hour after that until he is caught!"

Somebody started to sob. Gradak paced up and down in front of his captive audience, his appearance hideous. His nose, bloody and purple, had swollen to twice its normal size, and his eye sockets were blackened and puffy. He looked like a bull maddened by the picador's needles, deranged by pain.

A movement in the shed's rafters caught Rolly's eye. At first he thought he was seeing things, then realized with a jolt that it was Pinkham. He was maneuvering himself directly over top of Turgut, clambering gingerly from truss to truss, a short length of pipe clutched in one hand. Evidently he'd climbed up there while everyone's attention had been on Ben down in the water tank, just before their captors had arrived. The diver-tender paused, shifting his feet, then moved forward again, his eyes on the big terrorist's head.

Oh, no, Rolly thought, mouthing the words. He swiveled his head quickly and saw Malice Tatum standing stock-still, his heavy-lidded eyes locked on Pinkham. He'd stopped chewing his tobacco. No one else in the crowd appeared to be looking up.

Don't do it, you stupid kid, Rolly implored silently. Just stay where you're at till they leave. Don't do it . . .

Shivering, Ben clung to the life jackets, floating in the pitch-darkness. He didn't know what had happened, but guessed that the terrorists had returned, forcing Rolly to hide the hole. He told himself that they hadn't discovered him and blocked his exit per-

Chapter Twenty-Four

Gradak paced up and down in front of the little crowd of men, pale eyes glaring out of his battered face. Those in front looked nervously at their feet to keep from meeting his gaze. He muttered something under his breath in Arabic and turned to Turgut.

At that moment, overhead in the rafters, Pinkham stepped from the truss he was on to one directly over top of the two terrorists. His foot dislodged an old bolt head that had sheared and become trapped in a bracing joint. It fell through the dusty air of the shed—in slow motion, it seemed to Rolly—narrowly missed Turgut, and bounced on the steel deck with a sharp clatter.

Gradak and Turgut flinched sideways as though stung, and jerked their heads back to stare up at Pinkham, frozen in the rafters.

For a moment nobody moved. Then, slowly, Gradak began to smile, his body relaxing. Turgut did the same, keeping his Skorpion trained on the diver-tender. Gradak started to laugh, an unpleasant, mocking sound.

"What are you doing, boy?" he shouted. "Trying to get to heaven?"

Pinkham responded in the only way his mind would allow.

"Come on, motherfucker!" he crowed, brandishing the short length of pipe. "You and me, one on one!

A fair fight, and the best man wins! Let's see what you got!"

He just don't get it, thought Rolly, dreading the next few seconds.

Gradak looked around at the crowd, arms spread, his expression one of amused incredulity. "Fair?" he echoed. *"Fair?"* he gave a bellowing laugh, genuinely taken off guard. "Hussein's Beard," he exclaimed, "you people really do believe that life is a Hollywood movie."

He jerked his pistol up and fired once at Pinkham. The bullet hit the young man in the ribs, on his right side. His expression changed instantly from belligerence to blank disbelief. The pipe slipped from his hand and fell to the floor as he clutched the wound, swaying between the two trusses.

"You shot me," he said in a small voice. "It hurts."

"But you're a hero," Gradak replied mockingly. "You'll jump down, kill us all, and ride off into the sunset."

Pinkham's knees began to shake. "It hurts," he whispered.

Gradak shot him twice again, hitting him in the breastbone. The impact of the slugs lifted him up off the trusses and turned him backward. He fell silently, hit the deckplates with a reverberating thud, and lay still, staring sightlessly up at the rafters. Blood bubbled freely from the holes torn in his chest.

"One hour!" Gradak shouted. "And then three more!"

He turned on his heel and walked out of the shed, followed by the other terrorists. The steel door banged shut, cutting off the light, and the interior went dim once more.

"Bastard," somebody said.

"Jesus Christ," came another voice, "somebody help me cover them up."

Rolly pushed the nearby men off the plywood, and stepped back himself. He got his fingers under one edge and lifted it, exposing the opening into the water tank. "Hold dis," he whispered urgently to the men nearest him, and peered down into the hole.

"P-party over?" Ben asked, his teeth chattering. He was lying half on the life jackets, clutching the manila line, looking like a drowned rat. "Thought you'd s-sealed m-m-me up in here for good."

"Gimme your hand, cuz," Rolly said, reaching down. "Come outta dere."

"Good idea," Ben said, grabbing hold.

Rolly pulled him up to where he could grab the edge of the hole with his free hand. Malice Tatum seized his wrist, and together he and Rolly lifted Ben clear, dripping water.

"Agh," he exclaimed, spitting. "Thanks." He dropped to his knees on the floor and shook his head. "What the hell happened?" he asked, smoothing his hair back out of his eyes.

Rolly draped Ben's jacket over his wet shoulders. "Dey shot three," he growled softly. "Not including Ozzie."

Ben looked up. "Pinkham got shot?" he said. "Dead?"

"Yup."

"How the hell did that happen?"

"He made a stupid move," Rolly said, shaking his head. "Too much gung ho an' not enough judgment."

"Too young," Tatum muttered, his eyes distant.

"Ahh, shit." Ben put his face in his hands for a moment, rubbing his temples, then looked up again. "Where's Karen Marriot?"

Rolly blinked in surprise. "Jeezus, bro. . . . Ah dunno. She gotta be in here somewheres. Karen! Karen, where you at?"

The girl came through the crowd, looking very small

among the men. Her face was set hard, composed, but there were streaks under her eyes where tears had mixed with grime. She forced herself to smile a little.

"Hi," she said.

Rolly put a protective arm briefly around her shoulders. "Where you been hidin'?" he said. "You all right?"

"I guess. I've been over by those shelves, trying to look invisible."

"Good," Rolly said. "Dat was smart. You just hang on. Everything gonna be okay."

She nodded, staying close beside him.

Ben sneezed. "Agh. Look, I need a hacksaw. You guys wanna start looking around? Get a good blade in it if you can." He turned to Rolly and Tatum. "Think you can find about thirty feet of strong rope? Or maybe even some cable or a sling."

"I'll get it," Tatum responded, moving off through the crowd.

Rolly squatted down on his haunches beside his friend. "What you up to, cuz?"

"I'm gonna cut the dog off the hatch," Ben replied. "Drain the water out of the tank."

"Shit, you got—what? Eighteen feet of water pressure behind it? Dat thing gonna blow off like a fuckin' champagne cork."

"Probably," Ben nodded. "And I don't want to go with it. So I'm gonna tether myself to you guys with a long line. Karen—toss me that safety harness behind you, please." The girl handed him the tangled bundle of heavy straps. "Thanks."

Rolly looked doubtful. "Ah don't know about dis, cuz."

"What we'll do," Ben said, working the webbing up over his legs, "is this: tie one end of the rope to those welded-down bench legs over there. Then I'll swim it down to the hatch, pull it tight to get the right length, and come back up to tie it onto my harness. I'll use just enough length to reach the dog with the hacksaw. I'll go back down, cut it, and when the hatch blows, I'll pull myself back up the line while the tank drains."

"What if you cain't?" Rolly said. "What if it sucks too hard on you?"

"Then, you guys'll pull me up."

"What if we cain't neither?" Rolly persisted.

Ben sighed and looked at him. "Then, I'll just have to hope the tank drains down to where I am before I drown."

"Ah don't like it. Dere's gotta be another way."

"If you can come up with one in the next two minutes, I'll be glad to switch plans," Ben said. "Otherwise, I'm gonna try to make this work." He buckled up the heavy harness straps.

"I got the rope," Tatum said, stepping out of the crowd. He dropped a coil of one-inch polypropylene beside the hole. "It's pretty new, an' I cain't see no nicks in it. We got fifty feet there. That do?"

"Ought to," Ben said. "Should be more than enough."

"Dis is crazy," Rolly grumbled, pulling one end over to the workbench and clove-hitching it around a leg. He picked up a large rag from the deck and brought it back to the hole. Ripping it, he began to wrap it around the rope as a chafe preventer. "Edges of dat openin's sharp," he declared.

A man stepped forward and offered Ben a heavy-duty hacksaw. "Got a new high-carbon blade in it," he said. "We found a whole boxful on that top shelf."

"Great." Ben took the saw and tightened the wing nut that secured the blade, then set it down beside the hole. "Okay. Give me the end of that rope."

Rolly handed it to him, and he sat down on the edge of the opening, his legs dangling over the dark water. He took a couple of deep breaths, then pushed himself forward, half turning with his arms tight to his body as he dropped into the tank. There was a muted splash, and the loosely coiled poly snaked quickly into the hole.

Rolly knelt, flicked on his lighter, and peered in as Ben resurfaced. "Okay, cuz?"

"Yeah. Feed me the rest of that line, will you? I'm gonna need to pull it tight when I reach the hatch."

"You got it," Rolly said, taking up the slack. He dropped the bight in carefully, trying not to create a tangle. "Dat gonna work?"

"It's a beautiful thing," Ben said, treading water. He looked around. "I think the hatch is over there. I'm going down the wall again. Hopefully, I'll end up right on top of it the first time. Hopefully."

He breast-stroked over to the side of the tank, the yellow line floating after him. The water seemed colder now, but he knew that it only felt that way due to his own loss of body heat. Five minutes of trying to hacksaw through a steel bar underwater would change that, he thought to himself.

He took four deep breaths, inverted himself in a surface dive, and headed down. Finding the edge of the hatch right away, he positioned himself just above it, made sure he could just reach the dog, then pulled the rope tight and gripped it in one hand at the proper length. Then he pushed off the wall and headed back up to the surface.

He followed the line and popped up directly below the hole. "Here," he said, panting and holding up his fist. "Add eighteen inches more and cut it."

Rolly reached down with his belt knife, measured back another foot and a half, and sliced through the poly with one quick stroke.

"Anything else?" he asked, pulling up the excess.

"Just the hacksaw," Ben said, pedaling his feet rapidly as he tied the rope to the D-ring of his harness.

"The rest is up to yours truly. Oh, by the way, if you hear anything weird and the water in this tank starts getting shallower real quick, you might think about getting a few guys on that line and pulling my ass back to the surface." He grinned up at his friend. "See ya."

There was a soft *ploof* as he ducked back under the water.

Ari clutched his aching ribs and leaned back against one of the generator room's immense transformers. The relentless scream of the big diesel power plants hurt his ears and numbed his brain. He'd hidden inside the chopped-off cooling-water pipe for nearly half an hour, hoping to give the two terrorists hunting him time to move on. When he'd finally emerged, cramped beyond endurance, they'd been nowhere in sight.

Moving on to the far side of the generator room, he found a narrow passageway, its walls lined with runs of wire and conduit, that led to what looked like a switching room. Sandwiched between two ceiling-high panels covered with lights, meters, and knobs was a watertight door. Drawing a deep breath, Ari rotated the dogging wheel as quietly as he could, brought his pistol up to the ready, and gingerly pushed it open.

There was nothing behind it but a small landing and a flight of empty stairs—no sign of his pursuers. He waited a moment, then stepped over the high threshold and pulled the door to behind him. The whine of the generators faded back into the general hum of the rig.

He began to ascend the stairs, pausing at each landing to glance around the corner before continuing. The staircase was leading back up through all the deck levels. He passed the galley deck, the main deck, and entered the bridge superstructure.

The final landing was four levels up. Kneeling, he cracked open the heavy steel door and looked down the hallway. It was deserted, the dim wall lights reflecting dully off the polished tile floor. As on the levels immediately below, there were a half-dozen doors in each side of the hallway, most likely crew's quarters and offices.

Ari padded silently over to the nearest door and tried it. Locked. Moving on to the next one, he found it open and stepped inside, pulling the door shut behind him.

The room was dark and smelled of disinfectant. Two bunks, each with a metal stand-up locker at its foot, lay along opposite walls, separated by a simple nightstand. Heavy curtains were drawn over the single window.

Ari pulled the curtains aside slightly with one finger and looked out through the smudged glass. The sun had already gone down, but there was still enough daylight to see the entire main deck of the NAOC-X. A black-clad, heavily armed terrorist still sat outside the shed where the crew of the rig was being kept, smoking a cigarette. At the far end of the deck, another dark figure hurried along the railing, carrying a backpack, and disappeared down an external stairway.

Ari let the curtain close gently and sat down on one of the bunks, favoring his injured side. The intelligence report he'd read on Gradak a week previously hadn't specified the number of men the master terrorist planned to use on this operation, but Ari felt that from what he'd seen, the number was small, probably no more than six. That was good; it should be relatively easy to find a secure vantage point and hide for a while. They wouldn't have time to look for him—not until the rig was completely mined, and they'd still have to leave one or two men guarding the captive crew.

He lay back on the bunk, fatigued almost to the point of numbness, and closed his eyes. He'd just relax for a minute, to rally what little energy he had left. A wry smile crossed his face. The fools trying to kill him didn't know it, but he was really their ace in the hole, in a manner of thinking . . .

He was still smiling as he dropped off to sleep.

Ben broke the surface, gasping, and grabbed hold of the bundle of life jackets floating below the hole. As he regained his wind, he held up his right hand near Rolly's lighter flame and examined it, scowling. Watery blood streamed down his wrist and forearm in little rivulets; he'd barked his knuckles badly.

"I slipped," he panted. "I was sawing on the bar like crazy, and the blade jumped out of the kerf. I punched my hand right into the fucking thing."

"What you do dat for?" Rolly inquired.

"Dunno," Ben deadpanned. "Probably just wanted it to be a little more exciting."

Rolly leaned farther into the hole, bringing the lighter closer. "How's it goin'? Almost through?"

Ben nodded, breathing deeply. "Yeah. About three quarters cut. Two, maybe three more dives, and she oughta blow." He coughed. "I was thinking about changing the saw blade, but I think I'll just go with what I've got."

"You sure? Ain't no problem to change it."

"Nah, it's fine."

"Sure wish I could help some," came Tatum's lazy drawl from behind Rolly, "but I don't figger I'd do too good."

"Yeah?" Ben said, grinning up wearily. "Why's that?"

"I cain't swim," Tatum replied.

Ben nodded. "Yup. That'll more or less disqualify you for this kind of work. Okay," he said. "I'm going again."

"Watch your hand dis time," Rolly called as Ben's

head submerged. "Good thing dere ain't no triggerfish in here," he muttered to himself.

"Triggerfish?" Tatum said. "Why?"

Rolly sat back up from the hole, stretching his aching neck. " 'Cause he's bleedin'," he said. "They're like vampires when they smell blood. Come swarmin' in an' bite at you 'til you cain't hardly work no more."

"That don't sound good," Tatum reflected.

"It ain't." Rolly sighed and stuck a fresh Marlboro in his mouth. "Just another part of dis glamorous job we do."

Ben stroked directly down to the hatch without first going to the wall of the tank, well oriented after a half-dozen dives. The hacksaw was where he'd left it, stuck in the nearly completed cut through the threaded bar of the dog. As the carefully measured tethering line attached to his harness drew tight, holding him just above the hatch, he gripped the handle of the tool and began to saw rapidly. It was awkward, but he was able to brace himself by getting a foot back up on the underside of the horizontal pipe that spanned the tank. The leverage was poor, but it would have to do.

He cut frantically for about thirty seconds, his arm aching, then rested for a moment. He was already running out of air, and each successive dive reduced the time he was able to hold his breath. Steeling himself for a few more strokes before heading up again, he squeezed the saw tightly and drew it back through the kerf.

He flexed his arm muscles, bore down, and the threaded bar broke on the first stroke. The saw was ripped out of his hand, and he was spun into an upright position, water sucking at his legs and torso with incredible force. There was a dull roaring sound.

The sudden violence of it made him gasp in surprise, losing half the air in his lungs. His legs vibrated uncontrollably; he'd been sucked into the hatch opening up to his knees. The safety harness slid up tight around his armpits and shoulders, cutting into his flesh like a garotte wire, the tethering line as taut as a bowstring.

He tried feebly to get a grip on the line as the dull ache behind his breastbone intensified and his head began to throb. It was like trying to move through a torrent of wet cement. The air hunger became so severe that he scarcely noticed the pain of his knees and ankles banging against the sides of the hatch.

The tunnel vision a drowning man often experiences began to close in around his mind's eye. Then all at once the pain subsided. The ache in his chest and the pounding behind his eyes disappeared, to be replaced by a warm, floating feeling. He was aware that something was tearing at his body, but he felt separated from it, as though it was happening far away. The tunnel became smaller and smaller, until there was only blackness . . .

Rolly nearly dropped his lighter as there came a sudden loud crack, and the entire inside of the water tank seemed to heave in and out like a giant bellows. The steel deckplates on which he was lying began to vibrate, and a muted rushing sound began to come up through the hole. Ben's tethering line cracked as it became drum-tight, quivering under the strain.

"Shit!" Rolly grabbed the line and shook it. It had no more play in it than a steel bar. He tried to pull back on it, but could get nothing.

"Malice!" he shouted, scrambling to his knees. "Grab ahold!" He gripped the line with both hands just below the lip of the hole and heaved.

Tatum knelt and got his hands on either side of Rolly's. Together they hauled until their legs shook and their spines felt about to separate, but succeeded only in scraping the calluses off their hands.

"Godfuckindammit!" Rolly cursed, frantic. He lay down again and stuck his head into the hole. Flicking on the lighter, he saw that the water's surface was now eight feet below him and dropping fast.

"Get on dis here line!" he barked to the men standing nearest the opening. Two of them jumped forward. "De water's gettin' lower real quick! De shallower it is, de easier it's gonna be to haul Ben outtta there!" He seized the rope again. "Pull!"

The four men heaved for a full thirty seconds, to no avail. Then all at once something gave, and they began to gain back line a foot at a time. Rolly dropped prone immediately and flicked his lighter in the hole. The rope was nearly vertical, stretching down to the waterline some fourteen feet below.

The men gave one more heave, and Ben's head and shoulders broke the surface. He was limp. Rolly felt himself go numb inside. He was about to yell at the men on the line to pull Ben up when his friend's head lolled back and he began to cough weakly. One of his arms stirred and came up to his face.

"Hold it, hold it!" Rolly said over his shoulder. The water was below Ben's knees now, and he dangled like a puppet in his harness, rotating slowly at the end of the tethering line. He hung just below the long horizontal pipe that spanned the tank. Rolly pushed the line to the side of the hole, gaining an extra foot of clearance, then nodded to the men.

"Okay, pick 'im up. Gentle, now."

They brought Ben up slowly, grunting with the strain of lifting his dead weight. As his head and shoulders appeared in the opening, there came a loud sucking sound from the bottom of the tank; the water level had dropped below the top edge of the access hatch. While he got his arms under Ben's and lifted, Rolly caught a glimpse of white light shafting into the tank's interior.

They laid Ben back on the deckplates, a bundled-up coat under his head. His eyes were still closed, his face waxy and pale. His breathing was ragged and interrupted by convulsive swallowing. Rolly took his pulse; it was rapid, fluttering.

"Is he drownded?" someone asked.

"Yeah, basically," Rolly replied, one hand behind Ben's neck, the other monitoring the pulse under his ear. "But he's breathin' on his own, and his heart's still pumpin'. So we just gotta wait—keep his airway open and make sure he don't get no worse."

"Where's that med tech, um, Merriweather? Where's he at?" asked one of the onlooking men.

"He's layin' up front under that canvas with Bo an' them other two poor slobs," another man said quietly.

"Oh."

"Hey, gimme a couple of coats down here," Rolly interrupted, feeling Ben shiver under his hands. "We wanna warm him up some."

They tucked several work jackets around Ben's chest and legs. The men pressed in close, watching silently. Karen stepped out of the crowd and knelt beside Rolly. She took one of Ben's hands in hers and began to massage it. "He's cold," she said.

"Yeah," Rolly muttered. "He was in dere way too long. I hope he don't go into shock on us."

Ben's eyes fluttered open. "Shock?" he said hoarsely. "Not me, bro."

There was a collective sigh of relief from the onlookers, and Rolly grinned at his friend. "What you tryin' to do, cuz? Scare de fear of God into me?"

"Hell, no. I wouldn't waste my time trying to do the impossible." Ben coughed and turned his head to spit water. "Hey, Karen. How you doin'?"

"Okay." The girl smiled from ear to ear. "We were afraid you'd gotten yourself killed."

Ben shook his head. "Nah. Not this time."

"It was a pretty good try," Rolly growled, sitting back on his haunches and digging for his cigarettes. "Smoke?"

"Hell, no. Right now it'd probably do me in."

The burbling sounds echoing up out of the tank diminished and then ceased entirely. Tatum knelt and stuck his head into the hole. "Water's down to the bottom of the hatch," he announced. "She's as empty as she's gonna get."

He sat back on his lean haunches. "That's it. Back door's open, y'all."

Chapter Twenty-Five

"Okay," Ben said. "Listen up, everybody."

He was sitting on the edge of the hole, one hand gripping the descent rope. Rolly and Tatum had retied it to an overhead beam so that it hung straight down into the water tank.

"The way I see it, the most important thing we all have to do is get the hell off this rig and away from these assholes with the guns. The best way to do that is to abandon ship using the lifeboats." Ben paused for a moment. "Only do it really, *really* fast."

A low mutter rose from the crowd as Ben went on:

"We've all been divided into four different groups, each corresponding to lifeboats A, B, C, and D, right? Anybody not know which lifeboat group they were assigned to when they came aboard this rig?" Silence. "No? Good. Where are the four muster captains?"

There was a general shuffling as four men moved to the front rank of the throng. Texas was one; the other three Ben didn't know.

He cleared his throat. "Here's the deal: we organize ourselves into the four boat groups. Then each muster captain leads his group, as quickly and quietly as possible, to the proper boat. We load up, lower the boats, and float away." There was another awkward silence. "If anybody has a better idea," Ben said dryly, "now's the time."

"Well, shit," came Duane's whiny voice from somewhere in the back of the crowd. "What if'n we run into them dudes on the way to the boats? What about the storm? What if'n it takes too long to lower the boats an' they catch us? What if'n they come back here while some of us is still waitin' to go? What if'n— "

"Will you shut the fuck *up,* Duane!" Texas exploded, balling his fists and vainly trying to glare at the other man in the darkness. "Cain't you say somethin' helpful for a change, instead of bringin' up the worst things that can happen? We all know what them guys'll do if'n they catch us. You don't have to remind us, you little cockroach!"

"Easy for you to say," Duane began. "You ain't got the family responsibilities that I—"

"All right, all right!" Ben shouted. "We don't have time for this!" He lowered his voice and continued, eyeing Texas. "If you don't stop to do all the safety checks first, how fast can you drop those lifeboats to the water?"

"Pretty quick," Texas replied. "They've got a new system on 'em. It's almost like a controlled free fall: throw one lever an' they drop like stones to 'bout twenty feet above the surface, then a friction brake kicks in to slow 'em up before they splash down. We've done it a few times, runnin' drills. Works pretty good, but that last jolt can really rattle your spine."

"Is it better than being shot full of holes?" Ben asked.

"Oh, yeah."

"Okay, so basically everyone can just pile in at top speed, slam the hatch, and the boat can drop, right?"

"Right," Texas said. "Throw the releases on the lowerin' cables an' we all drift away downwind."

"And they sho' ain't gonna follow us, cuz," Rolly remarked. "Ah'd bet mah big money on dat."

"All right," Ben said. "That's it, then. Keep to the

lower catwalks, move quickly, and keep your eyes open. When you get to your boats, don't wait—go. If anybody can't keep up with their group, they're gonna get left, so stay with your people. Rolly?" The Cajun stooped down beside Ben. "You and I are going to go down first and see if the way's clear, as far as we can. Karen? Come here for a second." The girl stepped forward. Ben got to his feet and put a hand on her shoulder. "Who's in charge of lifeboat A?" One of the muster captains raised his hand. "She goes in the first boat with you," Ben said, ushering Karen toward him.

"Hey," a voice whined. "She gets to go in the first boat? What about women's lib an' all that shit?"

"Shut up, Duane," snarled a dozen or so men in unison.

"My partner and I are going in the last boat," Ben continued. He glanced down at Rolly, who shrugged and nodded. "Whose boat is that?"

Texas waved a finger. "That'd be me."

"Good." Ben blew a deep breath out one corner of his mouth. "Well, ol' buddy," he said, dropping a hand to Rolly's shoulder, "you ready?"

"Ah was born ready, cuz," the Cajun rasped.

Ben gripped the descent rope firmly, stepped off the edge of the hole, and slid carefully down into the water tank. Below, the pale light emanating from the blown hatch illuminated the lower walls of the tank, revealing rust and slime. The interior echoed with the sound of dripping water. The air was dank and smelled metallic.

Ben's feet dropped into the knee-deep water at the bottom with a soft splash. Looking up, he gripped the rope and motioned to Rolly. With deceptive agility the Cajun slid down the line, and a few seconds later was standing beside Ben.

"Didn't think ol' Rolly had it in him, didja cuz?" he whispered, panting.

"Bullshit," Ben retorted. "I've seen you move like Muhammad Ali when you wanted to." He waved his hand. "Let's take a look." They waded over to the hatchway, trying not to lose their footing on the slimy bottom. The humming of electrical motors on the pumping stations outside grew louder, and the scent of clean, salty air cut through the fetid humidity of the tank's atmosphere. Ben stooped down and looked cautiously outside.

"See anything?" Rolly whispered.

Ben shook his head slowly. "Uh-uh. Not so far." He leaned forward and stuck his upper body out through the hatch.

A sudden reverberating thump and splash made them both start violently, Ben banging his head as he withdrew from the opening. They turned to see Malice Tatum sitting in the water at the bottom of the rope, his bony knees sticking up in front of him He flailed for a moment, then regained his feet, dripping.

Ben rubbed his smarting head, willing his heart to slow down and not beat its way through the muscle of his chest.

"Malice!" he exclaimed. "What're you doing?"

The big man approached. "Sorry I startled you," he said. "I lost my grip." The slow smile came over his face. "Good thing it weren't no deeper." Ben noticed a two-foot steel crowbar stuck through Tatum's belt. "Thought maybe y'all could use some help. I'm on the last boat, anyway."

Ben smiled, nodding. "Sure thing. Thanks." He turned back toward the hatch. "We don't see anything out here. Yet."

He began to step through the opening, but Tatum reached out and put a hand on his arm. The big man's eyes were suddenly very hard and bright in his care-worn face.

"How 'bout you let me take a look-see, Ben," he said softly. "Recon's my job."

When Ben hesitated Rolly added, "De man knows dis rig better than you an' me, bro."

Nodding slowly, Ben withdrew from the hatchway. Tatum smiled, pulled the crowbar from his belt, and ducked through. "Back in a few minutes," he said over his shoulder.

The two divers watched as he crept forward into the maze of pipes and conduit outside the tank, until he worked his way out of their line of sight.

Rolly dug a mangled cigarette out of his shirt pocket and lit it with his Zippo. "Think dere's any regulations against smokin' inside a water tank?" he growled.

The seconds seemed to pass like hours as they waited for Tatum to return, both of them half expecting to hear sudden bursts of gunfire. The constant dripping echoed through the tank like the ticking of a loud clock, fraying their already worn nerves. At the hole above, Texas and the muster captain of the first lifeboat watched silently.

Ben had just about decided to go out and see what was taking so long when a shadow passed across the hatchway and Tatum's head and shoulders appeared.

"I went all the way down to the second boat on the port side," he panted. "Didn't see nothin'. Then I took the lower catwalk over to the starboard side; ain't no sign of 'em there, neither." He paused and grinned. "Looks clear."

"Let's hope it stays that way," Ben said. He turned and gestured up at the hole. "Okay. Let's go. Boat A."

The man beside Texas grabbed the rope and slid down with some difficulty. Karen Marriot followed, pausing midway to set a foot on the horizontal pipe traversing the tank and rest her arms. Rolly moved to the rope and steadied her as she slid down the last eight feet into the water.

"All right, *cher,*" he said, squeezing her shoulder. "Good job." She smiled at him, looking scared but in control.

Within five minutes, the first lifeboat group was assembled in the water tank, the men crowding around Ben and Rolly at the hatch. Tatum was crouched outside, scanning the immediate area for signs of movement.

"Rolly," Ben said, "you and I'll lead off toward the first boat and make sure the way's still clear." He turned to the muster captain. "What's your name, bud?"

"Jim," the man answered, his voice hollow.

"Okay, Jim. You and your people follow us in single file. Stay back about ten feet. We'll wave you on around the corners after we make sure none of these banditos are in the way. Got it?"

"Uh-huh," Jim mumbled. Ben had never seen anyone look less sure of what he was doing in his life.

"Second boat, follow right behind the first, same side," he called softly up to the hole. Texas nodded and waved.

Ben set a foot on the edge of the hatch trunk. "Let's go," he said.

Tatum moved aside as he stepped out into the light of the sub-deck pump station. Rolly dropped his cigarette butt in the water and followed. Tatum gestured toward a passageway visible through the tangle of pipes and mouthed the words, "port side." Then, to be heard above the loud humming of the pump motors, he moved close and spoke into Ben's ear.

"I'll watch the back entrance to this area," he called. "Maybe put a hurtin' on anyone tryin' to flank us." He waggled the crowbar. Ben nodded, and the

big man moved off through the piping and around the
far side of the tank.

The floor of the sub-deck was made of galvanized
grating, and two hundred feet below Ben and Rolly
could see the foam-streaked waters of the Gulf surging
through the uprights and vertical conductors of the
rig. The wind had dropped from a howl to a moan,
and shafts of sunlight were streaking through the partially open sides of this lower level.

Ben headed toward the passageway, wondering
what he was going to do if one of the black-clad gun-
men should appear. As he passed a welder's tool
bench, he spotted a couple of large chipping hammers.
He took one, wielding it in his right hand, and passed
the other back to Rolly. The Cajun rolled his eyes.
But it felt better than nothing at all.

They paused at the passageway entrance. It led to
a catwalk deck that ran along the entire port side of
the NAOC-X, a steel bulkhead on its inboard side, a
railing and the open Gulf outboard. About a hundred
feet from the entrance and then again at the far end
of the catwalk hung the two lifeboats in their mecha-
nized davits.

Ben studied them for a moment, taking more of an
interest in their design than he had earlier during the
lifeboat muster prompted by the helicopter crash.
They bore little resemblance to traditional oar-pow-
ered boats of any kind. Constructed of thick orange
fiberglass, they looked like nothing so much as a pair
of children's spinning tops: spherical capsules twenty
feet in diameter, completely enclosed, with large entrance hatches on the inboard sides and thick port-
holes set above the waterline. Each one could
accommodate forty passengers, seat-belted into place,
and carried enough emergency rations and bottled
water for two weeks. In addition, there were several
radio beacons aboard that activated automatically

when the boat hit the water, plus VHF units for spo-
ken-word communication.

There was no sign of anyone on the catwalk. Ben
signaled to Jim, crouched with his lifeboat group back
in the piping, and began to jog lightly down toward
the second boat. He swallowed hard, trying to ease
the constriction of his throat. A light metallic clatter
arose as the line of men behind him began to run
along the grating. He tried to will the noise away. He
could hear Rolly panting at his shoulder.

Ben sprinted the last twenty feet to the boarding
dais of the lifeboat station, leaped up its three stairs,
and spun the dog on the capsule hatch. Rolly gripped
one of the handles as the seal broke and together they
heaved on it. The watertight door opened upward,
gull-wing style, revealing the lifeboat's orange plastic-
padded interior with its rows of seats.

Ben stepped to the side and looked urgently at Jim,
who was just arriving at the foot of the dais, drawn
and pale. Karen was right behind him, followed by the
straggling file of men. The muster captain hesitated,
looking confused.

"Don't stop!" Ben hissed, his teeth clenched. "Get
aboard, dammit!"

Jim lurched forward into the capsule, taking up his
station beside the onboard descent controls. Karen
took just enough time to glance uncertainly at both
Ben and Rolly, then ducked through the hatch. She
took a seat near the center of the craft, looking back
up at them.

Rolly smiled quickly at her. "Buckle de seat belt,
cher," he called. "Gonna be a rough ride."

The rest of the men piled through the hatch almost
on top of one another, their weight making the boat
sway slightly in its davits. Ben glanced back the way
they had come. The second group was already boarding the other capsule at the far end of the catwalk.

As the last man clambered past him, he reached up and grabbed the edge of the hatch.

"Don't wait!" he ordered the ashen Jim. "As soon as I shut the hatch, dog it and drop her!" He nodded briefly. "Good luck."

He and Rolly yanked the door down and slammed it with a heavy thump. The external dog latched shut as one of the men sealed the hatch from the inside. The two divers stepped down hurriedly from the dais.

There was a loud metallic *clack,* and the whole dais vibrated. The capsule suddenly dropped from view, the support cables paying out from the freewheeling friction winches. Ben and Rolly looked over the railing to see the lifeboat hurtling down toward the surging swells far below.

Just as it appeared that the boat must smash into the water at full speed, a low screech emanated from the friction wenches and the dais shook again. The lowering cables went drum-tight as the brakes took the strain of slowing the plummeting craft. Smoke began to stream from the brake drums, and then the capsule hit the surface of the water with a tremendous splash. The cables slackened and snapped back and forth as the lifeboat wallowed in the swells.

"Turn loose! Turn loose!" Rolly fumed, pounding the handrail with his fist.

The capsule rolled sickeningly in the heavy seas, was yanked over almost ninety degrees, and then the straining cables popped free of the craft as the internal releases were thrown. The lifeboat righted itself like a stand-up punching bag and began to drift rapidly off to the northwest amid the driving swells.

A wave of relief washed over Ben and Rolly, and they turned in time to see the second lifeboat drop from its davits. It too braked properly, did a controlled crash into the water, and turned loose its cables. Narrowly missing being swept into one of the NAOC-X's massive legs, it wobbled off in pursuit of the first capsule.

Rolly grinned at Ben, triumph in his eyes. "Two down, cuz. Only two to go!"

Leaning back against one of the galley tables, Gradak pressed the wet towel to his throbbing face and ground his teeth against the pain. Riad was stooped in front of him, applying a gauze dressing to the lightning burn on the leader's knee. The wound was ugly— the skin charred black and the bone of the kneecap exposed.

The terrorist leader's eyes were manic. "I want him found! I want him found, and I want him dead! *Aaaggh!!* Be careful, you idiot!"

Riad looked up sideways at Gradak, then lightly applied the final piece of tape to the bandage. He knew the excruciating pain of a fresh burn wound, but had no anesthetics on hand.

Turgut spoke. "He's hiding, Ojim. He knows his way around these pipes and passageways like a rat knows its sewers. We could spend hours hunting and never find him." He shook his head. "It makes no difference, anyway. When we blow the rig, he'll go with it."

Gradak lurched forward and grabbed him by the throat. The bigger man's hands automatically came partway up, then went back down. His face purpled as Gradak squeezed, but he did not resist.

"It makes a difference to *me*!" The terrorist leader's voice was a hoarse shriek. "I am going to find him, and you are going to help me!" With his free hand he jerked his pistol out of its shoulder holster and jammed it against Turgut's forehead. "Tell me, now: do I have a soldier or a traitor in front of me?"

Turgut gasped for air. "A soldier."

"Good." Gradak abruptly released his grip and lowered the handgun. Turgut reeled back against the edge of the table, rubbing his throat and inhaling noisily. Riad stood carefully off to the side, watching Gradak with wary eyes.

"We go to the upper deck," the leader commanded. "Take the hostages out of the shed three at a time, and shoot them. Then three more, and three more, until he comes out!"

"Suppose, *agh,* suppose he still doesn't show himself?" Turgut said with some difficulty.

"He will!" Gradak shouted. "He may not give himself up, but if we kill enough of his friends, he will try to stop us! And to do that he will have to show his face! And then he's ours!" He waved his automatic. "Come with me."

Riad hefted his submachine gun. "Ojim, we haven't made contact with Daoud in Pass Christian. We have no escape route. How are we going to get off this installation before we detonate the charges?"

"Lifeboat," Gradak answered. "There are four large escape pods on this platform. We'll keep six of the hostages with us to use as bargaining chips later. Whoever picks us up eventually won't be expecting any trouble. We'll commandeer their vessel and be in Cuban waters in two days." He winced as a spasm of pain shot through his leg. "Remember," he grimaced, "no one knows we're here. And after we destroy the platform, there'll be no one left to tell the story. So you see, I have this operation well under control." His unearthly amber eyes fixed in turn on Riad, then Turgut. "But first, I want our sewer rat."

He turned and limped out of the galley to the main deck stairs. Riad and Turgut followed, their submachine guns at half-port. Sunlight was streaming through the small windows in the doors at the top of the stairway.

Gradak threw open the doors, and they hurried

across the main deck of the NAOC-X toward the
prison shed. The previous night's rain had left large
puddles of standing water everywhere the deckplates
were low, but the wind and brilliant sun were drying
them quickly. Saeb, still on guard outside the shed,
stood up stiffly as his three companions approached.
His arm, almost yanked from its socket during the
wild swing from the *Circe* to the rig leg, was aching
nearly to the point of paralysis. The fractured wrist of
his other arm had been throbbing for so long that he
barely noticed it.

"Open it!" Gradak barked, brandishing his pistol.
Turgut and Riad stood on either side of him, their
Skorpions at hip level and trained on the shed door.
Saeb pulled the pin from the locking hasp, gripped
the door handle, and heaved it open.

Caught in the sudden flood of bright daylight, four
startled and very unlucky men—the only occupants of
the shed—stared out at Ojim Gradak in horror. They
were clustered around what seemed to be a suspended
rope, which hung down into a hole in the floor . . .

With a wild shriek of pure animal rage, Gradak
threw up his automatic and began firing into the little
knot of men. Without hesitation Turgut and Riad
opened up as well. There were screams as the victims'
bodies jerked and contorted under the hail of bullets.
As one of them grabbed the rope and vainly tried to
hold himself up, the gunfire cut it in two and he fell
through the opening in the deckplates.

Gradak rushed into the shed, unmindful of his injured leg, and dove to the deck at the edge of the
hole. Eighteen feet below in the empty, damp-smelling
tank were two men, one halfway out an open hatch,
the other standing beside him and staring with saucer
eyes at the dead body that had just fallen from the
opening.

Texas glanced up from the hatchway, muttered

"Shit!" under his breath as he saw Gradak train his pistol on them, and dove out into the pump station. Duane had time to throw up his hands and scream a barely intelligible *"Nooooo!"* before Gradak's first shot punched through his left eye and blew off the back of his head.

Gradak jerked himself up from the hole. With the rope severed they could not follow. He gestured wildly with his handgun. "The lowest deck!" he screamed. "The pumping stations!"

Turgut, Riad, and Saeb sprinted out of the shed, splitting up and heading across the main deck for three different stairways. All but frothing at the mouth, Gradak followed Riad at a limping trot.

He was in the mood for a slaughter.

Ari awoke with a start. The pistol slid off his chest and clattered onto the tile floor of the sleeping quarters. The sound of sustained automatic-weapons fire was still coming from outside on the main deck. Ari reached down for the dropped handgun, gasping as knifelike pains stabbed through his chest and side, retrieved it, and rolled into a sitting position on the bunk. He slid over to the window and peered out cautiously from behind the curtain in time to see four black-clad terrorists running across the open deck, away from the large shed where the crew was being held. One of them was limping badly, unable to keep up with the others.

The Mossad agent gathered his strength and got to his feet. Something had gone wrong, gotten out of Gradak's control. He blinked hard, trying to clear his head. Perhaps word had somehow been passed to the mainland of Gradak's seizure of the rig, and a counterraid was already under way. Federal agents? A SEAL team?

The Mossad team he'd left stranded in Houston?

No. The first thing Gradak would have done would have been to lock down all possible communications with the outside world, and even if a brief message fragment had gone out, it would likely not have been intelligible through the electrical interference of the storm. The Mossad team hadn't had time to find alternative transportation. No, it had to be something else.

He glanced back out through the window. The door to the prison shed was open, swinging in the wind.

The crew. The crew had freed themselves, and Gradak and his men were hunting them down.

Perfect.

Ari couldn't help smiling to himself as he crossed the room and opened the hall door.

All the distraction was going to make his job much easier.

Chapter Twenty-Six

Texas came careening around the corner and onto the starboard catwalk, nearly knocking Ben over.

"Them bastards is comin'!" he howled. "They done shot Duane!"

He ran past the last six men filing into the fourth and final lifeboat and barged through the hatch. Two of the men fell on the stairs of the dais, holding up the others. Ben looked down at the far end of the catwalk, where Rolly was just slamming the hatch shut on the third capsule, all its crew on board. It swung for a few seconds in its davits as the Cajun stepped back, giving the thumbs-up signal, then dropped free, trailing its cables.

Ben was watching it near the water when a sudden metallic *clack* made him jerk his eyes back over to the nearby lifeboat. In a panic, Texas had thrown the descent lever with the hatch still open.

"Wait!" Ben yelled, flinging out his arm.

But it was too late. The lifeboat dropped like a stone, the open hatch door coming down like a pile driver on the head of the next man trying to board from the dais, snatching his body away like that of a rag doll. In horror Ben leaped to the handrail in time to see the hapless crewman hit the water just ahead of the slowing capsule. A second later it splashed down and immediately twisted in a wave trough, submerging its open hatch. The cables writhed and

snapped back and forth like angry snakes, shock-load-
ing to the breaking point with every surge that tore
at the foundering lifeboat.

Ben looked up wildly. Rolly was pounding down
the catwalk toward him at a dead run. The five remaining crew members were crowded around the dais
staring in shock at the scene below. A loud crack came
from one of the davits; it bent downward suddenly,
twisting as the metal failed under the strain. The lifeboat tilted crazily, still hanging from one good cable.
The hatch rolled clear of the swells for an instant,
spilling out men, gear, and seawater, then wallowed
back under again.

Rolly reached Ben, gasping. "Dey're dead!
Sonofabitch!"

Ben did not answer. He was focusing in over Rolly's
shoulder on the black figure that had just stepped into
view at the far end of the catwalk.

"Scatter!" he shouted, seizing his friend by the la-
pels and driving him sideways over the threshold of
an open companionway near the dais. As they crashed
on top of each other to the floor of an interior landing,
a volley of machine-gun slugs from Turgut's Skorpion
tore into the lifeboat station. Screams of agony came
from the five men outside.

Ben and Rolly scrambled to their feet and dashed
up the ascending stairs four at a time. Landing. No
door. Next flight of stairs. Landing. Door. As one,
they barged through it at full tilt.

And came back through it at full tilt as Saeb, just
down the hall, threw up his submachine gun and
opened fire. He was a fraction of a second too slow;
his bullets sprayed on down an empty hallway.

Ben in the lead, they raced to the top landing and
burst through the door onto the main deck. The sides
of the vast expanse of grating were jammed with
equipment and construction materials, creating a vir-

tual maze for a man to walk through. The two divers sprinted to the starboard side and dodged into a small forest of eight-foot-high cable spools.

A few seconds later Turgut emerged from the access door, followed by Saeb. They paused, searching the deck before them. Then Turgut waved his comrade over to the port side and proceeded himself to starboard. He stopped at the first cable spool, eyeing the area ahead over the barrel of his weapon.

Some thirty feet ahead of him, Ben and Rolly crouched behind a large compressor. Rolly was wheezing for air, trying to do it quietly, his face beet-red from the effort. Ben glanced at his friend, putting a hand on his shoulder. Rolly nodded slightly.

"All right," he managed to croak.

Hardly daring to breathe himself, Ben sneaked a look around the frame of the compressor. He could see only about ten feet through the obstacle course of oil drums, pipe sections, and machinery. There was no sign of their pursuers. He drew back again.

"Ah'd give mah left nut for dat ol' Winchester deer rifle of mine right now," Rolly whispered. Ben nodded helplessly.

They worked their way back through the equipment and stacks of drilling pipe until they reached the starboard railing. With the wind whistling past them, they looked down at the driving blue seas far below. The sky was cloudless, a hazy blue.

"Nice day for a funeral," Rolly said bitterly.

A movement from back the way they'd come caught Ben's eye. Some thirty feet away he saw a black shape duck out from behind a fuel tank and back behind a rack of acetylene bottles.

Motioning Rolly to follow, he crept along the handrail on his hands and knees, passing several large racks of high-pressure oxygen cylinders. They slid behind an immense stack of thirty-foot sections of steel pipe, neatly laid horizontally, about six feet high by twenty wide. Each section was at least fifteen inches in diameter, and Ben could look back the way they'd come by sighting down a particular pipe as though it was the inside of a giant gun barrel.

A gun barrel . . . As Rolly crawled up beside him, the pieces of a desperate idea began to assemble themselves in Ben's mind. He looked around. There was a rack of green oxygen cylinders within arm's reach. Several heavy three-foot pipe wrenches hung from hooks on the handrail. He pulled down on the loose blue tarpaulin that hung from the top of the pipe stack, hiding himself and Rolly from any approaching eyes, and batted the Cajun on the arm.

"Help me get two of these cylinders," he whispered. Rolly looked at him questioningly, then shrugged and got to his feet, keeping his head low. Trying not to clang them together, they pulled two full oxygen bottles from the nearby rack—each one five feet long by ten inches in diameter and made of heavy steel—and slid them bottom end first into two side-by-side pipe sections at chest level. Ben motioned to Rolly to unscrew the safety caps and expose the on/off valves, then turned to the handrail to lift two of the big pipe wrenches free of their hanger hooks.

He handed one to Rolly, making a chopping motion in the direction of the cylinder valves. The Cajun's face suddenly broke into a grin of understanding. He backed off to one side of the oxygen bottle nearest him. Ben pulled the tarpaulin down over the pipe ends beside his body and took up a similar position at his cylinder. Rolly upended a large wooden skid against the pipe stack to conceal himself from view, then crouched and raised his wrench above the valve of his cylinder, watching Ben.

Ben brought his wrench up into striking position, steadied himself, and peered with one eye out from

behind the tarpaulin and down the pipe section next
to his head. There was no sign of movement, and no
sound but the wind whistling and moaning around the
steel structures and equipment. He swallowed hard. If
the terrorist was too sharp-eyed . . . If he decided to
detour behind the pipe stack as they had done, instead
of walking in front of it . . .

Turgut stepped out from behind a cylinder rack
barely five feet from the far end of Ben's viewing pipe.
He paused, and Ben could see his eyes flickering over
his surroundings, missing nothing. For one heart-stopping instant, diver and gunman locked gazes—Ben
knew he must have been seen—and then Turgut
turned away, stepping past his line of sight.

And into line with the cylinder-loaded pipes. Ben
shot Rolly a fast look, then brought the heavy pipe
wrench down on top of the cylinder valve with all his
strength. It broke and blew off with a banshee scream
of escaping high-pressure gas. Rolly's valve shot off a
half second behind Ben's.

The heavy cylinders took off like missiles down the
two pipe sections, caroming frenziedly off the steel
walls. Turgut had just enough time to wheel full-on
to face the sudden cacophony before Ben's cylinder
rocketed past his right shoulder.

The butt end of Rolly's cylinder hit him full in the
chest, driving him off the deck and backward through
the air a full twenty feet before crushing him with a
wet thump against the unyielding steel plate of a crane
pedestal. A great gout of blood erupted from his
mouth on impact. He fell forward onto his face,
twitched once, and lay motionless. Beside him, the
nearly drained cylinder hissed out the last of its gas.

Ben scrambled around the end of the pipe stack
and dodged through the gas racks toward the crane
pedestal. Reaching the terrorist's body, he heaved him

over onto his back and seized the barrel of his submachine gun, trying to pull it free.

Then he stopped in dismay. The breech and clip of the weapon were slick with blood—and smashed flat. The impact of the cylinder had driven the gun into the man's chest, destroying it. The shoulder holster was empty. Frantically, Ben searched with his hands for another weapon. Nothing.

"Oh, *shit*!" Rolly came diving past him as another burst of gunfire sent hot slugs ricocheting through the standing equipment. Ben scrambled after Rolly behind the pedestal, tossing a glance over his shoulder that revealed Saeb running across the main deck from the port side, firing as he came. Lead rang on steel, and paint chips flew as the bullets zipped around them like angry hornets.

It was time to bail out. They rose and dashed pell-mell across thirty feet of open deck between the crane and a group of four small compressor skids. Saeb halted, trained his Skorpion on them, chuckling, and got off two rounds before the firing pin clicked on an empty chamber. With a curse, he ripped the spent clip from his weapon, banged home another, and began to run toward the sheds in pursuit.

Ben and Rolly ducked into the rear-most shed and shut the door. Grabbing short lengths of pipe from a bin beside a small tool bench, they took up positions on either side of the entrance, panting. After a few seconds, Rolly looked hard at Ben, his face twisting with helpless fury.

"Look at us, bro," he rasped through gritted teeth, "with dese damn bits of pipe. We need a better idea right now, or we gonna get shot, you an' me!"

"Yeah," Ben replied. He looked around quickly. Nearly a third of the shack was taken up by a huge vertical volume tank that held a reservoir of compressed air. High-pressure air—the master gauge on

the side of the tank read 1200 psi. There was an access
manifold at its base with quarter-turn valves and tap
fittings on it. And there were three- and four-foot
lengths of threaded pipe . . .

Ben looked up at Rolly. "If it worked once—" he
said in desperation. Rolly lowered his pipe.

"Ah ain't got no better ideas," he said. "How you
wanna rig it?"

Ben pointed at the three-foot pipe in his friend's
hand. "That's threaded. Get a fitting from the tool
bench and tap it into that volume-tank manifold.
Make sure the pipe points right at the door, about
halfway up."

Rolly spun and began to rummage through the pipe
fittings on the tool bench. Ben grabbed an open can
of welding rods and extracted a handful; each was
fourteen inches long and a little over an eighth of an
inch thick. Like blunt steel knitting needles.

The sound of a door banging followed by a short
burst of gunfire came from outside. The terrorist was
sweeping the other compressor sheds. Rolly worked
furiously over the manifold, trying to wrench the pipe
into place.

"Remember, line it up with the door," Ben hissed.

"Ah'm gettin' it, cuz," the Cajun seethed, grimacing
with effort.

As he torqued the length of pipe into place, Ben
fed the handful of welding rods loosely into its open
end. Then he stepped to the tool bench and grabbed
a coil of thin, flexible wire. Working quickly, he
wrapped one end of it around the handle of the valve
that controlled the airflow to the short pipe, then
backed away to the far corner of the shed, paying out
wire as he went. Rolly finished tightening the pipe,
checked the alignment, and stepped quickly around
behind the volume tank.

Ben crouched low in his corner behind several large

bags of cement mix and drew up tight on the wire.
There was a sudden thump on the wall of the shed,
as though a running man had just flattened himself
against it. For a few seconds the only sound was the
rising moan of the wind.

With a violent crash the door was kicked open, and
the deafening chatter of Saeb's submachine gun shook
the air. Sparks flew as bullets ricocheted off the volume tank, walls, and equipment.

Lying behind the cement bags, Ben somehow managed to make himself wait until the black-clad figure
filled the door frame. Then he yanked back on the
wire with all his strength.

A sudden whooshing blast nearly drowned out the
submachine gun's hammering. Ben buried his face in
his arms as a choking cloud of cement dust enveloped
him. Then, abruptly, the gun stopped firing. An odd,
strangled wail came from the direction of the door.

Ben ground his eyes with his knuckles, trying to see.
As his vision cleared, he saw that the doorway was
open, empty. The submachine gun was lying on the
floor of the shed.

He clawed his way over the torn cement bags, eyes
and throat burning from lime-based dust, and dove
across to the weapon. Grabbing it, he rolled to one
knee and brought it to bear on the doorway, its heft
and grips unfamiliar in his hands.

He didn't pull the trigger. Instead, he watched as
Saeb wobbled backward step by step, his hands
clenching and unclenching, the awful wail issuing continuously from his throat. More than a dozen welding
rods, turned into steel arrows by the tremendous blast
of air from the volume tank, protruded from his abdo-
men and chest. Two more had hit him in the face.
One had penetrated deeply below the left eye; the
other had transfixed the right jaw.

The terrorist's heels hit the raised edge of a deckplate, and he fell stiffly onto his back. The wailing stopped. His hands continued to clench and unclench in the air for a few more seconds, then dropped limply beside him.

Ben stepped to the door, fascinated and repelled, and looked down at the body of the man who had just tried to kill him. Blood was beginning to soak through Saeb's black jumpsuit and pool beneath him. His lifeless eyes stared frantically skyward, as though not accepting death.

Ben moved forward and knelt beside the dead terrorist, suddenly not wanting to look at his face any longer. Quickly, he pulled an extra machine-gun clip free of the twitching body, removed the pistol from the shoulder holster, and backed away. It occurred to him that all the firing should have drawn the attention of the others, but there was no sign of movement on the main deck.

He stepped back inside the shed. "Rolly!" he called softly. "That guy's had it. I've got his weapons."

There was a wet cough from behind the volume tank.

"Dat—dat's good, cuz . . ."

Ben's insides went numb. The Skorpion and the pistol clattered to the deck as he stepped forward.

Rolly was lying on his back behind the tank, his head propped up against the shed wall. His craggy face was calm, set, as though concentrating on a problem. A large red stain was soaking through his shirt in the center of his chest.

"Jesus, Rolly!" Ben dropped to his knees and ripped open his friend's shirt. Red blood bubbled freely from a small, ugly hole in Rolly's sternum.

"Ricochet, Ah believe," the Cajun grunted, his breathing shallow and labored. "Shitty luck."

"Christ . . ." Ben wadded up the torn shirt and pressed it over the wound, trying to stanch the flow.

"Oof . . . Not too hard dere, cuz." Rolly half grinned through the grimace of pain on his face. "Kinda knocked de wind outta me. Just . . . just gimme a minute . . ."

"Hang in there, Rolly! Hang in there, you hear me?" Helpless desperation seeped into Ben's chest like cold poison. He lightened the pressure on the soaking bundle of rags and gripped Rolly's hand tightly.

"Tell—tell you what, bro," the Cajun said weakly. "We gonna just smoke us a cigarette . . . lemme catch mah breath . . . an' then go find dem other pea-pickers an' kick some butt . . ." He groped a crumpled, torn Marlboro from his shirt pocket and stuck it in his mouth, his hand shaking. "Where . . . where's mah lighter . . ."

"Here," Ben said, trying to keep his voice steady. He pulled the silver Zippo from Rolly's jeans pocket and flicked it, holding the flame to the cigarette. But instead of drawing on it, the Cajun began to laugh— a shallow, rasping sound. He locked eyes with Ben.

"You know, Benjamin," he gasped, breathless, "maybe Ah oughta quit . . . Dey say . . . dey say smokin's bad for your health . . ." He winced, squeezing his eyes shut, and swallowed convulsively twice. Then a long, rattling sigh came from deep within him, and he lay still.

"Rolly," Ben whispered, squeezing his friend's hand and gently shaking him by the shoulder. "Wait . . ."

But he was gone.

Ben sat for a while—he didn't know how long— checking a pulse that wasn't there, watching for breathing that had long since ceased. It wasn't right to leave his old friend lying hurt in this drafty little shed; Rolly'd wake up and wonder where he'd gone. The tough, grizzled face with its laugh lines and worry lines and battle scars looked peaceful, merely asleep.

After a while longer, Ben took off his jacket, made a pad of it, and placed it beneath Rolly's head. He draped one of the sleeves across his closed eyes, took the crumpled cigarette from between his lips, and tucked it into his limp right hand. Then he rested a hand on his friend's head for a moment, and looked at him one last time.

"Till another day, bro," he said softly.

Ben got to his feet, picked up the automatic pistol and machine-gun clip, and stuck them both in his belt. Then he retrieved the Skorpion, hefting it, examining it—locating the safety, firing selector, and magazine release. It was a first-class piece of weaponry; beautiful, functional, and deadly.

Ben brought the submachine gun up to hip level, at the ready, and walked out of the shed to find a backup life raft or inflatable boat that would get him off the rig. Or to run into the two remaining terrorists.

He didn't particularly care which.

Chapter Twenty-Seven

Gradak and Riad stood beside each other near the damaged launching dais, looking down over the railing at the wallowing, half-suspended lifeboat below. There were no men left in it. Those who hadn't been spilled into the ocean initially had clawed their way out to avoid being drowned or battered to death in its interior. They were all gone, swept away downwind by the driving seas.

Gradak kicked the body of one of the crewmen Turgut had gunned down ten minutes earlier. The other boats were gone; there was no way off the rig. The only thing that gave the terrorist leader any pleasure at the moment was the faint, sporadic sound of gunfire coming from the upper decks as Turgut and Saeb hunted down the last remaining members of the escaped crew.

"How do we get off?" Riad said tonelessly, expecting no response. The rig had to be blown, whether they escaped or not. That was the mission.

Gradak's pale eyes suddenly narrowed as he stared out at the horizon.

"Perhaps," he replied, pointing to the northeast, "there."

Riad followed his finger. No more than a mile away, plunging forward through the seas, was a sailing vessel, a yacht, heeling heavily as it worked its way upwind. It was coming straight for the NAOC-X.

Gradak spun to face his young accomplice. "We will signal by waving white sheets from the boat-landing level. The seas are calming down, and it is daylight. If we can draw that boat in close enough, its crew will see the damaged lifeboat and assume that we need to be rescued. They will do all they can to get us aboard. It will be much easier than it was last night."

Riad nodded. "The weapons?"

"Leave the Skorpions and battle harnesses," Gradak said. "We must look like oilfield workers. We will take only our knives and pistols in one of the knapsacks, along with extra ammunition and the remote detonating unit."

"I'll get the others," Riad said, shedding his harness and shoulder holster. He dropped the submachine gun at his feet. "They must have killed the other crewmen by now."

"No!" Gradak's voice was harsh. "The boat is coming. There is no time!" He pointed at the companionway with his automatic. "Strip two sheets off one of the beds in those quarters and come with me to the lower level."

Riad hesitated momentarily, then ducked through the doorway. He emerged a few seconds later with an armful of white sheets, and the two terrorists jogged along the catwalk toward the open-air descending staircase that led to the boat landings far below.

"Why not contact them by radio?" Riad panted. "We have the small handset; the Americans use sixteen as an open channel for all marine traffic. We could—"

"No radio!" Gradak cut him off. "Nothing on the air."

"But, Ojim—" Riad protested, and then Malice Tatum stepped from behind a cluster of pipes and hit him in the temple with a short crowbar. The young terrorist fell into Gradak, knocking them both down.

The knapsack containing the pistols skidded off under a pump housing. Gradak barely had time to roll over and see what had happened before Tatum was on him, swinging the crowbar.

He struck him twice, glancing blows on the head and shoulder, before Riad, bleeding, tackled him and sent them both crashing through a tool bench. The crowbar clanged away out of reach. The two regained their feet like cats, circling each other. Gradak lay dazed, barely conscious.

Both men, trained killers, adopted martial-arts fighting stances—Riad upright, savate-style, and Tatum in a curious sideways crouch, his arms twisting hypnotically like a pair of cobras. Riad leaped forward, kicking out, and Tatum parried the attack with a windmilling, slithering sidestep. As the young terrorist's momentum carried him past, the lanky vet's arm stuck out with serpent's speed, digging rigid fingers into the nerve plexus near the collarbone. Riad gasped, stumbled, then regained his feet.

"You know, boy," Tatum said, flashing a quick glance at the still-stunned Gradak, "when you spend six years of your life crawlin' around the mountains in 'Nam an' Cambodia, you learn a whole lotta fightin' styles." He side-wound away easily from a lightning series of combination punches that Riad threw at his head, kicking him in the knee as he did so. "Some of 'em, like the ones the secret societies of the Montagnards use, don't even have no names."

He stepped forward slightly, and in what seemed like slow motion gouged Riad's right eye with a rigid thumb. "I don't know what they call this one," he said conversationally, "but I was always partial to it, myself."

He wheeled suddenly and delivered a shattering reverse roundhouse kick to Riad's ear. The terrorist sagged to one knee, his vision darkening on that side.

"How d'you like it?" Tatum inquired, his arms weaving the air. He was enjoying himself. He was in another place, another time, twenty-five years ago . . .

Two pistol shots cracked, and the vet staggered. One more followed, and he pitched forward onto his face, three bullet holes in the center of his back.

Gradak rose from behind a pipe run, one hand holding his smoking automatic, the other clutching the knapsack. He stepped over the pipes, nudged Tatum's dead body with his toe, then looked over at Riad.

The young man was seated, reeling, blood running from his ears. He couldn't get his balance. Sagging over further, he raised an arm to his leader.

"Ojim," he croaked. "Help me. I can't see on my right side. I—I can't stand up . . ."

"Ah," Gradak said, shaking his head, "that would be because your brain is hemorrhaging. It's only going to get worse, I'm afraid." He kicked Tatum's corpse casually in the ribs. "He really was quite good, wasn't he?"

"Ojim . . ." Riad pleaded, slumping to his side, "help me . . ."

Gradak's pale eyes were flat, cold. "Of course," he said, and shot the young terrorist between the eyes.

Slinging the knapsack over his shoulder, he pocketed the pistol, grabbed one of the sheets, and ran toward the descending staircase.

Ari pushed open the door that led from the central quarters complex out onto the main deck. At the far end of the rig, a man carrying a submachine gun was just disappearing down one of the exterior stairways. It wasn't one of the Arabs, Ari noted. He was wearing faded blue jeans and a khaki-colored work shirt.

Interesting, the Mossad agent thought. Things don't seem to be working out entirely in Gradak's favor.

He clutched his side as a spasm of pain gripped

him, then slowly ebbed. Taking a few deep breaths,
he moved carefully out onto the deck, working his
way toward the far stairway from cover to cover. As
he paused behind a large valve tree, he caught sight
of one of the terrorists lying crumpled beside the pedestal of one of the deck cranes. A green gas cylinder
was lying beside him. He didn't look as though he was
going to get up and cause any trouble. The Mossad
agent smiled grimly and moved on.

As he reached the stairway, he suddenly heard faint
pistol shots—two, then one more. Fingering his small
automatic, he brought it up to the ready-to-fire position and began to descend the staircase.

Sass took a half-turn crank on the jibsheet winch
and nudged the wheel a bit, keeping the *Teresa Ann*
pointing hard up to windward. The powerful hull
surged through the steep swells, throwing out sheets
of spray that were whipped back over the house and
deck by the wind. Sass turned her head quickly as a
particularly drenching spray battered droplets of hard
water against her foul-weather gear like a volley of
hailstones. She saw Caesar stick his big head up into
the open main hatch, whine a little, then disappear
back down to his rough-weather berth beneath the
galley table.

Too much water was dashing over the *Teresa Ann*'s
topsides for the companionway to remain open. Sass
tied off the wheel for a moment, then stepped across
the cockpit and pulled the hatch shut. No sense in
trying to air out the main cabin when the air was
mostly salt water.

She looked up at her target, the NAOC-X. The
giant platform was very close, less than half a mile
away. Her navigation had been dead on; the rig had
first appeared on the horizon only two compass points
off her steering course. She was pleased with herself.

Not bad for nighttime sailing through the remnants of a near hurricane.

This was the first time she'd ever seen the structure. Ben had told her about it, the scale of its construction, but she hadn't been able to appreciate the sheer size of the thing until now. It was easily ten times larger than any of the conventional oil platforms in the Gulf.

Amazing, she thought as she trained her binoculars on it. A floating city. Odd, though . . . It looked as if one corner of the top deck had been damaged. Tangled metal hung off it, moving slightly in the wind, and that whole area appeared blackened as if by fire or smoke. Sass chewed her lip. They must have had some kind of accident.

She let the binoculars roam over the rest of the rig. It looked fine, except for the large orange thing twisting in the water near the base of one leg . . .

Abruptly, she dropped the binoculars from her eyes and stared hard at the platform. The orange thing was a deployed lifeboat, hanging from its cables. She refocused the glasses on the lower deck. There was another davit station, but no other lifeboats. She thought she could make out a set of cables hanging down almost to the waterline.

Seizing the hand mike of the VHF radio from its hook on the steering pedestal, she pushed the transmission key and began to speak rapidly.

"NAOC-X, NAOC-X. This is the sailing vessel *Teresa Ann* approaching on your northeast side. Do you read, over." Static. She tried again. "NAOC-X, NAOC-X. Come back, please. Over."

More static. She squinted into the binoculars again, her alarm growing. The rig was less than a quarter mile away now, and she couldn't see a single person moving on it anywhere.

"NAOC-X, NAOC-X! Answer please! NAOC-X, please respond . . ."

It was futile. Sass jammed the hand mike back on its hook in frustration. Something was very wrong; there was always someone on duty at the radios on the big modern rigs. And they didn't leave deployed lifeboats smashing around in heavy seas on the ends of their cables. Ben, she thought . . .

A movement near the base of one of the leeward legs caught her attention. She trained the glasses on it. Something white was flapping furiously from the boat-landing level, just above the water. She focused. A man was waving what looked like a bedsheet.

Letting the binoculars hang around her neck, she spun the *Teresa Ann*'s wheel hard and tacked. The sails shook violently as the boat bucked around through the wind, then filled on the opposite side and began to draw again. The big double-ender heeled over and picked up way directly toward the leeward leg.

Ben paused at the base of the stairway and wiped his brow with the back of his hand. It wasn't hot, but rivulets of sweat mixed with cement dust were running off his forehead and stinging his eyes. A wave of fatigue passed over him, and he realized, vaguely, that he hadn't slept all night. He leaned against the handrail and rested a moment.

The unmistakable sound of a light footfall echoed through the stairwell. Ben jerked up the Skorpion and shrank back into an alcove, holding his breath. A few seconds later a man came padding quickly down the stairs. He wasn't dressed in the black garb of the terrorists. In his clean gray work shirt he looked more like a mechanic. But in his hand was a small automatic pistol.

As he reached the bottom of the stairs and began to turn toward the alcove, Ben lined up the submachine gun on his chest and shouted, "Hold it!"

The man froze, then turned slowly to see Ben looking at him through a ring sight. Slowly, he spread his hands out to his sides, the pistol dangling from one finger.

"I'm not moving," he said.

"Who the hell are you?" Ben demanded.

"Smith," Ari replied. "I'm an engineer. I was just—"

"Stay still!"

"Sorry, sorry." Ari put his hands back out to the sides again.

"An engineer I've never seen, prowling around with a pistol," Ben said. "Where'd you get it?"

Ari thought fast. "From the dead terrorist up near the crane pedestal," he said.

Ben shifted the submachine gun up slightly, remembering the empty shoulder holster on the man they'd killed with the oxygen cylinder. "Lie to me again," he said through clenched teeth, "and I'll cut your head off. You're not one of them, I can see that. But you're no engineer. Now, tell me who you are."

Ari sighed. "I'm a special agent who was sent to track the men who are trying to blow up this rig." When Ben didn't move, he added, "That's the truth."

Ben lowered the gun a few inches. He stared at the other man in silence. There was no reason to believe anything he said. "Tell me more."

"The terrorist team is made up of members of a violent Shiite Muslim faction from the Middle East," Ari recited. "We think they are being led by a man named Ojim Gradak."

"Who's 'we'?"

"The Mossad," Ari said. "Israeli secret service. Maybe you've heard of us?"

"I've heard of the Mossad," Ben said. "So you're an Israeli agent? All alone, on an American oil rig in the Gulf of Mexico. What is that, magic?"

"I told you," Ari explained wearily, "I've been tracking Gradak and his men—"

"I don't know how you got here," Ben said tersely, cutting him off, "or why you look hurt, or why I should believe anything you're saying. A whole lot of things don't add up, friend." He paused, unsure of what to do. He knew he wasn't going to shoot a man standing quietly in front of him with his arms outstretched, but he wasn't going to turn his back on him, either.

"The helicopter!" Ari exclaimed. "You must have been here when it crashed last night!"

"Yes," Ben said.

"I was the pilot," Ari went on. "Don't you remember? They took me to the infirmary. You must have seen me then."

Ben reshuffled events in his mind, gazing at the other man. There was an explosion, men fighting the fire, and a stretcher being carried into the main quarters . . .

"That's right," Ben said finally. "You're him." He lowered the submachine gun to his hip. "Which proves exactly nothing, except that you're a lousy pilot."

"Actually," Ari said, smiling slightly, "I'm very good. I just had a bad night." He let his hands come back slowly to his sides. "You need to trust me, you know."

"Why is that?" Ben demanded.

"Because you obviously don't want to shoot me, and if we stand here much longer, I assure you that this rig is going to blow up under our feet. And," he added, "Gradak and his men will escape."

Ben stood his ground, considering, then finally lowered the Skorpion's barrel toward the floor. "Two of them won't," he said, tight-lipped. He looked out of the stairwell at the waters of the Gulf. "I guess you've convinced me."

Ari stepped forward, his face reassuring. "We can find the rest of them, you and I," he said. "We can make them pay for what they've done. Maybe stop them from blowing the rig. They're not a suicide team; they must have planned a way off. But we need to move now. Are you ready?"

Ben didn't answer. He was looking out into the Gulf, at a very familiar sail emerging from behind one of the rig legs. The *Teresa Ann* heeled hard, then tacked crisply in the heavy wind, revealing a lithe figure clad in foul-weather gear at the cockpit wheel, wisps of blonde hair streaming out from beneath her dark sailor's watch cap.

Ben felt his heart stop beating.

He'd forgotten.

Sasha.

Chapter Twenty-Eight

Sass spun the wheel and settled the *Teresa Ann* onto a course paralleling the NAOC-X's boat landing, some fifty feet away. The man in the black coveralls had stopped waving the sheet and was now gesturing to her to bring the boat in closer. He was shouting as well, the words difficult to make out over the noise of wind and waves sloshing against the hull.

"Danger . . ." came his voice. "Explosion . . . help . . . must get off . . ."

That was enough for Sass. The man obviously needed help, wanted off the rig. And he might know where Ben was. She'd seen that all the lifeboats had been deployed; maybe he was aboard one of them. She wouldn't allow herself to think that he'd been hurt—or worse.

She fired up the *Teresa Ann*'s engine and put the bow into the wind. The sails luffed wildly, filling the air with rackety noise. Slowly, the boat inched up-sea, plunging over the swells as she made headway toward the man on the boat landing. He'll have to jump, Sass thought, but I can put the bow in close enough to make it easy. She glanced up at him. He didn't appear to be badly injured, but there was something wrong with his face . . .

A woman. And alone, apparently. Gradak couldn't help smiling to himself. Could it be so easy? He waved again, nodding his head in encouragement. She handled the big yacht expertly, her movements skilled and sure. She was going to be of great assistance to him, very shortly.

The bow was only ten feet from the landing now, pitching up and down as the swells rolled under the hull. Pale blue fumes billowed from the stern exhaust as the woman gunned the boat's engine, coaxing the vessel forward, forward . . .

Some six feet from the boat landing the bowsprit and pulpit dropped into a deep trough, and Gradak leaped. His momentum carried him well past the jibstay, and a second later he sprawled heavily on the rising foredeck. He slid immediately on the wet teak, heading over the side, and came up abruptly against the *Teresa Ann*'s hefty starboard rail.

The diesel roared, and the prop cavitated as Sass backed down hard, pulling her boat away from the unforgiving steel of the landing. Seeing that her new passenger was still aboard, jammed up against the starboard shroud chainplates, she laid the *Teresa Ann* over on an easy windward beat that would take her at least thirty feet clear of the corner leg up ahead, and cut the engine.

The man had regained his feet, and was picking his way quickly along the rail toward the cockpit. She looked at his face and caught her breath. His nose and mouth were a swollen purple mess, and most of his beard was caked with dried blood. From beneath dark, heavy brows his pale eyes gleamed at her like two chunks of ice.

She drew back involuntarily, then just as quickly regained her composure. The man was hurt. She put a hand on his arm as he clambered over the coaming and into the security of the cockpit.

"My God," she said, "what's happened to you? Sit down and let me find something to put on your face."

Gradak grinned at her, something between a leer and a snarl, and backhanded her across the mouth with his closed fist. The blow sent Sass reeling across the cockpit, crashing hard into the leeward coaming.

"Thank you, no," Gradak said, moving forward.

Ben sprinted along the lower-deck catwalk leading to the rig's leeward legs. He'd seen Gradak make the jump to the *Teresa Ann*'s foredeck and now, as he watched, the double-ender fell back from the boat landing and began a slow beat to windward alongside the NAOC-X. He raced toward the leg that his boat would bypass as she cleared the rig, looking frantically for a ladder, a staircase—anything that would take him down to the landing level. A railing barred his way, and he stopped short. The catwalk dead-ended at the leg; there was no way down—no ladder, nothing.

He glanced back. The Mossad agent was hurrying along the catwalk far back at the other end of the rig, holding his side. The only descending stairway Ben could see was several hundred feet away in the center of the platform. He looked down to see the *Teresa Ann* plunging ahead, only yards from the massive leg. As he watched, he saw Sass stagger to her feet and swing a roundhouse right at the terrorist who shared the cockpit with her. The dark-clothed figure easily parried the blow and delivered a vicious openhanded slap to her face that draped her across the steering pedestal.

Ben's vision blurred with rage, and he dropped the submachine gun. Ten feet away, the nearest boat-landing swing rope was shackled into a U-bolt on the underside of a support girder. Used as handheld support when a man was transferring from workboat to rig, it hung down more than one hundred and fifty feet to the landing level below.

Without thinking, Ben climbed up on the railing,

set a foot on the top horizontal, and launched himself out into space toward the rope. His hands snatched it, the heavy manila burning through his palms as it took the full weight of his flailing body. The automatic pistol in his belt slipped free, tumbling end over end into the water.

He loosened his grip and dropped like a stone down the length of the rope, ignoring the searing pain in his hands. Squeezing hard to slow himself as he reached the end, he kicked inward and jackknifed his body onto the grating of the boat landing.

The *Teresa Ann* was right beside him, heeled far over on a port tack, showing her bottom paint. He couldn't see the cockpit or its occupants. Scrambling to his feet, he ran to the nearby leg and out onto its small circular catwalk.

The boat was going to pass the leg by twenty feet in a matter of seconds. Ben kicked off his heavy boots, climbed over the handrail and dove.

He hit the cold salt water with a jarring splash and pulled hard, coming up in a deep trough. The next swell lifted him high, and he spotted the *Teresa Ann* mere yards away. Dropping his head, he stroked madly to intercept her.

He could feel more than see his boat approach—the vibration in the water as the big hull plunged up and down—and when he raised his head again, the *Teresa Ann*'s bow was poised directly above him, a huge white wedge about to slash downward.

It drove down on top of him like a pile driver, knocking the wind out of him, the barnacles at the waterline tearing at his legs. The dolphin-striker ground into his shoulder, and he hooked it with both elbows, hanging on with all the desperate strength he had left.

The bow rose over the next swell, dragging him clear of the water, and he managed to use the air time to shift himself upward, get his legs over the striker, and gasp in a lungful of air before he smashed down into the next trough.

He was nearly torn free as the boat lifted him into the air again, but he hung on, and as the bow paused at the apex of its upward surge, he flung an arm and leg over the bowsprit and heaved himself up onto it. The bow plunged down again, but he remained clear of the water, hanging on like a limpet.

Lungs burning, hands raw and bleeding, he dragged himself onto the *Teresa Ann*'s foredeck, keeping low behind the house. He could hear a harsh, gutteral voice coming from the cockpit. Blinking the salt water from his eyes, Ben crept aft along the high port side. At the shroud chainplates he stopped and cautiously raised his head.

Over the top of the deckhouse, he could see Gradak's back, wide and black. Sass was close in front of him, bent back over the wheel. One of her eyes was swollen shut. The terrorist had her by the hair. He yanked it viciously as she made a feeble attempt to claw his face.

Ben came over the top of the deckhouse in two steps and hurled himself at Gradak. His one hundred and eighty pounds took the terrorist full in the shoulder-blades and knocked him headfirst into the starboard coaming. Sass twisted off the wheel to the opposite side of the cockpit.

Ben landed two hammering punches to Gradak's right kidney before the terrorist leader jabbed backward with an elbow that cracked hard into Ben's ear, stunning him momentarily. Gradak twisted around to face his adversary, coming up with the pistol from his belt, and Ben drove his fist straight into his upper lip with a crunch that was either teeth or knuckles, or both. The terrorist's gun hand sagged, and Ben mashed it against the coaming with his foot, knocking the pistol loose.

Gradak jabbed upward for the eyes with rigid fingers. Ben drew back instinctively, and received a tremendous kick in the groin for his carelessness. The wave of pain and nausea doubled him over, and Gradak punched him in the back of the neck.

Sass swung at Gradak with a short boathook and caught him on the side of the head. He staggered into the front of the cockpit, but as she drew back for another swing, the terrorist's hand landed on his pistol and he whipped it up in front of him. Sass froze. On the floor of the cockpit, Ben stopped trying to regain his feet and gripped the edge of the lazaret, breathing hard.

"Sit!" Gradak shouted, steadying himself against the main hatch. He looked like something from the deepest pit of hell, with his bloodied face, ragged hair, and otherworldly eyes. Sass sat back against the lazaret, her hand fumbling for Ben's shoulder. He could feel her trembling.

Behind Gradak, Ben saw that the *Teresa Ann* was sailing herself back past the massive steel legs of the NAOC-X again. She must have jibed herself in the confusion, he thought dimly.

Gradak leveled the pistol at him. "I have use of the woman," he snarled. "But not of you."

Ben closed his eyes.

There was a shot, not as loud as he expected . . .

But no pain. No impact.

He opened his eyes. Gradak wobbled, his amber eyes staring, the pistol drooping in his hand. Blood welled from his mouth. He took an uncertain step forward, then fell over sideways into the leeward lazaret. In the center of his back, about three inches down from the base of his neck, a small hole oozed blood.

Ben and Sass stared at each other, then over at the

rig leg that was passing by less than a hundred feet away. Braced against the catwalk handrail, looking over the barrel of the Skorpion he'd just fired, was the Mossad agent.

Ari permitted himself a brief moment of self-satisfaction. Not a bad shot with a short-barreled weapon, even one of this high quality. He switched the Skorpion's selector back to full-automatic from single-shot and slung it over his shoulder.

The yacht was luffing her sails, turning into the wind to approach the boat landing once more and pick him up. He stepped down off the leg catwalk and walked along the grating toward the landing, his injured side throbbing. It was going to need some proper attention soon, he decided.

The man he'd encountered in the stairwell was standing on the foredeck of the boat, beckoning as it drew closer. The sails hammered in the wind, the sound echoing off the rig's vast network of support members.

Ari waited for the right moment, then jumped onto the tip of the bowsprit as it rose past the edge of the landing and grabbed the pulpit railing. He stepped into the pulpit, trying not to strain his side, and took Ben's offered hand to make it the rest of the way onto the foredeck.

Sass backed the *Teresa Ann* down and let her fall off the wind. She was slacking the sails to let the boat run off on a gentle broad reach when Ben and Ari climbed down into the cockpit. Ben helped her finish cleating off the sheets.

"You all right?" he asked, touching her swollen eye gently.

"No," Sass said. "But I plan on being."

Ben looked at her for a moment, his face taut with

concern, then kissed her on the forehead and turned to face Ari.

"Sit down," he said, slumping behind the wheel himself. Ari eased back onto the cockpit seat near the main hatch and clutched his side, looking at Gradak's corpse. Ben regarded him with eyes that showed near-exhaustion.

"That was one helluva shot," he said. "I want to thank you. The bastard had me." He looked over at Sass. "Had us both."

Ari nodded. "Yes. The world is now rid of one extremely nasty piece of work." He spat in Gradak's direction. "I'm not going to miss him."

"My name's Ben Gannon," Ben said. He gestured over his shoulder. "This is Sasha. Sass for short." He looked expectantly at the other man.

"Ari," Ari said, after a long pause. "From Israel," he added, smiling.

"Israel?" Sass commented.

Ben looked over at her. "It's a long story."

Ari leaned forward, grunting, and picked up the sodden knapsack Gradak had dropped into the cockpit when he'd first come aboard. Casually, he began to rummage through it.

"Actually, it's all quite simple," he said. "Would you like to hear my version of what's been going on out here over the past twenty-four hours? I think I owe the man who fought Ojim Gradak to a standstill that much."

"I'd love to hear it," Ben said.

Ari pulled a couple of ammunition clips from the knapsack and put them on the cockpit seat. "Several weeks ago, the Mossad received an intelligence report which outlined a terrorist operation that Ojim Gradak—the so-called 'Avenger of the Tribes'—was planning against the United States. Naturally, we felt that some action was required on our part. I was assigned to track the terrorist team, and then lead a Mossad team out to intercept them at their target—an American oil rig in the Gulf of Mexico." He pointed a finger at the NAOC-X. "That one, as it turned out."

"Where's your team?" Ben asked suddenly.

Ari's smile was thin. "They . . . never reached the United States. I had to come alone."

Ben looked troubled, but said nothing. Ari continued:

"I flew out here by helicopter early last night. The idea was to blend in with the crew and watch for Gradak's team to arrive. Unfortunately, as you know, Ben, I had a slight accident on landing." He smiled ruefully, pawing through the knapsack. "I wasn't in any condition to check all the rig's access points, and the terrorists made it aboard some time during the evening."

Ben's face had darkened. "Why," he interrupted, "didn't you and your people just do the obvious and inform the American authorities? Wouldn't that have prevented the whole thing?"

"The answer to the first part of your question," Ari replied, "is time and substantiation. There's something else, too, but I'll get to that in a few minutes. There wasn't time to go through the necessary channels to stop Gradak, and we didn't have enough substantiation—hard facts—to back up our intelligence report.

"As to your second question: no, it wouldn't have prevented anything. It would only have complicated things for the Mossad. You may not believe this, but highly sophisticated intelligence services, like your CIA and FBI, can often move like blundering dinosaurs when speed is of the essence."

Ari removed the remote-control detonator from the knapsack and held it up.

"Gradak's task was to set charges on the NAOC-X

and blow it up," he said. He jabbed a thumb over his shoulder. "It's fully mined as we speak.

"A great many things went wrong for him on this operation, needless to say. He must have had some kind of escape route planned, some pickup arranged. But I've seen nothing like a fast boat or helicopter in the area. I suspect that the storm prevented the team's means of escape from arriving." He looked at Sass. "That's why Gradak was so anxious to get aboard your boat." Sass glanced down at the body and shivered.

"I don't understand any of this, Ben," she said, holding onto his shoulder. "I mean, what's he saying? Terrorists invaded the rig you were working on and— what? Took it over so they could blow it up? Here in the Gulf?" Ben nodded up at her. "That's crazy!" she exclaimed. "Who'd want an American oil rig destroyed?"

Ari shrugged. "The Iranians. The Iraqis. The Libyans. Gradak had recently been linked to a particularly violent sect of Shiite Muslims. Perhaps them.

"And remember," he added, "this is not just any oil rig. This is the NAOC-X. The first of a fleet of floating production platforms that will likely render the Arabs and their oil inconsequential to America. It's a highly visible target, both for what it can produce in terms of oil, and for what it represents." The thin smile again. "Fanatics are big on symbolism, and they want this particular symbol destroyed."

Ben watched him silently, his face set hard. Ari smiled briefly at him and began to examine the remote-control detonator, pulling out the short antennae and lightly fingering the switches.

"So you were sent here to stop this . . . Gradak," Sass said. "Stop him from blowing up the rig and killing innocent people."

Ari looked up, still smiling, but didn't reply.

Ben spoke: "That part about stopping innocent people from being killed didn't work out so well, did it?"
He waited, but Ari just kept fingering the detonator.
Ben leaned forward. "You know," he said quietly,
"what you're saying doesn't add up. This guy"—he
indicated Gradak's body—"was no friend of yours, but
in spite of what you say, if your intention was to protect the lives of the men on the rig, you'd have seen
that they were warned of the danger." There was
anger in his voice.

"Ben—" Sass said, squeezing his arm.

"I'm not an expert on antiterrorism or intelligence
practices," Ben went on, "but lines of communication
in U.S. national security aren't that slow. Everyone's
hot-wired into guarding against terrorists these days."
He pointed a finger at Ari. "The United States listens
to Israel. You knew days beforehand what was going
to happen. If your people had informed ours that a
rig was going to be hit in the Gulf of Mexico, there'd
have been a net of military security dropped over the
oilfield that a gnat couldn't have gotten through.

"And those men would be alive." He glared at the
Mossad agent. "My friend would be alive."

He felt Sass stir beside him. Later, he thought. He'd
tell her about Rolly later.

Ari was no longer smiling. He met Ben's stare coolly.
His eyes, so warm and animated moments before as he'd
spun his tale, were strangely dead, devoid of emotion.

"Well," he said finally, "since you don't care for the
story I've just told you, I'll tell you another that you
might like better. But first, do you think either one of
you could tell me about how far we are from the rig
right now?"

Ben blinked, taken off guard. He and Sass turned
their heads and looked astern at the NAOC-X, huge
and immobile against the blue sky.

"About a half a mile," Ben said. "What—"

"Perfect," Ari said, and pressed a button on the detonator.

Simultaneously, at fourteen different critical locations on the giant rig, a faint radiowave pulse closed a tiny servo switch, permitting battery current to flow to the lead wires of a standard U.S. Military, M-6 blasting cap. The cap was buried deep inside ten pounds of Czech-made Semtex plastic explosive, which in turn had been molded like putty around a wellhead feed line, primary check valve, or natural gas bleed line.

Simultaneously, the fourteen Semtex charges exploded, the gases created moving outward at nearly eight thousand meters per second. The heavy steel pipes and housings to which they had been attached vaporized instantly.

From the cockpit of the *Teresa Ann,* Ben and Sass heard and felt the air shudder with a sudden, lightning-fast *crackcrackcrackcrackcrack* . . . Fingers of fire and white-hot metal fragments erupted visibly from a dozen locations on the NAOC-X's massive superstructure. The giant rig trembled like a great animal suddenly struck by a poleax.

At nine separate wellheads, three primary feed lines, and two bleed lines, thousands of gallons of high-grade crude and thousands of cubic feet of volatile natural gas burst forth into the sunlight, inundating the entire upper deck.

The natural gas was the first to ignite, instantly transforming the clear air around the superstructure into a seething cloud of fire. Fresh gas screamed from the molten ends of the ruptured lines, feeding the wild inferno. A few seconds later, the crude oil covering the upper deck from stem to stern reached its ignition temperature.

With a tremendous *whoosh* a tidal wave of fire

swept down the length of the NAOC-X. Storage tanks containing aviation fuel, diesel, and gasoline went off like bombs. Then the main fuel tanks for the rig's electrical generators, built into the supporting under-structure of the upper decks, exploded with four shat-tering detonations.

The belly of the NAOC-X blew out and downward in a great gout of flaming fuel and charred metal. Gut-ted, the rig staggered, the structural strength of her steel insides torn out. From deep within her came the rising shriek of ripping metal.

And then the superstructure broke in two, stem and stern sections collapsing in on one another—almost in slow motion, it seemed to Ben and Sass. The rig's legs went next, buckling and toppling inward, breaking away from the underwater pontoons that supported them. As the huge sections of half-molten, burning metal hit the water, they produced immense clouds of hissing steam.

Finally, the two pontoons, freed from the weight of the superstructure and legs, erupted through the wa-ter's surface, breaching upward like great whale forms. Hanging against the sky for a long second, tilting, then crashing back into the deep blue water in an explosion of white foam, they bobbed, rolled, turned . . . and then slowly sank beneath the dark swells of the Gulf.

Less than a minute later, all that remained was an oil slick, a rapidly dissipating cloud of steam, and the relentless, driving sea.

Chapter Twenty-Nine

As the fiery spectacle of the NAOC-X's destruction ended, Ben whirled to face Ari.

"You son of a bitch," he said in a choked voice, stepping forward.

The Mossad agent had already unslung the submachine gun. One-handed, he brought it up to bear on Ben's chest.

"I understand how you must feel," he said sympathetically, shaking his head. "You just can't get a break today. Here you are, in your own boat, right back in the same position you were in fifteen minutes ago." He smiled. "It's nothing to do with you, really. You're caught in events beyond your control. Just think of it as fate, with a capital F."

"Capital F is right," Ben muttered under his breath. He leaned back a little, touching Sass. "Got any other surprises for us this morning?"

Ari wedged himself into the front corner of the cockpit and propped the machine gun against his knee, the business end trained on Ben and Sass. He motioned for them to sit. They did.

"You know," Ari said, "you look like a nice couple. You don't look for trouble, but you handle yourselves well when trouble finds you." He glanced at Sass. "Both of you. And you obviously care about each other." Pause. "I envy you. I really do. And because I do, I'm going to finish my story. You remember—

the one I said I'd tell you just before the big firecracker went off." He grinned and glanced at the date
on his watch. "By the way, it's the fourth of July.
Happy Independence Day. Fireworks included."

"I've had enough of your stories," Ben said.

"Oh, you'll like this one," Ari continued pleasantly.
"Just give it half a chance." He waggled the barrel of
the Skorpion. "I insist."

Ben just looked at him, unsmiling. Ari began:

"Once upon a time in the Bekaa Valley," he said,
his tone mockingly theatrical, "there dwelt a certain
Shiite Muslim cleric-slash-rabble-rouser, his household, and his bodyguards. At least, he dwelt there for
a week or so earlier this year. Though not widely
known in the western press, this particular cleric was
one of the prime motivators of terrorism in Israel's
occupied territories—one of those religious fanatics
whom that bastard Arafat claims publicly to disown,
but in reality cooperates with and helps keep one step
ahead of the Israeli military.

"Things had not been going well for Israel in recent
months. There had been some embarrassing incidents
between the U.S. and my country regarding some in-
dustrial spying, as well as a lot of unfortunate news
footage that appeared to show Israeli troops beating
the living hell out of some unarmed Palestinian civilians. Those Palestinian civilians had, moments before,
been throwing rocks and Molotov cocktails at those
same troops, without provocation, but of course you
don't see that on the nightly news. At any rate, these
things were combining to reduce our sympathetic position in western eyes—particularly in Washington.

"Unpleasant talk was starting to circulate in Congress about cutting back military aid and funding to
Israel. The U.S. has a short collective memory, and
we were starting—quite unfairly, I might add—to look

like the bad guy in the Middle East to a lot of American lawmakers.

"So a few of us in the Mossad—the ones nobody else listens to because we believe in doing what is necessary, not just what is politically expedient—decided to do something to remind America and the western world who the bad guys really are."

Ari shifted a little, never taking his eyes off Ben. He grunted, settling his injured side against the cockpit coaming, and went on:

"Our little internal group had pinpointed the location of this Muslim cleric in the Bekaa Valley; Mudeen was his name. A commando team—our team, not one sanctioned by Mossad Central Command—was sent in for a night strike, and they got him—along with about two dozen members of his household. Before they were extracted, they left a few . . . calling cards, which would indicate that the raid had been an American operation.

"Then we waited, and kept our ears to the ground. A few weeks passed and then—jackpot! We got an intelligence report indicating that Ojim Gradak was going to take out an American oil rig in the Gulf of Mexico. He and his masters were angry, you see, at the assassination of a Shiite cleric by a U.S. hit team. And a lesson needed to be delivered."

"But we didn't do it!" Sass blurted. "You did!"

"Calm down, calm down," Ari cooed, motioning with the machine-gun barrel. "In this world, it doesn't matter whether you did or didn't do something—it only matters whether you *appear* to have done it. The Shiites jumped to the wrong conclusion, just as we hoped they would, and ran a revenge operation against the wrong country.

"Their mistake, of course, is our gain. Americans tend to get very emotional about anyone who threatens them or blows up their property. Can you imagine the political currency generated for Israel by the de-struction of *any* high-tech oil rig in American waters? Much less the rig which symbolizes one of America's fondest wishes—to be free of reliance on Arab oil? Follow our thinking: the terrorists would openly claim responsibility for it, the idiots—the result being that an enraged U.S. military and congress, in response to an enraged U.S. population, would pour money and weapons into Israel like the Potomac filling Chesa-peake Bay.

"And so, you see, we get what we want. What we need. Our congressional funding and military support remains substantial. Our public image in the western press as the first line of defense against the hordes of Islam remains intact. Several of our very worst ene-mies are killed or pressed hard to remain alive for a few months, and"—he stopped and grinned—"the next time our troops get filmed cracking a few Arab heads, they'll be applauded instead of condemned."

He stopped talking and cleared his throat. Ben and Sass sat silently, close together, digesting the rogue Mossad agent's lecture. Sass brushed her wet hair back from her forehead.

"Then what are you doing here?" she demanded. "You were going to get what you wanted. They were going to blow up the rig and then take the blame for it. Why'd you come out here to get in their way?"

"He didn't come out here to get in their way or stop them," Ben said. "He came out here to make sure they didn't fail." He turned to Ari. "Isn't that right?"

Ari nodded slowly. "Partly. All covert missions have primary and secondary objectives. Ideally, our group wanted several things from this operation. The main thing was to ensure the destruction of the NAOC-X, ostensibly by the Arab terrorist team, thereby guaranteeing the flow of money and material to Israel for the foreseeable future.

"Secondly, we wanted to take advantage of a rare opportunity to rid ourselves of Ojim Gradak. Our secret group's interests and those of the Mossad proper coincided here. We were able to conceal our independent operation within the Mossad's less ambitious plan, at least for a while. For once, we knew both when and where Gradak was going to be.

"The difference was, the Mossad command wanted to execute another Adolf Eichmann-style operation—prevent the rig's destruction *and* take Gradak alive for a show trial in Israel." Ari paused and smiled. "Our group had other, better ideas. He's caused us—and the rest of the civilized world—a great deal of trouble over the past ten years." He gazed at the terrorist's limp body with an expression of genuine loathing. "I consider putting a bullet through him to be a high point of my professional life.

"Our group positioned me as the setup-and-transport man for the Mossad operation. To prevent their team from interfering with Gradak—and *our* group's plans—all I had to do was maroon them on the mainland, without enough time to find alternative transport out here."

Ben was nearly halfway across the cockpit when Ari jerked the submachine gun up, stopping him in his tracks. He dropped a hand to the coaming to steady himself against the boat's roll, every muscle tensed.

"Now, now," Ari said, his tone patient, "none of that." He shook his head. "Just when we were getting along so well. Sit down, Ben. No, not close to me. Back where you were." Ben slid back to the seat beside Sass. "That's better."

Sass gripped his arm and touched her fingers to his cheek. Her eyes were wide, frightened. "What are you doing, Ben?" she said in a half whisper. "You can't run into a machine gun."

"He just tried to do the only thing he could, Sasha," Ari said, "because it's suddenly occurred to him that I can't possibly tell you all this and let you stay alive." He pursed his lips. "I really wish there was some other way, but . . ."

Sass, part of her body hidden from Ari's view by the steering pedestal, let her hand drift up to the becket securing the wheel. Out of the corner of his eye, Ben saw her release it. She hooked a thumb through the wheel's spokes to stop it from turning.

"I don't suppose it'd make any difference if we promised to keep our mouths shut," Ben offered.

"It's really not a risk I can afford to take," Ari replied. He stood up, hefting the machine gun. "And as a matter of fact, I think we've wasted about as much time as I can permit." He pulled the bolt back on the weapon.

Ben saw Sass turn the wheel slightly. Not much, just enough to start the *Teresa Ann* veering more directly downwind, off her broad reach. Ben glanced aloft. The mainsail was still full, pulling hard in the stiff breeze. More time. They needed a little more time.

"I hope you've got some sailing experience," he said. "This boat doesn't get you where you want to go on wishful thinking."

"Not a problem," Ari said. He winced suddenly, favoring his injured side. "You know," he said, breathing heavily, "I think I'm tired of talking to you." He brandished the Skorpion. "Get on your feet."

Sass tweaked the wheel a little more. The boat wobbled as it turned directly downwind, then began to work its way back onto a broad reach on the opposite tack, the mainsail still pulling on the wrong side.

Ben got slowly to his feet, bracing his knee against

the seat. The boat heaved up on a huge swell. The mainsail trembled as the wind got behind it.

"I think I'll let the lady live a few minutes longer," Ari said, "just to be polite." He trained the Skorpion on Ben's chest. "Hold still. This'll only hurt for a second." He smiled the icy smile of an assassin. "Any last words for her?"

"No," Ben said, his fists clenched at his sides. "Just for you."

"Really?" Ari said. "What are they?"

"Jibe-ho."

With an earsplitting crack the mainsail filled out on its opposite side and jibed. The heavy boom whistled across the cockpit, narrowly missing Ari's head, and slammed to a halt on the new tack with a tortured jangle of sheets and blocks. The *Teresa Ann* heeled ninety degrees on her beam ends and laid the end of her main boom in the water. Ari clutched wildly for a handhold, missed, and was thrown across the cockpit toward the downwind rail. There was an angry stutter of machine-gun fire as he squeezed the Skorpion's trigger by reflex. He crashed hard into the coaming, and the weapon went over the side.

Ben let go of the steering pedestal and dove at him. His weight crushed the Mossad agent down onto Gradak's body, and he hooked a forearm across his throat. He could feel the Israeli grappling frantically for something in his belt.

Ari got his right hand on the butt of the little Beretta and yanked it out of his trousers. He tried to bring it around to fire backward beneath his left arm into Ben's body, but he wasn't quick enough. Ben seized the wrist of his gun hand in a desperate grip and dug his fingers deep into the tendons.

They rolled off Gradak's body, kicking and thrashing on the floor of the cockpit. Sass, clinging to the wheel of the wildly veering boat, fought to regain her

balance and bring the *Teresa Ann* under control. The
Beretta fired, the slug crashing into the steering pedestal and shattering the compass, showering Sass with
glass shards and fluid.

Ben smashed the agent's gun hand into the edge
of the seat, keeping his forearm locked across Ari's
windpipe. Twice more, and the pistol clattered free
into the corner of the cockpit. Grabbing Ari's hair,
Ben drove his face into the cockpit floor, then kneed
him in the injured side. The Mossad agent gasped,
then twisted, heaved upward, grabbed Ben's hair, and
abruptly ducked forward.

Ben somersaulted over his back and sprawled heavily into the rear seat, losing his grip on Ari's throat.
The agent reeled forward toward the companionway
hatch, fighting for air, and yanked it open.

In a blur of black-and-tan motion Caesar erupted
from the companionway and attacked, his jaws snapping at Ari's wide-eyed face. The big dog's weight
forced the agent back into Ben, who was in the process of flinging himself after his opponent, and the
three of them tumbled into the rear of the cockpit
again.

Sass disengaged herself from the tangled melee of
legs, fists, and teeth and scooped the Beretta up from
the floor. As she turned, Ari broke free of Ben and
the dog and grabbed the gun. Spinning her around,
he fought to tear it from her hands. She held on like
grim death, and the two of them reeled around the
front of the cockpit, lurching from side to side as the
boat rolled.

With one tremendous wrench, Ari ripped the gun
free and hurled Sass to one side. In that split second,
Ben stepped in and brought the *Teresa Ann*'s short,
heavy wooden boathook around in a whistling Hank
Aaron swing. It hit the rogue Mossad agent just above
the ear with a wet crack, driving his head over onto

his shoulder. His body jinked sideways, falling. As the boat rolled, his knees hit the edge of the coaming and he toppled out of the cockpit and over the lee rail. There was a splash, and he disappeared. A second later his body bobbed to the surface under the stern, facedown, and receded rapidly in the *Teresa Ann*'s wake.

Ben slumped to his knees in the leeward seat, staring at the agent's motionless body. "He's sinking," he said. Sass crawled up beside him, her face bleeding, and watched with him. For a moment the corpse continued to bob around in the lacy white foam of the wake, a red halo spreading around its head, and then it was gone.

Sass made a little choking sound, and Ben turned to her. Taking her face gently in his hands, he kissed her, then held her tightly as she crushed herself against him, sobbing.

In a minute or two she quieted herself, sniffling, and drew back. "Sorry," she whispered. "Rough trip."

Ben rubbed the back of his neck. "Yeah. Rough." Sass thought that she'd never seen so many lines in his face.

She ran her hands over her own face, brushing back her limp hair. "I guess I look a real mess," she said, trying to smile. She reached down and scratched Caesar's big head. The rottweiler whined and gave her his quizzical look.

Ben pulled her close again. "Not to me," he whispered into her hair.

Chapter Thirty

A week had passed since the destruction of the NAOC-X. A week full of doctors and hospitals, reporters and cameras, and interview after interview with Coast Guard and FBI investigators. There had even been an unnerving two-hour debriefing with a team of dark-suited, utterly humorless men from Washington, whose terse questions centered mainly on the rogue Mossad agent named Ari. "C.I.A." a New Orleans sheriff's deputy had whispered to Ben.

And now it was over.

The *Teresa Ann* rocked gently over yet another tugboat wake as she made her way along the Mississippi ship channel toward the Gulf of Mexico. The night was very clear, and even the corona of light from New Orleans couldn't dim the brightness of the stars spackled across the velvet-black sky. Streams of car headlights flowed along both river banks, and the river itself was crowded with ship traffic. Ben kept the boat tight along the starboard side of the fairway, all her topside lights lit along with her running lights to increase her visibility.

A warm glow was emanating from the open companionway, and presently Sass emerged carrying two mugs of coffee. She stepped over Caesar, who lay on his side across the cockpit floor, and held one of them out. Ben smiled and took the offered cup, looking her over. Her eye was no longer swollen shut, and several small facial cuts were healing nicely, but the bruises around her cheekbone and nose were turning several different shades of purple and yellow. She sat down beside him and pulled her old Cherokee blanket up around her shoulders. He thought she'd never looked so beautiful.

Ben shifted in his seat behind the wheel, aggravating a dozen different bruises on various parts of his body. He sat still, waiting for the pangs to subside, and sipped his coffee. Sass took his free hand and turned it over gently.

"How're they doing?" she asked.

"Tender," Ben answered, "but getting better." He was still putting large amounts of salve on his palms, which had lost most of their skin when he'd slid down the swing rope. He found the injury particularly annoying. It was hard to get anything done when your hands were out of commission.

Using two fingers, he gingerly extracted Rolly's battered silver Zippo from his shirt pocket and held it out to Sass. She took it, and he picked up a short, thin cigar from the steering pedestal's small side shelf.

"Last of that box Rolly gave me for my birthday about three years ago," he said. "His favorite. Genuine Havana cigarillos." He laughed. "God knows what kind of scam he ran to get hold of 'em." Sass laughed with him a little, and wiped a finger along her eye.

"He was good people," she said, "with all his rough edges."

Ben's face softened. "Salt of the earth," he said quietly. "The best." He bit the end off the cigar and spat it over the side. "Here's to you, old friend," he whispered, holding it up to the sky. Sass flicked the lighter, and he lit the thin Havana, rolling and drawing until the entire tip glowed with a bright, even coal.

Sass snapped the top of the Zippo shut. "Well," she said, leaning against him, "what now?"

Ben blew a long, slow stream of smoke into the night air. He didn't answer right away. An oncoming tug pushing a huge chemical barge upriver was crowding the starboard side of the ship channel. Ben tweaked the wheel with his knee and brought the *Teresa Ann* in close to the next marker buoy, giving the barge extra room to pass. It slid by on their port rail, displaying massive gray-black sides, blue deck lights, and finally the big tug cabled to the stern, its powerful diesels thrumming at high rpm. The sound ebbed as it moved astern and continued up on toward the New Orleans refinery docks.

Ben put his arm around Sass. "I think," he said, "if it's okay with you, we'll just sail for a while. Stop by the marina, check on things a bit, and then go. Just go sail together, you and me." He drew on the cigar and looked off into the night. "Maybe head south, to the Caribbean."

Sass put a hand on his chest. "Do you want to come back?"

Ben looked into her eyes. "No," he said. "Right now, I don't."

He looked away. "And when you feel like that about a place, even a place that's supposed to be your home, it's best to leave for a while so you can . . . appreciate it again, later."

Sass laid her head on his shoulder and put her hand on his chest.

"Sounds good to me," she whispered.

EPILOGUE

The big Oceanic Whitetip cruised silently about five feet beneath the surface of the Gulf. It was a pelagic shark; a species which was found almost exclusively in the open sea far from shore. A few black-and-white-striped pilot fish schooled near its nose, opportunists hoping for scraps from their host's next meal.

The shark was homing in on an intermittent low-frequency vibration it had sensed during its solitary patrol. Such vibrations were often caused by the thrashing of injured fish or birds, and usually meant an easy meal. The Whitetip's head veered from side to side as it used the sensitive ampullae on its nose to determine the direction of the impulses.

The Gulf was flat calm. It was one of those days when the water's surface is as slick as oil, and the sea seems to breathe ... up ... down ... up ... down ... like a great sleeping animal. Surface disturbances of any kind are particularly apparent under these conditions.

The shark drew near the source of the vibration: a piece of flotsam perhaps four feet across. Something white was churning the surface, flashing and contrasting with the deep blue water. The motion excited the shark, but like all predators it was wary of injury. Following a pattern of behavior millions of years old, it would investigate first. It flicked its tail, darted in, and bumped the flashing white object with its nose.

"Aaaagh!" Sligo screamed, jerking his feet up into the air. He floundered for balance, bug-eyed, as the white-tipped dorsal fin cruised past. After a few more seconds of thrashing, he calmed his sun-addled mind enough to curl into a tuck position, which kept his entire body clear of the water, and held still.

He was sitting on the *Circe's* helm chair, which was stuck through the middle of one of her large life rings. The chair's heavy steel pedestal hung down below the ring, lowering its center of gravity and giving it the stability of a stand-up punching bag. On this unlikely raft Jeremiah Sligo had spent the last eight days, slowly going out of his mind with thirst, sun, cocaine withdrawal, and solitude.

The only reason he hadn't expired from dehydration already was that short squalls of rain had been frequent, enabling him to suck fresh water from his clothing almost daily. Nevertheless, his face, arms, and legs were encrusted with salt sores, and burned an angry crimson by the relentless sun.

For no apparent reason, after circling the chair raft twice more, the shark went away, as sharks will often do. Sligo remained in a tight tuck in his seat, his toes resting on the edge of the orange life ring, cramping horribly.

After a while, he swiveled his matted head and stared off to the south, his watery blue eyes twitchy and crazed in his blistered face. Far away in the distance, just above the horizon, he was sure he could see a coastline.

A very familiar coastline.

Cuba.

He glanced around apprehensively at the sapphire-blue sea, muttering to himself, then lowered his feet back into the water and began to kick.

PENGUIN PUTNAM

online

Your Internet gateway to a virtual environment with hundreds of entertaining and enlightening books from Penguin Putnam Inc.

While you're there, get the latest buzz on the best authors and books around—

Tom Clancy, Patricia Cornwell, W.E.B. Griffin, Nora Roberts, William Gibson, Robin Cook, Brian Jacques, Catherine Coulter, Stephen King, Jacquelyn Mitchard, and many more!

Penguin Putnam Online is located at
http://www.penguinputnam.com

PENGUIN PUTNAM NEWS

Every month you'll get an inside look at our upcoming books and new features on our site. This is an ongoing effort to provide you with the most interesting and up-to-date information about our books and authors.

Subscribe to Penguin Putnam News at
http://www.penguinputnam.com/ClubPPI